Praise for *Deliver*

The kind of novel "Ripped from the headlines" was meant to describe. Compelling.

—James Scott Bell, best-selling author of
Try Fear and *Deceived*

To say *Deliver Us from Evil* was a riveting read is an understatement. Caroll's new book is the perfect blend of romance and suspense! Highly recommended!

—Colleen Coble, author of *The Lightkeeper's Daughter*

With great plot twists, strong characters, and just the right amount of romance, *Deliver Us from Evil* is a high-octane, must read! Robin Caroll nailed the gritty, tough world of law enforcement and brought to light the tragedy of human trafficking in this powerful novel.

—Mark Mynheir, homicide detective and author of
The Night Watchman

In *Deliver Us from Evil*, Robin Caroll has done what most novelists fail to do. She has discovered the holy grail of fiction; she has found the truth.

—Brandt Dodson, author of *Daniel's Den*

Deliver Us from Evil is packed with plenty of action and adventure to keep the pages turning. But Robin Caroll goes beyond the typical expectations of the genre to bring attention to one of the most devastating crises of our generation. Well done.

—Rene Gutteridge, author of *Ghost Writer*

Robin Caroll hits it out of the park with this thrilling new novel. *Deliver Us from Evil* picks you up on page one and takes you on a ride you'll love page after page. And when all is said and done, you'll want to read it again just for the pure pleasure of wonderful storytelling. Can't wait for the next novel from this author. A must read!!

—Wanda Dyson, best-selling author of *Shepherd's Fall*

a novel

Deliver Us from Evil

Robin Caroll

B&H
PUBLISHING GROUP

NASHVILLE, TENNESSEE

978-0-8054-4980-8

Published by B&H Publishing Group,
Nashville, Tennessee

Dewey Decimal Classification: F
Subject Heading: RESCUE WORK—FICTION \ CHILD
ABUSE—FICTION \ GREAT SMOKY MOUNTAIN
NATIONAL PARK (TN)—FICTION

Scripture quotations or paraphrases are taken from the Holy Bible,
New International Version (NIV). Copyright © 1973, 1978, 1984
by International Bible Society. Used by permission of Zondervan
Publishing House. All rights reserved.

Publisher's Note: The characters and events in this book
are fictional, and any resemblance to actual persons or
events is coincidental.

1 2 3 4 5 6 7 8 • 13 12 11 10

To Case . . .
You're my William Wallace and Maximus Decimus Meridius
rolled into one amazing man.
I thank the Father for you in my life every day.
Love always, RC

ACKNOWLEDGMENTS

AS MANY AUTHORS DO, I've taken great liberties with facts where needed to suit my plot. These instances are intentional and in no way reflect on the information provided by the many who shared knowledge and information with me.

Special thanks to Chuck Justice for his flight detail information and for enduring my endless questions regarding Life Flight policies and procedures. These men and women who work in this field simply amaze me with their dedication and knowledge. May God bless you one and all.

My most heartfelt gratitude to my medical professional sources: my cousin Dr. Shannon Wahl, my neighbor Dr. Skipper Bertrand, and Deborah Gilbert (and the ladies who put me in touch with her—Leslie Pfeil and Crystal Bencken). Thank you so much for sharing your knowledge of the intricacies of the human body and leading me into the research of drugs I still can't pronounce.

The careers I chose for my characters are noble and full of valor, but I hadn't a clue as to the enormity of what these people deal with on a daily basis. Their dedication and knowledge awes me. Special thanks to those who provided me with facts, gave the basic layout of the Great Smoky Mountain ranger stations, and shared with me a little about ranger life: Bob Miller, Management Assistant, Great Smoky Mountains National Park; Bill Wright, Chief Ranger, Great Smoky Mountains National Park; and Ranger Roy Appugliese, Abrams Creek Ranger Station/Cades Cove District, Great Smoky Mountains National Park. Thanks to David Turner with the US Marshals Public Affairs Office; Steve Bius, chief, Training Management Division, US Marshals; and the men employed by the Marshal Services at the federal courthouse in Little Rock. Thank you to the US Coast Guard Admissions Office.

Many thanks to the members of ACFW who helped me with details of certain injuries—I so appreciate you sharing your painful experiences with me.

Heartfelt thanks to my awesome first readers who provided me with such detailed feedback: Lisa Burroughs, Krystina Harden, Tracey Justice, Ronie Kendig, Dineen Miller, Cara Putman, and Heather Diane Tipton. I couldn't do this without you!

Special thanks to agent, Kelly Mortimer, who believed in me from the beginning and always has my best interest at heart!

I wouldn't have stuck with writing if it weren't for my mentor and friend, Colleen Coble. Lady, you inspire me.

Camy Tang, Pamela James, Cheryl Wyatt—you ladies rock, and I'm so grateful I have you to share this journey with.

Thanks beyond compare to Karen Ball for believing in this project and letting me grow. Deepest thanks to Julee Schwarzburg, who gave me the exact editing I needed. You ladies are true gems.

Huge thanks to my family, who support and encourage me in ways I can't even begin to describe: Mom and Papa, BB and Robert, Bek and Krys, Bubba and Lisa, Brandon and Rachel, Willie and Connie, Bob and Linda Casteel, Scotty and Jan Casteel, and Kasi, Laci, and Cody.

Special acknowledgment to my grandmother, Una Abi Brannon Shannon, for instilling in me such a deep and great love for the written word and letting me borrow her maiden name for my spunky character.

My deepest gratitude to my children—Emily, Remington, and Isabella—I love you girls more than life itself, and I'm so blessed to have you in my life.

Finally, all glory to my Lord and Savior, Jesus Christ.

But what does it say? "The word is near you; it is in your mouth and in your heart," that is, the word of faith we are proclaiming: That if you confess with your mouth, "Jesus is Lord," and believe in your heart that God raised him from the dead, you will be saved.

—ROMANS 10:8–9

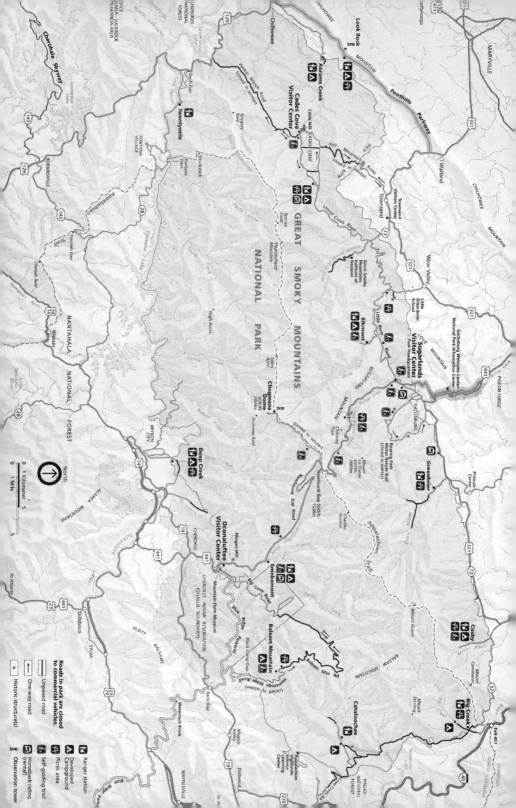

PROLOGUE

WHERE WAS BACKUP?

Roark Holland squinted past the harsh streetlight glare to the vehicle that had arrived only minutes ago. A van parked in a darkened part of the street. At the curb of the old building housing the Pugsley family in Witness Protection. The family that Roark needed to move to another safe house.

The Pugsleys' cover had been blown. With their whereabouts known, their enemy would seek the total annihilation of anyone who could identify them, namely Mr. Pugsley.

Roark glanced in his rearview mirror. Still no team.

A light flipped on inside the van, just for a fraction of a second. But in that heartbeat Roark took in the black jackets. The guns.

Grabbing his Beretta 98 in one hand, he pressed the transmit button on his radio with his other. "Demott, we have movement on the street. Where's my backup?" He wasn't prepared to go in alone—no tactical equipment, no comm, no extra ammo.

"Stay put, Holland. Team's ETA, less than five minutes."

The van door slid open.

"No time to wait. I'm going in." Roark's grip tightened on the Beretta.

Three men, decked out in black, stepped onto the road.

"Wait, Holland. Don't go in without backup. That's an order."

But he could control the situation. "There's three of them. No time." Roark turned off the radio and slipped it into his coat pocket, eased open the door, and stepped onto the pavement.

The men circled toward the back of the brownstone building.

Roark ignored the pounding of his heart as he crept to the front door. He used the key he'd been given and pushed inside. He knew the layout—had studied it for just such a scenario—and headed to the staircase.

He moved lightly but fast, his steps tapping against the metal stairs. He passed the second-floor landing and kept climbing.

A steady hum echoed off the concrete walls of the enclosed staircase. The elevator? Roark picked up speed as he moved up from the third-floor entry. The thud of his footsteps rose.

Ding!

He froze at the door to the fourth-floor hall and inched it open. The elevator doors parted with the speed of a snail. Through the crack he counted all three men emerging from the elevator car. The center man pointed toward one end of the hall, then the opposite. The other two nodded and moved toward their respective ends.

Good. They didn't know which apartment was the Pugsley unit.

He turned on his radio. "Demott, where in tarnation is my backup? If I don't move, Pugsley's dead."

"Wait. Marshals are en route. Don't move in."

Roark shook his head and turned off the radio. Don't move in? Five more minutes and the family would be taken out. He couldn't wait. Wouldn't. He steadied the barrel of the Beretta through the crack. Roark put the leader in his sights, drew a deep breath, then squeezed the trigger.

The man fell into a heap on the ground, a hand against the widening red spot on his chest. Guns at the ready, the other men ran toward their fallen comrade. Roark shut the door and took slow, steady breaths. He'd have to take them out in quick succession. He tensed, then relaxed his arm and leg muscles, turned toward the door, and gripped the knob in his left hand.

Pop, pop-pop-pop!

Roark flattened himself against the wall as the barrage of bullets slammed into the door.

Silence echoed in the aftermath. Where was his backup?

Roark held his breath. One . . . two . . . three—he opened the door and stepped through, his gun out and finger in the trigger well.

Nothing. Only the dead man in the center of the hall.

Roark spanned right, then left. No sign of either man.

Then he noticed the open door to the Pugsley apartment.

Pop! Pop!

Adrenaline surging into his legs, Roark pushed through the doorway, his firearm extended. Mrs. Pugsley lay dead at his feet. A fatal shot into the neck. Roark felt for a pulse, just to be sure. No thrumming under his fingers.

He stood and cross-stepped around the living room. Timmy, the Pugsleys' nine-year-old son, was draped over the back of a couch, a crumpled bag of Cheetos still in his hand.

Bile scorched the back of Roark's throat. He swallowed and kept moving down the hallway, two members of the Pugsley family still unaccounted for—Mr. Pugsley and his six-year-old daughter, Mindy.

Muffled voices reached him. Angry, hard voices. And a masculine response, whiny. Begging. Pleading.

Roark crept along the corridor, pressing his back against the wall and holding his gun at the ready. He paused at a doorway and listened. The voices were too muffled to be coming from this room. He spun across the threshold. Maybe a connecting closet would allow him to sneak up on the men.

White lace curtains fluttered beside a froufrou canopy bed. Mindy's room. Roark checked out the window that faced the street. No sign of an unmarked car. Why hadn't backup arrived on-scene? He peered into the open closet. No sign of the child. Could she be with her father? Were the men using her to torture Pugsley? He had to be sure.

Roark crouched and lifted the bed skirt. He met the stare of a tear-filled, wide-eyed little girl with blonde hair.

He lowered the gun and reached for her. Thank goodness he'd met the child on previous occasions so she recognized him. He pulled her from under the bed and stood, holding her in his arms.

Her little body shook as she sobbed in silence against his neck. Roark's throat tightened.

He'd get Mindy to safety, then return to take care of the shooters. And maybe, just maybe, have time enough to save Mr. Pugsley.

Poking his head into the hallway, he ensured all was clear, then made fast tracks to the front door. He stood in the corridor, clutching little Mindy. Where could he put her? Someplace safe but close.

Pop! Pop! Pop!

Mindy turned her head free of his neck. "Dadddddddy!" Her sob bounced off the hallway walls, reverberating.

Running steps thudded from inside the apartment. No time to hide. No time to think.

Ding!

Roark plunged into the elevator just as the men cleared the apartment. He lowered Mindy to the ground and fired as the men appeared. The doors closed. He slunk to the ground, his breathing coming in bursts.

They would take the stairs and wait for them. Roark couldn't let them hurt this little girl any more. They'd already stolen her family.

He jabbed the emergency stop button between floors two and three. Think. He needed to figure something out. Checking his coat pocket, he calculated how much ammo he had left. Enough to take care of those two, that was for sure, but not with Mindy as a target. He turned on his radio. "Demott, Pugsley family all taken out except for the little girl. I have her. Is backup here?"

No response except static. He tried again, still no response. He pocketed the useless radio. Had to think. Had to find a way out.

Mindy hunched over and cried harder.

He stroked her tear-stained face. "Shh, honey. It'll be okay. I'm not gonna let them hurt you."

She continued sobbing, huddling in the corner. His heart ripped in two.

Had his backup arrived yet? Why didn't he hear gunshots exploding around them? He had no doubt the shooters waited on them. They wouldn't leave . . . not with Mindy as a witness.

He stood, closing his eyes. *God, help me out of here.*

His eyes popped open, and he stared at the emergency hatch at the top of the elevator. Maybe . . . maybe he could get back onto the third floor that way, and the shooters wouldn't know where they were. Sure, they'd eventually figure it out, but by then backup would be on-site.

Dare I risk it without a team in place?

Mindy's breathing hiccupped. Roark didn't have a choice. He had to move now.

He lifted the end of his Beretta, then jumped and pushed open the hatch. He holstered his weapon, then reached for Mindy. "Come on, sweetie. We're going out."

She clung to Roark but didn't speak. Shock. He lifted her into the open space of the shaft. "That's right. Just climb up there and sit down. I'll help you."

Her feet disappeared. The elevator shook. Mindy cried out. Were they trying to bypass the emergency stop?

Roark took a deep breath and leapt, gripping the edge of the hatch tight. Using his upper-body strength, he pulled himself into the shaft.

Metal scraping sounded from above, but Roark couldn't make out anything in the darkness.

"Mister, I'm scared." Little Mindy sat huddled against the cables.

He closed the hatch door and grabbed her to him, taking in his surroundings. The ladder. Had to be one around somewhere—all shafts had one. "We'll be fine. We just have to find a way out."

The car shuddered, then groaned.

She sobbed harder, pressing her wet face against his. "I don't like it here. It's dark and scary."

"I know, honey. I know." He needed to figure something out, and quick. His gaze bounced off the walls. There, near the right corner . . . the metal rungs. He lowered her to the cold metal.

More scraping echoed in the shaft. Mindy's sobs intensified. The car jerked. He lost his balance, then grabbed the cables to steady himself.

"Hang on, Mindy. I think I've found our way out." He picked his steps as he moved away from her to the built-in ladder.

He reached the rung, grabbed it, and yanked. It held. Yes! He turned back to Mindy. "We're gonna be—"

The elevator hummed. The car jerked again, harder. Then, with a snap, it began to descend. Fast. Free-falling. Roark's grip tightened on the rung.

God, help us.

"Misterrrrr!"

The car shuddered and jerked, stopping as suddenly as it had descended. Roark breathed a heavy sigh and relaxed his grip. "It's gonna be okay. I'm coming to you."

Flames erupted, barreling up from the shaft. Engulfing the elevator . . .

"Help! Help!" Mindy's big blue eyes reflected the bursting blaze. Her blonde hair sparkled beneath the flickering flames drawing closer to her. Closer. Nearer.

Roark dropped to the roof of the car. Heat and fire licked his face.

Mindy's screams filled the shaft, clawing at his soul. *Please, God, save her.*

He reached for Mindy, but just then the cable snapped. The car slipped down into the darkened pit.

"Awwwww." Her cries of pain seared him more than the fire.

Hot metal slapped him across his cheek and jaw. Pain radiated throughout his body. He fell to his knees.

Mindy screamed for him, cried out in pain, yelled. Why hadn't he waited for backup? Better for the little girl to have died instantly by a bullet than burn to death in this fiery coffin.

White dots danced before his eyes. Darkness overtook him.

ONE

Tuesday, 3:30 p.m.
FBI Field Office
Knoxville, Tennessee

JONATHAN'S THROAT CLOSED AS he stared at the building from the parking lot. He gripped the package tight in his arthritic hands. Could he do this? Turn over evidence that would implicate him?

His heart raced and he froze. Not the best time for his atrial fibrillation to make an appearance. Despite being on the heart transplant list for eight months, it looked like his progressed heart disease would do him in. The most important reason he couldn't go to prison—he'd never get a heart and would die. While Carmen wanted him to confess his crimes, she wouldn't want him to die. The memory of saying good-bye to his beloved mere hours ago scorched his soul.

Her eyes fluttered open. Those blue orbs, which had once sparkled even in the absence of light, now blinked flat and lifeless.

He swallowed hard.

"Jonathan," her voice croaked, "it's time."

Tears burned the backs of his eyes, and he rested his hand over her parchmentlike skin. "No, Carmen. Please, let me get the medicine."

Her eyelids drooped and she gasped. Air wheezed in her lungs. "Sweetheart, the fight's . . . gone from me." She let out a hiss, faint and eerie. "The cancer's . . . won."

Jonathan laid his lips against her cheek, her skin cold and clammy, as if in preparation for the morgue. How could she continue to refuse the medicine? Even though she didn't approve of his means of acquisition, the drugs had kept her alive for five years. Five years he cherished every minute of. He'd do anything to keep her alive and the pain at

1

bay—the intense pain that had become her constant companion these last two weeks. It killed him to witness her agony.

She licked her bottom lip, but no moisture soaked into the cracked flesh. "You've done . . . your best by me, Jonathan. I know . . . you meant . . . no harm to . . . anyone." Her eyes lit as they once had. "Oh, how I've enjoyed loving you."

His insides turned to oatmeal. Stubborn woman—she'd allow herself to die, all because she discovered how he'd gotten the money.

"Promise me . . . you'll . . . tell the . . . truth. Admit what . . . you've done." Her breath rattled. "What you've . . . all done."

Pulling himself from the wretched memory, Jonathan breathed through the heat tightening his chest. He'd secure himself the best deal possible—immunity—or he wouldn't decipher the papers. And without him no one could make sense of the accounting system he'd created more than five years ago. Officials hadn't a clue.

With a deep breath he headed to the guardhouse in front of the fenced FBI building. His legs threatened to rebel, stiffening with every step. He forced himself to keep moving, one foot in front of the other.

At the guardhouse, a man behind bulletproof glass looked up. "May I help you?"

"I need to . . . see someone."

"About what, sir?"

"I have some information regarding a crime." He waved the file he held.

"One moment, sir, and someone will be with you."

Jonathan stared at the cloudy sky. He could still turn back, get away scot-free. His heartbeat sped. The world blurred. No, he couldn't lose consciousness now, nor could he go back on his promise. He owed it to Carmen. No matter what happened, he'd honor Carmen's dying wish.

"Sir?" A young man in a suit stood beside the fenced entry, hand resting on the butt of his gun. "May I help you?"

Jonathan lifted the file. "I have some evidence regarding an ongoing crime ring."

The agent motioned him toward a metal-detector arch. "Come through this way, sir."

Jonathan's steps wavered. He dragged his feet toward the archway.

A car door creaked. Jonathan glanced over his shoulder just as two men in full tactical gear stormed toward them. He had a split second to recognize one of the men's eyes, just before gunfire erupted.

A vise gripped Jonathan's heart, and he slumped to the dirty tile floor, the squeezing of his heart demanding his paralysis.

Too late. *I'm sorry, Carmen.*

Two Weeks Later—Wednesday, 3:45 p.m.
Golden Gloves Boxing of Knoxville

OOOF!

Brannon Callahan's head jerked backward. She swiped her headgear with her glove.

"You aren't concentrating on your form. You're just trying to whale on me." Steve Burroughs, her supervisor and sparring partner, bounced on the balls of his feet.

"Then why am I the one getting hit?" She threw a right jab that missed his jaw.

He brushed her off with his glove. "Don't try to street fight me. Box."

She clamped down on her mouthpiece and threw an uppercut with her left fist. It made contact, sending vibrations up her arm.

He wobbled backward, then got his balance. "Nice shot."

It felt good to hit something. Hard. Sparring with Steve was the best form of venting. The energy had to be spent somehow—why not get a workout at the same time? She ducked a right cross, then followed through with a left-right combination. Both shots made full contact.

Steve spit out his mouthpiece and leaned against the ropes. "I think that's enough for today, girl. I'm an old man, remember?"

She couldn't fight the grin. Although only in his late forties, the chief ranger looked two decades older. With gray hair, hawk nose, and skin like tanned leather, Steve had already lived a lifetime.

She removed her mouthpiece, gloves, and headgear before sitting on the canvas. "Old? You're still kickin' me in the ring."

He tossed her a towel and sat beside her. "So you wanna tell me what's got you all hot and bothered this afternoon?"

She shrugged.

"Come on, spit it out. I know something's gnawing at you, just like you were picking a fight with me in the ring. What's up?"

How could she explain? "I'm not exactly keen that the district feels there's a need for another pilot in the park." She tightened the scrunchie keeping her hair out of her face.

"That's a compliment—having you on staff has been so successful they want to expand."

"But I have to train him. Did you notice his arrogance?" She ripped at the tape bound around her knuckles. "He's nothing more than a young upstart with an ego bigger than the helicopter." While only thirty-six, she often felt older than Steve looked.

"You're so good, you can come across a bit intimidating at first, girl." Steve grabbed the ropes and pulled to standing, then offered her a hand. "Give him a chance."

She let Steve tug her up. "Yeah, yeah, yeah. Even if he had maturity, I still have to train him. With all the rescues we've been called out on of late . . . well, I really don't have the time." She exited the ring. "Like those kids yesterday." She shook her head as she waited for Steve to join her on the gym floor. "Their stupidity almost cost them their lives."

"They were young, Brannon."

"Please. Any amateur with half a brain should know better than to try to climb Clingmans Dome in winter." Didn't people realize if something happened to them they'd leave behind devastated family and friends? Loved ones who would mourn them forever? She fought against the familiar pain every time she participated in a search and rescue. All because people hadn't taken necessary precautions.

"They didn't know any better."

"It takes a special kind of stupid not to have researched your climb." Most SARs could be avoided if people planned a little more. It ripped her apart that so many parents, grandparents, siblings . . . fiancées . . . survived to deal with such grief. She'd tasted the bitterness of grief—twice—and the aftertaste still lingered.

Steve paused outside the locker rooms and shifted his sparring gear to one hand. "I agree, but most people don't see the dangers we do every day." He tapped her shoulder. "Hit the showers, champ. You stink."

She laughed as she headed into the ladies' locker room. Maybe Steve was right and the new pilot just made a lousy first impression. Maybe he'd be easy to train.

Please, God, let it be so.

Friday, 2:15 p.m.
US Marshals Office, Howard Baker Federal Courthouse
Knoxville, Tennessee

"YOU WANT ME TO escort a *heart*?" Roark struggled to keep his voice calm. He tapped the butt of his Beretta, welcoming it back to its rightful place on his hip.

Senior US Marshal Gerald Demott glared. "Look, I know you think this is a slight, but it's important. And for your first assignment back on the job . . ."

"IA cleared me of all wrongdoing. I'm seeing the shrink and everything." He gritted his teeth and exhaled. "I've been released to return to active duty."

"This *is* active. It's a field assignment, and it's important. Here's the case information." Demott passed him a folder, then glanced at his watch. "You'd better hurry or you'll miss your flight."

Roark grabbed the file and turned to go.

"Holland."

He looked back at his boss. "Yeah?"

Demott held out Roark's badge. "You might want to take this with you, too."

Roark accepted the metal emblem, then clipped it to his belt before marching out of Demott's office. A heart. His job was to escort a human heart from North Carolina to Knoxville. Any rookie could handle that. But no, they still didn't trust him enough to handle a *real* assignment.

He'd done everything they asked—took a medical leave of absence while Internal Affairs went over every painful minute of his failed mission, saw the shrink they demanded he speak to every week since Mindy's death, answered their relentless questions. The shrink reiterated he'd been forgiven for acting on his own.

Maybe one day he'd forgive himself. How many innocent lives would he have to save for his conscience to leave him be?

Roark slipped into the car, then headed to the airport. But to be assigned a heart transport? Not only was it wrong, it was downright insulting. After almost fifteen years as a marshal, he'd earned the benefit of the doubt from his supervisors. Especially Demott. His boss should know him better, know he'd only disregard orders if it was a matter of life and death.

But Mindy Pugsley died. They'd all died.

He pushed the nagging voice from his mind. Even Dr. Martin had advised him not to dwell on the past. On what had gone wrong. On disobeying a direct order.

If only Mindy didn't haunt his dreams.

Roark touched the angry scar that ran along his right cheekbone to his chin. A constant reminder that he'd failed, that he'd made a mistake that took someone's life. He'd have to live with the pain for the rest of his life.

He skidded the car into the airport's short-term parking lot. After securing the car and gathering the case folder, Roark grabbed his coat. Snowflakes pelted downward, swirling on the bursts of wind and settling on the concrete. The purple hues of the setting sun streaked across the mountain peaks beyond the runways, making the January snow grab the last hope of light.

Yes, he'd handle this mundane assignment, then tell Demott he wanted back on *real* active duty. Making a difference would be the best thing for him. Would make him feel whole again.

TWO

THEY WERE FALLING TOO fast.

The tickling vibration against her palm made Brannon loosen her grip. Wind pushed against the HH-65 Dolphin, slamming the helicopter into more turbulence. The vertical speed indicator dropped a notch. She pulled back on the collective, piloting the helicopter steady over Great Smoky Mountains National Park.

She kept her gaze locked on the landscape for any unnatural movement. Far below them the mountain peaks jutted out from the snow-covered red maples like a snaggle-toothed beast baring its teeth. The tree canopy blocked most of the ground from their sight.

"Is it always like this?" Jefferson Montgomery, new pilot in the National Park Service, asked over the headset.

"Sometimes, but we still have to do flyovers. It's our job."

"I know it's our job. Was just trying to get a feel for what I'll face every day."

For the millionth time in the hour flight, Brannon resisted putting Jefferson in his place. "We'll head back now."

"Want me to fly us in?" He rubbed his hands together.

As if she'd let this newbie fly her baby. "No, just pay attention to the horizon and treetops. Weather like this makes you fly by gauges and instinct." She pushed the foot pedal to turn the helicopter and moved the cyclic.

He sighed over the comm. Disappointment? She didn't have time to care. The wind shoved the Dolphin at least eight degrees off course. She made the adjustment and piloted toward the heliport at the ranger station.

"Do you know when my bird will be ready?" His ambition and competitiveness would make him a liability, not an asset.

"Nope. When they deliver it, I suppose." She pulled the helicopter into a level altitude, then used the collective to cushion the landing. She'd served thirteen years with the Coast Guard flying this model. But still, the weather could make even the best pilot get sloppy.

Using the pedals to align the landing gear with the ground track, she settled with little more than a bump. After shutting down the engines, radioing to Control, and marking her logbook, she yanked off her headset and hung it on the clip above her head.

Jefferson didn't bother completing his checklist before jumping from the Dolphin. Brannon let out a long breath, did her own walkaround, then rushed into the Abrams Creek ranger station, snow crunching under her feet.

The bell tinkled over the door as she pushed inside, a blast of wind and snowflakes sweeping in with her. The fragrant aroma of simmering coffee filled Brannon's senses. A fire crackled in the rock-front fireplace, the pops and hisses a welcome greeting from the frigid temperatures outside. She stood in front of the fire, holding her hands as close to the orange flames as possible. Tingles shimmied into her fingers as the warmth seeped through them.

"Temperature's dropping fast." Her partner and best friend, Lincoln Vailes, stomped inside the back door and hung his issued coat on the hook beside his rig.

She grinned. "Couldn't ride your bike in today?"

"Are you kidding? I wouldn't dream of getting my Harley out in this mess."

"Supposed to have a blizzard heading this way." Steve slurped a sip of coffee before he set the mug back down. "Everything clear out there?"

Brannon hung up her belt beside Lincoln's and shrugged out of her coat. "All clear. No sign of anybody." She tossed her jacket over a chair and backed up to the fire. She pulled the scrunchie from her hair, ran her fingers through the damp strands, then secured it again into a ponytail at the base of her neck. Little beads of snow fell, melting before they landed on the scuffed wooden floor.

"Let's hope the free-skiers have enough common sense to stay off the terrain." Lincoln plopped down on the threadbare couch and propped his boots on the coffee table. "I don't want to get a call to go out anytime soon if the storm hits."

"That'd be nice, for a change." Steve took another noisy swallow of his java. "Maybe we'll have a slow weekend." He nodded at the newcomer. "How'd you do?"

"I'm ready to go." Jefferson dropped onto the chair closest to the fireplace.

"Easy there, Ace. You still have a lot to learn about the park." Brannon moved to the coffee station in the corner. She lifted the carafe and stared at the thick mire in the bottom of the glass pot. With a mental shrug she pulled out a mug. No matter how much it resembled sludge, bad coffee was still better than no coffee.

Temptation for a cup of fresh java almost made her cross the mudroom and enter her living space. Exhaustion stopped her. If she went anywhere near her bedroom, she'd curl up and sleep, and she still had two hours left on her shift.

Lincoln laid his head back. The ends of his dark hair curled up at the tips. "Once the weather slacks, I'll take you around on ground."

"For what? I'm a pilot."

"You'll still need good knowledge of the area." She dumped several spoons of sugar into the cup, then stirred. It still looked like something you'd have to slog through in a swamp.

"Whatever." Jefferson snorted.

Brannon chose to ignore him and moved to the television, flipped on the local news station, and hovered in front of the screen. "Let's see what's happening in the outside world." Her hand paused over the remote as a newsbreak flashed across the screen. She backstepped to her seat, eyes glued to the image of two men rushing out of a hospital.

"In a joint endeavor between the FBI and the US Marshals, a donor heart is being rushed to a recipient at Parkwest Medical Center in Knoxville, Tennessee. Unidentified sources reveal the heart is intended for a government witness who has information on the largest child-trafficking ring in American history, being run out of Tennessee. We're live from the New Hanover Regional Medical Center in Wilmington."

The screen focused on the reporter shoving a microphone in a man's face. A very handsome face framed by a blondish silver crew cut. His eyes were as dark as the depths of the Snake River, but she couldn't tell if that was a play of the lighting. A long, fresh scar on the right side of his jaw marred the smooth tan of his face. Decked out in a pair of khakis and a button-down shirt—with gun and badge displayed—the man pushed the microphone from his face and let out a gruff, "No comment."

A man shorter and blonder than the marshal, wearing hospital scrubs beneath a coat, carried a small cooler. Round glasses magnified eyes in his young face as he pressed close to the marshal. Cameramen and reporters crowded them.

Lincoln rested his elbows on his knees and let his hands dangle between his legs. "They're heading our way."

Brannon held up a finger and stared at the screen as the two men rushed into the helicopter. While the rotors whipped, the cameraman got close enough to capture the marshal buckling his seat belt and scowling at the mass of media. The aircraft shook as it warbled, then rose into the sky.

Brannon switched the station to the local weather and narrowed her eyes.

"What?" Lincoln leaned forward.

"I can't believe it." She pointed at the radar map on the television. "They're flying after dark into an oncoming blizzard."

Steve shook his head. "Weather says it's just a winter storm."

She rubbed her arms. "I know better. We've seen these so-called winter storms that intensify into full-blown blizzards."

"How bad do you think it could be?" Steve stood and rubbed a hand over his face.

"I think this storm will grow into a blizzard like we haven't seen in years. And if I'm right and that Bell flies over the Smokies and hits an air wave, that helicopter's going down. It wasn't designed to fly in such conditions."

Friday, 6:00 p.m.
Airspace over North Carolina

ROARK SHIFTED HIS FEET. The aircraft's constant vibration caused a headache to pound against his temples. The instrument panel in the cockpit illuminated the dark helicopter in an eerie green glow. Why did the helicopter have to feel so cramped? So close? He gritted his teeth.

He glanced at the flight medic beside him. Thomas fiddled with the little pack sitting atop the cooler.

The cooler holding a human heart.

The idea bothered Roark almost as much as being given this babysitting assignment. Almost as much as being in such a confined space. "So, that gonna be okay sitting on the floor?" He raised his voice over the hum of the engines and cocked his head toward the cooler.

Thomas followed his gaze. "Sure. No problem. The heart'll be good for four hours."

"Kinda cutting it close, isn't it? This is over a three-hour flight."

"I have several doses of pyruvate and perfluoroperhydrophenanthrene-egg yolk phospholipids ready to inject."

"What does all *that* mean?"

"Oh." Thomas chuckled, his high-pitched voice squeaking in the confined aircraft. "It's a new compound mixture that will extend the organ's viability for up to forty-eight hours." His fingers grazed the small zippered pack. "Cutting edge stuff."

"Yeah." Roark turned to stare out the window. Snow blew haphazardly. No moon lit the night sky. No stars twinkled against the black backdrop. He still didn't understand all the medical mumbo jumbo, but he no longer cared. Getting the heart to the hospital in time to save the witness was his only concern. End of discussion. He'd read the file on his flight to North Carolina. Demott had been right—this was an important case.

Snow crashed against the helicopter in silent assault, whirling around on steady gusts of wind. The helicopter pitched and bounced. Thomas picked up the cooler and gripped it in his lap. Roark released his seat belt, then inched toward the cockpit. An ozone-burning stench infiltrated his nostrils as he glanced around the instrument panel. The pilot's lips formed a white straight line.

"121MCE to ATC Tennessee," the pilot said into his mouthpiece. "121MCE to ATC Knoxville, come in ATC."

Roark couldn't hear the radio. He rubbed his palms on his jeans.

"121MCE to ATC Knoxville, come in ATC."

Determined to be heard over the roar of the helicopter, he leaned closer to the pilot. "What's going on?"

The pilot cut his eyes over to Roark, then to the control panel. "I can't raise Air Traffic Control in Knoxville, and the blizzard's moving in. Too much wind and precipitation." He tapped another button on the radio controller. "I'm on the right frequency."

"And that means what, exactly?"

Both of the pilot's hands stayed in motion on the control sticks. "Just sit back and buckle in, please. This is gonna be a bumpy ride."

Roark pushed back, slipped the seat belt over his thighs, and then locked the catch. Great. His heartbeat kicked up a notch. He glanced at Thomas, who stared bug-eyed behind his glasses. The dimmed lights spilled from the cockpit, reflecting against those thick glasses, making him appear much younger than his years. His scrawny frame seemed to diminish as the helicopter shook and rattled.

Roark gave a curt nod. "Just some turbulence." At least he hoped so. He tapped the butt of his gun, drawing comfort from its mere presence. A reminder that he was back in control.

The flight medic turned a whiter shade of ashen and hugged the red cooler to his chest.

Sheets of snow blasted the helicopter, shoving it hard to the left. The aircraft surged down and up, then the rhythmic *thump-hum* of the rotor engine sputtered.

Metallic creaks shot across the aircraft, no longer masked by the growl of the engine.

The pilot cursed. A lot.

Roark leaned as far forward as his seat belt would allow. The instrument panel flashed yellow and white. Gauge needles bounced like Mexican jumping beans. Despite the freezing temperatures, the pilot's forehead glistened with sweat.

Roark's adrenaline spiked. He gripped his knees and stared out the bubble window. Zero visibility. All he could make out in the aircraft's running lights were tight tornadic spirals of white assailing the helicopter.

And he was stuck in a metal coffin.

Just as the nose of the aircraft dipped, red warning lights flickered in the cockpit. An alarm beeped, drowning out the hum of the engines.

Na-na, na—naaaaaa!

The helicopter shuddered.

"Hold on, I'm gonna do an autorotation," the pilot hollered.

Like Roark knew what *that* was. He shot a glance at Thomas's face. The poor kid looked like he'd lose his supper any minute.

The helicopter lurched. The engine sputtered, then died.

Free fall.

THREE

"NO MORE, NO MORE." Mai drew her legs to her chest, then wrapped her arms around them, locking her hands together. No clothes, shivering, and curled up, she dropped her forehead to her knees, her long hair shielding her face from the prying eyes of the American towering over her. "No more." Her accented English gave way to sobs.

Rough fingers dug into her shoulder as Poppy Fred jerked her upright.

Why did this American demand she call him by a familiar name? He was not her family—none of them were. Her family had sold her for food, which was almost as humiliating as what the American did to her. She blinked at him from beneath jagged bangs and breathed against the drum of her own heartbeat.

She shook as cold forced its way into her bones, like Poppy Fred had forced himself on her. Tears burned tracks down her face. Why had she believed the Americans, even for a second?

She had been so excited yesterday, ready to start a thrilling adventure in a new land. For years she had studied everything American. Was obsessed with learning their language and customs. Now her dreams had been shattered in the most nightmarish way, lying splintered and shredded at her bare feet. Mai hiccupped as she cried.

Poppy Fred reared back his beefy hand and brought it down.

A sharp sting prickled her face as her head snapped from the blow. She scraped against the cold hard wall of the suffocating room. She lifted her hand to her face, the heat on her cheek searing her palm.

"Get used to it. This is your life now." His face twisted, not at all the appearance he had when he and Aunt Betty offered to help her escape poverty and get a real American education. At least that was what her father had told her when he let her know she had no choice in leaving.

She hugged herself, hunching her back to better cover her exposed chest. This was not what she agreed to, not what she wanted. America was supposed to be different, the land of the free. But now she found herself imprisoned again, punished for wanting a better life. She should not have to endure such pain. Unless she got schooling. Then the suffering might be worth the pain. Maybe this . . . this *thing* with Poppy Fred was payment for that—she knew how expensive school was.

Mai lifted her eyes to the man who zipped his trousers. "I go to American school now?"

His cackle bounced off the bare, dirty walls, making her ears hum. "This is the only kind of American schooling you'll be getting."

Fear sat like lead in the pit of her tummy while her body shook with sobs. The stench of Poppy Fred's sweat mixed with the reek of stale cigarette smoke made her want to gag. Maybe she could pull further into a ball and just die.

"You be nice now. Uncle Milt will be here in a minute to test the goods, too." Poppy Fred flashed the smile that had made her happy to be going to America, the one he used to get her to leave her family and homeland at the age of fourteen. But now it made her stomach turn.

"Remember, we hold your papers and can turn you in to the bad police here." His lips curled back. "And they do painful things to bad little Oriental girls."

Mai squeezed her arms until her nails dug into her skin. She winced. "I be good, Poppy Fred." Nothing could be worse than this.

"Be a good girl and you'll survive." He tucked his shirttails into his trousers and stalked out.

Alone in the tiny room, Mai glanced around. Chills came in waves, racking her body. Why had Poppy Fred taken away her clothes? Her teeth rattled from the shivers. She pushed off the cold floor and rubbed her palms together. Even the mattress, with patches of springs poking through the quilted top, didn't have a sheet or a blanket.

Spotted moonlight streaked through the window, but the beams did not shine on her. The panes were so tiny, even she would be too big to pass through it.

Wind swirled around the building, whistling through the trees.

Keys clanked in the hall. Mai shoved herself in the adjacent corner, pushing back as far into the space as possible. The frigid wall pressed into her spine.

The door swung open, and the biggest man she had ever seen filled the frame.

She opened her mouth to release the scream trapped in her throat, but no sound emerged. Only her own raspy breathing resonated in her head.

Like a gorilla, the big man did not have a neck—his bald head sat right on top of his broad shoulders. Sucking up all the air and space with his bulk, he turned and locked the door. Looking back at Mai, he smiled, his white teeth flashing against his chocolate-colored skin. "Fred tells me you're a good girl."

"I be good. Poppy Fred say so." She crossed one leg over the other, yearning for covering, and this time not for protection from the chill.

The big man ran his tongue over inflated lips, then slipped it back in his mouth with a slurping pop. "I done called Nancy, but we're running a little late." He took a step toward her. "We have a little time to get to know each other better. Ain't that nice?"

She had no way to escape, no place to hide. She was too small to fight him, her limbs refused even to try. Mai pinched her eyes shut and begged her mind to take her far, far away.

Her mind was already cursing America when Milton laid his hands on her.

Friday, 6:30 p.m.
Howard Baker Federal Courthouse
Knoxville, Tennessee

EVEN IN THE DISMAL winter weather, a crowd of media pushed against Congressman Warren McGovern. The air sucked his lungs dry with each reporter shoving against him. Lights from cameras shone on his face as paparazzi swarmed in front of him. Warren paused under the arch of the four-story annex at the courthouse and held up his hands. He waited for the clamor and shuffling to stop, smiling down on the press like a king addressing his subjects. Wouldn't his father be proud?

The reporters and cameramen juggled umbrellas, microphones, lights, and cameras, but none would leave this impromptu press conference. Tonight, on all the local 10:00 news channels, Warren's sound bite would be the lead-in for the segment.

"Fellow citizens, I am as outraged by the allegations set out by the US Attorney's office as you are. In just a moment, I'll be meeting with Mr. Noah Markinson, the US attorney, to discuss this most serious issue."

Warren let his gaze kiss each attentive face in the media. "As many of you are aware, I sit on the Coalition Against Child Trafficking, consulting with investigators empowered by the Justice Department. In my capacity with this organization, I have received no information regarding this alleged child-trafficking ring, nor of the key government witness who's awaiting the heart transplant televised not long ago." He'd had to see the newscast to get the information—no one bothered to inform him, which made his blood boil.

The wind picked up, pushing snow across his face. Warren dusted off the shoulders of his trench coat. "Ladies and gentlemen, I assure you I'll get some answers and report back to you as soon as they are confirmed. Thank you."

He ducked into the courthouse, ignoring the reporters' questions. Warren's nose wrinkled as he entered the old building. It had been renovated in 1998, but the air still reeked of stale body odor and lack of ventilation.

Kevin, his aide, dabbed at the water marks on Warren's Armani suit as they marched down the long, empty hall. Great. It would cost him plenty to have the water stains removed.

"Sir, Mr. Markinson is waiting for you in the conference room."

"I just bet he is." Warren shoved away Kevin's hand. "He'd better have some answers for me. I still can't believe his office leaked this information without calling me first." A crucial investigation like this . . . well, it could help his reelection campaign beyond measure. Not to mention he headed up the Coalition. How bad did it look that he hadn't been informed?

"I know, sir. It's unthinkable."

Warren stopped outside the closed conference room and patted Kevin's arm. "You stay close, boy, and I'll show you how the real game of politics is played." Time to find out what was going on. He squared his shoulders, then blew into the room.

Clouds of yesterday's cigarette smoke hung in the air, even though the building boasted a no-smoking policy. Warren recognized several of the players lounging around the time-weathered table. Some sat in the cushionless chairs, some hung out by the coffeepot, and more leaned against the wall. He nodded to the head investigator in charge of the Coalition. The Justice Department flunky assigned to the Coalition stood vigil by the coffee machine with a man Warren didn't know. A good turnout for a meeting called after quitting time.

Pressing into the center of the room, Warren spied the one who hadn't thought to bring him into the loop: the US attorney. "Noah, what's all this nonsense about having a government witness in protective custody?"

All heads snapped at his entrance.

Markinson waved toward the chairs. "Let's have a seat and go over the details."

Warren moved to the head of the table. His father, a lifetime military man, had instilled in Warren the need to live by rules and policies. And rule one—always appear to be in charge. People respected the leadership attitude, and with respect came information.

He settled in the chair, which creaked as he shifted, then stroked his chin with his thumb and forefinger. "Fill me in, Noah." Rule number two—call someone by his first name—it shows superiority.

The US attorney emitted a long sigh. His gaze darted around, landing on each person's face briefly, then focused on Warren's. "Two weeks ago a potential witness tried to enter the Knoxville FBI office. He had documents, which we now know are regarding a large child-trafficking ring based right out of the state."

Raising an eyebrow, Warren released an undignified snort. "Child-trafficking ring in Tennessee?"

Snickers erupted from the men.

Markinson shook his head. "I know how ludicrous it sounds. Trust me, I was as skeptical as any of y—"

"How can you take this seriously? What did this alleged witness say?" Warren interrupted before the man could finish his sentence. Rule number three—always bring the focus back to yourself—you get more respect that way.

"I'm getting to that, Congressman." Markinson lifted a folder but didn't open it. He waved the file around like a white flag. "The man had documents showing the money trail of this ring: cash deposits in amounts less than ten thousand dollars at a time so as not to garner any currency transaction reports, fielding the money through dummy corporations and finally landing in offshore accounts."

Heat rose up the back of Warren's neck. He shifted in his chair, causing it to groan again. "So why haven't arrests been made?"

"The documents prove the money trail, but we can't uncover who owns stock in the corporations or who owns the offshore accounts. At least not without the witness, who was the obvious moneyman in this ring. The code to get the information is in his mind."

Perspiration clung to Warren's back, dampening his button-down shirt. "But what does this witness claim?"

"That's the problem. Someone shot at him as he tried to enter the FBI building and went—"

"Somebody shot the man *at* the FBI office?" Warren slammed his palms against the table. "That's outrageous."

Markinson held up his hand. "It was in the parking lot. No one was injured. The witness wasn't hit."

"Did agents arrest the shooter?"

"No, he got away."

Warren crossed his arms over his chest. "What an example of fine federal lawmen we have here in Knoxville. It's an absolute disgrace." He shook his head, furrowing his brow. Had the FBI turned into the Keystone Kops? How could this have happened?

Markinson laid down the folder. "That isn't the issue, Congressman. The issue is the witness dropped the folder, then went into cardiac failure and lost consciousness. He was rushed to Parkwest Medical Center."

"You don't say?" Warren leaned forward, resting his elbows on the scuffed wooden table. So . . . they *did* have something to go on.

"The man suffers from heart disease and has been on the transplant list for months. Getting shot at sent him into failure."

"Well, surely he's been stabilized in two weeks." Why wouldn't Markinson just spit everything out? What was he hiding?

The US attorney sighed. "Yes, he was—is—stabilized. However, because of his condition, the doctors determined it would be in his best interest to keep him in a drug-induced coma until a donor heart could be located."

"And the documents can't be interpreted by anyone else?"

"We've had the FBI, NSA, and CIA looking into it. As of yet they've found nothing of use."

"How can that be?" Surely all the government entities could decode one set of documents.

"According to the NSA decoders, these guys are good. We suspect the accountant, our witness, layered and hid the money well. As I said before, the key to the evidence is in our witness's head."

"Who is this man?" Warren's tone left no room for arguing, tired of having to pull out information that should have been provided.

"Jonathan Wilks, a retired IRS agent. We can only assume he has the knowledge and capabilities to back up the documentation."

"But what do you know about him?"

Markinson scanned the file. "After running a check on him and getting a warrant to search his residence of record in Rockford, we discovered he'd recently lost his wife to cancer, had no children of his own, and lived within his means. A stepson called in the wife's death and requested an autopsy. That's all we know right now." He shut the folder. "We're still investigating. Some reports take more time than others."

"Ah." Warren nodded, as if granting approval. Time for action. "What's the game plan, Noah?"

"The man has a rare blood type, AB negative, but was at the top of the list for a heart transplant. The surgeons said it was only a matter of time before he dropped dead without one."

"Was?" Warren folded his arms across his chest again, tucked in his chin, and pinned Markinson with his glare. "What's the status now?"

"As you've heard, we located a heart in North Carolina that matches the witness's. Of course, Jonathan Wilks is in ICU with armed marshals guarding his room and unable to be transported to the hospital in North Carolina. As we speak, the donated heart is en route to the hospital where the surgeons will perform the transplant. If all goes as the medical staff has led us to believe, after Wilks has the surgery, his prognosis will be good." Markinson tapped the file.

"Let me get this straight—this witness is dying." What was he missing?

"No, not dying. The heart surgeon—and trust me, we have the best available in the state on standby to perform the transplant—assures me the surgery should be successful and the witness will be able to speak and function clearly."

"As long as the transplant goes well."

Markinson nodded. "The only thing left to chance at this point is the heart getting to the hospital in time."

"Is this an issue?"

"Well, generally speaking, the heart is only viable for four hours after removal. The helicopter flight from Wilmington to Knoxville is a little over three hours in normal weather conditions." Markinson ran a hand over his mouth. "Due to the approaching blizzard, the medical technician transporting the heart has certain medications he can inject that will extend the viability for up to forty-eight hours. So it should all be fine."

Warren shoved to his feet. "Keep me abreast of the situation, Noah. I'm heading to the hospital to be there when the witness comes out of surgery. I want to hear his testimony firsthand." No way would he be left out of the loop again.

With a nod toward the other men at the table, he turned and left the room with Kevin right on his heels.

Friday, 6:45 p.m.
Abrams Creek Ranger Station
Great Smoky Mountains National Park, Tennessee

BRANNON STRODE TO THE radio control center, her senses humming, and lifted the mike.

"What're you doing?" Jefferson rose to his feet and moved to the desk, staring at her.

"I'm going to try to get that Bell pilot's flight plan to see which route they're taking." She twisted the knob, changing the radio frequency, and squealed the mike. "RCM986 Tennessee to North Carolina ATC."

The radio squalled.

"RCM986 Tennessee to Wilmington ATC, come in, please."

Nothing but static filled the air.

Wind gusted around the ranger station, whistling and whipping against the wood cabin. Brannon tried to hail air traffic control again but with no response. She slammed down the microphone and chewed the skin beside her fingernail. The storms must have knocked out the ranger station's communication capabilities with ATC.

"What're you thinking?" Steve took a long slurp of coffee, staring at her over the rim of the cup.

"Pull up the radar screen." She nodded toward the computer linked to the National Weather Service. "I want to see where the storm's moving right now. If that pilot's any good, he'll veer off course to avoid the brunt of the blizzard."

Steve's fingers flew over the keyboard until the screen pulled up the latest satellite radar of the storm front. Brannon leaned over his shoulder to study the monitor, inhaling the familiar scent of Old Spice and cigarettes. She traced the straightest path from Wilmington to Knoxville. The worst area of the storm was right in the line she'd drawn.

"They're flying right into it!" Jefferson said.

Brannon shook her head. "Not necessarily." She tapped the screen again. "Look here. If he alters about forty degrees off course, he'd miss the bulk of it." She narrowed her eyes. "That would put them right over the Appalachian Trail . . ."—she glanced at her watch and did a quick mental calculation—"in an hour or so."

"What do you want to do?" Lincoln sat on the edge of the desk, letting one leg dangle.

Straightening, she chewed the hardened skin by her nail again. Steve would go with her judgment. As the pilot, she had the responsibility of making the call. She stared at the screen once more. If that Bell didn't veer, the helicopter would go down. But any pilot worth his weight would shift off course. Then again, those Life Flight flyboys weren't always trained for countermaneuvers. Most often they flew local flights—straight shots from one hospital to another. Brannon dropped her hand and sighed. "I don't know."

Lincoln touched her shoulder. "What's your gut telling you?"

She closed her eyes, letting her subconscious take over. All she could envision was the helicopter going down in the park, in the storm. No way could they survive the elements if they even survived the crash. Brannon opened her eyes and locked gazes with Lincoln. "We need to go back up."

Her partner hoisted to his feet. "Now?"

She glanced at the clock, then shook her head. "Not right this second. I'd like to start patrolling the area in about forty-five minutes, though. We'll start around the Smokemont station and double back to here."

"In this weather?" Steve tapped the weather satellite screen again. Big clumps of red and yellow covered the entire park's perimeter. The blizzard had arrived in full force.

"The Dolphin can handle the blizzard." Brannon ran a hand over her hair, smoothing down the wisps that had escaped the scrunchie.

"Can you?" Steve met her gaze. He wasn't doubting her abilities, just asking as her supervisor.

She took no offense. "Of course I can. This storm is nothing compared to some of the typhoons I had to fly SAR in when I was in the Coast Guard."

"Okay, then." Steve reached for the mike. "You guys go gas up the chopper, and I'll keep trying the radio."

"I'll copilot." Jefferson all but bounced with excitement.

"No. You aren't trained in park rescues yet." Brannon glanced at Lincoln. "You up to it?"

"Lead the way, sweetheart. I'm right behind you."

FOUR

Friday, 7:00 p.m.
Suburb South of Townsend, Tennessee

MAI STARED OUT THE cracked, dirty window, her body shivering in response to the cold. The oil lantern on the dresser emitted a dull glow over the room, but it did not provide warmth. What happened to freedom? The backs of her eyes burned, but she would not cry, not again. She touched the bruise on her cheek, a constant reminder of how tears were not allowed.

Snow fell so hard she could not see more than a couple of centimeters from the window. The moonless night settled around the run-down building. The wind sounded like screaming through the walls with cracks large enough for small rodents to slip through. A layer of snow covered the ground outside the small building that housed more than twenty-five girls like her. The men who came called it a *brothel*. Mai was not sure what the word meant but knew what they would call her back in Thailand.

She had so wanted to be American. Did everything she could to fit in. But she never learned about the hell she lived in now.

A vehicle screeched to a halt outside, sliding on the ice in the driveway. Outside lights came on, lighting the pathway to the road. Mai pressed her nose against the icy windowpane. The side of the large white van opened. Milt—she would not allow herself to think of him as an uncle—stepped out and strode toward the building.

Mai moved to the opposite corner of the room she shared with five other girls. She was alone now, the others "entertaining." Could Milt be returning for her so soon?

The door slammed so hard the windows rattled in their chipped wooden frames.

Mai ran to the window and stared outside once more.

Milt trudged through the snow and opened the back of the van. Girls about her age and younger spilled out. Dressed in tattered and threadbare long shirts, their feet uncovered, they shuffled toward the door. Several slipped and fell, only to be yelled at.

More girls like her—tricked into coming to the United States with empty promises.

Mai lifted her hand to bang on the glass, to warn them to run— run far away. She balled her palm into a fist, then dropped it to her side, hiding it in the folds of her own tattered and threadbare long shirt. Milt would beat her if he caught her.

How many had already learned what they were to do here? Mai swiped a silent tear from her face.

Loud voices echoed down the hallway. Six bedrooms lined the hallway right next to the office, as Madam Nancy called it. At the end of the hall was the working corridor holding twenty rooms. These had nice furnishings and heat, but the girls were not allowed to sleep there. Oh no, those were only for the visits from the men who came in and out all day and night.

Mai pressed her ear against the wall closest to the office. She was able to make out Madam Nancy's squeaky voice. "These all look real fine, Milton. Here's your money."

"This may be the last shipment for a while." His booming voice echoed. Mai moved a fraction of an inch away.

"Why's that? I like getting fresh batches. Keeps the men interested. And I have my other locations to think of as well."

"We've had a little glitch in our system. It's being worked out now, but until everything's all clear again, we're stopping all shipments."

"I hate interruptions, Milton."

A chair creaked over the wind. Mai bit her bottom lip.

"Yeah, well, better safe than sorry. We all have a lot to lose here, Nancy."

"I suppose. Would you like a drink? I have some of my special Scotch hidden away."

"Lawd, woman, you must be reading my mind. I'd love a shot. It's colder than an ice sculpture out there."

Madam Nancy's high-pitched laugh hurt Mai's teeth.

"Thanks. This hits the spot mighty nice."

"Anything else I can do for you?"

"Well, now that you mention it, there is this one girl I had the pleasure of getting to know. Brought her in from Thailand about an hour or so ago. Didn't get her name though."

"Hmm. I just sent a group to the Colorado location. Can you describe her?"

"All them girls look alike, you know that." His deep chuckle rumbled. "But she had this little birthmark, right about here."

Mai touched the tiny mole just below her hairline. She backed away, turned, and huddled in the farthest corner of the darkened room. Hot urine trickled down her legs.

Friday, 7:30 p.m.
Airspace over North Carolina, Heading Northwest

THE ABSENCE OF THE engine brought out every creak and screech in the helicopter. Roark gripped the back of the pilot's seat. "What's going on?"

The pilot didn't turn his head to answer. "Too much wind. The currents are blowing the snow right into the rotors. The engine's shut down."

"What do we do?"

"Sit back and be quiet. And hold on."

Roark tightened his grip. Be quiet? While the ground rose up to meet them? At a fast pace, no less?

"Are we gonna crash?" The flight medic's face reflected fear. Raw fear.

Scooting back in his seat, Roark patted Thomas's shoulder. "I don't think it's that serious. I'm sure the pilot's trained for storms and emergencies. We'll be fine."

The man in scrubs didn't light up with hope. Instead, he appeared downright pasty in the blinking lights from the cockpit.

"Not the ones I've flown with. Most don't go up in this kind of weather. Especially after sunset."

Roark looked out the window, pondering Thomas's assessment. He couldn't see a thing. According to the case file, they hadn't planned to transport the heart at night, but the donor hadn't been able to hang on to the fragile string of life. He'd passed on, and the surgical team had no choice but to harvest the organ.

The helicopter took a sharp left. It pitched forward and down.

Thomas made little squeaking moans.

The pilot spewed more curses.

From the beam of the running lights, he could make out mountains. A crest. All approaching way too fast. He forced himself to breathe.

The hum of the rotor engine roared to life, followed by the reassuring *thrwump-thrwump* of the blades picking up speed. The helicopter steadied, then gained altitude.

Roark grinned at the flight medic. "See, told you it was going to be fine." He ignored the thumping of his own heart.

Thomas nodded. His hands, holding the cooler in a death grip, were still as white as his face. The lenses of his glasses fogged over, although there was no heat in the aircraft.

"Well, *that* was fun," the pilot announced.

Roark laughed and clapped the pilot's shoulder. "Good work, man. Good work."

"Are we almost there?" Thomas's voice shook as he spoke over the engines and rattles.

"I've had to veer off course to avoid the main line of the storm. It might put us off schedule by about an hour."

"Will that be a problem? With the heart, I mean?" Roark asked.

Glancing at his watch, Thomas raked his upper teeth over his bottom lip. "It might."

"What do you mean, *it might*?"

"Well, the cardiac surgeon told me if I didn't land in three hours to give the first injection. It's already been two hours since the heart was harvested."

"Then go ahead and give the injection." Roark cracked his knuckles.

"It's just . . ." Thomas gazed down at the floor of the helicopter.

"What?"

"The procedure is very delicate. I need to be as still as possible, and I need light."

Roark shook his head. "You've got to be kidding me. Still? In a helicopter?"

"That's the only way to do it. It's not fair. We didn't anticipate a storm of this intensity coming upon us so quickly. Why did this have to happen to us?"

Roark had never been able to tolerate whining. "You'll have to do it despite the turbulence."

"I'm not trained to inject hearts." Thomas's bottom lip protruded. "The cardiac surgeon should've come."

"But he didn't and you did." Roark laid a hand on the man's shoulder. "You can do it, Thomas." He whipped out the flashlight fastened to the side of the copilot's chair. "I'll hold the light for you."

The flight medic hesitated a moment, looking like he was gnawing on the inside of his mouth, then nodded. "Okay."

Roark flipped on the flashlight and tapped the pilot's shoulder. "Thomas needs to make an injection. Can you keep this as steady as possible?"

"I'll try, but the wind and snow are really pushing us."

"Just do your best."

Thomas unzipped the pack, then laid it open on the seat beside him. Four syringes snuggled inside. He set the cooler on the floor, then lifted the cover.

Not knowing what to expect, Roark held his breath and peeked into the container. There wasn't a river of blood, only a pink tinge of liquid surrounding a bluish lump. Clear, liquid-filled bags surrounded the organ.

Thomas freed one of the syringes from the pack, then hovered over the heart. His Adam's apple bobbed once. He lifted his gaze to Roark.

Roark smiled and focused the beam of light. "Go ahead, you're doing great." Not that he would know if the guy wasn't, but he couldn't tell Thomas that. Part of his job was to be a calming presence to those on the edge.

Lowering the syringe, Thomas leaned over the cooler.

The helicopter shoved to the left.

Thomas jerked the needle upright. A sheen of sweat glistened on his upper lip. "I can't do this."

"Sure you can." Roark tapped the pilot's shoulder again. "Try to keep her as steady as possible for a minute."

"I'm trying," the pilot growled.

Roark directed the flashlight again. "Go ahead."

Thomas licked his lips before hunching over again. He lowered the syringe. This time, the needle pierced the tissue of the organ. He pressed down on the plunger.

After pulling the needle free, Thomas locked it back in the pack, then closed the lid on the cooler. He wiped the side of his face with his shoulder before looking at Roark and smiling. "I did it. That gives the heart another twelve hours."

Roark shifted on the seat, the worn vinyl rubbing against his jeans, and let out a hiss of air. Finally. It was done. "Then we're all good." But Roark wasn't so sure. He clicked off the flashlight, then snapped it back into its holder.

"Look guys, the Great Smoky Mountains National Park," the pilot announced, as if this were a guided tour.

Although he'd seen the park many times, hiked and camped there even, Roark still stared out the window. Beneath the helicopter's running lights, the peaks and valleys protruded, but the snow and shadows limited any details. "Did we miss the line of the storm?"

"I think so. It's still pretty bad, but at least the wind currents are less intense now."

The helicopter evened out. Although the wind continued to batter the sides, the current seemed to have stopped fluctuating so rapidly. Roark sat back, shoving aside the formidable warning in his head.

They'd just entered a false sense of security.

Friday, 7:45 p.m.
Congressman McGovern's Office
Knoxville, Tennessee

"I'M A UNITED STATES congressman, for pity's sake. I don't ride in taxies. Get me a car to take me to the hospital," Warren barked into the phone. What kind of runaround did these imbeciles think he'd accept? His father would turn over in his grave if Warren dared to allow himself to be treated as ordinary.

"Sir, I understand your situation, but we have a blizzard, and it's late. No car is available right now. I can call you a taxi."

Warren needed to get to the hospital, and fast. He sucked in air, held it until his lungs screamed, then let it whoosh out. "Just find me a car—and not a taxi."

"I'll see what I can do, sir."

"Do it quickly." Warren slammed down the phone and gazed around his office. The dark paneling and soft track lighting did nothing to soothe his irritation.

A knock rapped against the door.

"Come in."

Kevin scuttled in, carrying a folder that he set on Warren's desk. "Here are the papers Mr. Markinson had, sir."

Warren raised an eyebrow. "Does he know you got these?"

Kevin smiled. "I was able to copy and return them without his realizing I had them."

"And no one saw you?"

Kevin's head shook like a washing machine on spin cycle. "Oh no, sir. No one."

"Good job. Good job." At least he'd get an idea of what Markinson wanted kept secret. Warren flipped open the file and scanned the first page. His blood pressure spiked as he skimmed the documents.

"Is there anything else, sir?"

Warren looked up at his young aide. So naive and guileless, trusting and earnest. Nothing more than a mouse of a man, really.

Warren's father would have hated him. "Yes. Find me a limo to take me to the hospital, pronto."

"Yes, sir." Kevin rushed from the room, all but bowing before he left.

Warren smiled. Rule number four—always instill a reverential fear in your subordinates. You'll never know when their eagerness to please you will come in handy.

He returned to the file—meticulously documented accounting records, down to the last detail. The deposits of cash, the transfers from one corporation's account to another to yet another, and the wires to offshore accounts—nine of them. Warren shook his head. None of it made a lick of sense to a layman, but if Jonathan Wilks got his heart transplant and came out of the coma, he'd roll over and bust this ring wide open.

Data on Wilks reflected he'd been married for twenty-five years to the same woman: Carmen. While Wilks didn't have a child of his own, the wife had a son when the couple married. This stepson hadn't been to the Wilks's home in several months. The stepson had reported his mother's death, requested an autopsy, received said copy, then dropped off the radar. No additional information was provided. The FBI was looking for him, but it didn't appear that finding him was a top priority.

Nothing Warren could see that Noah Markinson wouldn't want out in the open. So why did the man act so coy?

He closed the folder with a decisive snap, then lifted the phone and dialed.

Rule number five—always have contacts who could assist you in getting around obstacles tossed in your path.

FIVE

Friday, 8:00 p.m.
Abrams Creek Ranger Station
Great Smoky Mountains National Park, Tennessee

BRANNON DID HER PREFLIGHT assessment under the bright
security lights of the heliport, then placed her Sig Sauer in the
box. Strapping herself into the pilot's harness with a deep breath,
she clenched and unclenched her fingers, steeling her nerves.
She started the engine and radioed her takeoff to the air traffic
control tower while Lincoln fastened his harness. They bowed their
heads for a quick moment, asking for God's hedge of protection
to surround them, just as they did before every takeoff. Brannon
whispered an additional prayer of protection for those in the Bell.

The rotor engine hummed as Brannon blew on her hands to
warm them, refusing to lose the *feel* of her controls by wearing
gloves. With the helicopter light on the skids, Brannon increased
the Dolphin's power to a forty-knot pitch altitude. During takeoff
she pulled the collective until she reached the power setting of just
below maximum. She made a quick jab with the left pedal, and the
helicopter lifted into the air.

"Where are we headed first?" Lincoln asked over the headset.

"Toward Clingmans Dome. If that pilot shifted to avoid the
worst of the weather, he'd adjust to the west of the direct path.
I want to try and raise him on the pilot-to-pilot comm." She pushed
the cyclic, shoving the helicopter into a hammerhead turn. Her sense
of control surged, and she smiled into the darkness.

"Man, this blizzard's nasty. Haven't seen this much of a mess
in years."

"Mmm." In the shroud of night, with the weather moving in so, she would have to fly by the gauges. Brannon squinted to make out the crests of the mountains below them. Wind rocked the aircraft, blowing snow at them from all directions, like flying inside a blender set on puree. The *ting-ting* of the sleet hitting the windshield competed against the whirring of the rotor blades.

"And the bad stuff hasn't even gotten here yet." Lincoln rubbed his gloved hands together.

Brannon sighed, her breath making puffs in the frosty air. "I hope that pilot has some type of training in weather like this." *Please, God, let him have had some.*

"Don't all you pilots have to?"

"In flight school, yeah, but let's be honest, it depends on where you fly the majority of the time. Most who aren't flying in this stuff all the time forget how to do it."

"Use it or lose it?"

She nodded. "Something like that." She pressed the radio trigger on the cyclic with her right index finger, opening the general channel in her headset. "RCM986 to Bell pilot bearing into GSM."

Static snuggled against her ear, comforting her. At least the radio worked in the Dolphin.

"RCM986 to pilot bearing into GSM, come in Bell pilot."

"RCM986 this is Knoxville ATC."

"Knoxville ATC, I'm in flight to intercept Bell206B3 helicopter flying in direct line of blizzard. Over."

"ATC has lost radio contact with the aircraft. Can you raise on pilot-to-pilot comm? Over."

"What's his call sign?"

"Call sign is 121MCE."

"Stand by, Knoxville ATC." Brannon hit the trigger again to access the pilot-to-pilot comm, then cringed as the channel change squealed over her headset. "RCM986 GSMNPS calling 121MCE." She paused a moment. "Calling Bell 121MCE, come in."

Another squeal erupted over her headset, then a static-filled response. "121MCE here."

Brannon let out a long breath. "What are your coordinates?"

Lincoln switched on his direct light before jotting the numbers in his spiral notebook as the pilot spouted them off.

"Stand by, please. Notifying Knoxville ATC of your location." She triggered the channel back to the main frequency, reported the Bell's coordinates to the air traffic controller, and waited for their message to the pilot. Brannon glanced down at her own coordinates and calculated that she could reach the other helicopter within thirty minutes. Would that be enough time?

"Knoxville ATC, please stand by. Contacting 121MCE for status report. Over." Brannon clicked the channel trigger. "RCM986 hailing 121MCE."

"121MCE here. Go ahead." The static over the connection had decreased.

"How're you doing in the weather?" Brannon pressed her lips together as she awaited his response.

"Weather is brutal. Zero visibility and high winds. I've never seen anything like it. We don't get much weather in North Carolina. Not like this."

A chill that had nothing to do with the weather seeped into her. "How's your craft handling?"

"Not so good. I veered off course to miss the bulk of the storm. Comm is also acting up."

Which explained why Air Traffic Control couldn't reach him. "How're you on fuel?"

"Half a tank."

Brannon breathed a silent prayer of thanks. "Stand by." She clicked the channel back to the main frequency. "Knoxville ATC, this is RCM986 again. Over."

"Do you have a status on 121MCE?"

"Affirmative. Pilot states he has half a tank of fuel but is off course. Pilot reports regular radio is out as well. Please advise. Over."

"Knoxville ATC requests you intercept Bell and escort to Knoxville. Can you confirm? Over."

"Confirm, Knoxville ATC. Intercept and escort. Over." She twisted the channel knob back to the pilot-to-pilot comm and informed the Bell pilot of ATC's instructions.

The loud response sounded over the headset. "Yes, I copy. Thank you."

"Copy that. We should intercept you in approximately twenty-five minutes. What are your current coordinates?"

As the pilot read out his coordinates, foreboding spidered down Brannon's spine. She cut her eyes over to Lincoln, who scribbled in his notebook.

"Got it, 121MCE. Will keep the frequency open."

"Thanks, RCM986."

Brannon switched off her mike. "I have a sick feeling this will turn into a SAR." She shook her head. "We'll intercept them right about Mount LeConte. Great. Had to be one of the high areas."

"'O, you of little faith.'"

She narrowed her eyes at Lincoln but let the Scripture soothe her fears. "Too easy. Luke 12:28."

Lincoln chuckled, the familiar rumbling calming her just as their quizzing of Scripture did. It'd been the one thing Lincoln used to pull her out of the darkest grief she'd ever lived through. Without the coping mechanism and Lincoln, she didn't know if she would've survived.

Brannon shifted in the seat, keeping her eyes peeled on the shadowed horizon. A sudden gust of wind thrust the Dolphin down and to the right. She tightened her grip on the collective and pushed on the right pedal. The helicopter jostled, then steadied. "Storm's moving in right on top of us."

"We'll be fine."

"'He got up, rebuked the wind, and said to the waves, "Quiet! Be still!" Then the wind died down and it was completely calm.'"

Lincoln shook his head. "Simple. Mark 4:39."

"Right. Now if we could just get the wind to calm down for us, I'd be one happy camper." *God, we could definitely use some of Your rebuking right about now.*

Lincoln's face twisted into seriousness. "Let's pray."

"Already on it."

Friday, 8:15 p.m.
Great Smoky Mountains, Tennessee

ROARK RUBBED HIS PALMS on his jeans and flexed his fingers. Why didn't helicopters come equipped with heaters? Because no idiot would be out in this kind of weather.

A gust of snow and sleet, shoved by the unforgiving wind, plowed into the side of the aircraft, pitching it nose first into a plunge. The helicopter's engine sputtered and coughed, made an ear-piercing screech, then stalled. Lights flashed inside the cabin. Alarms reverberated off the metal frame.

The lack of engine noise hung colder than the air, heavier than wet snow.

"Hold on!"

Roark stared at the pilot as the helicopter dropped. "What are you doing?"

"Autorotation, now be quiet."

Thomas's eyes widened to the size of silver dollars. He set the cooler on the floor, placed his feet on either side, and tightened the cinch of his seat belt.

Bracing his own feet on the floor, Roark kept his attention trained on the cursing pilot.

An odor similar to ethanol seeped into the cabin. Roark swallowed back the acidic burning in the back of his throat.

The pilot lowered the control in his left hand, all the way down. His right leg stiffened and pressed down on the pedal.

The nose of the aircraft pitched down. Shifting under them, the helicopter lost airspeed.

With his right hand the pilot lifted the control. The needle on the RPM gauge of the instrument panel spun counterclockwise.

"121MCE to RCM986. Mayday! I repeat, Mayday! We're going down."

The air crackled with the wind and vibration. The rancid stench of fear overpowered the smell associated with electrical charges.

Roark clenched his jaw. It was one thing to suspect they might crash, but it was an entirely different matter to hear the pilot call out a Mayday.

The pilot yelled into his headset. "No, there's no place to land. Can't recover from the autorotation." He tapped a gauge, then yelled out coordinates.

Thomas whimpered. Roark couldn't comfort him this time. Not now, when it was obvious they were about to crash and burn.

The helicopter plummeted toward the mountain summit and outcrops—rapid and inflexible. Wind pummeled the body of the aircraft, causing it to creak and quake.

Roark's stomach flipped as if he were soaring down the highest peak of a roller coaster. He tightened his seat belt, then gripped the side of the seat.

"Hold on, guys. This one's gonna be rough."

As if they needed the announcement. Roark didn't blink as he stared out the front bubble window. The mountain drew closer and closer. Trees grew bigger and bigger. Every muscle in Roark tightened, squeezing . . . choking.

Thomas heaved, emptying his stomach contents all over the floor.

The bitter stench almost caused Roark to gag. He jammed his feet against the rubber tracks where the copilot's chair was anchored to the floor and pressed his back into the seat.

Trees brushed against the windows, scraping and rasping. Limbs snapped. The helicopter shuddered.

A boom exploded in Roark's ears. He jolted forward, his seat belt pinning him to the seat. The windshield shattered, then clattered against metal. A blast of frigid air swooshed into the cabin.

Then all was still. Silence loomed over the helicopter.

Roark struggled to regain his breath, his heartbeat ringing in his head.

Drip . . . drip . . . drip!

The unmistakable odor of fuel filled Roark's nostrils. He opened his mouth to breathe and struggled to get his fingers around the seat belt release.

A thunderous explosion sounded. No, Roark *felt* the explosion. Unbearable heat lanced out at his face. He squinted, forcing himself to disengage the belt. Dots surged before his line of vision, just out of focus. He shook his head and fought to keep his eyes opened.

Not again!

Orange and red flames licked up at the pilot's feet. He screamed, the agony chasing away every other sound.

Friday, 8:25 p.m.
Congressman McGovern's Office
Knoxville, Tennessee

"CONGRESSMAN, YOU NEED TO see this." Kevin passed him a single sheet of paper.

Warren scanned the information and ground his teeth.

RCM986 with GSMNPS has picked up an
emergency Mayday call from 121MCE.

Warren's pulse spiked. He glanced at his aide. "Is that Mayday call from the helicopter transporting the heart?"

"Yes, sir."

Warren continued reading down the page.

121MCE is down. RCM986 GSMNPS search-and-
rescue team dispatched.

Warren glanced again at Kevin. "Who's heading up the search and rescue?"

"From the ATC conversation I've been monitoring, a ranger-pilot from the Great Smoky Mountains National Park, sir."

"So they're going to find the helicopter?"

"As I understand it, this National Park Service pilot has been in communication with the Bell pilot for some time and is already on her way to intercept."

"Her?"

"The ranger-pilot is a woman."

Long minutes ticked by, as if peanut butter had crept into Father Time's clock.

A woman pilot? How absurd. The heart needed to be recovered, and they were entrusting a *woman* to do the rescuing?

"Anything else, sir?"

"Did you hear when the search-and-rescue unit should arrive at the crash site?"

"The land crew should be there within thirty minutes."

"And the ranger woman?"

"Should be there any moment, sir, if not already. I'll continue monitoring."

"Very good, Kevin. Keep me updated."

The young man rushed from the room.

Sitting back in his leather chair, Warren peered out the window into the dark void. Swirls of pristine snow danced around, but he paid little attention. His mind tripped over tidbits of information. Shifting in his seat, he reached into his Armani jacket pocket, pulled out his private cell phone, and pressed speed dial number six.

The situation had escalated. Now Warren had to act.

SIX

THE SMALL BUILDING HUMMED with activity—music blaring, girls giggling, and doors slamming. The perfume Madam Nancy doused them in mixed with the stench of body sweat and liquor, hanging in the air like heavy clouds. As Friday night arrived, so did the men willing to brave the foul weather and long distance to make a visit.

Mai had vomited after Milt's call, enraging Madam Nancy to the point where she had been beaten, but at least she was excused from "entertaining" for several hours. Huddled in the corner of her room, Mai rested her head against the rough wall. She had to find a way out. But how? She was smart but in unfamiliar territory.

The office door slammed, causing the thin wall to rattle and shake. Mai lifted her head, then pressed it back against the chipped paint when she heard voices.

"I don't know what we're going to do, Bucky. Milton says they're closing down operations for a while," Madam Nancy's voice screeched.

"What's going on with them? They've never been behind schedule before." Mai didn't recognize the man's voice.

"I don't know. He just said there was a glitch in their system and they're working to straighten it all out." A cabinet banged, then glasses rattled. "I don't know what to do. I was ready to ship this current group off to Colorado when the new ones arrived." Madam Nancy's words echoed against the wall. "I swear this throws our whole system out of whack."

Creaks of wooden chairs came from the office. Mai hugged her legs tighter to her chest.

"Sounds to me like something's seriously wrong, Nancy. If I were you, I'd check it out." The man's belch vibrated the wall, making Mai shudder. Just like all the repulsive Americans.

"You think?"

"No telling what's going on, but if I were you, I'd sure want to know."

"You have a point, Bucky." Glasses clinked before clattering against wood. "Have any suggestions on who I could get to look into this for me?" Madam Nancy's voice sounded smooth and silky now.

"Well, now, I just might."

The wooden chair creaked again.

"Maybe you and I should go to the hall back there and discuss this a little further."

Madam Nancy laughed, but it did not sound ugly like normal. "Don't be crass, Bucky, those are for the girls. I happen to keep a special room for myself and some very special customers. Would you like to see it?"

Mai pinched her eyes closed tight, her firsthand knowledge of what Madam Nancy was about to do with the strange man filling her mind with visuals she did not want. The acid in her stomach churned, and she retched, but nothing came up. She had nothing left to purge.

She would find a way to flee Madam Nancy's before she was sent to this Colorado place. She had to. Her survival depended on her escape.

Friday, 8:29 p.m.
East of Mount LeConte
Great Smoky Mountains, Tennessee

"HOLD ON," BRANNON HISSED as she took the Dolphin into a deep pitch. The pilot-to-pilot comm had remained silent for several minutes, no matter how much she hailed the Bell. *Please, God, let them be okay.*

Lincoln reached down to the metal box snapped below his legs as Brannon dropped the helicopter lower. He yanked out the night-vision goggles, then shoved them over his eyes. "Tell me when to start looking."

"Now." She squinted against the driving sleet and snow before glancing down at her instrument panel. The little voice inside her head screamed that she might be too late for the people in the Bell. She increased the Dolphin's airspeed as she dropped altitude, increasing her prayer as well.

Peering out into the sheets of precipitation descending, Lincoln tapped his fingers against his knee. In a fluid movement he reached over and gripped Brannon's shoulder. "About thirty degrees to your left. See it?"

She jerked her gaze to where Lincoln had indicated and squinted. Faint hues of orange danced off in the distance. Flames! Brannon increased the airspeed, pushing the craft into maximum load as she careened over the tall trees. Three more knots clicked off her gauge, and she decreased their altitude again, slipping lower and dodging the pines with their branches covered in snow.

The dense forest whipped past the helicopter as Brannon kept her eyes glued to the fire cutting into the landscape, drawing brighter and closer. She tightened her hold on the controls, careful not to let her hands slip against the sweat coating her palms.

Lincoln pressed a hand against the bubble window, lodging himself against the seat as the helicopter dipped lower and lower. He pushed the goggles tighter on his face and peered out the window.

Despite her training in the Coast Guard, Brannon bit back fear. The searing at the back of her throat burned with familiarity. It scorched her each time she searched for a crash and prayed to find survivors. The pain associated with losing her parents, then Wade, always sat at the forefront of her memory.

Please, Lord, let us find them alive.

As she flew closer, the orange hue flickered against the sullen night like a serpent's tongue hissing out into the darkness. Despair shot through her as she searched for a landing area close to the crash but not close enough to endanger the Dolphin. A small clearing next to the valley opened, and she aimed for it. The edge of Roaring Fork nature trail. If only the Bell pilot had been able to hold out for a couple hundred more feet, the helicopter could've stayed intact.

Wind gusted against the swooping helicopter, causing her landing to bounce and skid. Brannon shut down the engine, unfastened her harness, and jumped from the Dolphin right behind Lincoln. The two raced toward the crashed helicopter, their boots slipping on the icy valley bed.

The Bell, which now blazed in yellow and orange flames, lay on its nose like a crippled bird fallen in flight. A dancing blue flame shot up the middle, stopping Brannon cold. She grabbed Lincoln's shoulder. "Be careful. The fuel is leaking, and it's gonna blow."

He nodded but continued on toward the wounded aircraft. Jerking open the passenger cargo door, he reached inside. Brannon pushed to the pilot's door and wrenched it open. White heat blew against her face, forcing her to stumble backward. The rank stench of burning flesh assaulted her nostrils. She turned her head and retched before turning back to the cockpit.

The pilot's head lolled to the side as the flickering blaze ate up his legs. The pilot had passed the point of saving. Brannon pressed her lips together, tears pooling in her eyes.

Lincoln moved into the backseat. "Help me with these two." He dragged an unconscious man to the icy ground. Beneath his coat, his white shirt was soaked red in a large patch. Lincoln turned toward the helicopter again.

Brannon swallowed hard, then beat her partner to the remaining man. While Lincoln gripped his feet, she reached for his arms. Her gaze settled on the man's face—handsome and rugged with a fresh scar—the US marshal she'd seen on television. Her mind replayed the news segment as she struggled to help Lincoln pull the man free from the inferno building in the helicopter. The heart!

After letting the man sink to the ground, Brannon rushed once more to the crushed Bell.

"We can't save the pilot, Brannon. Let it go." Lincoln hollered as he raced forward with the fire extinguisher from the Dolphin.

"The heart," she tossed over her shoulder as she pushed into the body of the aircraft. A red cooler with a black pouch on top leaned

against the back of the pilot's seat. The crackle from the engine
prickled the flesh on Brannon's arms. The stench of burning flesh
seared her throat. She snatched up the cooler and the pouch.

Lincoln sprayed the cockpit with the extinguisher to no avail.
Brannon screamed at him to get out, then turned, took two steps,
and dove for the ground.

An explosion rocked the earth as if an earthquake occurred.
Heat surrounded the valley area.

Brannon kept herself flat, covering her head with her hands.
Bits of debris danced on the wind before falling to litter the snow-
covered terrain.

"Are you okay?" Lincoln's hand on her shoulder brought imme-
diate comfort and relief.

She rolled over and stared into his hooded eyes before accept-
ing the hand he offered. "I'm okay. How're they?" She nodded
toward the two men lying on the ground.

"Unconscious. One's got a cut on his shoulder, and the other
has a gash on his head."

Brannon retrieved the cooler and black pouch, then followed
Lincoln as he picked his way back to the men. Her pulse rocked as
she scanned the crash site. Only bits and pieces of the helicopter lay
scattered and smoldering in the midst of the forest.

That had been close, too close. *Thank You, God, that no one else
was killed.* But her heart ached for the pilot. *Why couldn't we have
gotten here in time?*

No reply came in the stillness of the explosion aftermath.

Lincoln dropped to a knee beside the man whose shirt stuck to
his chest with the spreading red stain. He snapped open the emergency medical kit from the Dolphin, clicked on the flashlight, and
pressed clean gauze to the man's injury.

Lowering herself beside the marshal, Brannon pushed her bangs,
dripping with melted snow and sleet, aside. She laid her fingers on
his forehead to inspect the cut, then glanced at the man's handsome
face. She sucked in cold air, then rocked back on her heels.

Eyes like liquid black stared up at her.

Friday, 8:40 p.m.
Crash site
Great Smoky Mountains, Tennessee

ROARK'S FOREHEAD BURNED WHERE the nymph touched him. The outline around her was fuzzy, distorted. He blinked. Did he die? Was this a dream? Flecks of snow and sleet assaulted his face. No, he was alive and awake, and the woman gazing down at him with wide eyes was no nymph or angel. He dug his elbows into the cold, wet ground and struggled to sit. He tapped the butt of his gun, and his heartbeat steadied.

The woman's hands moved to his shoulders and eased him back. "Don't try to sit. You're okay, but I need to treat the cut on your head. I'm Brannon Callahan with the Great Smoky Mountains National Park Rangers. We're here to help." Gauze appeared in her hand, and she dabbed at his forehead.

No, he didn't need anyone to take care of him—he was always in control. He waved the ranger's hands away and pushed into a sitting position. The wind carried a sharp burning odor on its gusts. "What happened?"

"Your helicopter crashed." Her voice caressed his ears, smooth and gilded.

Roark scanned the area, catching sight of hunks of metal scattering the ground, wisps of smoke rising from their mounds. He glanced back at the woman hovering over him. Her auburn hair hung over her shoulder in a loose ponytail. "What about the other—"

"We got the other passenger out." She gave a jerk of her head. "My partner, Lincoln, is attending to his injury."

"And the pilot?" He had to focus. Keep to the task at hand.

Her big eyes blinked with moisture, then bore into him, pinning him to the spot. How unusual—one green eye and one blue, yet both shimmering almost iridescently by the glow of the flashlight. She shook her head. "He was already dead when we got here."

Panic shot into his bloodstream. Had he failed his mission? "There was a cooler. It held a—"

"We got the heart out." She smiled as she interrupted, laying her hand on his shoulder again.

Frowning, he stared up at her. His fingers sought the butt of his Beretta. "How did you know about the heart?"

"I watched the news. You're the marshal, right?"

"Roark Holland." He dug his palms into the ground, the ice stinging his flesh, then pushed into a standing position.

She rose as well, a good eight or nine inches shorter than his six-foot-two height. She had a good, athletic build, not like the skinny figure his youngest sister had.

He brushed past Brannon and towered over the man tending to Thomas. "How is he?"

"He's lost a lot of blood. I think a main artery may have been severed by metal shards." The dark-haired man in a ranger coat glanced up at him, then gazed over to the woman. "We need to get him to a hospital ASAP."

"Let's get to the helicopter. You can work on him in the air." Brannon moved to Thomas's feet.

Roark walked around her, then leaned over to help the man with Thomas.

She laid a hand on his shoulder, jerking his attention back to her determined face. "You just get in. You're in no shape to help carry him. That head gash is pretty nasty." She flashed him a gentle smile.

Roark stomped out of the way, lamenting her logic under his breath. He. Had. To. Stay. In. Control. He lifted the cooler with the black pouch, then squared his shoulders. "We have to get this heart to the hospital in Knoxville immediately." The sharpness of his tone cut through the howling of the wind.

Brannon jutted out her chin. "Of course. And he"—she tilted her head toward Thomas—"needs the hospital as well."

Roark clenched his jaw. She kept staring at him, trying to read his expression.

"Fine. Let's get to that helicopter of yours." Still gripping the cooler and medicine pack in his right hand, he scooped up the medical case from beside her partner with his left, then hitched a brow as he stared back at the woman.

She sighed and broke eye contact, then bent and grabbed Thomas by the legs while her partner hoisted Thomas's shoulders. Together, the two lifted the flight medic and swayed as their boots slipped on the icy ground.

The wind whistled through the trees as the odd group rushed toward the aircraft a mere five hundred yards away.

Roark passed them, heading toward the waiting helicopter. While bigger, it didn't matter. In this weather, it was still an airborne coffin. He could only hope the woman's partner was a better pilot than the previous one.

Crack!

Roark groaned as something slammed into his back and tackled him to the ground. He twisted to see what it was, his hands pulling into thick, soft auburn hair.

The woman ranger straddled him.

He moved to shove her aside when a limb crashed to the ground with a sickening thud, covering his footprints in the snow where he had stood minutes ago. Flecks of ice splattered him and the woman, sending shivers over his body.

Brannon gave him a casual shrug, then pushed to her feet and dusted the snow from her shoulders. "You're welcome." Her stare lingered a moment longer, then she shook her head and went to assist her partner as he dragged Thomas across the white ground.

Sure, she may have saved him from getting whacked by the limb, but what right did she have to come across so . . . so . . . what? Roark struggled to his feet, lifted the case, pack, and cooler, then stomped behind them. In control? He was supposed to be the one in charge.

When Roark jumped into the helicopter, Thomas lay across the backseat, buckled in tight. The shelter the aircraft provided from the blasting wind welcomed him aboard. Unlike the other helicopter, this one provided ample lighting to see. He shoved the case and cooler with medicine pack across the floor and wiped the snow from his brow.

Roark reached into his jacket pocket, pulled out his satellite phone, and stared at the LCD screen. No signal. What good was a satellite phone if the blizzard could block reception?

"Lincoln will stay with him in flight. You can sit in the copilot's seat." She rubbed her gloveless hands together and blew on them.

Do what? "Isn't he the pilot?"

Her chuckle was low and throaty. "Nope. That would be me." She patted the seat beside her. "Come on up. Lincoln needs all the room he can get back there."

Roark settled in the other chair in the cockpit and glanced over at her. Snowflakes caught in her eyelashes, drawing his gaze to her piercing eyes. He swallowed against the heat rising in his chest. This was a job and nothing more.

"What's your name again?" His voice sounded demanding to his own ears.

She raised an eyebrow. "Brannon Callahan. And the man back there is Lincoln Vailes."

"Again, I'm Roark Holland, US marshal."

"Do you always use your job title in introductions?"

He opened his mouth to reproach her snappy comment, but he needn't have bothered. She'd already slipped on her headset and flipped switches on the control panel. The helicopter vibrated as the engines hummed to life. "GSMNPS rangers, cancel call out to crash coordinates. I have the survivors and will deliver them to Parkwest Medical. Over."

From the backseat Thomas moaned. Roark turned. Blood soaked the front of his shirt. His face contorted into a grimace, and he emitted another groan.

Lincoln pulled a wad of dripping gauze from Thomas's chest. Fresh blood, bright red, oozed from a large gash near his right shoulder. Lincoln grabbed a fresh pack of gauze from the case, ripped it open with his teeth, then pressed it against the cut. Thomas cringed and forced out a breath.

"Copy that, base. Will notify Knoxville ATC as soon as I'm in the air. Over." Brannon slipped her headset down to rest around her neck and hollered over the roar of the rotors thumping. "Ready?"

Lincoln made a circular motion with his finger. "We're good."

She nodded and pressed a series of buttons and gauges on the panel. The aircraft vibrated in response.

Ping! Ping! Ping!

Roark's breathing froze. No mistaking that sound—the telling echo of bullets hitting metal. He released his Beretta from its holster in one fluid motion.

The rotor engine coughed, then smoke filled the air.

Brannon flipped switches, her eyes wide. "We've lost the engine." Her gaze jerked over the instrument panel, and she ducked her head. "And the rotors are out." She slapped the side of her fist against the instrument panel and glared at Roark. "Who's shooting at us?"

As if he knew.

SEVEN

Friday, 9:42 p.m.
Crash Site Near Mount LeConte
Great Smoky Mountains, Tennessee

BRANNON CLICKED THE TRIGGER, activating her radio frequency. "RCM986 to Knoxville ATC, come in. Mayday. HH-65 Dolphin down. Shots fired. I repeat, RCM986 is disabled on the ground."

No warming hum of static echoed against her ear.

Roark steadied his Beretta. "Get down!" His gaze locked with Brannon's for a moment as he slunk to the floor and eased around the copilot's seat.

No kidding, *get down*. This wasn't her first rodeo at being fired upon. Brannon tried again to raise a contact on the radio—no response. She yanked her headset from her neck and tossed it.

Slipping from the pilot's seat, Brannon moved to the floor and opened the box. She withdrew her Sig handgun and crawled behind Roark. She grabbed the hand radio, turned it on, and sent out one more distress call. Still nothing.

The metal *pinging* smacked against the crippled helicopter, hammering out any coherent thought Brannon could muster from the recesses of her mind. Why would someone shoot at them, especially in this weather? And in this area? Who knew where to look for them?

Roark opened the door to the helicopter a fraction of an inch. A bullet whizzed at the opening. He fell back into the cabin and slammed the door shut.

The flight medic, barely conscious, groaned. Placing another stack of gauze against the wounded man's shoulder, Lincoln hissed over the noise, "What's going on?" He kept his head low, level with the seat bottom.

Roark grunted as he pushed to a crouching position. A red splotch seeped through his jacket over his left tricep. "I'll handle this."

Brannon moved beside Lincoln, grabbed a clean pack of gauze, and offered it to Roark. "You've been shot."

He glanced at his upper arm and shrugged. "Just a graze. I'm fine." He ignored the gauze and turned back to the door. "Everybody get as low as you can."

She opened her mouth to tell him not to do something stupid, but he jerked open the helicopter door, then fired shots. The blast of the handgun's discharge reverberated in the metal Dolphin, drowning out the howling wind.

Brannon hunkered on the floor, her weapon at the ready. Fear like she hadn't felt since she led the Coast Guard rescue mission in Cuban waters swelled inside her. That had been the only time attempts were made to stop her search-and-rescue efforts.

She slipped her finger into the trigger well of the Sig. *God, please help us.*

Lincoln rested his hand on her shoulder. Over the *ping-ping* of bullets hitting the helicopter and the roar of Roark's firing, his soft voice whispered against her ear. "Our Father, who art in heaven, hallowed be thy name."

Weak at first, Brannon lifted her voice with Lincoln's. "Thy kingdom come, thy will be done, on earth as it is in heaven."

Thomas coughed, then his voice, wobbly and weak, joined theirs. "Give us this day our daily bread. Forgive us our sins, as we forgive those who sin against us. Lead us not into temptation, but deliver us from evil. For thine is the kingdom, the power, and the glory forever."

Roark jammed the door shut, slumping against the back of the copilot's seat. "They've backed off for now. We need to make a move—we're sitting ducks in this bird."

"Amen," Brannon whispered, studying Roark's eyes. She forced her voice to come out steady and solid despite the pounding of her heart. "Why in blue blazes is someone shooting at us?"

His upper lip curled into a snarl. "Obviously someone wants to kill us."

"You think?" She snorted. "Must be pretty determined to venture out in this weather and know our exact coordinates." Her gaze raked over him. "Any idea who would be crazy enough?"

"If I had to make a guess, I'd say someone who doesn't want that heart to make it to the recipient."

As she stared at the cooler, Brannon's mind replayed the newscast she'd watched. "A government witness, right?"

"Look, I'll explain everything later. Right now we need to get out of here."

"Where would you like us to go?" She cocked her head. "In case you've forgotten, we're smack-dab in the middle of a blizzard. The nearest ranger station is about twenty miles of rough forest away. We'll be safer staying in the helicopter, defending ourselves here. At least air traffic control will have the coordinates where we landed. And the Dolphin will provide us with some cover."

"Did you raise anyone on the radio?"

"No, but they had my location when we landed." She ran a hand over her wet hair. "They'll send someone for us."

"Who? I thought *you* were the rescue team." Roark added under his breath, "Some rescue."

The hairs on the back of her neck bristled like a pine in the spring. "How dare you." She and Lincoln had risked their lives, and her chopper, to come out in this mess to save them.

He raised a hand. "Just save it. The situation has changed. I'm in charge now, and we'll do things the way I say we will. So pack up. We're moving out."

Brannon stiffened yet her hands trembled. Everything within her very being told her not to leave her helicopter and to ignore the egotistical marshal. She was trained for SAR, especially in the Smokies. "Look, I'm the—"

Lincoln laid a hand on her shoulder. She turned and her gaze locked with his.

"He's a federal marshal, and he has the authority. Let it go. You can give him a piece of your mind later. Help me pack up the emergency supplies."

His voice pacified the indignation surging through her. She nodded and replaced the spelunking equipment with food and survival supplies into the sturdy backpacks.

Roark inched open the door and peered outside. Didn't stop him from barking orders. "Hurry up, get that stuff loaded. We can carry the two backpacks and the heart—that's it. We'll need our hands free to tote Thomas. Let's go."

Brannon stuck out her tongue at his back. Childish, yes, but it made her feel a lot better. She slipped her gun into its holster on her belt. After loading the backpacks with all the water bottles, blankets, first-aid supplies, and packages of dried food, she slipped the hand radio into her pack, then slung one over her back and passed the other to Lincoln. Almost as an afterthought, she grabbed the black pack from atop the cooler, slipped it into the front compartment of her pack, and zipped it up.

"How should we carry him?" she whispered to Lincoln with a nod toward the injured medic. He had more EMT training than she did, and she trusted him. "He's regained consciousness."

"Let's try supporting him between us."

The man shifted, struggling to pull himself into a sitting position. "The glass cut my supraspinatus tendon." He ground his teeth together.

"What's that mean?" Brannon chewed her cuticle.

"That's the tendon under my rotator cuff. Until I can get surgery, my right arm is useless." His big eyes blinked behind his thick glasses. "Whoever supports my right side will have to do it all. I can't even lift my arm."

Lincoln nodded before staring at Brannon, his brow arched. She sighed and shifted under the flight medic's left arm.

"Ready?" Roark turned to the trio. "Good. When I open the door, run toward the woods to the left of the helicopter. I'll cover you."

"Why left?" Brannon stilled.

"Because the guys out there, the ones with guns and ammo, moved to the right. We don't want to go in their direction."

"Well, I'm assuming your master plan is for us to get to the ranger station, correct?"

He nodded.

"Then we need to go to the right. That's the direction of the station."

Roark paused for a moment. Brannon could almost smell the burn from his brain firing. He crouched closer to the door. "We'll head left for now, then once I'm sure we're safe, we'll double back to the ranger station." His stare collided with Brannon's.

"Whatever you say, Super Marshal." The sarcasm zipped off her tongue, leaving a bitter taste in her mouth.

"Yeah. That would be me." He gripped the door handle, his jaw muscles tightening. "On the count of three, you guys head to the left. I'll make sure they've dropped back. Keep as low as you can, but move into the trees as quickly as possible. Got it?"

"Got it, Ace."

Lincoln threw her a disapproving look. "'I will watch my ways and keep my tongue from sin; I will put a muzzle on my mouth.'"

Psalm 39:1. Brannon pinched her lips together and dropped her gaze to the floor, knowing she was being difficult but couldn't seem to stop herself. Something about the marshal just set her off, like rubbing a cat's fur backward.

She flipped on the flashlight and lifted her eyes to meet Lincoln's. She whispered as condemnation settled on her heart, "'But no man can tame the tongue.'"

Friday, 10:00 p.m.
Parkwest Medical Center
Knoxville, Tennessee

"CONGRESSMAN MCGOVERN, THIS WAY." Kevin motioned toward the elevator in the hospital.

Warren strode to where his aide waited with eagerness brightening his eyes. "What's the status on the witness's medical condition?" he barked as he slipped into the elevator, fighting the urge to hold his breath.

"The same, from what I've heard."

"Hmm." Warren straightened his tie and looked at Kevin. "I'll meet with this surgeon. I want you to get me all the information on the search-and-rescue team."

Kevin, like an eager lapdog, bobbed his head. Rule number six—use the little kiss-ups to your own benefit, then take all the glory.

The elevator beeped just before the doors yawned open. Warren pushed past the little suit and marched to the nurses' station. The stench of death hung in the corridors, creeping over the forced heated air and settling on unsuspecting patrons. Warren denied the shiver tickling his flesh. The last time he'd been in a hospital was at the age of thirteen, and look how that had turned out for him.

He cleared his throat to get the attention of the three women sitting behind the counter. "I'm Congressman Warren McGovern. I need to speak to the surgeon in charge of Jonathan Wilks."

A young RN with bright blue eyes blinked up at him, as if in awe. Warren puffed his chest out more. From behind him a hoarse voice spoke. "I'm Dr. Rhoads."

Warren spun around to face the doctor and fought to keep his face impassive. The doctor appeared much younger than Warren had expected for an expert heart transplant surgeon—dark hair with streaks of gray at the temples, eagle-sharp eyes peering behind thin wire-rimmed glasses, and standing well over six feet tall, towering above the congressman.

Warren handed the necessary paperwork to the doctor and introduced himself. "I need a status update on your patient's condition."

Dr. Rhoads scanned the paperwork, then waved him to a waiting area across from the nurses' station.

Warren strode into the room with its cheap carpeting and vinyl chairs, careful not to brush his suit against the backs of the sofas. "So, what's his status?"

"He's stable."

"Is he still in a coma?"

"Yes, the medication is keeping him under. His blood pressure is steady within normal limits."

"That's good?" Warren clenched his teeth together, moving his mouth into a weak smile. He hated when doctors and lawyers talked their specialized language, coming across as superior to regular laymen. He didn't like it at all.

"It's very good."

"May I see him?"

Dr. Rhoads studied Warren from behind his designer spectacles. "He's guarded by the Marshal Services."

"I know that. I want to see him—see for myself that he's holding on."

The doctor hesitated a moment, then nodded. "I can take you in for a minute. Follow me."

Warren matched Dr. Rhoads's wide stride as they turned down the hall into the cardiac unit. Here the presence of the Grim Reaper hovered heavier—thicker, denser, more determined to zap the life out of bodies. He balled his hands into fists, his palms coated with a sheen of sweat.

"Right this way." The doctor pushed through yet another set of steel double doors. The air whooshed as the doors pressed closed behind them, trapping them in the hall of demise. Beeps and chirps battered them from all sides, electronic monitoring equipment gone mad. Warren's head began to ache. The pain started at the base of his skull and worked upward until it throbbed in his temples.

Dr. Rhoads stopped in front of the room at the end of the corridor. A US marshal hunkered in a chair to the left of the door. The overweight man wrestled to his feet when he caught sight of Warren. "Congressman."

"Marshal." Warren nodded but didn't meet the man's eyes.

Dr. Rhoads pushed open the door and entered the room before Warren. "We haven't seen much change in his condition."

Warren moved to the foot of the bed, studying the man lying with tubes and wires hooked over his chest and face. He didn't look like someone involved with a child-trafficking ring. Narrowing his eyes, Warren peered into Jonathan Wilks's face, searching for any sign of consciousness. Nothing.

"We need to leave now," the doctor whispered.

He followed Dr. Rhoads. His feet itched to run free of this horrible place. Instead he forced himself to put one foot in front of the other, marching like a good soldier until he broke through the double steel doors. Then, and only then, did he suck in air.

"Congressman!" Kevin rushed toward him.

Nodding good-bye to the doctor, Warren intercepted his young aide. "What is it?"

"I've news about the helicopter."

"And?" Warren folded his arms across his chest. Must this little whippersnapper try his hand at drama right now? He just needed information.

"Air traffic control reports receiving a message from that woman pilot—the rescue one."

"And?" He could barely contain his impatience.

"She found the crash site but has since reported her rescue helicopter is down and someone is shooting at them."

"Shooting!"

"Yes, sir." Kevin's eyes were so wide they looked as if they'd split apart his face at any moment. "They managed to save the flight medic and marshal, but the Life Flight pilot died in the crash."

"And?"

"Air traffic control has been trying to raise her again on the radio, but it's dead."

"Who's dead?"

"The radio, sir."

"So we don't know who's shooting at them, if they're still alive, or what's going on?" Warren squared his shoulders and dropped his arms.

"No, sir." Kevin shifted his weight back and forth from one foot to the other.

"Then I suggest you find out."

Kevin took a step backward. "Y-y-yes, sir. I'm on it." He turned and all but ran down the hall, his feet slipping on the tiled floor.

Warren reached for his cell phone, then noticed the sign on the wall banning the use of the gadgets on the ICU floor. With a sigh he tromped to the elevator and slipped inside. He would make his call as soon as he hit the lobby area. Well, as long as no one loitered around who would ask pestering questions. Questions he couldn't answer.

Ones he'd refuse to answer.

EIGHT

Friday, 10:14 p.m.
Southeast of Mount LeConte
Great Smoky Mountains, Tennessee

ROARK LEANED AGAINST THE helicopter and kept his back to the group, listening as they rushed into the forest behind, their steps crunching and crackling in the frozen snow. As sleet battered his face, he focused his attention on the tree line opposite him, studying the landscape for any sign of movement.

Nothing—no limbs cracking as an unseen person moved to put Roark in the sniper's crosshairs. Aside from the hissing of the wind, silence prevailed. Even the clumsy steps of the group behind him had abated.

Keeping his Beretta drawn and aimed toward the woods, Roark backstepped around the downed helicopter until he moved behind it. He turned and made a hasty retreat into the thicket. Just ahead, in the cover of darkness and swirling snow, he could make out the faint halo of the flashlight beam from the group. He quickened his pace and joined the others, often glancing over his shoulder, expecting to face the barrel of a gun.

He hesitated, then took the cooler from Lincoln's hand—holstering his weapon to do so. Roark nudged Brannon's shoulder and tried to take her place in supporting Thomas, but she shoved him back.

"I can do it. This is my job." The tone of her voice cut him to the quick.

"But it's my job to protect you," he whispered in her ear.

She stopped in a heartbeat, almost causing Lincoln to stumble and pull Thomas down with him. By the glow of the flashlight, her eyes blinked cold fire. "Since when? I'm the ranger, the search-and-rescue person. It's *my* job to protect *you*, and you're injured."

A snort of laughter slipped out before Roark could stop it. Her eyes narrowed, and her lips pinched into a tight line. He pressed his own lips together.

"Let me tell you something, Mr. Marshal. I don't care how big and important you think you are—you will not make it out of these mountains without our guidance. So you can stop with the arrogance and know-it-all, take-charge attitude. We must work together to survive." Brannon shifted Thomas's arm higher over her shoulder and took off through the forest, leaving Roark no other option but to follow.

What was her problem anyway? She was a strange type of woman—fire and feisty yet praying aloud. Roark pulled the cooler higher to avoid bumping it against a fallen log. He still couldn't believe it. Here he was, traipsing around in the dense mountainside in the dead of night, in the middle of a blizzard, and toting a human heart. Shaking his head, Roark hadn't ever heard of something so ludicrous.

"We need to start rounding back, or we'll head too deep into the woods to make it to the station in time to save your friend." Brannon's words carried over the wind.

Roark paused, his trained gaze taking in the terrain, watching for any type of unusual movement. He detected only the wind pushing the ice and snow. He set down the cooler and touched the handle of his Beretta. Just that slight touch comforted him in the darkness.

Roark and his sidearm went way back—the one relationship he could depend on. Partners for life, unlike the two serious romantic relationships he'd endured that ended in nothing but misery and heartache for him. So what if Dr. Martin reported his affection for his weapon bordered on unhealthy? His Beretta would never cheat on him, would never lie to him.

"If we circle around now, we can stay in this valley, which will make for an easier hike. Rainbow Falls should be about five miles to the west." Lincoln spoke with quiet authority.

Roark directed his words to Lincoln and him alone, ignoring the stubborn spitfire. "Then let's start doing that. I don't know how many are following us, but we know they're armed." He ran his hand over his hair, now coated in a blanket of sleet, then lifted the cooler.

"We need to get to a safe location and set up camp." Lincoln gave a slight tilt of his head toward the flight medic. "We also need to rest a bit before the five-mile hike to Rainbow Falls."

Roark studied the flight medic's face. Pasty white, a line of sweat lay on his upper lip, an indication of the cost of his physical exertion. Thomas needed to rest. While Roark had a job to do, people to keep safe, he couldn't ignore the man's plight. "Is there any place close that might provide some shelter from the weather and whoever's hunting us?"

"I don't know." Brannon's words stumbled out amid a cloud. The temperature had dipped lower as the time ticked by. Her bottom lip quivered as the cold seeped around them like icy fingers tightening their grip.

"You don't know? You're a park ranger. How can you not know?" And *he* was accused of not being competent to do his job? The US Marshal Service should take a look at these two.

"We're based out of Abrams Creek, well west of here. This is a huge park. No single ranger knows every inch of it. In case you missed it, the park is so big it spans two states."

"But out-shacks are located throughout the park. If we head toward Rainbow Falls, we'll find something soon." Lincoln's gaze probed Roark's, as if looking for permission.

"Lead the way." Roark kept his head down as the rangers supported Thomas and resumed hiking. Cold cloaked his entire body. His corduroy coat wasn't enough protection against the raging blizzard.

As he walked, Roark pulled out his phone to see if he could get a signal—no such luck, just like always. Why should he expect anything different now? He grunted as his thoughts tumbled, causing a backward glance from Brannon.

No matter how much the woman annoyed him, yet attracted him at the same time, he wouldn't let himself get distracted. No sir, not now. Too much was riding on this particular assignment.

He'd waited long weeks to prove he was back to 100 percent—Internal Affairs inquiry, weekly visits to the shrink, the snide comments from some of the other marshals. Yes, he'd been reprimanded for not following orders, for trying to take control of a situation, but IA had cleared him back to active duty. Then what? They'd given him this menial assignment. Why? To prove that he was capable of handling the job again? If he failed in this task . . . well, Demott would never trust him with a real assignment, if he didn't fire Roark on the spot.

He wouldn't fail. Couldn't.

Roark shook his head and plodded onward. The exhausting trek went slow. Several times a member of the group would slip on the sleet freezing on the ground. Hiking five miles in this crazy weather with an injured man was a journey. Roark's own arm burned where the bullet had grazed him, but he refused to ask for so much as an aspirin from Brannon.

So deep in his thoughts, Roark didn't see the trio stop in front of him, and he ran right into Brannon's back. She spun around, daggers of fire blazing from her eyes. "Looks like we've found one of the out-shacks."

"Let me check it out first." He set down the cooler and grasped his Beretta, the leather creaked as the handgun moved free of the holster. It felt good, right, to have his partner back in his hand.

"For what, pray tell?" Brannon eased Thomas down to a rock outside the mouth of the lean-to and popped her hands on her hips. "It's a shack, for pity's sake, and a man's hurt." She brushed past him into the shanty, jerking the flashlight's beam around the small area.

The woman was insufferable—attractive with her quiet strength and mismatched eyes, yet ornery. Roark forced himself into the small confining space behind her. His breathing hitched, causing him to suck in air through his nostrils. This would be worse than being stuck in an elevator for hours on end.

And he hated small places. With a passion. Even though he'd tried to convince Dr. Martin otherwise.

The building leaned against the mountain. The room was maybe ten feet by ten feet of weathered-wood walls. A fire pit sat in the corner, a makeshift chimney climbing the rickety wall. The building itself rounded out at the top, making it appear domelike. Dark. Damp. Close—very close. Roark concentrated on keeping his breathing regular, not inhaling too deep or too shallow.

Brannon flung her backpack to the floor and pulled out a wool blanket. "We'll make a pallet for your flight medic."

"Thomas."

She glanced up at him. "What?"

"Thomas. His name is Thomas."

"Oh." Her hands smoothed the blanket flat on the dirt floor besieged with pine needles and twigs.

"Will someone know to check here for us?" Roark studied the small crevices etched into the walls.

"Not usually. This isn't on the tourist maps or anything. It's not on the beaten path, so to speak, and in this weather? I doubt it seriously." She finished straightening the pallet and pushed to her feet. "Let me help Lincoln get Thomas in here and build a fire. Then I want you to tell me what's so important about that heart that people would weather the storm to come after it."

Saturday, 12:30 a.m.
Near Mount LeConte
Great Smoky Mountains, Tennessee

BRANNON SMILED AS LINCOLN tried to coax Thomas into eating some of the beef jerky. His words were smooth, comforting. If anyone could get the injured man to eat, it would be Lincoln. He'd saved her from drowning in a pit of grief and depression, using faith and Scripture to pull her back from the edge. She pulled another package of the jerky from her backpack and left the warmth of the fire, approaching the marshal.

Sitting on a jagged rock just outside the door, Roark reloaded the Beretta's clip. The flashlight sat beside him, splintering the darkness around the shanty. He glanced up as she neared and jammed the magazine into the handgun with a resounding click, caressed the barrel, then holstered the weapon. He'd dressed the flesh wound on his arm. Now the chill settled over them like a bad suit jacket.

"Blessed are the peacemakers, for they will be called sons of God." She straightened her shoulders and made her way to him. She'd be the bigger person, the one to extend the olive branch.

"Hey." Maybe the adrenaline from being targets had caused them both to snap a little too much. Still, she wasn't keen on his must-have-control attitude.

"Hey." He nodded at her handgun. "How much ammo do you have?"

"Twelve rounds. Why?"

"Just getting a count in case we need it."

"Oh." She held out the package of jerky. "Here. You need to eat, keep your strength up and all that." She flashed him a tentative smile.

He hesitated, staring into her eyes with his dark, piercing ones. Then he took the offered food. "Thanks." With big hands he ripped the package open and bit off a hunk.

Brannon sat on an opposite rock and concentrated on eating. Why did the man's forearms seem to interest her so much? Sure they were corded with muscles, but what was the big deal?

They reminded her of Wade.

Heat crept up the back of her neck, and she shivered. She needed to ignore the foolish impulses of her betraying body and concentrate on the task at hand. She swallowed. "It's really cold out. Are you sure you don't want to come inside and warm up next to the fire?"

His face lost expression. "No. I prefer to be out here."

She sighed. So much for trying to help him. "So what's the story about the witness?"

Roark blinked twice, then his gaze settled on her face. The heat reached her ears, causing her to look down at the jerky in her hands.

"The witness can give details on a large child-trafficking ring. We have the documented proof, but we need this guy to tell us who is involved, how to connect the proof to the guilty parties."

Snow drifted, swirling around the air, some settling on Roark's hair, making it appear to glisten. She tilted her head as she tried to concentrate on the details. "Where's this ring acting out of?"

"Knoxville."

"Here in Tennessee?" Her hands curled around the jerky, squeezing it into a tight wad. "How can that be?"

"Happens all the time actually. The more remote the location, the better for these scumbags." Roark bit off another bite and shook his head as he chewed. "Occurs right under our noses," he said around the jerky, then swallowed. "But this time . . . this time we have a chance to catch the ringleaders and put them behind bars for a long, long time. Cut-off-a-snake's-head-and-the-body-will-die type of thing."

"How does the ring work?"

"We don't know all the details, can't until our witness comes out of a coma, which we're told will be after he has the transplant surgery." Roark wadded the package from the jerky into a ball, then slipped it into his pocket. "From what we can garner, girls between the ages of ten and fourteen are coaxed into coming into the States from Thailand under the pretense of adoption, English education, and such. Or their parents are selling them off." His eyes slipped a shade darker than ebony. "Once they get here, they realize they've been had, but it's too late."

"What happens to them?" She forced to keep her voice from wavering, the jerky she'd just eaten turning to cement.

"They're sold into prostitution rings."

Brannon gasped and covered her mouth with her hand. Her mind whipped as unrelenting as the wind. Girls, children really, sold into prostitution? A hollow pit opened in her heart, growing as she considered the plight of these children. Tears stung her eyes. "H-how many of them?"

"From the records we've procured, hundreds into thousands."

Nausea erupted from her stomach, blazing the length of her throat. She pinched her eyes closed, pushing down the pain searing her soul. Those poor children.

A cold hand covered hers. She opened her eyes and stared into Roark's face. He knelt in front of her, his hands over hers, his gaze soft and compassionate. "We'll be able to put everyone involved behind bars with this witness. That's why it's so vital we get the heart to the hospital in time."

Brannon nodded, reining in her despair and anger. "Then we need to get a move on. I brought the hand radio so I can try to raise my supervisor or the ATC again."

"I'll try my phone again, too." Roark squeezed her hands for the briefest of seconds, then stood and pulled out a satellite phone from his pocket.

She smiled at him, feeling the common ground strengthen between them. "This weather is blocking reception." She headed to her backpack, retrieved her radio, then moved back to the door. "We'll have a better chance of reception free of the mountain."

Roark nodded and followed her. He pressed buttons and held the phone toward the sky, moving it around like a beacon in the dark.

Flipping on the radio, she tried to raise Steve. Twice she radioed her location and situation—twice she received no response. She twisted the dial and changed frequency, then repeated her SOS message. Once more, nothing squalled from the radio. Maybe someone heard her call for help, but she couldn't receive the reply. *God, let that be true. Please.*

Shoving the phone back into his pocket, Roark met her questioning gaze and shook his head. She sighed. Things weren't looking so good. "Who do you think tracked us?"

"Honestly? I don't know. But I would imagine someone involved in the ring."

"Do they know you have this witness in custody?"

He gave a snort, his face crinkling into an expression of distaste. "We tried to keep it quiet, but the blasted press hounded us.

Someone talked and before we could act, it was all over the news so the entire world knew where we were headed and how."

Brannon rubbed her finger along her bottom lip. "But it has to be someone familiar with this area. Trust me, it's hard to hike this terrain, and in this weather they'd have to be really experienced." She hugged herself with her arms folded over her chest. "No other aircraft was in the area, so they had to be within driving distance."

She closed her eyes, letting the analytical portion of her brain take over. "A Hummer or a Jeep. Something rugged. To have gotten to the crash site from the time the news aired, that only gave them limited driving time, which means they had to be close to begin with." Her eyes shot open. "Did anyone know about the witness and his condition prior to the media hype?"

"Yeah. We've had the witness in custody for a couple of weeks, so lots of people knew. People we'd assumed could be trusted, but we see how that turned out." Roark shifted his weight. "Why?"

"Well . . . let's just say someone knew you had him and were waiting for an opportunity to get him. Why not go after the witness himself?"

"He's in the cardiac ICU, in a coma, under guard of the marshals. I don't think anyone would take the chance of trying to get to him there." He shrugged. "Besides, the man's going to die without the heart transplant. They probably figured if they can stop or delay the surgery long enough, they'd be home free anyway."

"Will they?" Her pulse pounded inside her skull, making her head ache.

"More than likely, yeah."

"But you said you had documented proof . . ."

"Proof we can't decipher." He raised a hand before she could interrupt. "We've had the best of the alphabet-soupers working on decoding it for two weeks now. Hasn't been broken yet."

"Alphabet-soupers?"

Roark gave a wry smile. "CIA, FBI, NSA—all the government initial organizations."

Despite the situation, she chuckled. "That's good. Never heard them called that before."

"Insider joke." He nodded toward Lincoln and Thomas, who dozed in the warm glow of the fire. "We need to rest, get Thomas's wound cleaned again, and then head out."

She gestured to his arm. "Yours as well."

"Nothing but a graze. I'm fine." His gaze shot toward the sky. "We'd better get some rest while we can. Dawn will be here before too much longer, and then we're visible targets."

NINE

Saturday, 3:00 a.m.
Parkwest Medical Center
Knoxville, Tennessee

WARREN LOITERED OUTSIDE THE hospital's main entrance, hovering over the ashtray as he puffed away at his cigarette. The stinging wind bit against his exposed neck and face, but he refused to acknowledge his discomfort. He needed the nicotine fix more than he needed warmth.

"Congressman McGovern."

He turned toward the doors, squinting in the bright overhead lights as he tried to discern the voice calling out to him.

"Congressman McGovern." Kevin marched with prissy strides toward him.

After crushing out his cigarette, Warren straightened and strode to meet the effeminate man now rushing to greet him. Couldn't a man get a little privacy around here? "Yes?"

"Dr. Rhoads has called a meeting with the marshals. We thought you'd want to be included."

As if anyone would consider excluding him? He'd been kept out of the loop quite enough, thank you very much. He squared his shoulders and moved to the doors, losing his footing only once on the sheet of ice on the sidewalk. "Has something happened?"

"I don't know, sir. They're meeting in the waiting room up on the ICU floor."

Warren sighed as he strode into the elevator and jabbed the button. He'd have to endure the fingers of death tickling his spine again. Shaking off the shudder, he gritted his teeth. Ever since his mother had died in a hospital when she'd been admitted for

a minor treatment, he'd known hospitals weren't a place of healing. They were halls of loss. Human error and a lawsuit later, he
still swallowed the bitterness when he thought of the sloppy doctor who had murdered his beloved mother. Leaving him on the
brink of manhood to be raised by his father with strict rules and a
militant lifestyle. His father married his Asian mistress not even a
week after burying Warren's mother. Unfair. But Warren had made
a name for himself—had gotten into the political game to help
people, which helped his own career. But that was beside the
point.

The elevator dinged as the doors slid open at an excruciatingly
slow pace. Warren's heartbeat sped in contrast, like the hare waiting
for the tortoise to catch up in the race.

He moved into the corridor, then spun on his heel, and stalked
down the hall to the waiting room. Maybe this meeting would mean
his luck had finally changed. His career needed a kick-start.

Dr. Rhoads leaned against the wall of the waiting room,
crowded by a semicircle of US marshals. Gerald Demott, chief of
the marshals, stood front and center. This was serious business.

"What's going on?" His voice boomed in the otherwise silent
room.

Looking up, Dr. Rhoads nodded. "Now that we're all here, let me
fill you in on the patient's condition." He ran a hand over the errant
hair brushing the tops of his ears. "Mr. Wilks has taken a turn for the
worse. His blood pressure is dropping." He held up a finger to hush
the spattering of gasps and beginning of questions. "He is currently
in stable condition, but that's not expected to hold out much longer.
If it takes much longer for the heart to get here, he may not survive
the surgery."

"Where's the heart, Gerald?" Warren glared at the chief, as if
the delay were his personal fault.

Demott cleared his throat. "Our last report is that the heart
survived the crash in the Great Smoky Mountains. We know our
marshal got it out safely, and a National Park Service helicopter
landed." He hauled in a deep breath. "Unfortunately, we received
a report of an unknown assailant firing upon the rescue team and

disabling the helicopter. It appears the occupants of the helicopter
are now stranded."

"So the heart and your marshal are stuck out in the mountains
somewhere?" Warren folded his arms across his chest and stared
down his nose at Demott. Rule number seven—learn how to intimi-
date by your size, and use it when necessary.

"Yes. We know the rescue rangers are with our marshal, as well
as the flight medic. Air traffic control has their coordinates, and the
Air National Guard helicopter is en route to that location now."

"When will it reach them?" Dr. Rhoads interjected.

Demott shrugged. "We assume it'll take approximately an hour
and a half to get to the crash site from their current location, considering the weather." He glanced at his watch.

"Can the heart survive that long?" Warren waited for the
doctor's answer.

"Normally, no. But the harvesting surgeon prepared a pack of
new drugs to go with the heart. Upon each injection the viability of
the heart is extended for twelve hours. Four injections were sent."

Warren ran a finger alongside his nose. "So that heart has about
thirty-something hours left?"

"As long as the injections are given within the twelve-hour window." Dr. Rhoads tapped his pen against the metal chart he held.

"Will our witness last?" The chief marshal swallowed hard.

"That's in God's hands, Mr. Demott. We'll do our best to help
him hang on." Dr. Rhoads slipped the pen into the jacket of his
white coat. "That's the update on his condition." His gaze settled
on Gerald Demott's face. "Let me know if you hear anything more
about the location and condition of the heart."

Demott nodded. Dr. Rhoads strode from the room, heading
toward the steel double doors. To check on his patient, no doubt.
Warren turned his attention to Demott. "Have you heard from your
marshal yet?"

"We've tried to raise him on the satellite phone, but the blizzard's blocking reception."

"I see." The creepy feeling of death's proximity breathed
down Warren's back like the Grim Reaper hovering over his

shoulder. "Let me see what I can find out. Maybe I can get more information."

"Good luck."

Warren pressed the button for the elevator, stiffening his legs to stop their quivering. Such a small time window, considering everything—the weather, the distance, and the fact that someone stalked the heart. Warren tightened his lips as he pressed into the elevator and descended.

If Wilks didn't make it, could Warren blame the FBI's incompetence and gain further support of his constituents by his outrage?

Saturday, 7:15 a.m.
Outbuilding
Great Smoky Mountains National Park, Tennessee

BRANNON PACKED THEIR MEAGER supplies while Lincoln cleaned and rebandaged Thomas's injury. The man had lost a lot of blood, but the flow seemed to be diminishing now, although his ragged breathing echoed in the small cavern.

Heavy snow clouds enveloped the sky, blocking the sun's first rays. Winds shifted, pushing the falling snow in every direction. The temperature continued to drop, throwing the group into a frosty wonderland.

Brannon lifted the collar of her coat and shivered. How could Roark stand the elements much longer? He refused to come inside the shelter to warm by the fire. Did he need to prove he was Superman? Their tentative truce could be shattered with his control-freak attitude.

After checking and rechecking his gun, Roark pushed the cooler toward the front of the shack. Thomas struggled to speak. "We need to give the heart another injection." His eyes widened. "Black pack? It was . . . on the cooler." His voice raised an octave, each word choked out. "Where is it?"

"I put it in my backpack." She retrieved the case and held it up. "For safekeeping."

"Have to do . . . injection . . . heart won't be . . . viable."

"Okay, okay. Calm down. I'll get the heart for you." She grabbed the red cooler and pulled it beside Thomas, then opened the cover.

The organ rested in a mushy solution of clear liquid and melting ice. She pushed the cooler against Thomas's leg.

"Can't do . . . it."

"What?" Brannon's heart thumped in her throat. "Why not?"

"Can't use . . . right arm." The flight medic shook his head. "You will have . . . to do it."

She rocked back on her heels, almost falling backward. She'd experienced a lot in the Coast Guard but never sticking a needle into an exposed human heart. Now wasn't the time to start, either. She stared at her partner, who had received extensive emergency first-aid training. "Lincoln, you're the best qualified."

His eyes widened and one brow shot up. "I don't think my first-aid training is preparation for this kind of thing."

His ability to appear to read her mind bothered her more times than not. This was one of those times. She moved farther away from them, closer to the opening of the shack. "At least you're confident holding a syringe." Brannon sat cross-legged on the floor, holding out her hand to show the shakiness.

"Someone . . . do now . . . while I can talk . . . you through it. I'm getting . . . sleepy." Thomas's head rolled against the wall of the cave.

"Okay." Lincoln moved closer to Thomas.

She smiled as she stared into her partner's eyes. "'The man of God may be thoroughly equipped for every good work.'"

Shaking his head, Lincoln muttered, "Simple. Second Timothy 3:17." He leaned closer to Thomas. "Tell me what to do."

The flight medic tossed Lincoln a look that appeared to be a combination of relief and pain. "Pack."

While Lincoln did as Thomas instructed, Brannon glanced at Roark. He sat opposite her, his gaze avoiding the two men's move-ments but flickering over the shack and finally landing on her.

Heat crept up her neck, spreading to her ears and cheeks. She dropped her stare and focused on the ground. What was it about the man's scrutiny that made her feel stripped to the soul, her spirit lying bare in front of him? She lifted her finger to her mouth and bit at the hardened cuticle.

"Why do you do that?" Roark's voice shattered her thoughts.

"Huh? What?"

He nodded at her fingers. "Why do you bite your nails?"

She dropped her hand into her lap. "I don't bite my nails."

"Then what are you doing?"

She opened her mouth to give an answer, but Thomas let out a groan and an "oh no."

Both she and Roark shot to their feet and hovered over Thomas and Lincoln, who stared up at her. "One of the vials is broken."

"What exactly does that mean?" She laced her fingers in front of her body, squeezing them together.

"Means," Thomas began with his forced words, "heart just lost . . . twelve hours."

Saturday, 7:28 a.m.
Northwest toward Rainbow Falls
Great Smoky Mountains National Park, Tennessee

ROARK STOOD IN THE opening of the out-shack, studying the landscape. He rubbed his arms against the frigid temperature. Snow and ice battled in the air, fluttering like thick drapes in the wind. He couldn't make out more than ten feet in front of him, a dangerous disadvantage when he needed to get the group moving. With the broken syringe they would have to push farther, faster, to get the heart to the hospital in time. Twelve hours was all they had until they'd have to inject again. And they only had one vial left.

"We're ready." Brannon's words were hot in his ear. He turned his head. The woman had grit, as his sister would say, and it made her very attractive. Too attractive. Hadn't he sworn off women after his last romantic fiasco? Being lied to and cheated on still stung, even after more than a year. And Brannon was too similar in personality to Dr. Martin. Roark would bet the good doctor had advised Demott to give him simple assignments for a while. To continue his therapy. He didn't need therapy. He needed to work.

Roark straightened. No time for rehashing past failed relationships or his current situation. Right now he had to concentrate on the job and complete it. He pulled out his trusty Beretta and studied the rangers. "Stay as close to me as you can. The storm's right on top of us."

Brannon and Lincoln propped Thomas between them. Roark lifted the cooler and stepped free of the shanty's protection.

Pecks of sleet slipped under his collar, slithering down his back like an icy snake. He clenched his jaw, ignoring his discomfort, and glanced over his shoulder at the trio behind him. He had an assignment to succeed at and people to protect. Those innocent girls trafficked in . . . . Their fate sat in his hands. He couldn't let more young girls die. Not on his watch.

Thomas seemed barely conscious, his head lolling to rest on one shoulder, then the other. Brannon's face was lined with determination. Roark's muscles tensed as he fought the desire to carry her burden. He couldn't—he knew that—he had to be ready to react to any trouble. That was his job.

The group descended a rocky trail, losing traction as fresh ice joined the slick layer covering the ground. Wind nipped at their exposed flesh, chafing it raw. In less than an hour, Roark's face burned, and he had to keep regripping his gun as feeling fled from his fingers. Squinting, he made out the valley before them, level and even. He increased his pace, pushing one foot in front of the other faster, harder.

Crack!

Roark released the cooler, spun, and crouched, in one fluid movement, with his Beretta aimed in the direction of where the gun had been fired. "Get down!" Adrenaline coursed through his veins, thawing his extremities.

As one, Brannon and Lincoln dropped to a squat, pulling Thomas down with them. Brannon withdrew her Sig, Lincoln only a second behind her.

"Get behind me," Roark barked as he maneuvered around them. His attention shifted over the rocky terrain, studying each shadow of trees as he hunted for movement, human movement.

Pop-pop-pop!

The rapid gunfire erupted over the valley. Thomas yelled out, pain twisting his voice, making his words incoherent.

Roark raced into action. His feet sought steady ground while he ran where the gunshots originated. Brannon's gasp and murmurs reached his ears as he continued toward the tree line above and to the left of them.

A flash of light flickered in his peripheral vision to the right.

Crack!

He squeezed the Beretta's trigger just as Brannon yelped. He glanced back toward the group—they'd hunkered down behind two fallen trees. He spun to where he'd seen the gun flash, then fired four more shots in quick succession.

The lingering echoes of the gunshots rippled over the valley. The shooter's, his, Brannon's, and Lincoln's—all meshed together into a chorus of explosion.

Keeping his eyes locked on the gunman's location, Roark crept in that direction. He crossed the valley and pulled himself up the embankment. Losing his footing on the ice and snow, he slipped back to the valley bed.

Pop! Pop!

Lifting his Beretta, he returned rapid fire.

A soft thump sounded, followed by a groan. Twigs snapped, then a thud.

Roark climbed up the steep incline, pulling on trees with his left hand. In his right he gripped his handgun. Once he reached the top, he stood still with his head tilted a fraction.

Another groan. Labored breathing.

Roark spotted the fallen gunman by his breath puffing in the cold. He brushed aside limbs and underbrush as he approached the form lying at the base of a tree, never letting the gun waver.

The shooter lay still except for the labored rise and fall of his chest. Roark towered over him, studying his face. He didn't recognize the man decked out in full tactical gear. Not even a remote resemblance to any mug shot he'd seen in the perp books. Squatting, he shoved the barrel of the Beretta against the man's temple. "Who are you, and why were you trying to kill us?"

The man's eyes blinked. A croak escaped his lips. Blood oozed through the left side of his coat. Roark took in the location of the wound—a heart shot. The shooter had mere seconds to live. "Who are you? Who sent you?"

Once more he groaned and blinked twice. His chest lay still, not rising any longer.

Roark felt the man's neck—no pulse. He let out a sigh, then reached into the man's coat pockets. His fingers wrapped around cold metal. He yanked his hand out, pulling a SAT phone free. No wallet, no driver's license, no form of identification. Nothing but the phone and bullets.

"Roark!" Brannon's cry filled him with dread.

Without a backward glance, Roark rushed to the embankment and scrambled down to the valley bed.

TEN

A DOOR SLAMMED, MAKING the walls vibrate and rattle. Mai arose from her restless sleep, still huddled against two of her roommates. The bedroom door swung open and crashed against the wall. Mai pushed herself off the mattress and scooted into the far corner, staring at Madam Nancy looming in the doorway.

"Your three other roommates have been transferred." She reached behind her tubby frame and pushed a young Thai girl into the room. "This is your new roomie for now."

The girl, eleven at most, stumbled into the room, tripped over the edge of the mattress, and fell face-first onto it. A soft whimper escaped from the cracked lips of her tear-streaked face.

Madam Nancy's face wrinkled into a frown. "You girls teach this one the rules around here. I don't want to hear no more sobbing from her." She wagged a sausagelike finger. "If she keeps crying all the time, I'm holding you three responsible." With that, she stomped from the room.

Tears flowing, the new girl curled into a ball on the mattress. Mai's two roommates, Sunee and Prasert, headed toward the washroom. They were older, sixteen and seventeen, and had been with Madam Nancy for a couple of years. Their experiences had hardened their eyes. Neither one had shown Mai any compassion when she had arrived, and it did not appear they would with this new girl.

Moving beside the girl, Mai wrapped her arm around the girl's bony frame. She whispered shushing sounds and stroked her long hair. *"Bpen khoon gaw di?"*

79

The girl looked up. "Am I okay?" she repeated in broken English. Her eyes as black as night spilled more tears. "I am Kanya."

"I am Mai." She smiled at the younger girl and reverted to her native tongue. "How old are you?"

"*Sip saam.*"

"Thirteen? Really?" Mai let her arm drop from Kanya's hair. "I thought you were younger."

Kanya smiled, revealing a row of white, straight teeth. "I am small for my age, *khaa*?"

"Yes." Mai chuckled, then remembered where she was. "I am fourteen." She pressed her lips together and leaned next to Kanya's ear. "When did you get to the States?"

"Last night." Fresh tears streamed from Kanya's eyes. "*Gra maawm glap baan.*"

Mai's eyes overflowed with tears. "I want to go home, too."

Saturday, 8:46 a.m.
Northwest toward Rainbow Falls
Great Smoky Mountains National Park, Tennessee

BRANNON IGNORED THE FIERY pain in her left ankle, concentrating on the fallen man beside her. Her hands trembled as she holstered her weapon, pushed back his bangs, and straightened the glasses on his face. His breathing grew fainter, until it was nothing more than a gravelly whisper. Gurgling came from him, liquid filling his lungs.

God, no. Please, not someone else. Another life lost due to these criminals. To consider it ripped at Brannon's soul.

"Give me something else to cover the wound," Lincoln snapped as he shoved wads of gauze into Thomas's gut. Blood soaked through the white clump.

Bile seared the back of her throat. While it had been a while since she went through more than just a basic first-aid course, she could recognize a dying man when one lay in front of her. She stroked Thomas's brow once more.

"I need—" Lincoln's gaze locked with hers, and understanding passed between them. He pushed against the bundle of saturated gauze stuck to Thomas's abdomen.

Thomas took a wheezing breath, shuddered, then his muscles went slack.

Shoulders slumping, Lincoln reached up and closed the flight medic's eyes. Brannon's breathing hiccupped.

"He's gone." Lincoln laid a hand on her shoulder and squeezed. "There's nothing more we can do for him."

Brannon closed her eyes. Fierce tears burned down her cheeks. As if the heavens heard her sobs, the winds died down, and snow-flakes drifted instead of plowing over them. *Why, God, why?*

Thrashing of snow-burdened branches from the incline behind caused her to jerk her attention over her shoulder. In a smooth movement she withdrew her firearm.

Roark slipped and stumbled toward them, his face etched in concern. "Are you guys okay?"

Brannon holstered her Sig and shook her head. "Did you get the guy who shot at us?"

He nodded. His gaze stopped on Thomas, lying still in the snow. Roark plopped to his knees. "Is he . . . ?"

Lincoln cleared his throat. "He got shot in the gut. He bled out."

"Where's the cooler?" Roark stared over the area.

"The cooler?" Brannon pushed his shoulder. He swayed as he gave way to lack of balance and slumped to the side. She didn't care. "A man just died—shot to death—and all you can think about is *the heart*? What kind of unemotional deviant are you?" Red flashed before her eyes.

"Look, I'm sorry Thomas died, but there's nothing we can do about it." His voice sure sounded steady, even if he was out of breath.

"You could at least mourn him for a moment." It was a human life—gone forever from this earth. She shoved her palms into the frozen ground and pushed to her feet. She put weight on her left leg, causing a bolt of pain to shoot up from her ankle, and crumbled back to the ground with a groan.

Roark knelt and reached for her leg at the same moment Lincoln touched her shoulder. "What is it?" her partner asked.

She spoke from between clenched teeth. "My ankle. I think I twisted it." Pain throbbed, ripping away her grief.

With nimble fingers Roark unlaced her hiking boots. A flash of heated attraction swelled inside the pit of her stomach, making her light-headed. Then a fresh shot of pain rushed through her leg. "Ouch!" She tried to jerk her leg free of his hands. "What're you doing?"

"We need to check your ankle. I'm taking off your boot." He pulled the boot free and set it on the ground, then gingerly felt along her ankle area.

She opened her mouth to argue, but Lincoln squeezed her shoulder again. "He's right."

"Then *you* check it out for me."

Lincoln took Roark's place without another word. His hands were just as gentle, maybe even more so, but his touch didn't cause a burst of heat to swim through her veins. Brannon fidgeted on the cold ground, not sure if she felt disappointed or relieved.

"Definitely twisted." Lincoln eased her foot on the ground before reaching into his backpack. "I need to get it wrapped."

"We need to get moving." She spit the words out, attraction and common sense battling within her and making her more irritated than injured.

Now, God? Seriously?

"I'll wrap your ankle, slip your boot on loosely, then we can get out of here." Lincoln pulled the Coban wrap from the backpack and began unrolling. "I need your sock off so I can wrap your bare ankle, then we'll put the sock on over it."

Before she could lift her leg to comply, Roark lifted her foot and tugged off her sock. His fingers burned into her bare flesh as his thumb stroked her tattoo. "What's this?"

"My pilot wings." She tried to wrench her foot free, but he held firm and pulled it closer to him.

He leaned over her foot, inspecting the gold wings and anchor tattoo. His thumb brushed over the inked spot again, sending spirals of exhilaration coursing through her. Without a conscious thought, she sighed.

"Very cool." His voice came out as a whisper, raspy.

She glanced at his face—it flushed a tinge of crimson, right up to the tips of his ears. The lines around his eyes carved deeper while his dark orbs appeared intense. She dropped her gaze to her ankle, which seemed to be swelling already, but that felt like the least of her worries at the moment. Was he feeling the bite of physical attraction as well? She wet her lips, then felt his stare burn into her. The passion flickering in his gaze nearly undid her self-control.

Lord, what am I doing?

Lincoln cleared his throat. His questioning glance went from her face to Roark's, then back to hers again. "I need to wrap your ankle now."

Roark released his hold on her foot, and it headed for the ground. At the last moment she tightened her leg and hovered her foot about six inches above the icy terrain. Her stomach muscles quivered.

With deft movements Lincoln wound the wrap around her ankle, secured it, then slipped her sock and boot back on. The tightness of her boot around her swollen ankle felt like pinpricks of needles against her flesh. She gritted her teeth, vowing to keep the pain to herself.

"We need to mark the coordinates here." Her voice felt thick in her throat. "So we can send a team out for the . . . others."

While Lincoln shoved the first-aid supplies back into the pack and pulled out the GPS, Brannon shifted to stand. Roark's grip on her elbow held her steady. She tested her weight on her injured ankle. The pain still made her grit her teeth, but if she used only her toes for balance, she could manage. Heat spread from her elbow up and down her arm. She jerked her arm free from Roark's electrifying touch, glaring as she did.

She'd never experienced such raw attraction before—not even with Wade. Why was it happening now? She stared at the ground while firming her equilibrium. She didn't know if she even liked

Roark Holland and couldn't fathom why she'd feel such an intense draw to the puzzling man.

One thing was for sure: She couldn't allow another complication to intrude on the goal of the moment—to get them safely to the station and get the heart to the hospital. There'd be time later to sort out all the conflicting emotions, but not now.

Saturday, 9:41 a.m.
Northwest toward Rainbow Falls
Great Smoky Mountains National Park, Tennessee

ROARK SWUNG BRANNON'S BACKPACK over his shoulder, hoisted the cooler, and followed behind her and Lincoln. He controlled his breathing, determined to ignore the pull to take her into his arms and kiss her breathless. What was it about the woman that drove him insane with her mere presence? She confused him by arousing his senses, intrigued him by such sharp contrasts in her personality, and intoxicated him just by being near.

Touching her had been a mistake. A big mistake. He couldn't get the softness of her skin out of his mind. To be so strong and domineering on the outside, her skin was as smooth as a frozen pond. And that tattoo! What woman had a tattoo of her pilot wings on her ankle? Coast Guard, unless he was mistaken. How'd she go from Coast Guard to park ranger? And she held and fired a gun well. He bit back a chuckle. Brannon Callahan was definitely a woman he wanted to know better—needed to know on a much more personal level.

Another big mistake in the making.

"We'll send someone back for Thomas's body as soon as we get to the station," Lincoln told Brannon.

"And the shooter's," Roark added.

Lincoln glanced over his shoulder, his concerned gaze studying Roark for a moment before turning back to Brannon.

The look spoke volumes. He swallowed but remained silent. *Was* there something between the two rangers, something more than just the closeness of partners? Of longtime friends?

Their progress wasn't as quick as Roark would like, but Brannon seemed to hold her own, considering her ankle. Why couldn't she whine and complain like the women he'd been involved with before, who'd be sniveling and demanding at a time like this? Brannon's strength and assertiveness seemed to stir all kinds of conflicting thoughts inside of him.

His own arm ached from toting the cooler. Roark shook his head over the absurdity of it all. The entire trip seemed surreal— escorting a human heart around in a cooler designed for picnics and tailgate parties, the helicopter crashing, being found by the alluring Brannon limping in front of him, being shot at, and killing the shooter. Crazy, that's what it was.

Lincoln looked over at Brannon. "Do you need to stop and rest?"

"We can stop for a few minutes," Roark interjected.

Her head jerked. "I'm fine. I don't need a break." Her words were clipped and delivered with the right amount of sharpness to deter any other man.

But not Roark. "I'm just saying I could use a little break myself. We can try to raise someone on my satellite phone and on your radio."

Lincoln stared at the sky for a moment, then switched his attention to Brannon. "He's right. The storm's lessened. We might have reception now."

"We'll never get reception down here." Her eyes lifted to an overhanging area about five hundred yards above them. "We're close to Rainbow Falls. Let's head up toward that cliff."

"Gonna be hard for you to climb, isn't it?" Roark wanted to take the words back as soon as he said them because of the scathing look Brannon flung at him.

"'But those who hope in the LORD will renew their strength. They will soar on wings like eagles; they will run and not grow weary, they will walk and not be faint,'" she mumbled.

Letting out a full laugh, Lincoln hugged her. "Very good, girl."

She returned his chuckle. "Book, chapter, and verse?"

"Uh." Lincoln stroked his black mustache with his left fore-finger. "Let's see, Isaiah?"

"Chapter and verse?" When she smiled, a single dimple on her left side deepened.

"Chapter 40, verse 31." Lincoln laughed again as he answered her.

What was this little game these two played? They quoted Bible stuff back and forth, and it unnerved Roark. Ever since God failed him in his time of need, Roark avoided anything biblical or religious. He couldn't chance being disappointed again.

"Good." She hobbled toward the rise of the embankment. "Now help hoist me up."

Lincoln climbed a couple of steps, then turned and grabbed Brannon's hand. She wobbled for a moment, her injured leg hovering out to the side before she grabbed a tree and balanced.

Roark watched them continue in this manner for a few more minutes, his impatience gnawing away at him. After another ten excruciatingly long minutes, he couldn't take it any longer. With sturdy and sure steps, he climbed up the embankment, reached the two rangers, handed Lincoln the cooler, then lifted Brannon into his arms and marched past Lincoln.

"Put. Me. Down." She ground her words out, as if speaking through clenched teeth.

"We'll get there faster if I carry you."

"I'm quite capable of making it on my own."

He hauled in a deep breath—lugging her up the uneven and rocky mountainside was exhausting. "I'm sure you are, but we need to hurry it up."

Lincoln's low chuckle behind them made her tense under his grip. But she didn't say anything. Unless a growl counted.

When he reached the level area, he eased her down. Her eyes narrowed at him. "Thank you," she spat out.

"See, that wasn't so hard." He lowered the backpack to the ground, then rolled his shoulders, wishing the knotted muscles would stop aching.

"What wasn't so hard?" Her stare dared him to offend.

"Thanking me." He chuckled as her mouth dropped open. She was going to let him have it, of that he was certain. Lincoln stepped beside them, and she didn't have the opportunity.

Crack! Boom!

Roark startled as the earth beneath him shifted. Then, disappeared.

A thunderous roar filled the air.

The three fell as empty space met their weight. Down . . . down . . . falling.

Time was suspended.

Thud! Roark's side landed on rocks. Hard. His insides jostled.

He couldn't see a thing, couldn't feel anything but cold closing in. He lowered his chin to his chest, fighting to breathe against the stabbing pain.

Trying to inhale was no use—his lungs burned. He opened his eyes, wondering what he would see.

Nothing. Total darkness.

The only sound he could hear was the thudding of his own heartbeat.

ELEVEN

Saturday, 9:45 a.m.
Parkwest Medical Center
Knoxville, Tennessee

WARREN LEANED AGAINST THE outer wall of the hospital, puffing long tokes off his cigarette. The blizzard's fury had been spent—a carpet of snow and ice encased everything. The winds had died, leaving nothing but bitter cold in their wake.

Warren shifted, lifting the collar of his coat to protect his neck, and took another drag off his cigarette. Being outside in the weather, at this time of day on a weekend . . . Yeah, he needed a smoke.

"Congressman McGovern." Kevin rushed toward him, pumping his scrawny legs as fast as he could on the slippery ground.

Groaning, Warren tossed his cigarette into the sand-filled ashtray, not bothering to grind it out, and pushed off the wall. His aide would never venture outside and invade Warren's quiet time unless there was news of some sort. By the look on the young man's face, the news wasn't good. Had Wilks taken a turn for the worse?

"Sir," Kevin reached him, his breathing coming in spurts, "Marshal Demott has received a report that the Air National Guard helicopter landed at the coordinates given by the National Park Service pilot. They found the NPS helicopter and the crash site of the Life Flight helicopter but no sign of the marshal, rangers, or the flight medic."

"Any particulars reported yet?" Warren picked his steps across the slick sidewalk, heading toward the hospital's entrance.

Kevin's head shook as he tried to match Warren's long stride. "Not yet, sir. The marshals are trying to raise their guy on the satellite phone."

"Any news on the heart?"

"No, sir. The ranger supervisor has been hailing the rangers on a radio but hasn't gotten a response yet."

Warren stopped outside the hospital's automatic doors and peered down into Kevin's face. "So we don't know anything of the group's status?"

"No, sir. Not yet."

Lifting his finger to tap his chin, he considered his options and what would benefit him. What would his father, the colonel, do? Warren let out a long sigh and dropped his ungloved hand. "You go back in and find out what you can. I need to think for a moment."

"Yes, sir." The aide stepped on the mat in front of the glass doors—they whooshed open.

"Kevin."

He stopped and turned to stare up at Warren. "Yes, sir?"

"Keep your ears open, son. They might not share all the information they receive with you. Understand what I'm saying to you?"

"Yes, sir."

Warren waited until Kevin had crossed the foyer before pacing toward the end of the building. Avoiding the icy sidewalk, he moved to the area normally covered in grass. His dress shoes crunched in the snow, soaking his feet. He glanced down, irritated he'd ruined his new Kenneth Cole suede loafers—he'd just broken them in.

Rounding the side of the building, Warren yanked out his pack of Camels, shook a cigarette free, and lit it with his engraved lighter. The smoke filled his lungs, sending calming sensations through his body. He exhaled, flicking the lighter's lid open and closed as he considered his next move.

Click-click. Click-click.

He shoved the lighter into his pant's pocket, then pulled the cell phone free from his breast pocket. Warren never could understand why the general population had a fetish with belt clips and holsters for cell phones. Didn't they realize it looked tacky, messed up the natural line of a suit? His father had been a stickler about appearances. Warren had never been allowed to wear baggy jeans and shirts in his teens. No, sir. Not the son of Colonel McGovern.

His fingers, stiff from the frigid air, punched in the number. The call connected, and he pressed the phone to his ear. After four rings the computerized voice came over the line, inquiring if he wanted to leave a voice mail or enter a numeric page. Warren flipped the phone closed and shoved it back into his pocket.

Where was Tom Hurst?

Saturday, 9:48 a.m.
Underground
Great Smoky Mountains National Park, Tennessee

BRANNON COULDN'T BREATHE. SHE fought to take short, shallow breaths, reminding herself not to hyperventilate.

Helpless. Complete and utter helplessness. A feeling she detested—ever since losing Mom and Dad in a boating accident.

Her heart thumped so hard that her chest bounced with the beat. Snow and ice settled on her eyelashes, distorting her vision.

She sat on frozen ground with her ankle throbbing and a new burning in her shoulder, but she discarded the pain and discomfort. She had more important things to worry about, like how the others fared.

Brannon tensed her muscles, then glanced around in the darkness. She couldn't make out any sounds or movement. Alone, all alone. Darkness wrapped around her, cloaking her in its icy grip.

God, please don't let us die like this. Not like Mom and Dad and Wade. Please, God, help us. Do something.

Droplets of beaded ice showered over her shoulder. She froze. Had she done that?

More movement behind and above her. Crunching registered in her mind.

"Lincoln? Roark? Are y'all okay?" Pushing past the pain, Brannon waited for a response.

Nothing.

Air whooshed from her lungs. Panic catapulted her into action. She felt around in the darkness, her palms grazing the hard, slick rocks. She couldn't tell if she was inching away from the other two or not.

She called out again, this time her voice weaker and shakier to her own ears. Her voice echoed in the dark coffin around her.

Saturday, 9:57 a.m.
Underground
Great Smoky Mountains National Park, Tennessee

ROARK SHIFTED, TESTING HIS limbs. A groan came from the left. Unless his orientation had been distorted during the fall, the sound came from where Lincoln had been standing. Which meant the ranger was alive. But . . . what about Brannon?

Lincoln had grabbed Roark when the ground vanished under them. Brannon had been sitting on the ledge. If his calculations were correct, she should be near his right leg. *Should* being the operative word.

Bits of ice fell from the break in the ground above him, but he refused to acknowledge the icy frigidness. He needed to find Brannon. Not that he could explain why, but he just needed to find her and make sure she was okay.

He reached out again. This time, instead of grabbing air, his fingers grazed against something. Something that moved against him. Something warm. Brannon!

The darkness fought against him. His breathing came in spurts. No, he wouldn't think about how small the area had to be. He had to concentrate on reaching her. "Brannon!"

"Roark?" But it wasn't her angelic voice responding. Lincoln shifted against him. "Have you heard Brannon yet?"

"Nothing. What happened?"

"We fell into a dormant cave."

A cave. Just great. The rock formations seemed to close in around him, even though he could see nothing in the pitch darkness.

No, he wouldn't let that happen. He steeled his mind and concentrated on regulating his breathing. In and out. Slow and steady. In through his nose, out through his mouth.

"I'm trying to find my flashlight." Lincoln's jacket rustled in the darkness.

Roark pushed to standing, then went still, letting his strained muscles relax and rest. The humming of a familiar tune drifted up to him. Soft and muffled, the droning sound soothed him. What was it? He held his breath while trying to discern where the sound came from.

Below and in front of him. Brannon! She hummed a song.

Roark tilted his head to the side. What song was that?

Recharged, however briefly, Roark jabbed the void where Lincoln rustled. "Can you hear that? Is it her?"

Lincoln chuckled. "That's her all right. Humming 'Amazing Grace.'" He flicked on the flashlight and cast the beam around. "Hey, Brannon, can you see me?"

Brannon stopped humming. She screamed.

Roark's heart nearly stopped beating.

Lincoln jerked the flashlight around the space. Four stone and dirt walls closed in on them, making their space only about twelve feet by twelve feet. Above them, the gap they'd fallen through stood about thirty feet overhead. Stalactites hung over them, jagged spears of rock ready to pierce them.

But no sign of her.

"Brannon!" Lincoln inched forward, then reached out his palm to brace against the wall.

"Lincoln!"

He shone the light down, not even three feet in front of Roark. A six-foot drop-off of about three feet wide opened beneath them. Brannon lay below them, shielding her eyes from the brightness as she looked up at them. "Are y'all okay?"

Lincoln glanced at Roark. "We're fine. How about you?"

"I-I'mm j-just cold." But her voice sounded weaker to Roark.

Must've sounded the same to Lincoln. "We're coming to you. There's no way out up here. Can you see an opening down there?"

"N-no. It's just d-d-dark here."

Roark touched Lincoln's arm and lowered his voice to a whisper. "Even if there isn't a way out there, we need to check on her. She doesn't sound so good."

"No, she doesn't."

Roark sat on the edge. "Let me lower you down to her. You'll need to move her out of the way for me."

"I can lower you."

Assessing the slight differences in their sizes, Roark shook his head. "Nah, you're the first-aid guru. She'll need your help. Besides, I'm well over six feet—I should be able to lower myself easier."

Lincoln nodded and set the flashlight on its side. "Brannon, I'm coming down." He lowered himself alongside the edge.

Roark took hold of his hands, then swung him over the rim of the rock.

Lincoln let go as soon as he was free of the jagged edges. He squatted next to Brannon, then Roark could no longer see either of them. A long minute passed before Lincoln moved into view. Brannon was nowhere to be seen. He held up his hands. "I'm good. Toss down the flashlight."

After throwing the light to Lincoln, Roark laid on his stomach, letting his feet dangle over the edge of the drop-off. He eased himself lower, glancing over his shoulder to gauge the distance. When his hands reached the jagged rim, he hung about a foot off the ground. He let go, landing on the icy rock and slipping, then regained his footing and moved toward Brannon.

Her head rested against the side of a rock, her eyes pinched closed. Blood caked the sleeve of her right arm. Roark bent to get on eye level with her. With numb fingers he touched the side of her face.

Her eyes stared into his. The pupils were dilated, almost appearing fixed, like she couldn't focus. Little drops of frozen tears rested on her red and chapped cheeks. Her breathing came in spurts.

"Brannon . . ." Roark kept his voice low and tone even. Could she be in shock? He touched her shoulder, shaking her just a bit.

She blinked again, and again, then her eyes filled with moisture. "Roark," she croaked as she lifted her arms and encircled his neck. She squeezed him so tight he thought she'd choke him.

He swallowed back an emotion he didn't dare name. She clung to him like Saran Wrap, her body trembling as she sobbed warm tears against his neck. Lost as to what to do, he held her tight. "You're okay," he whispered. Crying women didn't affect him, but something about Brannon's tears undid him. Maybe because she was normally such a pillar of strength.

"Not like Mom and Dad. Not like Wade," she murmured, her breath hot near his jawbone. What was she talking about? Was she delirious?

Lincoln grabbed her shoulders, laying her back and running a hand over her head, stroking her wet hair. "No, not like them. We're okay."

Roark narrowed his eyes, locking them on Lincoln.

"Later," the man whispered over Brannon's head.

Feeling his heart pound, Roark nodded. She wasn't hysterical.

Lincoln moved away from her as he flipped off his backpack. Then he held her by the shoulders and scrutinized her face. "Brannon, look at me." Her sobs continued to fill the air. "Brannon, look at me!"

Her head jerked up.

Lincoln smiled. "We're going to be okay. Do you hear? We'll be fine. Not like your mom and dad. Not like Wade."

"Oh, Lincoln." She flung herself against his chest. He tucked her head under his chin and held her.

That strange sensation snaked around Roark's stomach. Jealousy . . . envy, he didn't know, but he still didn't like it. He stared at the ground. Anything to avoid seeing the two rangers embrace so intimately. When was the last time he'd held a woman just to comfort her? What would it be like to feel Brannon's heart beating against his?

Roark froze.

The heart!

TWELVE

MAI OFFERED HALF OF the stale toast to her new friend. Kanya snatched it and tore a big bite free, smacking as she gulped it down. The girl had finally stopped sobbing long enough for Mai to realize she now had an ally in this dungeon.

"*Khaawp jai,*" Kanya said around the food in her mouth.

"You are welcome." Mai took a bite, chewing as an idea niggled into her brain. "You know why you are here?"

Kanya's mouth hung slack, and she answered. "Yes. The man who brought me here made sure I knew."

"It's horrible." Mai took another bite and studied her friend. "I hate it."

"Me, too." Kanya finished the toast in one bite. "I want to go back home. I wish I had never left." She swallowed. "I believed their lies."

"We all did. Now we know better." Mai dusted the crumbs from her lap. Even her father bought into the lies. At least Mai chose to believe he had been lied to. She could not bear the thought of his agreeing to sell her for what she was forced to do. "We could do something about it."

Kanya's round eyes widened as she switched to English. "What can we do? We are mere *dek aawn.*"

"Yes, we are children, but we can do something. We have to." Mai darted her gaze around the room, even though only the two of them were present. She lowered her voice. "I cannot stay here. I would rather die."

"Me too. But what?"

Mai leaned forward and kept her voice to a whisper. The walls were, after all, thin. "We can leave."

"*Laa!* Where would we go? How would we go?"

"Shh." Mai scooted closer to Kanya. "I do not know, but we at least have to try."

Kanya blinked her dark eyes as if considering Mai's idea.

"The only other option is to stay here and *sang waat* with these dirty American men. Is that what you want?"

Kanya shook her head.

"Then we must plan our escape." Mai licked her cracked lips and let her gaze roam over the room. "We will need supplies."

"How?"

"Each time we are taken back to the *entertaining rooms*, we need to steal stuff."

"Like what?"

Mai shrugged. "Clothes, shoes, socks . . . anything we can use."

"And food. What will we do about food?"

"When we are given our sandwiches, we will only eat half. The other we will hide away to take with us."

"And drink?" Kanya folded her arms over her chest.

"We can get a can of that diet soda Madam Nancy keeps in the cabinets back in the rooms. One every time we have to go back there."

"Yes, we can do that." Kanya seemed to be more interested and excited now. "Should we tell the other girls?"

"No!" Mai lowered her voice again. "Some of them feel like this is home to them. They have certain men who come back again and again to see just them. They think these men will one day take them away from this life." Mai snorted. She still could not believe some of the girls were so stupid. "We must keep this between us, *gaw dai*?"

"Okay."

Mai stuck out her hand. Kanya took it, and the two girls shook hands. Anticipation filled Mai—she had a friend, a plan, and a goal. What could go wrong?

Saturday, 10:05 a.m.

Underground

Great Smoky Mountains National Park, Tennessee

HAD ALL THIS BEEN for nothing?

Roark grabbed the flashlight from beside Brannon and Lincoln, shining it around the space. It was even smaller than before. At least where he and Lincoln had fallen had airspace above the rocks. Here there was nothing but stone on all four sides and a rock ceiling no more than seven feet above them. Roark's chest ached, but he had a job to do. He had to find the heart, and the cooler wasn't here in the confining area.

"Hey, I need the light to dress Brannon's shoulder." Lincoln unzipped his backpack and pulled out the first-aid kit.

"Did you see the cooler?" Roark struggled to keep his voice steady, even as his breathing felt labored.

Brannon's eyes went wide. "I didn't."

"It's not here. Lincoln, did you see it before we came down?"

Lincoln frowned. "I don't remember. I didn't even think about it, to be honest. I was worried about finding Brannon."

"I need to go back up and check." He stood where he'd lowered himself and Lincoln. If he jumped, he could grab the edge and pull up. Maybe.

Lincoln moved beside him. "I can give you a boost, then hand you the flashlight."

Much better idea. "It shouldn't take me but a minute to see." Roark glanced at Brannon, trying to gauge by her expression how much pain she was in. "Can you wait a few moments to see to your injuries?"

"Sure. It's really nothing more than a scrape. Go find the heart." She waved him off, still pale, but sounding stronger.

Lincoln bent and laced his fingers together, cupping his hands to make a step. Roark placed a toe in Lincoln's hands and reached for the jagged edge.

Pebbles dug into his palms, but he pulled himself up until he rested his waist against the edge. He popped a leg up, then lifted himself.

"Ready for the flashlight?" Lincoln's voice sounded farther away than he really was.

Roark lay on his stomach, his arms dangling over the edge.

"Catch." Lincoln tossed the light.

With ease, Roark caught the flashlight. "I'll only be a second." He stood and pierced the darkness with the beam.

No, not there. Not there either.

His pulse spiked. If he couldn't find the heart, the mission was a failure. And the lives of two good people were lost for nothing. Not to mention the case would collapse.

The light danced over something red. Roark jerked the beam back to the rounded corner to the right.

The cooler, sitting on its side.

All the air left his lungs. He hadn't failed. Not yet.

He had no idea if the fall had damaged the heart, but at least he had it. Lincoln would probably be able to tell him if the organ was okay.

"Found it!" He snatched up the cooler. He returned to the edge and shone the light below.

Lincoln smiled up at him. "Way to go. Hand it down to me."

Again, Roark lay on his stomach and passed the cooler down, followed by the flashlight. He repeated his movements to get back down to Lincoln and Brannon, even though he hated going into the small space. But there was no way they could get out from where he'd fallen. Maybe there'd be another way out from the smaller space. He could hope.

This time, as he took the cooler from Lincoln and set it on the stone floor, he noticed the temperature had dropped even lower. His body shivered, and he blew into his hands. His gaze scanned the small space. They had to find a way out, or they'd die.

The four walls closed in on him.

"We need to get some heat going," Lincoln whispered. "She's doing better, but I think she's in shock. She needs to rest a little and refocus. If she doesn't, I don't think she'll be able to make it. Once she's resting, we can try to find a way out."

"I don't see a fire pit anywhere."

Lincoln chuckled. "There's moss on some of the stalagmites. We can use that to start the fire. I have matches in my pack."

"But won't a fire smoke us out?"

"Nah. Using just the moss and any twigs that dropped in the fall, the fire won't be big enough. The little bit of smoke it'll produce will go straight up and out where we fell through."

Roark rubbed his hands together. "Then I'd better get busy collecting moss and twigs."

Lincoln grinned and went back to Brannon's side. Her face lit up brighter than the flashlight beam as her partner sat beside her and reached for her arm.

Again Roark's stomach twisted with an emotion he couldn't name.

Or wouldn't.

Saturday, 10:18 a.m.
Underground
Great Smoky Mountains National Park, Tennessee

SITTING WITH HER BACK against the rock wall, Brannon's nerves returned to normal even though exhaustion weighted every limb. Roark continued to collect moss and twigs off the formations and cave's sides. Lincoln finished bandaging the gash she'd incurred in the fall and patted her knee. "You did just fine, girl."

"No, I didn't. I panicked, Lincoln." She fought against the tears. "I let fear get the best of me. All I could think was that I was hurt, alone, and possibly going to die."

Lincoln made clucking sounds and stood. "Don't beat yourself up, hon. 'Those who look to him are radiant; their faces are never covered with shame.'" He turned and shoved the first-aid supplies into the backpack.

Psalm 34:5. Lincoln had done it again—read her heart and mind and reminded her that God was in charge, not her. She considered her partner as he zipped the backpack and wondered for the umpteenth time what great thing she'd ever done to have gotten such an amazing friend.

Lincoln was an attractive man with his dark eyes, dark hair, and trimmed mustache. Physically he looked like a Greek god. Inside, Lincoln loved the Lord with all his heart and soul. His spirit was as gentle as a lamb's. And that spirit had been what pulled her back from the ledge when Wade had died.

Wade . . . handsome and charismatic Wade. The man she'd intended to marry. The man who'd brought her to Tennessee and introduced her to Lincoln Vailes.

The man who'd died in a hiking accident and left her all alone.

Roark let out a whoop, his face red and raw, as a little flame rose from his small pile. She couldn't help but grin.

The marshal raised her awareness of physical attraction. Why did she have to be drawn to a man who was a control freak and sometimes obnoxious? It just wasn't fair. The many facets of Roark Holland confused her. What perplexed her the most was why she would be attracted to such a man in the first place. He was nothing like Wade.

Maybe that's why she *was* attracted to him.

She tilted her head as Roark and Lincoln engaged in an animated discussion. Several times Roark pointed, and Lincoln would shake his head. She should get up and join the discussion, but she just didn't have any fight left in her. Her emotions were too raw right now.

Suddenly the subject of her scrutiny spun around and locked gazes with her. Roark hitched up a single brow. Heat shot up the back of her neck, spreading across her face.

"You should rest a little." His voice didn't tremble as he bent and set the moss and twigs in a pile nearby. Maybe he was unaffected by her.

The thought disappointed her more than it should. She licked her lips. "I can go on."

"But we aren't going anywhere real soon." Roark gestured around the cave. "Why don't you rest, and I'll try to raise someone on the satellite again?"

"He's right, Brannon. I need you at 100 percent to get us out of here. I'll use the radio and see if we get anything." Lincoln squeezed her shoulder.

She shook her head. "We need to figure out a way to get out of here."

"Look." Lincoln squatted beside her. "We'll get some heat in our bones, and we can all rest a little. Humor me, okay?"

She didn't want to admit how heavy her eyelids were. "For you." She gave a weak smile, then closed her eyes.

THIRTEEN

Saturday, 10:45 a.m.
Underground
Great Smoky Mountains National Park, Tennessee

THE LITTLE FIRE CRACKLED beside Brannon as she slept. Roark leaned against the wall of the cave, studying her partner who tended the flames. "Can I ask you something? Personal, I mean?" The question slipped out before Roark could stop it.

Lincoln shrugged. "I guess."

How to word his juvenile question without sounding like . . . well, a juvenile? "You and Brannon seem really close."

A silence hung heavier than the warmth keeping out the iciness of winter.

The ranger cleared his throat. "We are. She's my best friend, but that isn't a question."

Unexplained relief swelled in Roark's chest. "I'm just curious why . . . well, why you two aren't involved."

Lincoln's quiet chuckle echoed off the cave's walls. "I've never seen her in that light. Oh, don't get me wrong, she's pretty and great, but I love her like my little sister." His eyes darkened at their subject of conversation, still in slumber. "She almost was." His voice dropped to a whisper.

Roark recognized the pain in the ranger's words. "What do you mean?"

A soft sigh sounded over the popping of the fire. "You heard her mention Wade, right?"

"Yeah, and her parents."

"Wade was my older brother." His voice hitched. "And Brannon's fiancé."

Roark's mouth went dry.

"She was flying SAR choppers for the Coast Guard, based out of Florida. Wade, well, he was always an adventure junkie. Addicted to the adrenaline rush."

Roark remained silent but knew just what Lincoln described. At one time he'd sought out thrills just for the excitement, too.

"Wade met her at a survivalist seminar the Coast Guard put on. He was instantly attracted to her. He called me the night he met her and told me he'd found my future sister-in-law." Lincoln chuckled. "That was Wade—knew what he wanted as soon as he saw it. Told me that night he just had to convince her he was the man for her."

What would it feel like to be able to make such decisions so spontaneously? Roark couldn't imagine. Then again, his entire life had been planned to the T. But somehow he'd gotten sidetracked.

No, the incident with Mindy had sidetracked him.

"Wade proceeded to woo Brannon. It's a wonder she didn't get caught up in the whirlwind of his romancing." Lincoln's eyes held that faraway glossiness of being lost down memory lane. "She held out, taking it slow. But finally, after almost two years, she agreed to marry him. Boy, was he jazzed."

"I can imagine." Roark's gaze shot to Brannon, still curled up by the fire.

"By that time she'd fulfilled her obligation to the Coast Guard. She put in for her release, planning to move here and marry Wade." Lincoln paused, as if searching for the words. "He brought her home, and I was wowed as soon as I met her. So down to earth and strong. A good Christian woman."

"And she applied for the ranger job?"

"Not right away. I don't think she planned anything at first. Wade loved taking her around the park, introducing her to his friends, and going to church. I really don't know if she'd have even wanted to work if they'd gotten married."

"So what happened?"

"Wade and his buddies always took a hiking trip every year. The guys kept it up through college and well after. That year they'd planned to go to the Grand Tetons in Wyoming."

Beautiful country. Roark had hiked there once upon a time.

"Off they went. Brannon and I were looking at some property Wade had fallen in love with. They wanted to build a house."

Roark had a feeling where this was going but couldn't stop Lincoln in his tale. He just *had* to know.

"We got a call two days into their trip from a park ranger. An avalanche had hit, and their hiking group was missing." Lincoln scrubbed a hand over his face. "For two more days we waited for word. Nothing."

Leaning forward, Roark noticed the raw pain in Lincoln's expression.

"And then we heard. They'd gotten stuck in the avalanche and couldn't get out. They died because no one could reach them."

How horrifying. Roark couldn't imagine the pain Lincoln felt over the loss of his brother. And poor Brannon . . .

Lincoln looked at Brannon. "She came undone. She'd lost both her parents at seventeen to a yachting accident. To lose Wade . . . well, it almost did her in."

The words lodged in Roark's throat. He gave a cough. "What happened then?"

"I stayed on her hard. She lost her will to live, everything. I wouldn't give up on her. Got angry. Yelled. Got in her face." Lincoln shook his head as if to erase the memory. "It was a long haul, but she finally came around. Faith got her through."

Faith. Why had it failed Roark when he needed it most? It'd disappeared like a wisp when he was trapped in the burning elevator with Mindy.

"Since she'd left the Coast Guard and her parents were dead, Brannon decided to stay here and build a life. I was the only person she had."

Roark couldn't imagine how she'd gone on.

"She decided to apply to the NPS. With her college and military history, she was able to get on rather quickly. She worked for a couple of years as a regular ranger, then the super was able to get funding to buy her a helicopter and upgrade her as the pilot."

"She seems happy enough now." An unfamiliar lump sat sideways in Roark's stomach. She'd been through so much—he could easily forgive her attitude at times.

Before Lincoln could reply, Brannon struggled to sit. She blinked several times, then focused on Lincoln. "Hey. Were you able to raise anybody on the radio?"

He moved beside her. "Glad you got some rest. How're you feeling?"

She sat up. "Fine. Good to go." Her eyes met Roark's. "Did you reach anyone on your phone?"

Roark shook his head. "Still no service."

"I got some static on the radio," Lincoln said. "The blizzard's pretty much passed."

"We should try again. Toss me my backpack. Maybe with the weather calming, Steve can pick up my distress call." She nodded to Roark. "Use your satellite phone again—with the clouds gone, you should be able to get some type of reception."

Roark handed her the pack, then dug in his pocket and pulled out his SAT phone. Back to all business now. But that was okay. He understood her a little better.

And it only made her more appealing.

Saturday, 11:50 a.m.
Underground
Great Smoky Mountains National Park, Tennessee

ROARK'S MOVEMENTS, WHILE EFFICIENT, appeared graceful. Brannon shook her head to rid her mind of the fanciful thoughts. Maybe the fall had knocked her in the head. She jerked the radio from the pack and flipped it on. After giving her call sign, she tried to hail Steve back at base.

A squawk of static filled the air, then a crackling noise. Her heart jumped. Finally!

"Brannon, that you?" Steve's voice had never sounded so good.

"It's me. We're okay, but we need some help."

"What's going on?"

She closed her eyes, recalling the fear she could still taste. "Listen, we need you to get in touch with the National Guard to come get us. I've twisted my ankle so hiking out of here isn't feasible."

"I'll get right on it. What's your location?"

Brannon looked at Lincoln. He answered without hesitation. "We're about a mile north of Rainbow Falls. In an unmarked cave. SAR will have to bring equipment to get us out."

She relayed the information to Steve, along with how many were in their party and their condition. Unbelievable that a SAR team would have to rescue her. The irony smacked her square between the eyes, and it stung.

"Take care, you and Lincoln both."

"Thanks, Steve." She shoved the radio back into her pack and looked at Lincoln. "At least help is on the way."

"That is something." Lincoln brushed off snow from his shoulder. "But we're the best SAR team in the park, and you know it. The Guard will have to hunt for us."

Brannon touched his arm. "'The LORD will guide you always.'"

"Isaiah 58:11." He smiled. "No fair using the same Scripture you have posted in the Dolphin."

"All's fair in love and war, my friend."

Lincoln shook his head.

"So what's that?" Roark asked.

"What's what?" Brannon gazed at Roark.

"The book whatever for that saying. What is it?"

"Huh?" She had no idea what he was talking about. He made no sense.

Lincoln chuckled. "That wasn't Scripture—that was just an old adage."

"Oh." Roark's face flushed and he lowered his head. A long moment passed before he spoke again. "Why do you guys do that?"

"Quote Scripture?" Lincoln asked.

"Yeah. You guys do it back and forth. A lot."

"I don't know." Lincoln shone the light along the floor of the area. "Just something that keeps us focused on what's really important in this life."

"It's something we just started doing. Challenging each other on Scripture memorization, but it also comforts us." It was what Lincoln used to reach out to her years ago. What brought her back from the brink of deep depression. She ran her gaze over the top of the stone walls. "Why?"

"I was just curious."

"Are you a Christian, Roark?"

"Do I believe in God?"

"Yes."

A heavy pause settled. Brannon kept her mouth closed, refusing to push him for an answer. Her heart beat so hard, she was sure he and Lincoln could hear it.

"I believe in God." Roark's voice could barely be heard over her racing pulse.

"But?"

"Well, let's just say me and the Big Guy upstairs haven't been communicating much lately."

She couldn't stop herself from asking yet another question. "Why's that?"

"I was raised with a mom who was a Christian—took me and my sisters to church and all that. But once I got out on my own, well . . . I just had a couple of bad experiences with so-called Christians."

Brannon bit her tongue so she wouldn't keep prying, but his stance screamed there was more to his story. She nudged Lincoln.

"Uh, that happens sometimes," her partner said.

How profound! She could have done better than that. "There are a lot of people who profess to be Christians, Roark, who talk a good game but don't live the life. Is that what you meant?"

He glanced over to her, his eyes caressed her. "Kind of." A cloud dropped over his eyes, masking further expression, like a door slamming shut. Roark stared straight ahead, not looking at her.

How had she offended him this time? Her prying questions? Had she been too nosy? Maybe she had, but only because she felt as if she had a vested interest in Roark's spiritual standing. Not that she did, but her heart told her to push, so push she had. Now he seemed to be ignoring her.

Brring!

Roark pulled his phone from his coat pocket, then pressed it against his ear. "Demott? Holland here." Roark shoved snow around with the toe of his boot. "Yeah, we're okay."

Lincoln crossed over and lowered himself to the boulder beside Brannon. Both of them kept their eyes glued to Roark.

"No, we're okay." He paused for a moment. "We don't have to worry about the shooter anymore. I took him out." He lifted his eyes to settle on Brannon's face.

She averted her gaze but kept his movements in her peripheral vision.

"The heart is safe and sound. It got an injection before the flight medic was shot." Roark checked his watch and shook his head as if the person he spoke with could see him. "The rangers have contacted the station, and they're working to get another helicopter out here to pick us up."

Brannon crossed her arms over her chest and snuck another look at him.

He paced as he talked. "No, I don't know the exact coordinates. The chief at the ranger station knows our location." He sighed, glancing at Lincoln and Brannon. "What's the landline number to your station?"

Lincoln rattled off the numbers, which Roark repeated into the phone. "Yeah, you can try that. The chief's name is Steve."

Roark snapped the phone shut and slipped it into the backpack. He shook his head as he stood and slung the pack over his shoulder. "I hate to do this, guys, but we gotta try to find a way out of here."

"Why?" Brannon asked. "Steve will get somebody out here to us before too much longer. We don't have any equipment to get out of this cave."

"Why not? You must get calls for people stuck in caves."

Lincoln nodded. "Tennessee has more caves than any other state, but the ones that are logged in the park are closed to the public."

"We had to remove the spelunking cables and anchors to bring food and first-aid supplies." She didn't appreciate Roark's accusing tone. They'd left the gear behind because *he* rushed them from her Dolphin.

Roark shifted his weight, staring at the ground as if avoiding her look. "We've got to get this heart to the hospital pronto."

"I don't think we'll make enough progress to beat the helicopter coming to get us." She chuckled. "Besides, like you said, the heart will still be viable for several more hours."

"You don't understand." He lifted his face and stared at her. "The recipient—you know, the witness who can put away the child traffickers? Well, he's not doing so hot. He needs the surgery *now*. Otherwise, he won't make it."

Brannon's stomach roiled. "What would happen then?"

Roark's stare seemed to go straight through her, right into her very soul. "The child traffickers get off—free to keep selling young girls into prostitution like slabs of meat."

She couldn't let that happen. Not if she had anything to say about it. Pushing to her feet, Brannon glanced at Lincoln. "Come on, it won't hurt to check for another way out."

Lincoln hesitated, then nodded. He didn't look convinced.

She set her jaw and concentrated on finding a way out, all the while keeping her ears on alert for the helicopter. Steve would find someone to come get them—he was as dependable as the day was long. But would help come in time to save the witness?

Something caught her eye. "Lincoln, there." She directed the flashlight's beam. About four feet up, maybe five, was a small hole in the stone wall. "Is that a pancake crawl?"

Please, Lord, let it be a way out.

FOURTEEN

ROARK'S MIND ATTEMPTED TO wrap around what Brannon had said as she and Lincoln studied the hole in the cave. Did she really believe in all that Bible talk?

Could *faith* be real? Could he depend on it again? He had for a long time, but God had abandoned him in that elevator shaft. Had abandoned little Mindy.

"It is a pancake crawl!" Brannon's voice was tinged with excitement.

Roark jerked his focus back to the present, where Brannon pointed in the cave. "What's that?" He didn't like feeling so out of the loop. So out of control.

"It's a small connecting tunnel, if you will, from one underground room to another." Lincoln set the flashlight on the floor before inspecting the space. "I see light, which means there has to be an opening on the other side."

"But it's not big enough to crawl through." Roark's heart hammered.

"We lie flat and slide through." Lincoln grabbed the rock Brannon had been sitting on. "Help me push this over so I can see inside."

Before Roark could move to help, Brannon helped Lincoln shove the small boulder under the hole in the cave. The injury on her shoulder must be a surface wound, like she'd claimed. Lincoln stood atop the stone, peering into the space.

Roark eyed the hole. It couldn't be much larger than three feet in diameter. Lie on his back and slide through? No way.

B-ring! Brr-ring!

Brannon glanced over her shoulder. "Roark, your phone's ringing."

He shook his head. "My phone doesn't have a ring like that." His pulse spiked. "Wait a minute." He dug into his coat pocket and pulled out the SAT phone he'd taken off the shooter. He glanced at the caller ID—*Zimp*. What kind of name was Zimp? Pressing the cell against his ear, he held up a finger to silence Brannon and Lincoln.

"Tom, where in tarnation have you been? The boss has been calling me every five minutes to see if I've gotten in touch with you. Man, glad you finally have reception." The squeaky voice on the phone paused for a moment before launching into another tirade. "Boss is anxious to find out your status. Have you taken care of the heart yet?"

Roark stood still, even calming his breathing.

"Tom . . . you still there, man?"

"What is it?" Brannon moved beside Roark, her eyes soft as she studied his face.

He held a finger over his lips.

"Tom? Man, the phone must be cutting out again. Listen, if you can hear me, the boss said to take out everybody in that group. Got it? Take them all out. He's sent Milt your way to help."

Roark pressed the end button, his mind racing and his adrenaline surging. Pulling his own satellite phone from his pocket, he dialed as fast as his almost frozen fingers would allow. "Demott, it's Holland. We have a serious problem."

"We've talked to the ranger station—they're sending one of the National Guard units out. Also sending out a rescue land unit to recover the bodies from the coordinates that ranger gave."

"Fine. Listen, Demott, when I took down the shooter, I lifted a phone from him. I just got a call on it."

"What? You didn't mention a phone before."

"It slipped my mind since the weather kept blocking reception. But here's the deal: The caller ID showed the man who called is named Zimp. Z-I-M-P. Run it through the systems, will you?"

"Got it. *Zimp*. What's the number of the phone you have?"

Roark pulled the shooter's phone out again, went into the directory, and located the phone number. He recited it to his supervisor. "Listen, this Zimp who called said the boss had sent some guy named Milt my way. Have you heard how long it'll be until the National Guard shows up?"

"An hour at the earliest."

Great. "Send the Guard as fast you can and let me know what you find out about Zimp and the number." He shut his phone before turning to Brannon and Lincoln.

"What's going on?" Lincoln had moved beside Brannon, his arm rested over her shoulders.

Roark explained. "How many rounds do each of you have left?"

Both rangers checked their weapons. Brannon answered first. "Ten."

"Nine," Lincoln added.

Roark did a count. He had two magazines left in his pockets and six rounds left in his Beretta.

"When will the Guard be here?" Brannon's face didn't reflect fear but rather quiet strength and fortitude.

"At the earliest, an hour."

"We need to get out of here and to a place that has cover but close to a clearing where the chopper can land." She pushed to her good foot, swayed a moment, then used the toe of her injured leg to balance.

"That would be ideal." Not only had she thought of getting cover, but she also considered a landing area for the helicopter. Yep, she was back at the top of her game. Cool under pressure.

Her eyes closed, as if making a mental map. She lifted her finger to her mouth, chewing on her skin the way she often did. Why did he find her so charming and engaging? He swallowed hard.

Brannon grabbed his sleeve. "We're pretty close to Rainbow Falls now. We can get there and have plenty of cover and still be able to access a clear area for the helicopter to land."

"Good idea. Let's get moving." Roark lifted the cooler containing the heart and swung one of the packs over his shoulder. Then froze.

That little hole.

"Is there no other way out of this cave?"

Lincoln shook his head. "Not without proper rigging."

Roark steadied his breathing. "Maybe we should just stay in here. It's good cover, and surely the National Guard will have the equipment to get us out."

"No place for the helicopter to land around here." Brannon shook her head. "Once we get to the other room of the cave, we'll be able to get out."

"Are you sure about that?" He could only hope he didn't sound as much like a wuss as he felt.

"Well, Lincoln saw light, which means there has to be a big enough opening to let the sunlight spill in."

"But what if it's overhead, just like how we fell in? We still wouldn't have the equipment to get out." Roark's pulse zinged.

"I'll go first and check it out." Lincoln moved toward the hole, Brannon at his heels.

They'd called it a pancake crawl. Pancake was about right.

"Let me go first. I'm smaller." Brannon balanced with one leg in the air. "Give me a lift."

"But your foot . . . your shoulder—"

"I'm fine, Lincoln. Help me up." She lifted her arms toward that little hole.

Lincoln gave Brannon a boost and passed her the flashlight.

A creepy finger traced Roark's spine. Was this Milt guy already here? Watching for them—waiting for the perfect shot to avail itself? Were they moving into target range?

Saturday, 12:25 p.m.
Parkwest Medical Center
Knoxville, Tennessee

WARREN CLOSED HIS PHONE and continued pacing. Things were not going as he'd hoped. Now what? He needed to think, needed to make a game plan. The heart was out in the open. Wilks wasn't doing so well. There had to be something he could do to put a positive spin on the Coalition. Otherwise, his political career might be as dead as Wilks in a few hours.

He headed to the elevator. While he waited for the car to arrive, an idea hit him. He glanced over his shoulder and called to his aide.

Kevin rushed forward, a puppy eager to do his master's bidding. Warren bit back a smile at the correlation. The elevator chimed a second before the doors slid open. Once he and Kevin were inside and alone, he forced a stern expression to his face. "I want you to call all the local news stations. I want to call a press conference."

"Here, sir?"

"Right outside the hospital doors." He chuckled at the ingeniousness of his plan.

"But why, sir?"

Warren shot Kevin a scathing look and gnashed his teeth. "Because the public has a right to know the status of such an important situation. The US Attorney's office let the fact that they even had a witness slip to the public before they contacted me. I figure turnabout is fair play. I'll let the public know about the dire situation of the government witness and the status of the donor heart." He rubbed his hands together, already imagining the look on the US attorney's face. "I need to put a positive spin on this, boy. Understand?"

"Oh. Yes, sir."

"Get it set up pronto." The doors slid open. Warren stepped into the foyer, pulling his lighter from his pocket. "Can I trust you to get it done?"

"Y-yes sir," Kevin mumbled as the doors closed.

Warren strode out the hospital's entrance, lighting his cigarette before he'd even cleared the second set of glass doors. The afternoon chill settled around him as he marched to the smoking area one hundred yards from the entrance. He could turn the situation around, make it work for him. Yes, he could come out of this smelling like a rose—he just had to make sure all the morons did their jobs properly.

Will that make you proud of me, Dad?

Saturday, 1:40 p.m.
Underground
Great Smoky Mountains National Park, Tennessee

BRANNON LAY ON HER belly, shining the flashlight toward the opening of the pancake crawl. The scrape on her shoulder burned, but she disregarded the discomfort. Only about twenty more feet and she'd be in the other room of the cave.

Lord, please let there be a way out on the other side. We need a miracle.

How could these child traffickers send someone else after them? Roark had killed the guy shooting at them. Wasn't that enough? Who would dare come out here in this weather? Had to be someone very knowledgeable of the area. Chills trickled over Brannon as she inched farther through the little tunnel.

Her hands hurt as she pushed the flashlight first, then herself over the jagged stone. Rocks dug into her stomach, but she ignored the pokes. Child trafficking, based out of Tennessee. The idea was ludicrous, preposterous, yet Roark said it was true. And someone was willing to murder numerous people to keep it a secret.

"How're you doing?" Lincoln's voice steadied her, just as it always did.

She used her uninjured leg to shove herself. "About five more feet and I should clear the crawl." And hopefully find a way out of this cave. *Please, God.*

The flashlight fell, landing with a thud. "Oh!" Her hands found nothing but air.

"Brannon, are you okay?"

"Fine, Lincoln. Reached the end of the crawl." She inched herself to the edge and glanced about.

The flashlight lay on its side, the beam casting eerie shadows on wet stone, but the chamber had plenty of natural light filling the area. The crawl's opening was only about four feet above the floor of the cave. Even with a bum ankle, she could make the drop. "I'm going to enter the other room now," she yelled over her shoulder.

This was going to be a doozy. There wasn't enough headroom for Brannon to sit and let herself drop legs first. Not even enough space to turn around. How would Roark and Lincoln make it through? She needed to figure something out. And fast.

Lord, I need a little help here.

Maybe she could get ahold of the edge above her. That seemed to be her only option. She rolled over onto her back and looked at the top of the pancake crawl's edge. Was that a rock jutting out? If she could just reach it . . .

She shuffled her back against the space, her shoulders clearing the crawl. She extended her right arm up as far as possible, despite the pain. There, just an inch more. Brannon scooted a little farther. Her hand made contact with the cold rock. She gripped it before using her left hand to brace against the edge.

Ever so slowly, she pulled herself free of the tunnel. She supported her body weight with her right toe as she stood at the mouth of the crawl. Whispering a prayer for a landing that wouldn't hurt her left ankle any more, Brannon let go of the rock and jumped to the ground.

Landing on the ball of her right foot, she bit back a cry as the weight pushed her to the ground. Soft dirt cushioned her fall. She sent up a prayer of thanks, then stood. "I'm in."

"Can you see a way out?" Lincoln hollered.

"Just a sec." That this chamber had a dirt floor held promise for a way out. She grabbed the flashlight for better viewing and shone the beam left, then right. Her heartbeat picked up as she spied where light spilled into the room. "I think there's a way out. A walking path."

Lincoln's woops brought a smile to her face.

"Come on. Who's next?"

"Hang on."

While she waited for Lincoln and Roark, she hobbled toward the keyhole squeeze. It'd be as tight vertically as the crawl had been horizontally, but she could smell the fresh air through the crevice.

"Uh, Brannon?"

She hurried back to the pancake crawl. "Yeah, Lincoln?"

"Roark's gonna come through first. He'll be coming feet first. Think that's a problem on your end?"

"Actually, that'd probably be the best way. Come on your stomach, Roark."

"He's getting in the crawl space now."

"Ready." She leaned against the wall, listening to her partner guide Roark. Why was Lincoln talking to him like a frightened child? The man was a US marshal—surely he could maneuver his way through twenty-five to thirty feet of a pancake crawl.

"You're doing great. Keep going."

Lincoln's words drifted to Brannon. She smiled. That was her partner, the encourager. Maybe Roark's broad shoulders made the tunnel too narrow for easy passage.

She pushed off the cave's wall and peered up to the crawl's opening. Little pebbles drifted down on her like the snow had earlier.

"Keep going, Roark. You're almost there." Lincoln definitely sounded too upbeat for something so easy.

"How would you know?" Roark growled.

Brannon bit back another smile just as a pair of feet came into view. "Whoa, Roark. You're here."

The feet froze.

"Just lower yourself to your waist and then drop. Go slow."

Before she could spout off any further directions, Roark stood beside her. His face was red and a bead of sweat lined his upper lip, despite the iciness of the chamber. She grazed his cheek. "Are you okay?"

He brushed off her touch. "I'm fine." But his words held both a snarl and a quiver.

"All okay on that end?" Lincoln asked.

"We're good." But she ran an inspecting glance over the marshal.

"I'm going to douse the fire and load the crawl with the backpacks and cooler."

"Holler when you're on your way." She turned to find Roark sitting against the wall, his breathing more labored than it should be. She sat beside him. "Seriously, are you okay?"

"I just don't like small spaces."

Ah. Claustrophobic. The pancake crawl must've been hard on him. But he'd done it anyway. She masked the respect she knew would reflect on her face. Time to deflect, change the subject. "So why did you become a marshal?"

He chuckled, and Brannon found herself wanting to hear more, learn all she could about this intriguing man.

"After my father died, my mother moved me and my sisters back to her family home. I was raised by my grandfather, and every night we watched *Gunsmoke* together. I always wanted to be Marshal Dillon." His eyes twinkled. "After graduating from the police academy and walking the beat for a couple of years, I realized I needed more mental stimulation."

His laughter was contagious, and Brannon found herself smiling at him.

"I knew I'd have to be on the force a long time to make detective, and I'm not exactly big on patience, so I looked for other avenues. The marshal training program was short. I applied and was accepted." He rubbed his knee with a distracted movement. "The rest, as they say, is history."

"It's as good a reason as any."

Roark's face grew pensive. "Funny thing happened, though. I found I really liked helping people, protecting them." He let out a long sigh, one wrought with regret and sadness. "There's so much evil and ugliness in the world—I like to think I do my part to protect people from it."

She swallowed hard. "I can understand that."

He touched her arm. "Does your faith help you deal with the ugliness of the world?"

Brannon weighed her answer before she spoke. "Yes, it does. Because no matter what happens on this earth, I know everything's in God's hands. I may not understand why things happen, at least not on this side of paradise anyway, but I do know there is always a reason." She hugged her arms around her torso. "And knowing that is what helps me sleep at night."

Roark shifted. His thigh brushed against her, sending ripples of exhilaration up her leg. She gasped as her pulse escalated. Why did just his touch do such strange things to her? Part of her wanted to scoot closer to him, but the smart, logical side won the mental argument. Brannon maneuvered away from him. Once she freed herself of the contact, her breathing regulated to a normal pattern. "How're you doing, Lincoln?"

"Fire's almost out."

She rubbed her hands, wondering what could be taking her partner so long. Lincoln was nothing if not efficient.

"Why a helicopter pilot?"

Roark's deep baritone jolted her from the inner musings. She glanced into his eyes—an error on her part, a big one. His dark orbs penetrated her façade as if seeing who she really was on the inside. She lifted her finger and chewed on the cuticle.

"Brannon?"

"Yeah?" She jerked her hand into her lap.

"What made you decide to become a helicopter pilot?"

"Oh." She hated to answer—it seemed that people wanted to know more why she took a job normally held by a man than her motivation for doing it. "Well, I wanted to help people, save them. I joined the Coast Guard when I was seventeen. After I finished my training and education at the Academy, I found myself pulled to flying." Visions of the rigorous training and the men who abused and heckled her paraded across her mind. She stared into Roark's eyes again. "So I applied for flight school and was accepted."

"Why didn't you stay with the Coast Guard?"

"I gave them thirteen years, won the Distinguished Service Medal, and opened the door for women to become pilots in the Guard." She shrugged. "I guess I felt I'd given all I could. When it came time to re-up, I chose to leave."

No need to dig up everything about Wade. She still couldn't talk about him without feeling like a part of her had died, even though it'd been more than five years.

Roark scrutinized her. More than ever the scar running along his jawbone appeared more visible. "So you decided to become a park ranger?"

"My degree is in marine biology, and I love working with nature. Lincoln suggested I apply." She popped her knuckles. "So I prayed hard, and God showed me that this is where He wanted me to be."

That suspicious, guarded look crossed his face. "Do you really believe God takes an active part in your everyday life?"

"Yes. Yes, I do." Brannon fingered the area of her injured arm. "I can't imagine not going to God for direction in my life."

"Even when the world is horrible?"

"Especially then." If He hadn't sent Lincoln to befriend her after Wade had died, well, she didn't know how she would've made it.

Roark ran his hand over his head. "So you believe there's a master plan and everything happens for a reason?"

"I have to believe that." She stared at the crawl opening. "Otherwise I'd go insane." What was taking Lincoln so long?

Roark didn't reply, and she didn't press him. Over the years, being exposed to macho types in the Guard had taught her many things, but mainly that they needed space and time to grasp a bigger picture than their minds were accustomed to seeing. Brannon continued to stare at the passage, not letting on to Roark that she was sending up prayers on his behalf right this very moment.

After a long pause he spoke. "I guess I never considered it that way before. It's something I'll have to think about."

"Good." She couldn't hide her smile. "So tell me about your sisters."

He chuckled. "They're all older than me. Two are married with kids. Rosalyn is only a year older than I am, and she's quite the career woman." His expression softened. "Quite a handful."

"What's her profession?"

"A high school principal."

"Wow." Brannon couldn't imagine the responsibility of all those kids.

Roark's face softened even more. "Yeah, she's pretty special."

"Heads up!" Lincoln's yell echoed off the walls. "I'm coming feet first, too, and will be kicking the packs and cooler ahead of me."

Finally. "Waiting on you, bud." She stood and peered at the opening.

Roark stood as well. Brannon tilted her head and eyed his jaw. "So, how'd you get that scar?"

He ran a finger along the angry scar. "Let's just say my reflexes were slow that day."

"Oh." Heat fanned her cheeks.

Pain crawled over his face—fresh, raw pain. Her heart ached for him.

Lord, call him back to You so You can ease the burdens he carries.

FIFTEEN

Saturday, 3:10 p.m.
Suburb South of Townsend, Tennessee

MAI SNUCK INTO HER room, hiding the two diet soda cans under her robe. She shut the door behind her and glanced around. This was resting time, per Madam Nancy's orders. But Mai had other things to do.

Kanya sat in the corner, her knees drawn to her chest and her eyes filled with tears. The two older girls snored. Mai moved to the mattress, lifted the threadbare sheet, and sought out the small slit she and Kanya had ripped earlier. She shoved the two cans into the mattress, replaced the sheet, then moved to kneel beside her new friend.

"I hate it here." Kanya's native tongue whispers tore into Mai's heart.

She, too, was sick of being used and discarded. Mai laid a hand on Kanya's arm. "But this is only for a little while longer. We have a plan, and we *are* going to get out of here."

"But when?"

"Soon." She patted Kanya's arm, then withdrew her hand. "I stole two drinks from the cooler. What did you get?"

Kanya lifted a shoulder. "I took a package of beef jerky off the last guy."

Butterflies swarmed in Mai's stomach. "You are not supposed to take anything from the men. They might notice and tell Madam Nancy." She wrapped her arms around her midsection. "That can get us caught."

"He did not notice." Tears fell down Kanya's cheeks. "He did not even know how to open the door to leave."

Mai glanced over her shoulder toward the hall, then swiped the tears from her friend's face. "You cannot let them see you crying.

122

They will hurt you." She stood, fisting her hands on her hips. "We have to stick to the plan if we are going to get out of here." Softening her tone and her expression, she squared her shoulders. "Come on, Kanya, you can do this. We have no other choice."

Even more tears spilled from Kanya's eyes. "That is just it. I had a choice to come and I did." She threw her hands in the air, waving them about. "And look how it turned out."

A reflection of that same dismay shot through Mai. She knelt again beside her friend. "Did Uncle Fred and Aunt Betty bring you over?"

Kanya's dark hair bobbed around her face.

"Me too." Mai ran a hand over her own long hair. "We were lied to, misled. We did not know any better." Or did her father know?

"Only a *ngang* allows themselves to be so deceived."

Mai jerked Kanya's shoulder. "This is *not* our fault! We are not fools."

Kanya snorted. "We let ourselves be sold into this . . . this . . . slavery." The dejection in her voice enraged Mai.

She shoved Kanya, then stood and glared down at her. "We were tricked, yes. But we can do something." The fury subsided, leaving her despondent. "We cannot give up now, not before we have even tried."

Kanya didn't look up.

"Look, we have to try. To do something to help ourselves." Mai jumped as a braying laugh filled the hall. She lowered her voice. "I am going to do this with or without you. I can at least say I refused to accept the situation."

Kanya sniffed and lifted her gaze to lock with Mai's. "Okay."

Mai held out her hand and pulled her friend to her feet.

"I will see what I can get tonight." Kanya wiped her face clean of tears.

"We better try and sleep—Madam Nancy will notice if we look tired." Although how the woman expected them to nap was beyond her. Then again, most everything was beyond her.

Except her plan to escape.

Saturday, 3:25 p.m.
Underground
Great Smoky Mountains National Park, Tennessee

"SHOULDN'T THE NATIONAL GUARD be here by now?" Roark stood beside the cramped hole that would take them out of the cave.

"They'll get here as soon as they can. We need to get to an area where the helicopter can land anyway." Brannon nudged past him. "Let me see if we'll be able to make it through the keyhole."

Before he could say a word, she squeezed into the little space. An area even more confined than the tunnel. His mouth went dry. How much more could he take?

"You could just tell her why you don't like tight places." Lincoln stood beside him, his quiet voice unnerving Roark.

"I'm fine."

"You know, both Brannon and I are pretty good listeners."

He knew Lincoln was right, which was why he chose to keep his mouth shut. Having to share with Dr. Martin was bad enough. Exposing his weakness to Brannon would be . . . well, unthinkable. At least until he figured out what exactly he felt for her.

Because he definitely felt something.

"Guess that would be a no."

"Nothing personal, Lincoln. It's something I have to deal with."

"Guys, it'll be tight, but I think y'all can fit." Brannon's voice sounded so far away. "It's only about eight feet long, so just hold your breath and hurry."

Eight feet of walls closing in on him? The tunnel had almost done him in. Now this?

"You go first. I'll be right behind you." Lincoln laid a hand on Roark's shoulder.

"No. You go ahead. I'll bring up the rear." Less chance of Brannon seeing him like before—having a panic attack.

Lincoln cast a final glance at him, then moved into the crushing slit in stone, dragging his backpack behind him. As soon as he did, darkness swept over the room.

Roark's heart raced. He could do this. Mind over matter and all that. They had to get out. He had to get out. Had to get the heart out or there'd be more innocent victims. He gripped the cooler against his sweat-coated palm.

"All clear. Come on, Roark." Lincoln's voice drifted through the hole.

Roark took a deep breath. Turning sideways, he held his breath and shoved himself into the crevice.

The rock pushed against him. The air vacuumed from the space.

Roark froze. He closed his eyes, struggling to force air in through his nose. He couldn't move. His feet were cemented to the spot. Darkness shrouded him. White dots danced before his eyes.

"Mister, are we gonna be okay? I'm scared."

Roark gathered little Mindy in his arms. "We'll be fine. We just have to find a way out."

"I don't like it here. It's dark and scary."

"I know, honey. I know." Roark glanced around the elevator shaft, trying to catch a glimpse of anything. Any route of escape. He hadn't wanted to take the little girl this way, but what else could he do? Demott had said to wait for backup, but he couldn't. He had to take control of the situation.

Her parents and brother were dead, and Roark had to escape with Mindy into the elevator shaft. To save her life.

But their options now were limited. His options. It was his responsibility to get Mindy out alive.

The hum of the elevator started. The car jerked.

"Mister!"

The car jerked again and began ascending.

Roark threw Mindy beneath him. What was he going to do? God, help us!

But the elevator shaft burst into flames. Roark tried to roll on top of Mindy, but she panicked. Her screams filled the shaft as the fire grabbed her. He reached for her, but the cable snapped, catching him across the jaw and knocking him out.

He had awakened in the hospital with a scar and a fear of tight, dark places.

"Roark?" Lincoln called out.

Inhale through the nose, exhale through the mouth. Roark fought to shove the memories away.

"Roark, are you okay?" Lincoln called again.

His feet wouldn't respond, no matter how much Roark ordered them to move. He could make out voices but none calling to him.

Except the ghost of little Mindy Pugsley.

A soft hand grabbed his forearm. "Roark?"

He jerked, drilling his head into the stone. "Mindy?"

"It's Brannon. Come on. Follow me." She tugged on his arm.

He slid a step closer to her.

"Good. Just keep coming with me. You're doing great."

What felt like an eternity later, he cleared the hole in the rock. He dropped to the ground, gasping for air.

Brannon laid a hand on his shoulder. "Are you okay?"

His worst nightmare had come true—Brannon had seen his weakness firsthand. Now she'd see what a fake he was. What a phony. Why he didn't deserve her interest. She'd been through enough. She didn't need some wimpy guy who couldn't let go of the past.

Saturday, 4:15 p.m.
Parkwest Medical Center
Knoxville, Tennessee

THEY INTENDED TO KEEP him out of the loop.

How dare the FBI and US Attorney's office acquire information about the witness and not tell him—again. He sat on the Coalition. He was a US congressman. He was invested in the outcome of this situation.

Warren smoothed his tie against his shirt, wishing he'd had the forethought to grab another oxford on his way. The wrinkles and creases could work to his advantage, however, portraying him as a hands-on type of congressman, a working man's representative.

He smiled at his reflection in the hospital bathroom mirror, then twisted his face into different expressions. When he found the one that looked most earnest and sincere, Warren stepped back from the row of sinks. Yes, this expression would endear him in the hearts of his constituents.

Only through his aide had he learned more particulars. That Wilks's wife had died at home from a long battle with cancer. Wilks had called her son, then left, going straight to the Knoxville FBI office. He hadn't even waited until the son got there—just left his wife's dead body in the master bed and departed. The FBI were now reactivating the search for the son and had requested a copy of the wife's autopsy report. The information was nothing vitally important to the case, per se, but it annoyed him that no one had informed him.

The door swung open and Kevin scuttled inside. "Congressman, the press is waiting."

"Are all the major affiliates represented?"

"Yes, sir. ABC, CBS, NBC, FOX, and CNN. All here and accounted for."

"Good." Warren tossed a final glance at his reflection, smoothed down his thinning hair, and waltzed past his aide. One of these days he'd have to check out all those hair restoration infomercials. He certainly could afford it. First, however, he had to play to the public—his public.

Kevin doubled his steps to keep up with Warren. "Sir, Marshal Demott has caught wind of your press conference."

Warren slowed his pace and stared, with a single brow hitched, at his aide. "And?"

"He's not too happy, sir. He's trying to get a gag order."

"A gag order?" Irritation seethed through him. Hiding information, now trying for a gag order? What did the marshal know that wasn't in any of the reports? What didn't he want others to know? "Well, we'll just see about that now, won't we?" Warren strode toward the hospital's main entrance. He stomped on the mat, causing the glass doors to whoosh open.

Camera bulbs flashed, reporters called his name, bright lights from video feeds shone in his eyes. Warren straightened his shoulders and moved to the area set up with microphones and a podium, just right of the entrance. He held up his hands as he moved behind the wooden podium. "Ladies and gentlemen."

A moderate silence fell over the crowd as the reporters and cameramen scooted in front of the podium. Hushed shoving and pushing murmured over the group as media personnel vied for the best position.

"I'd like to make a statement, then I'll open the floor for questions." He gazed over them, the hungry buzzards. Time to give them what they wanted, what they craved. "The witness in the child-trafficking ring is stable, but the surgeon has updated us that the heart needs to get here as soon as possible for the transplant surgery to be successful."

Rumblings and questions popped up from the flock of vultures.

Warren cleared his throat and held up his palms again. "We know the helicopter transporting the heart crashed, but the heart and the US marshal escorting it survived the crash. A search-and-rescue helicopter from the Great Smoky Mountains National Park found the crash site but was prohibited from taking off when shots were fired."

Gasps moved through the crowd. Perfect. Now he had their undivided attention. "The marshal has kept the heart safe, folks, despite being fired upon. As we speak, a National Guard helicopter is en route to the area." He twisted his face into the concerned expression he'd practiced in the men's room. "Now, my time is very limited, but I'll field a few questions."

"Congressman, what about the child-trafficking ring?"

Warren darted his gaze through the mass of media until he found the rookie reporter who'd posed the question. He locked his stare on the young man. "As far as we know, the only person who has information regarding this alleged ring is the witness in protective custody."

"Who shot at the marshal?"

"We don't know that information at this time." Warren swung his gaze to Dineen Milner, the tall brunette who was the star field reporter for NBC. "I'm sure the marshal will be thoroughly debriefed upon his arrival and we'll know more."

"Congressman, have there been any casualties?"

Warren lowered his brows and set his jaw as he stared at Roni Kednig, the saucy reporter from ABC. "Sadly, yes. The pilot transporting the heart was killed in the crash. From the information we've received, which is limited at this time, the flight medic transporting the heart has also been killed."

"In the crash?" Ms. Kednig pressed.

"No, in the exchange of gunfire." Warren flicked his eyes to the up-and-coming reporter from FOX. "Next."

"What is the estimated time of arrival of the heart?" The reporter blinked as more camera flashes went off.

"The most up-to-date information we have is still vague, but we're anticipating the arrival within the next couple of hours or so."

Heather Tilton, the seasoned reporter from CNN, pushed to the front of the crowd. "Congressman, can you give us any further details on the child-trafficking ring itself?"

Kevin touched his elbow.

Warren glanced over and noticed Demott standing off to the side of the crowd, his arms crossed over his chest. Straightening, Warren shook his head. "That's all I have at this time. I'll keep you updated as the situation progresses." He slipped his hands into his pockets. "Thank you all for coming."

Kevin took Warren's place behind the podium and reiterated to the reporters that they would keep the media updated as they received information. While Kevin handled the little scavengers, Warren strode to face the chief marshal.

"Was that really the best thing to do, Congressman?" Demott's eyes narrowed to little slits.

Warren shrugged. "The public has a right to know."

"Not if it compromises the case or puts people in harm's way."

"How does holding a press conference put anyone in danger, Marshal?"

Demott's gaze scanned the crowd beginning to disperse. "Whoever is involved in the ring will soon be aware that the one person who can blow their cover is about to undergo surgery."

"And he's being guarded by US marshals." Warren cocked his head to the side. "Are you concerned your team can't handle it?"

Opening his mouth, then snapping it shut, Demott glared at him for a moment, then turned and marched back into the hospital.

Warren reached into his breast pocket and whipped out his pack of cigarettes. Some people smoked after sex—he smoked for the same reason but different circumstances. Satisfaction was still satisfaction, no matter the conditions. And winning people over made him crave the nicotine every time.

SIXTEEN

Saturday, 4:20 p.m.
Southeast of Rainbow Falls
Great Smoky Mountains National Park, Tennessee

THE LATE AFTERNOON SUN played peekaboo behind the snow clouds, the soft glow moving like shadows over the valley. Dusk fell over the landscape with a hush.

Brannon lifted the water bottle and took another sip. "How long do you think he'll be?"

Lincoln smiled. "Who knows? He saw footprints and had to track."

"Do you think somebody else is really after us?"

"You heard what Roark said. No mistaking the fresh footprints though. Somebody's been out here recently." Lincoln took a swig from his own bottle. "This whole situation reeks."

"Yeah." Brannon's mind flipped through her earlier conversation with Roark. "What do you think about his spiritual state?"

"Roark's?"

"Yeah."

Lincoln grimaced. "Why so interested?"

Heat flashed across her face. "Not so much interested as concerned. I mean, aren't we, as Christians, called to share the gospel?"

"Hmm." He hauled in a deep breath and exhaled. "Brannon, I love you dearly. But I'm not blind. I've seen the little interplay between you two—I'd have to be stupid to have missed it. So I have to ask you, are you worried about his salvation as a sister in Christ or for a more personal reason?"

Leave it to Lincoln to have the ability to see into her heart, even in a time like this. "Does it matter?"

Stroking his mustache, he tilted his head and studied her. "I think it does."

"How so?"

"Well, if you're concerned as a sister in Christ, you want to tell him about the gospel so his soul is saved from eternal damnation. You have no personal stake in his salvation at all."

"Right."

"But, on the other hand, if you're concerned because you want more of a relationship with him, then it's a selfish motive. You only want his salvation because it will suit your desires."

He had a point. Then again, he always did. "Still, if the end result is the same, what does it matter, the motivation?"

Lincoln closed his eyes and remained silent for a while. She sat quiet, knowing he was gathering his thoughts to temper his words. When he opened his eyes, they shimmered in the flickering moonlight. "True. Philippians 1:18 says: 'But what does it matter? The important thing is that in every way, whether from false motives or true, Christ is preached. And because of this I rejoice.'"

She let the Scripture roll over her. Yet the uneasy feeling still sent pinpricks up the back of her neck. "But?"

"But what?"

"I hear a 'but' in your voice." Brannon nudged her shoulder against his arm. "Come on, Lincoln, spit it out."

"We've been partners and friends for quite a while now, and we know each other pretty well."

"Just tell me what you're thinking. I respect your opinion and want your input."

He stroked his mustache. "I've never seen you like this before, with any man. Not even my brother. I can't help but think that Roark's salvation isn't the issue of your heart."

Stinging from his assessment, which was a little too close to the truth for comfort, Brannon touched his hand. "And?"

"I don't know. If your heart isn't pure, your testimony won't be as powerful." He laid his other hand atop hers. "My concern here is not only for his salvation but also your walk of faith."

She swallowed as she mulled over his words. Biting tears threatened to spill. Blinking them back, she hauled in a long breath. "I guess I'll just have to pray about it."

His hand squeezed hers, filling her with warmth, love, and simple joy. "I'll pray for you, too."

"Thanks. Now where is Roark? We need to start moving again." She tossed her scrutiny across the valley, now dark. "I don't want to give whoever's coming after us any advantage in catching up."

A loud thumping reverberated over the valley.

Brannon turned her gaze toward the sky. The *thwump-thwump-thwump* so familiar to her drew closer. She twisted Lincoln's coat in her grip. "The helicopter's here." Bursting into action, she lifted the flashlight and handed it to him. "Shine the light up so he can see where we are." She cupped her hands. "Roark!"

A blast of illumination from the sky scanned over the icy terrain, the helicopter's light searching for them.

She heard the click of the flashlight and Lincoln's steps as he moved free from the covering of the trees. Hobbling as fast as she could manage, Brannon neared the edge of the woods. "Roark!"

Saturday, 4:25 p.m.
Southeast of Rainbow Falls
Great Smoky Mountains National Park, Tennessee

HE WAS GETTING CLOSE, Roark could tell.

Easing his steps into the snow and ice, he continued to track the footprints. Exhaustion clawed at every muscle. Movement flashed in his peripheral vision. He spun behind a clump of foliage and peered between the ice-loaded branches. A large African-American man in full tactical gear held an assault rifle close to his chest as he crept through the woods. Heading right toward Brannon and Lincoln.

Roark tightened his grip on his Beretta and crouched lower. Watching. Waiting.

The man slunk closer to the bushes where Roark hid. His boots crunched in the hardened snow.

Beretta at the ready, Roark controlled his breathing. Slow and steady, shallow and silent.

The air seemed crisper than before and still—no breeze moved a single needle on a tree. Cold penetrated the woods. Silence hung in the air as heavy as the ice coating the ground. Roark tensed his leg muscles, itching to pounce.

The man drew nearer. Closer. Roark could smell the man's scent on the wind. He shifted his weight. A twig snapped. The man stopped. He lifted his assault rifle, peering through the scope.

No time to wait. Roark leapt, catching the man across the back of the shoulders. The weapon thudded into the snow.

The man shrugged Roark to the ground. He landed on a rock that dug into the small of his back. Roark flinched. The Beretta fell from his grip and skidded across an icy patch to the woods. He jumped to his feet.

Roark couldn't make it to his gun before the bigger man would cream him. He needed something to get an edge. Fatigue latched onto his limbs.

They faced off, rotating in a circle around each other. Gauging. Analyzing. Sizing each other up.

"Who are you?" Roark took another step left, staying out of striking distance.

The man mirrored Roark's movements. "Don't matter." Then he lunged. The back of his gloved fist slammed against Roark's jaw.

His head snapped back . . . his knees wobbled. The next blow hit his abdomen. Air whooshed from his lungs.

The man threw his massive fist again, but Roark ducked. The blow just grazed him. Roark executed a dodging spin, using the man's wide shoulders for support. The man blew by him and teetered on the ice.

Again they faced each other. Roark's breath came in pants and gasps. His jaw ached, and the bitter, metallic taste of blood filled his mouth.

The man's breathing came out erratic as well. Both cross-stepped, kept moving in a tight circle.

"Roark." Brannon's yell broke the silence.

Would she come to find him? Considering her profession, she probably would. Roark's heart pounded. He couldn't take that chance. Closing the space between the man and him, he executed a full crescent kick, landing the heel of his right foot solid inside the man's left thigh. The man grunted and bent.

Now was his chance. Roark's leg flew out again, catching the man's right temple with the side of his foot.

Ooof! The man dropped to his knees.

Now to finish him off. Roark charged, his right knee landing in the middle of the man's gut. He slammed the side of his forearm across the man's shoulder, sending the man backward into the snow.

With a quick exhale, he hit the man's nose with a perfectly placed heel-palm strike, forcing the bone up through the sinus cavity.

"Roark!" Brannon's voice sounded nearer.

He retrieved his Beretta and crept toward the fallen man. He kept his eyes locked on the still figure as he approached slowly, cautiously. With the tip of his boot, he nudged the man. No response. Bright red blood dripped from his nose into a puddle on the pristine snow.

Roark holstered his gun, then hunched down beside the hulk. Lifeless eyes peered back at him. He checked the pockets. No wallet, no identification, nothing but a cell phone.

He slipped the phone into his pocket, stood, then stepped over the dead man and sprinted back to Brannon and Lincoln. He spit out the blood, wondering how bad he looked. He didn't want to alarm her.

A thumping sounded as he approached. As he rushed into the clearing, Roark spied the National Guard helicopter landing in a whirlwind. The side door slid open and an armed National Guardsman jumped to the ground.

"Let's go," Brannon hollered over the drone of the engine. Her long hair whipped in the wind, blocking her face.

He limped forward, following her and Lincoln into the cargo bay of the helicopter. He reached for the cooler sitting on the floor.

The helicopter's engine revved as the pilot nodded to his partner. The other guardsman hopped into the aircraft and shut the door with a resounding slam.

Roark held tight to the cooler's handle. He'd done it. Accomplished his mission. No other innocents would die.

Saturday, 4:36 p.m.
Southeast of Rainbow Falls
Great Smoky Mountains National Park, Tennessee

BRANNON STARED AT ROARK, taking in the trickle of blood from the corner of his mouth. "Did you find anything?"

He held up a cell phone. "Just this."

She didn't respond, just considered what that meant. He'd found whoever had left the footprints. Fought with him. Dare she ask if the man was alive or dead? She pressed her feet against the helicopter floor as it rose into the sky. Searing agony shot up her leg. Brannon gritted her teeth. Twisted ankle or not, she would not cry out.

The pilot's voice filled the air as he keyed up the radio. "ATC this is National Guard in Great Smoky Mountains National Park. Over."

The pilot rattled off their coordinates, informed the tower of their rescue, and notified that they were en route to Parkwest Medical Center.

Tears of helplessness and disappointment clouded Brannon's eyes. She swiped them away, but not before Roark touched her shoulder. She cut her eyes to him and found his expression one of empathy as he glanced at her ankle.

How could he sense her feelings so accurately? Brannon was accustomed to Lincoln's reading her thoughts, but that was because they'd been partners, a team, for several years. She'd only known Roark for days.

God, help me to understand.

Recalling the way Roark made her feel when he looked at her a certain way, or how her knees had turned to mush when he'd touched her tattoo, she prayed her emotions weren't so obvious. Now that they were about to return to civilization, would the attraction they'd begun to experience disappear? Reality always did have a way of crashing into her fantasies.

She studied his movements as he inspected his gun clips, then shoved them back into his coat pockets. Where Roark Holland was concerned, it seemed her heart was lost in a deep fantasy. Would she be able to walk away cold once they landed? She choked at the thought.

Roark turned his gaze to her, his eyes confused.

She shook her head and smiled before staring out the window. No matter what, Brannon wouldn't let her heart become any more involved with Roark. Yeah. Right. And she had some lovely beachfront property right here in Tennessee, too.

SEVENTEEN

Saturday, 5:00 p.m.
Parkwest Medical Center
Knoxville, Tennessee

"CONGRESSMAN?" KEVIN STUCK HIS head in the waiting room.

Warren tore his gaze from the newspaper he'd been scanning. The article posed the possibility of the child-trafficking ring. It went further to question if these children were Asian, as implied. Warren still didn't grasp the outrage. He'd endured his Asian stepmother's tirades for four years before he could leave home. Hers and her demanding daughters' while Warren ached for his mother. To be forced to live under the same roof as his father's mistress . . . that foreigner who took over his home . . .

"Congressman?" Kevin crossed the empty room and stood before him.

"Yes?" He set the newspaper on the table and rose. "What is it, Kevin?" The news had better be important. Warren had finally found a little peace and quiet, a place where he didn't feel the Grim Reaper breathing icy blasts down his neck.

"Marshal Demott has received word via air traffic control that the helicopter is about twenty minutes out."

Warren raised his brows, a rush of adrenaline pumping through his veins. "Is the surgeon in place?"

"Yes, sir. They're prepping the patient for surgery now, and Dr. Rhoads is heading to the landing pad."

"Good, good." Warren pressed his lips together, his mind flipping through a mountain of options. "Where is Demott?"

"He's assembling his team so they can debrief his man and the others in the helicopter as soon as they land."

"I see. Where?"

"The chief of surgery has offered them his personal office and conference area."

Warren smoothed his suit jacket, lifted his coat from the back of the plain loveseat, and strode toward the door. He barked orders over his shoulder, not bothering to look at his aide. "Take me there. I need to be present at the debriefing."

Kevin dogged his heels. "Sir, they say only authorized members of the law enforcement team are allowed."

Warren jerked to a stop in the hallway, turned, and glared at Kevin. They were definitely trying to hide something. Enough of this runaround nonsense. He intended to find out what was going on. "We'll see about that. Authorized members, indeed."

His shoes squeaked on the polished tile floor, his long stride causing his feet to beat out a smooth and steady cadence. As he punched the elevator button and waited, a black cloud settled over him. He *had* to get into that debriefing. Find out what the marshal in the field knew.

Not waiting for the elevator doors to open all the way, Warren pushed inside and jabbed the button for the fourth floor. He stretched his neck from side to side, then straightened his suit jacket. Only authorized members of law enforcement allowed in the meeting? Who did they think they were? Didn't these idiots realize it was Congress who voted on their agency budgets? He'd remind them. Rule number eight—always throw out your trump card when necessary.

Good thing he happened to be a master poker player.

He stepped out of the elevator and waited for Kevin to lead the way. Warren followed, his mind already tripping over the demands he'd have to make to get into their little meeting. Yes, get inside he would.

Coming to a halt, Kevin nodded toward a closed door. "They're in there." The nervous little man looked as if he'd wring his hands at any moment.

Warren puffed out his chest, winked at his impressionable aide, then barged into the room. He paused for a moment, taking in the people milling about.

Agents from the US Marshals, CIA, and FBI stared as he entered the cramped room, then slammed the door behind him. Demott moved from behind the desk, a grimace on his face. "You can't be in here, Congressman."

"And just why not?" Warren wagged his finger through the air, keeping his tone even. "In case you've forgotten, Gerald, I sit on the Coalition Against Child Trafficking Committee, consulting with the Justice Department. I'm more than authorized to attend this meeting."

"It's not just a meeting, Congressman. It's a debriefing. I'm sorry, but the US Marshal Services don't allow nonlaw-enforcement members present during debriefings." Demott shrugged, wearing a smirk. "Company policy."

Blood pressure shooting into the red, Warren glared at the man. He hadn't liked Gerald Demott before this whole incident—he liked him even less now. "I think the guidelines of your procedures can be bent this time. Considering who I am and the extenuating circumstances."

Demott shook his head. "I don't think so, sir." His eyes danced as he crossed his arms over his chest. "Policy and rules still apply, no matter what the circumstances."

Warren opened his mouth to argue, then noticed the silence thickening the air. Every pair of eyes were glued to him, as if they all wanted to know which man would back down.

Rule number nine—if you can't win the battle outright, at least leave the impression you can, and will, win the war. "I see. I'll have to contact the Justice Department as well as the US Attorney's office in this matter. I'll see you soon." He spun, turning on his heel, and strode from the room before Demott could respond.

Outside in the hall Kevin lifted his head. "Well?"

"Shut up, Kevin." He fisted his hands, tightening the muscles in his arms. The Colonel would be ashamed of Warren. "And get me Justice on the phone."

Saturday, 5:10 p.m.
Suburb South of Townsend, Tennessee

MAI SHOVED THE CAN of diet soda as hard as she could into the hole of the mattress. It hit against tin, refusing to go in any farther—the end of it poked out of the fabric. She pulled the can free and stuck her hand in the hole. With all her might, Mai pushed the existing can farther into the hole, garnering an inch or so of play. She shoved the last can inside, then replaced the tattered sheet before standing.

The door creaked open, causing her to jump and spin around.

Kanya slipped into the room and handed Mai a disposable lighter and a crushed candy bar. "Here."

Taking the items, she stared into her friend's face. Tears streaked down Kanya's made-up face. Did it really matter to the men who visited what they looked like? Mai could not help but think not. All the men cared about was . . . well, she refused to think about that. She touched Kanya's arm and spoke in Thai. "Are you okay?"

"I hate America." Kanya sniffed, her eyes puffy and bloodshot from all the crying she had been doing. She had to stop—Madam Nancy would have one of her *boys* come teach Kanya a lesson if she continued. It had happened to another girl last night.

"Not much longer." Mai could barely keep the excitement from her voice as she counted their stolen bounty. "We need to tear another hole in the other side of the mattress—this one is full."

"Knowing we will escape is the only thing that makes life here bearable."

Kanya's depressed tone concerned Mai. Deeply. Tossing her friend an understanding look, Mai moved to the opposite side of the mattress. "Keep watch and make sure nobody comes in."

Mai removed the barrette from her hair, pried it open, and knelt. Using the rough edge of the hairpiece, she gnawed at the soft edge, ripping a hole. Once the opening was made, she stuck her hand inside and yanked out stuffing, hollowing it out as best she could.

"Someone is coming!" Kanya leaned against the door, her ear pressed close to the wood. "Hurry."

Heart pounding, Mai shoved the lighter and candy into the hole, jerked the sheet tight, and jumped to her feet. She pushed the barrette into her hair and clicked it closed.

Kanya scrambled away from the door just as it swung open, hitting the thin wall. The resounding clatter echoed in the room.

Madam Nancy stood in the threshold, her hands planted on her ample hips. "What are you doing hiding in here?" She grabbed Kanya's arm, shaking her. "I have customers lined up and waiting. Get yor bottom out there."

Kanya stumbled as she crossed the doorway. Mai moved forward, only to have Madam Nancy grab her upper arm and jerk her backward. Her pudgy fingers dug into the bony flesh, squeezing until Mai winced. "What were you girls doing in here?"

"W-w-we had to wash up."

Madam Nancy narrowed her eyes. "Don't you lie to me, or you *will* regret it."

"N-no, ma'am. I am not lying. We really were messy and needed to clean up before we came to find you."

The brawny woman glared down at her for a long moment. Then she huffed and let loose of Mai's arm, shoving her toward the door. "Then get on out there. Time is money and yor wastin' mine."

The knots in Mai's stomach loosened a bit as she staggered into the hall on what felt like boneless knees. *Just a little longer.*

Soon she would be in control of her life again.

Saturday, 5:18 p.m.
Knoxville, Tennessee Airspace

ROARK STARED AT BRANNON. She'd remained quiet through the flight, her eyes narrowed as she stared into the dim and cold night. How could the woman look so enticing without even trying? Shaking his head to remove the random thoughts, Roark questioned his mental state. He must've inhaled too many fuel fumes in the crash. His thoughts and emotions wouldn't behave—they seemed drawn to Brannon at the worst possible times. Like now.

The helicopter shifted with no jerks or abrupt jarring. "There's the hospital's landing pad." The National Guard pilot gave a curt nod toward a rooftop.

Bright lights shot through the darkened sky—some blinking yellow, some steady red. The entire roof glowed with a halo-type effect, casting a surreal feel to the situation.

Roark sucked in a deep breath as the helicopter pitched forward and dropped altitude. He pinched his eyes shut for just a fraction of a second, felt a gentle rocking motion, then heard Brannon's steady voice over the weakening hum of the engines. "We're here."

Lincoln pushed open the door. A team of men in paper surgical gowns stood at attention. Roark jumped from the helicopter, clutching the red cooler. The harsh glare of the spotlights burned his eyes. Brannon slipped from the seat. Roark gripped her elbow and helped her from the aircraft.

"Holland."

Roark turned at the sound of his boss's voice. He released Brannon and moved to shake Demott's hand. His supervisor gripped his palm, then took the cooler from his other. "This needs to go to Dr. Rhoads now."

The man in full surgical garb addressed him. "Can you remember when the last injection was given?"

Standing beside Brannon, just to the side of the helicopter, Lincoln answered. "Right about 7:15 a.m."

Dr. Rhoads glanced at his watch, nodded, then handed the cooler to a woman decked out in scrubs. "Let's go." The medical team rushed into the staircase.

Roark stared at the cooler disappearing behind the door. Suddenly exhaustion overtook him and weariness zapped his energy. Mission accomplished. He let out a long sigh. No more innocent girls would be lost. No, he couldn't bring Mindy back, but maybe this would ease the scars on his soul.

"Come on, Holland." Demott clapped Roark's shoulder, nearly knocking him to his knees. "We need to get you debriefed."

"Yes, sir." Roark faced Brannon and Lincoln. "You both need to come as well. We'll need your statements."

"Brannon needs to have her ankle and shoulder looked at first." Lincoln's stare met Roark's, sending obvious warnings with his eyes.

Roark moved toward her, but Lincoln intercepted and wrapped his arm around her waist. "I'll take her to Emergency. We know you have things to do."

As if he'd been sucker punched, Roark took a step backward. Why the attitude from Lincoln? He took note of Brannon's demeanor. Her face reflected pain not only in her expression but also in her eyes.

He glanced down at her ankle—the swelling had increased quite a bit, her skin puffed over her unlaced boot, a yellowish brown hue colored her flesh. A sinking sensation tightened in his gut, and he took another step toward her. "Brannon . . ."

Lincoln touched his shoulder. "You go. I'll get her to Emergency." The words were the same as before, but the ranger's tone had softened.

Darting his attention from Lincoln to Brannon, Roark stood still, as if his feet had grown roots. Gerald gripped his arm. "We have to go, Holland."

Roark hoped Brannon knew he'd rather make sure she was okay. "I'll meet you in Emergency as soon as I'm done."

She nodded. Her lips pressed so tight together they appeared white. Roark's stomach plummeted to his toes. With a final nod he followed his boss into the staircase.

Yet everything inside him seemed to leave him and stay with Brannon.

Saturday, 5:25 p.m.
Parkwest Medical Center
Knoxville, Tennessee

BRANNON ALLOWED LINCOLN TO take most of her weight as she hobbled down the walkway of the landing pad. Boots clattering on the metal stairs echoed in the cement enclosure, grating through her eardrums. She gritted her teeth against the sound and the agony of her ankle.

"Here we go," Lincoln said as the elevator opened to the floor marked EMERGENCY.

A line of sweat formed on her upper lip. She shot a puff of breath upward while Lincoln helped her through the steel door. A blast of warm air brushed across her face, drying out her eyes. She blinked against the heat as well as the bright lights from the bottom floor of the hospital. As they made their way to the emergency triage nurses' station, the sour odor of sickness masked by disinfectant permeated the corridor.

Children wailed with hurt and discomfort. Brannon eased onto the nearest chair and gripped the knee of her injured leg. How had the pain intensified so quickly? Lincoln went to speak to the triage nurse on duty while she got her bearings.

Blood dripped from a long gash across a young man's cheek. Angry welts decorated his face, yet he dared Brannon with his eyes to comment. She jerked her gaze to the next row of people in the waiting room. A little girl with blonde curls sticking to her face leaned against her mother's chest. The child's Caribbean-blue eyes drooped and her face was flushed. How long had this feverish child been waiting? Brannon glanced to the mother's face, taking in the etched lines of worry and concern.

Twisting in her chair to see Lincoln ambling toward her, Brannon nodded toward the mother and child. "That child needs help now, Lincoln. She's burning up with fever," she whispered as he hunched down beside her.

"They're really backed up right now and having to screen everyone coming in."

"Why?"

"Because of all the media hype about the heart. Before they move patients into Admitting, hospital officials need to make sure each case is genuine."

"That child is sick. Look at her—a child can't fake that pitiful look."

He stood. "Let me talk to the triage nurse and see what I can do, okay?"

She nodded, but her eyes locked on the mother's blank stare, then traveled down to the child's. The little girl stuck her pointer finger in her mouth, her little rosy lips puckering as she soothed herself.

"They're going to take her back next." Lincoln laid a hand on her shoulder. "The pediatrician on call is en route."

Brannon smiled.

"But they're ready for you now. Come on." He wrapped his arm around her waist and hoisted her to her feet.

Bursts of pain shot up her leg. White dots danced before her eyes. She swayed as the room shifted around her. Lincoln gripped her arm, steadying her. She pressed her lips together until her equilibrium returned, then nodded to him. With all the speed of a snail, they made their way back to the examining rooms.

Her shoulder was treated against infection and bandaged, then Brannon endured having her ankle x-rayed. Before long, she sat back in her examining room, the doctor tsking as he reviewed her films.

"Your ankle is sprained, and you've done additional harm by putting pressure on it after the injury." His young eyes flickered with annoyance. "What were you thinking?"

"Oh, I don't know—maybe that I needed to get out of there and deliver the heart?" She blew out the words in a huffed breath, then inhaled.

His shaggy brows crumpled into a unibrow as he bent down to finish wrapping her ankle. Brannon gnashed her teeth, another sarcastic remark burning her tongue. She lifted her finger and chewed at the cuticle.

"About done in here?" Lincoln moved from the doorway into the small examining room, leaning his hip against the counter.

She plucked her leg free from the doctor's touch, then hopped down from the table. She wobbled a bit, grabbing on to Lincoln's arm.

The doctor's eyes widened as he pushed off the stool and stood. "Actually, you'll need a pair of crutches."

"I'm fine."

A nurse sashayed into the room, carrying a set of aluminum crutches. "Here ya go, honey."

Brannon jerked the offensive sticks from the too-perky nurse, jabbed the rubber-coated tops under her armpits, and glared over at the doctor. Why couldn't people understand she hated feeling defenseless?

The doctor raised his brows and shrugged. "The nurse will get you your discharge papers." He took her chart and strode from the room.

Biting down on her lip, remorse filled Brannon. Maybe she'd been a little too snippy with the doctor, but couldn't he see how helpless her injury had made her?

The nurse smiled. "Let me go get those discharge papers."

Footsteps clattered in the hall outside the examining room. Pinpricks of awareness tickled the back of Brannon's neck, sensing Roark's presence before he marched into the room with the man he'd addressed as his boss.

Roark's broad shoulders overshadowed the small space. And although seriousness etched his face, his dark eyes glimmered as he stared at her. "What's the verdict on your ankle?"

"Fine." She shifted, using the crutches to move an inch or so forward.

"Good." His gaze caressed her face, sending spirals of heat across her cheeks.

The other man cleared his throat. "We really need to debrief you both." His nod included both Brannon and Lincoln. "We have the use of a couple conference rooms—will you join us?"

Brannon maneuvered the crutches to follow the red-haired man. "As if we had a choice," she mumbled under her breath. Lincoln touched her shoulder. She refused to meet his gaze, knowing she'd see a silent warning. Instead, she pressed her lips together and hobbled after Roark's boss.

The hallway floor, recently polished, provided little traction for the rubber tips of the crutches. She gripped the handles tighter, increasing her pace to keep up with the man in front of her. The crutch shifted. Brannon swayed, stepping down on her injured leg for balance, and a jolt of pain shot up her leg. She let go of the crutches. A strong arm wrapped around her waist.

Lifting her eyes, she stared into Roark's concerned face. She licked her lips. "Th-thanks."

"Why don't you let me help you? Lincoln can carry your crutches for you."

No matter how much she wanted to walk on her own, she knew she couldn't without help. Nor did she want to move out of his embrace. She leaned against him.

All too soon for her liking, they reached the conference area, and Roark released her. His boss motioned for her and Lincoln to sit across the long table from him, Roark, and two men in suits.

She grasped the edge of the wooden table, a strange sensation swarming in the pit of her stomach. Putting her hand under the table, she grabbed Lincoln's. Why was she so nervous? She'd endured many debriefs with the Coast Guard. Why was this one different?

Because Roark was there, watching and listening? Something about him made her nervous, but it had nothing to do with the rescue and everything to do with attraction.

The red-haired man pushed a button on a recorder, then shoved it in front of her. "I'm Chief Marshal Gerald Demott. This is the debriefing interview with Brannon Callahan and Lincoln Vailes."

She licked her lips again and squeezed Lincoln's hand tighter.

"First, Ms. Callahan and Mr. Vailes, we need to inspect your service weapons and bullets."

Brannon and Lincoln laid their guns on the table. A marshal took them both and left. Mr. Demott continued. "He'll bring them back to you before we're done. Now we need you to tell us what happened in regard to this search-and-rescue mission. From the beginning until you landed here tonight."

"Well, I saw the news report of the harvested heart on the local station. Being aware of the approaching blizzard, I tracked the course the helicopter would make, realized it would never make it, and decided to go up in my Dolphin to check things out."

Demott held up his hand. "What made you think they'd never make it?"

"Well, the wind currents over the Great Smoky Mountains can be quite dangerous in normal weather, and a Bell can't withstand all the updrafts from the blizzard." She shrugged. "I just figured if that bird did go down and I was already in the air, the rescue would be faster."

The debriefing continued until both statements were completed and the marshal returned their handguns to them. Brannon felt as if it'd taken a lifetime, yet she enjoyed staying in close proximity to Roark.

The conference room door swung open, hitting the wall behind it. A tall, wiry man rushed into the room, leaned over, and whispered into Demott's ear. Whatever he said, it wasn't news the chief marshal wanted to hear. His face contorted into a grimace and he nodded.

The newcomer strode from the room while Demott stood. "We'll have to get these typed up and your signatures later."

The other marshals in the room clamored to their feet. "What is it?" Roark asked.

"The witness is dead."

Brannon's heart free-fell to her feet. "W-what? How? We got the heart here in time."

Demott ran his hand over his red hair and sighed. "He died in surgery before they could even do the transplant."

EIGHTEEN

Saturday, 7:45 p.m.
Parkwest Medical Center
Knoxville, Tennessee

WARREN TIGHTENED HIS KENNETH Cole tie, straightened his suit jacket, and adjusted his cuff links. He loved having money and all that it provided him. Made him elite. Focus, that's what he needed. No slipups could be allowed. He would master the outcome. Hadn't his father drilled into his head that the son of Colonel McGovern was meant for great things?

"Congressman, the marshals are entering the meeting, sir, and the surgeon is on his way." Kevin stood a little taller as he sidled up next to Warren in the hospital's men's room.

Taking a step back to free his personal space, he frowned at Kevin. "Tell them I'm on my way and not to start the meeting without me."

Kevin spun on his heel to do Warren's bidding. As he lifted his hand to turn the doorknob, Warren stopped him with another order. "Additionally, as soon as you deliver that message, call all the media back out. I intend to hold a press conference as soon as the meeting is concluded."

"Are you sure you want to do that, sir? I mean, won't the FBI and marshals do that?"

How dare his aide question him? Warren straightened his shoulders, fighting not to show his displeasure. "I know what I'm doing, son. I'll be the one making the announcements. Understood?"

"Yes, sir." Kevin pushed open the door and fled.

Warren appraised his appearance a final time, smiled at himself in the mirror, then marched from the bathroom.

On the short walk to the conference room, he went over the questions he wanted posed in the meeting. He drew in a deep breath, held it, then exhaled and pushed open the door.

Agents from various government agencies milled about the room, some standing and chatting among themselves, others sitting at the table with heads bent as they whispered back and forth. Warren cleared his throat and glared at the woman in a dirty park ranger's uniform sitting near the head of the conference table. Her eyes appeared glazed, as if she'd been crying. Who was she, and what was she doing in the meeting?

Before he could ask, the door whooshed open, and the surgeon trudged into the room, still decked out in surgical scrubs and cap. He ran a hand over his chin. "I'm sorry to say that Mr. Wilks's heart wasn't strong enough to withstand the anesthesia. Time of death was 6:10."

Of course he'd died—didn't hospitals kill people? Warren's beloved mother had been a victim of such incompetence.

"Did he ever regain consciousness?" Demott asked. .

"No." The surgeon's pager sounded over the deafening silence in the room. He glanced down at the number. "I hate to cut this short, but I have another surgery. I'm truly sorry we couldn't perform the surgery."

"When will we have the official report?" Special Agent in Charge Greg Daly asked.

"You'll receive a copy by Wednesday at the latest. Now, if you'll excuse me, I have to run."

After the doctor rushed out the door, chaos erupted, everyone talking at once.

Warren pushed off the wall and whistled. All attention turned to him, and silence prevailed. "We need to decide the next course of action, gentlemen." He let his gaze settle on the woman's face. "And lady."

She gave a curt nod.

Warren looked over to the SAC. "Have the decoders come up with anything useful from the papers recovered from the witness?"

Greg Daly dabbed at his forehead with a cloth handkerchief. "Not yet. The only thing we know for certain is the account numbers are to a bank in the Cayman Islands. No information on whose names those accounts were in."

"Anything more come up on Wilks?" Warren would be relentless. This might be his only time to get information. And he needed that information.

"Not directly." The SAC pulled at files to read. "Autopsy report on his wife came back with some interesting toxicology labs. Traces of DCA, CV247, and ABT-737 were detected."

"And those are?"

"Cancer treatment drugs."

Warren shrugged. "Not so interesting when the woman died of cancer."

"She hadn't been under a physician's care in more than five years, Congressman. And those medications are still in trials."

"That means?"

Daly shook his head. "She was taking some sort of black-market cancer cocktail."

"Which Wilks would require quite a bit of money to afford for those five years. That's why it appeared he lived within his means." Warren nodded.

"The rescue team has recovered the three bodies." A junior FBI agent flipped papers. "They're on the way to the hospital now. We'll identify the shooters and see what we can find out there."

Warren shifted his gaze to Demott. "Do you have anything?"

Demott's jaw jutted out, and the tips of his ears turned an interesting shade of red. "No offense, Congressman, but this is a law enforcement situation. I don't think we should be sharing information with every Tom, Dick, or Jane."

"Then what's *she* doing in here?" Once more Warren tilted his head toward the woman sitting at the table.

Demott cleared his throat. "These are national park rangers Brannon Callahan and Lincoln Vailes. They were the rescue team who delivered the heart."

"What right do they have to be here? Yet you question my presence when I sit on the Coalition?" Warren folded his arms over his chest and looked down his nose at the marshal. What were they trying to keep hidden? From him? Or from the public?

A man stood suddenly, his chair shoving back so fast it made a horrid scraping sound against the floor. His hands balled into fists at his side as he scowled at Warren. "They have a lot more reason to be here than you do, Congressman."

"Ah yes, you must be the marshal who delivered the heart." He fisted his hands on his hips. "It's a shame you didn't get the heart here quicker—our witness may have stood a better chance had the surgery been performed earlier." Rule number ten—detract attention from yourself by instigating someone already appearing to be on the edge.

"My name is Roark Holland, and yes, I'm the marshal who delivered the heart." He took a step forward, his muscular build invading Warren's personal space.

Warren scrambled backward. Maybe he'd goaded the wrong man this time. "I need to know what information we're going to release to the media."

"The media?" Daly bolted to his feet. "I don't think we need to alert the media to any more details."

"The press knew the surgery was going to take place. We can't put them off." Warren took another side step away from Roark, who still looked as if he'd like to rip Warren's head off.

"Whose fault is that, Congressman?" Demott drew to his feet as well.

The SAC held out his hand. "This is still an ongoing FBI investigation. We can't release information that could compromise our case, especially not to the media."

"We can't just leave them in the dark." Warren crossed his arms again. "We need to make some kind of statement."

Holland looked ready to pounce. Demott laid a hand on the younger marshal's arm, tightening his fingers around the man's bicep. Then the chief marshal glared at Warren. "If this case is compromised, we'll never catch these scumbag child traffickers."

Warren opened his mouth to spout off another argument, only
to have the woman stagger to her feet. "Excuse me. I realize I'm not
working this case or anything, but what I do know is there is still
someone out there involved in this ring. I think someone should try
to find that person. Maybe then you'll get some answers."

The agents and marshals began discussing their options, while
the woman's gaze burned into his flesh. Making a mental note to
do a little checking on her, Warren slipped out of the conference
room.

Saturday, 8:10 p.m.
Parkwest Medical Center
Knoxville, Tennessee

ROARK CLENCHED HIS JAW, fighting to control his anger. The
stuffy and pretentious congressman had some nerve, insinuating he
belonged in the meeting and Brannon didn't. She'd put her life at
risk to save them, as well as to get the heart back to the hospital.
For the jerk to have implied it was their fault the witness died . . .
It made his blood boil. He saw the censure in Demott's eyes, and
Roark let out his breath in a huff.

He turned back to the congressman, but the man was gone.
In the burst of excitement, he'd snuck out. Roark nudged his boss.
"Sir, the congressman is gone."

"Probably making statements to the press. Time for damage
control," the Special Agent in Charge said as he rushed from the
room, a group of FBI agents dogging him.

"I guess they'll handle McGovern." Demott ran his hand over
his face. "I don't like that man."

Roark nodded. "There's something suspicious about him, boss.
He's much too interested in this case for a normal politician."

"Well, he sits on that committee our Justice Department set up
to oversee the child-trafficking reports." Demott shrugged. "I guess
he's worried about the reelection factor."

"I think there's more to his interest than that." Roark turned his
attention to the movement at the end of the room.

Lincoln held Brannon's elbow, assisting her to her feet. He pushed the crutches at her. She grimaced but took them. Lincoln turned his back to her, and Brannon stuck her tongue out at him. Roark bit back a chuckle.

"So what do you want us to do?" Lincoln rounded the table and addressed the two marshals.

"Let me see if I can find someone to type up your statements. All we'll need is your signatures, then you can wash your hands of this." Demott stuck his head out the door, whistling, then speaking in muffled tones.

"Can the ring be busted without the witness?"

Brannon's soft tone startled him. "We can always hope the departments working on the paperwork will get a break."

"That's it? That's the only way these . . . these child abusers will be busted?"

"It's in the hands of the FBI field agents." Roark shifted his weight from one foot to the other. How could he explain it to her when he, himself, couldn't understand the invisible lines drawn between government law enforcement agencies?

"So these men will get away with exploiting innocent children? That's just wrong."

"I know. My boss has assigned me to the follow up on the case, but until more evidence is uncovered, our hands are pretty much tied."

Chirp! Brring! Chirp!

Lincoln lifted a cell phone from his jacket and pushed it against his ear. "Hello."

Roark assessed Brannon as she stood beside her partner. She tugged her bottom lip between her teeth, making a slight hissing noise. His arms twitched as he recalled how it felt to hold her close, so close he could feel her heartbeat.

Lincoln flipped the phone closed and glanced at Brannon. "That was Steve. He's sending the new pilot to pick us up." He glanced at his watch. "ETA in about ten minutes." He looked to Roark. "We need to get up to the landing pad. Can we sign our statements later?"

They were leaving—*she* was leaving. Why did his heart feel like a giant vise had it in its grip and was tightening it with every passing second? He knew he'd have to say good-bye. He just wasn't ready. Not yet.

Demott returned his attention to Lincoln. "You say your ride is on its way?"

"Yes, sir. A helicopter is en route as we speak. We really need to rest, sir. We've been up for more hours than I care to count. Can we please reschedule the review of our statements?"

"Okay, okay. We can set up an appointment to conclude everything sometime next week, I suppose." Demott glanced over at Roark.

Still staring at Brannon, Roark wanted to shout, "No, they can't delay the statements. It has to be done now"—anything to keep her from leaving. She turned those intoxicating eyes on him, and his soul rocked full force from their penetrating impact. "Yeah, I suppose," he mumbled, yet never took his eyes off her.

"Great. You know where to reach us." Lincoln grabbed Brannon's crutches, maneuvering to offer her full support.

That strange sensation jabbed in Roark's gut again. Jealousy. Envy. He clenched his jaw muscles. He knew nothing was between Lincoln and Brannon except their friendship.

And then she smiled at him. "I just wanted to say it was a pleasure to have met you."

Did he detect a hint of disappointment in her expression? Hope surged. Facing his boss, Roark lifted a single brow. "I'll escort them to the roof."

Demott stared at him a moment, then a slow grin pushed across his ruddy face. "Okay. Meet you back here."

Roark turned and pulled Brannon against him. His eyes narrowed as he glared at her partner, silently daring Lincoln to try to take her away from him.

Lincoln's eyes widened, then he gave a slight nod. "Why don't you guys head on up? I need to, uh, stop by the restroom. I'll bring the crutches with me."

Tilting her head, Brannon studied Lincoln. "Are you sure? We can wait for you."

"No, it'll take you longer. I'll be right behind you." He stared at Roark, his meaning clear in his eyes.

Roark mouthed *"thank you,"* then led Brannon toward the elevator at the end of the hall.

They moved little by little, as Brannon favored her injured leg, but Roark didn't mind. He knew once she got on that helicopter and headed back to the ranger station, he'd lose someone special.

Had it really only been a little over a day since he'd met her?

He wanted nothing more than to get to know her better. On a much more personal level. Even though they didn't live too far from each other, they would both get back to their normal lives and wouldn't build on the friendship they'd begun. The realization saddened him.

Shoving open the door to the roof, cold air slammed against them, pushing them backward. He wrapped his arm tighter around her waist and turned her to face him.

Her eyes glistened with unshed tears, undoing Roark. The tip of her tongue darted out from between her chapped lips. A spiral of intense yearning tugged at him. His body moved of its own accord. Lowering his head, he pressed his lips against hers.

Heat wrapped around him, taking control of his senses. Roark pulled her close, wrapping his hand in her hair. He was right—it was as soft as silk against his calloused palms.

She sighed against his mouth, drawing him deeper into infatuation with her. Then honor shoved to the forefront of his brain. He stiffened and ended the kiss. Her eyes, glazed over, blinked up at him. The delicate skin around her mouth reddened from the stubble on his face, making him want to kiss her all over again.

"Oh, good, the helicopter's landing." Lincoln spoke louder than necessary, causing them to jump apart. He eased a hand under Brannon's elbow. "You ready?"

She nodded but kept her gaze locked on Roark. He reached out a finger and traced the line of her cheek, planted a quick kiss on her temple, then stepped back to let the rangers pass onto the landing pad.

He watched them duck into the waiting helicopter, his heart pounding so hard it threatened to jump from his chest. Roark knew the statistics of people in intense situations often finding themselves attracted to each other. This should have been just that—a statistic.

But he knew himself, and what he was feeling for Brannon was more. Or it could be.

He didn't have time to analyze what could be—he had a successful assignment that failed. Roark had to concentrate on salvaging his job, his career.

Yet he had a feeling that a certain set of mismatched eyes would haunt his dreams.

NINETEEN

Saturday, 9:15 p.m.
Helipad, Parkwest Medical Center
Knoxville, Tennessee

WHAT WAS WRONG WITH her?

Brannon blinked back the tears until Lincoln helped her into the copilot's seat. As the helicopter lifted into the air, she set the headset onto her head. Within seconds a voice hummed in her ear. "Well, hello, hotshot. How was your adventure?"

Just his voice twisted her insides into knots. She swiped her knuckles across her cheek and glanced over to her new coworker. A mass of shiny golden blond hair topped a tan and rugged face. Jefferson Montgomery was going to be a thorn in her side.

She keyed the controller to engage the headset. "Hi, Jefferson. Thanks for picking us up."

"Anytime. You know I love flying."

Brannon took stock of the helicopter. "Where'd you get this?"

"Local aerial tour company heard about your chopper getting shot up, so they loaned us this one."

Nice of them, but she couldn't help wondering what NPS would do for the future. She could only hope her Dolphin had been well insured. Otherwise, she and Jefferson might both be out of jobs. And her a home, since District demanded she live at the station 24-7.

"Heard you injured your ankle. How is it?"

"Doctor says I'll only need to stay off of it a couple of days or so." A sliver of competitiveness stabbed her heart. "I'll be back flying by the weekend."

"No hurry. I can cover all the flying needed." He pulled back on the collective.

Just what she was afraid of. She swallowed hard, forcing herself to think of something else. Her mind shifted to Roark. Of being in his arms. Of kissing him. Fresh tears burned her eyes. His kiss had been good-bye. She shouldn't care. Shouldn't give one iota that she'd never see him again.

But she did.

"I heard your rescue was a success."

Why did Jefferson continue to make small talk? "Partially."

"You got that marshal and the heart out. Must've been some adventure."

"Yes." The bitter burn of failure left a bad taste in her mouth. "But the pilot and flight medic died, and the person who was to receive the heart died anyway."

"Humph. That's not your problem, though, right?"

"Actually, it is. It's not only *my* problem but every upstanding citizen's, too. That witness was going to blow the lid off a child-trafficking ring. Now . . ." She spread her palms and stared out the bubble window.

"I see."

She wasn't in the mood to deal with this man right now. She wanted to crawl into bed and mourn her failures—losing those men and then the witness. And just as surely, losing Roark. She sniffed against a pity party.

Lincoln pulled her headset away from her ear and whispered, "'May the favor of the Lord our God rest upon us; establish the work of our hands for us—yes, establish the work of our hands.'"

Her heart lifted for a moment, and she smiled over her shoulder at him. He understood her better than anyone. "Too easy. You made me learn this when I became a ranger. Psalm 90:17." She let out a hiccupping breath. "Thanks, I appreciate it."

He winked, then leaned back in his seat.

"Am I missing something?" Jefferson tilted his head as he kept his eyes on the terrain.

Her spirits soared higher than the altitude of the aircraft. "Lincoln was just reminding me that I have control over nothing in this world." She smiled wider as Jefferson spared her a fleeting glance. "God's always in control over everything, even our jobs."

"You believe in God, faith, and all that?"

"One hundred percent." She wet her lips. "Don't you?" This conversation felt an awful lot like the one she'd had with Roark not too long ago.

Roark. The knife in her heart twisted another inch.

"Not really." Jefferson's breath wisped against his microphone. "Seems to me if there was a great and powerful God, such bad things wouldn't happen in the world. I think people dictate what goes on in their lives."

"That's where faith comes in. The believing in what you can't see because you know it to be true." She glanced at Jefferson, wondering if her words ministered to him.

He was quiet for a while. "Interesting way of looking at it. I suppose you use whatever you have to in order to deal with stuff."

She bit her tongue, knowing she should just pray for him and keep her mouth shut. He showed no inclination toward being witnessed to. Not right now.

"For instance, my mom died only a month ago. Did God do that?"

Brannon swallowed, choosing her words with care. "I'm sorry you lost your mom. I don't profess to know all the answers as to why things happen."

He shook his head, his eyes never leaving the airspace before them. "Cancer. She'd been fighting it for years."

"I'm sorry. Are you close to your stepfather?"

Jefferson snorted. "Not hardly. He didn't even bother to stay with her when she died. He called to tell me she'd passed away and to come to the house. When I got there, I found my mother's body, but my stepfather was gone. Just vanished. Not that I care, mind you, but he should've at least had the decency to stay around to bury her and settle their estate."

"That's awful."

"Yeah." He popped his knuckles. "How does God play into that?"

"He'll provide comfort, if you let Him," Lincoln said.

Jefferson harrumphed. The helicopter shifted. As Jefferson began the descent, regret filled Brannon's heart. Why hadn't she told Roark about her feelings for him? If only she could've witnessed to him more, been a better example, talked to him awhile longer—who knew what strides she could have made with him? Why hadn't she pressed the issue? Brannon gazed over her shoulder at Lincoln. Had his words halted her in witnessing stronger to Roark?

As soon as the skids touched the concrete, Brannon yanked off the headset and jumped from the loaned helicopter. Her momentary lack of acknowledgment of her injury came back in record time when she put weight on her left leg. The pain pills the doctor had given her didn't even mask the agony. Teetering as she hopped on one foot and gripped the helicopter door, Brannon gritted her teeth.

Lincoln handed her the set of crutches, smiling. Didn't he realize how horrid they were—an outward, visible sign of her weakness? She shook her head, making his smile spread into a full grin. He took the offensive sticks and wrapped an arm around her waist. "Let's get inside and check on Steve."

The wind cut through the air, chilling Brannon deep down into the warm recesses of her body. She shivered and shifted closer to Lincoln. If there was any justice in the world, it would have been Roark helping her.

She wouldn't dwell on Roark or what could have been between them any longer. She pushed him out of her mind as hard as she pushed open the station door.

Steve rushed to her side, pulling her from Lincoln and into a big bear hug. "Girlie, I was so worried about you." He scrutinized her, as if checking for himself that she was really okay.

"Oh, I'm fine, Steve, thanks for asking," Lincoln chuckled as he leaned the crutches against the coat tree.

Looking over to Lincoln, Steve laughed. "Well, I knew you weren't injured like Brannon here." His soft gaze rested back on her, pushing back the chill settling over her. "I'm just so glad you weren't hurt worse."

"Nah, I'm fine." She hugged her boss with a final squeeze, then hopped to lower herself onto the couch. Letting out a long sigh, she rested her head against the lumpy cushion. "But I sure am glad to be back home."

"Speaking of home, you ought to hit the shower, then to bed with you," Steve said.

"I *am* tired." She ran a hand over her face, realizing the fatigue of the past couple of days had crept up on her. "It's been a long day."

Lincoln stood in front of her and held out his hand. "Come on, I'll help you."

She let him tug her to a standing position. Dizziness swarmed, and she swayed. Lincoln pulled her to him. "You okay, Brannon?"

"Yeah. I think the pain medication is kicking in, though. The room feels like it's spinning."

"Get her to bed." Steve's voice boomed across the room.

Lincoln didn't wait for an argument, just took control. No good-byes were necessary, and she didn't know if she could muster the strength to find her voice. All Brannon was aware of was the ache in her leg.

He led her to the door separating the ranger station from her home, flipping on lights as they passed them. Brannon gritted her teeth, concentrating on making it to bed without getting sick all over the place.

Once Lincoln helped her to her room, he placed a kiss on her temple and left, turning off the lights as he went. She fell across the bed. The hum of the heater coaxed Brannon into a semisleep state.

Images flitted across her mind—the Bell engulfed in flames, losing a helicopter pilot, getting shot at, hiking through the woods, Roark's smile, Roark's eyes, Roark's kiss . . .

Sunday, 10:00 a.m.
Suburb South of Townsend, Tennessee

SUNLIGHT STREAMED THROUGH THE dirty window pane, spilling brightness into a room void of hope. A bird perched on the windowsill and tweeted, startling Mai. She jumped, staring over her shoulder. A long whoosh of air tore from her lungs and snuck past her lips. She took a moment to study the free creature preening his wings before turning back to her task. Freedom, would she have it again?

She pressed her fingers into the hole in the edge of the mattress against the third hidden supplies stash—the cache was full. A smile pushed into her face as her heart sped. Dare she allow herself to believe they could succeed? She pounced in the center of the mattress, almost landing right on Kanya.

Her friend groaned, rolled onto her stomach, and buried her face in the mattress. "I need sleep. Leave me alone." Her words were sleepy in her native tongue.

Leaning over, Mai hovered next to Kanya's ear. "We can leave soon," she breathed, then shoved away.

Kanya jerked around and upright in one fluid motion. Her eyes widened, and moisture pooled over the dark orbs. "We have enough supplies?"

"Enough for three days, if we are careful. That should be plenty of time to get to help." Mai drew her knees up to her chest and wrapped her arms around her legs. "Tomorrow is perfect, since Madam Nancy always leaves for a couple of hours on Monday nights. All the girls say so."

Kanya tucked errant strands of ebony hair behind her ear. "Where does she go? Every Monday night, I mean?"

"I do not know." Mai shrugged. "I do not care. The point is she leaves, and that is when we will make our escape." She swallowed. Sweet freedom whispered, calling to her. A shiver vibrated throughout her body. She would succeed. Or die trying.

Anything was better than staying here and doing nothing.

"What is our plan? Who will help us?" Kanya, being younger,

looked to Mai for direction and instruction. She blinked and sniffed.

For a moment Mai forgot the horrors they had endured—her friend had not yet lost the look of innocence. Would she, herself, ever get that back? Ever? Mai gave herself a mental shake. No, it was too late for her—she would never be innocent again. She had seen too much, lived through too much. She would never be the same. A part of her had been lost forever, stolen by the dirty American men. Hatred flamed her heart.

"Mai?" Kanya touched her shoulder, drawing her from her thoughts. The hope in her eyes filled the room with a light brighter than the sunbeams now dancing over the floor.

After days of snowstorms, was the appearance of the sun a sign that all would be okay? Mai wished it so. Determination gripped her in a tight hold. She would escape and lead Kanya to freedom as well. "We will wait until Madam Nancy leaves. Fred will come in, but we should be safe. He likes Oneia, and as soon as Madam Nancy leaves, he will go visit her." Mai shuddered. "That will give us an hour to get out of the house and through the woods in the back."

"We go through the woods?" Kanya's eyes widened even more. "Why can we not go down the street if Fred will be busy?"

Mai inhaled deeply, held it a moment, and then let it out in a rush. "Because we cannot risk someone seeing us."

She pushed to her feet and strode to the window. The snow clumped on the bare branches, weighing the limbs down until they bowed. Several inches of snow lay packed on the ground. The sun reflected off the pristine snow, causing Mai to blink. Even with her eyes closed, white dots floated across her vision.

She turned back to Kanya. The tips of her fingers resting against the sill chilled. "We need to find extra clothes. Can you lift some of Aelita's? Maybe her long underpants?"

"I can try." Kanya stood and joined Mai at the window, pressing her nose against the glass. "It looks cold out there." She turned her expressive eyes back to Mai's face. "Can we really make it?"

"We have to try." Seeing the uncertainty cross Kanya's features, Mai stiffened her spine. She wouldn't show doubt to her friend. "I have paid attention when Madam Nancy has spoken with the clients, so I have a mental map of the area. We will make it through the woods within an hour. After that, we will hit the valley of the mountainside. All we have to do is follow it for a couple of miles, and we will enter a national park."

"What does that mean?" Kanya wrapped a thick strand of hair around her finger, twirling and twisting the hair into knots.

"It means there are people in a national park who will protect us from Madam Nancy."

"How can we trust anyone?" Kanya frowned.

Mai shrugged. "We do not have a choice. I have heard these people are good—are the law here in America. We have to take the chance."

"Will Madam Nancy come after us?" Kanya shuddered. Her shoulders protruded out as she hunched over.

Mai shook her head. "She will send someone after us. That is why we have to move fast." She gripped her friend's shoulders. "We will have to run, Kanya—get a head start before she realizes we are gone. It is our only hope."

TWENTY

Monday, 8:10 a.m.
US Marshals Office, Howard Baker Federal Courthouse
Knoxville, Tennessee

THE SUN BEATING DOWN on the terrain the past several hours had raised the temperatures, but they hadn't crept above freezing yet. Most likely wouldn't. Roark almost slipped as he bounded up the stairs into the Knoxville marshals' office. He passed security with a flash of his badge, then paused at the elevator bay. As of late, he'd taken the stairs, but today, well, today he punched the button and waited for the elevator.

He caught his reflection in the polished steel doors. His eyes could be mistaken for road maps with all the red lines streaking through them. Roark ran a hand through his hair, trying to bring the strands under control. No way would anyone expect him to be back in the office so early. No one but himself. Then again, nobody would be surprised to see him, either. His dedication to the job was a given.

Even after the Mindy incident.

Stepping from the elevator onto the third floor, he strode toward the conference room. He knew where his boss would be—holed up reviewing the files. The rubber soles of Roark's shoes squeaked against the nondescript tile floor. He knocked on the door once, then turned the knob.

Gerald Demott nodded as Roark strode into the room and dropped into a vacant chair after tossing his coat across the end of the table.

"Couldn't get any rest, Holland?"

"Not when there's work to be done." And the haunting images of Brannon's eyes tormenting him hadn't helped any, either. Roark shook off the hours he'd tossed and turned in his bed the last two nights, only managing to twist his sheets into tight knots. "What have we got?"

"NSA is working overtime on the papers Jonathan Wilks had when he appeared at the FBI." He gestured over the mess of papers and files on the table. "If only he'd brought in a key to the stupid thing. We can only pray they'll figure out the accounting mess."

Roark chose to ignore the praying comment Demott had spit out so second naturedly. He was accustomed to his boss's religious statements and normally ignored them. But after being around Brannon and Lincoln, the comment seemed to jump out and smack him between the eyes. Was *somebody* trying to make a point? Was there a message he was supposed to get?

"Got positive IDs on both the shooters." Demott scrambled for the reports. "First one is Tom Hurst. No record, no rap sheet, but ballistics show the gun found on his body was the same used at the FBI office shooting at Wilks."

Roark slumped into a chair. "The heat of the operation?"

"Most likely." Demott grabbed another sheet. "Second body, the African-American you took down, is Milton Anderson. Rap sheet for petty convictions, couple of drug deals, stuff like that. Last known address is in Wildwood, Tennessee. FBI's checking that out and looking for known associates."

"What about the phone I nabbed?"

"Running checks. It's a disposable phone, though—no contracts, no traceable information. Ran the name Zimp and came up with nothing. FBI's analyzing the SIM card now."

"So we got nothing to go on?"

Demott slammed the file shut with a thump against the table and met Roark's gaze. "The National Security Agency is our best bet at breaking this code." He scraped the chair back, got up, and paced. "We'd better pray hard. Otherwise, this is all for nothing."

Two praying comments back-to-back? There definitely was a point being made here. He shoved to his feet. "Boss, are you trying to say you believe God will intervene in this nightmare?"

"I have a good relationship with the Big Guy. He listens when His people cry out."

Roark's mouth went dry. "Even though He lets bad things happen to really good people?" His tongue stuck to the roof of his mouth, feeling as if it'd swollen to twice its size.

"It's hard to explain, Holland. God *is* love, but the world is cavorting in sin. More so now than ever before."

"So all this"—Roark waved toward the file lying on the table—"is God punishing the world?" The back of the chair dug into his hip, but he paid no mind—he needed to hear his boss's answer, an explanation.

"We all must pay for our sins, Roark. We're given forgiveness and grace—it's a gift from God. But there are many unsaved, many who don't confess their sins and ask for forgiveness."

"Again, this is about the punishment factor, right?"

Demott shook his head. "Think of it this way. Everyone has free will. They choose how they'll act. God loves us like a father loves his child. Like a father will reprimand his child when he chooses to do the wrong thing, God will correct us because we're His children."

Roark crossed his arms over his chest. "You really believe that?"

"With everything I am."

"Hmmm." Roark pressed his lips tight together. "I guess it's a good thing to have something to cling to in times like these."

"It's more than that, Holland. My faith isn't something I only cling to when times are tough. This is my way of life. It's a part of who I am."

"But what about those girls sold into prostitution? What are those children being punished or reprimanded for?" What had Mindy been guilty of?

"I don't have answers to the reason of why things happen. I'm just saying I know people make their own choices, and I believe God is everywhere, and He knows all the reasons."

"He has a master plan, is what you're saying?" Roark shifted his weight from one foot to the other.

"Yeah, but our minds can't wrap around the complexities. Mortal minds can't comprehend—we're not supposed to."

Roark's cell phone vibrated. He jerked it off his waistband, staring down at the caller ID—his fellow marshal called. "Holland."

"Hey, pardner. Thought I'd give you a heads-up. Rumor has it a certain congressman has a bee in his bonnet and is on his way to see you and Demott."

"Thanks, Cole. We'll handle it." Roark slipped the phone back into its holder, then stared at his boss. "McGovern's on his way here, and Cole says the man's looking for trouble."

Monday, 8:30 a.m.
Howard Baker Federal Courthouse
Knoxville, Tennessee

A PUDGY MAN WITH a badge and gun at the security counter stopped him from entering the courthouse. Warren bit back his disgust. How could a human let himself go in such a way? Had the man never heard the term *diet*? How dare some rent-a-cop with a marshal's badge have the nerve to ask *him*, Warren McGovern, for identification? He dug in his breast pocket for his driver's license.

The possibility of his world crashing down on him sent Warren's blood pressure into the danger zone. He'd started his endeavor eight years ago when he needed the money for his campaign. Now he liked the lifestyle his income provided. He couldn't lose it now.

The Colonel's mocking laugh haunted his dreams. Oh, how Warren wished his mother had lived, that he'd been raised by her. She was the only good woman he'd ever known. The rest? Well, that *woman* his father had married sure wasn't any good.

Warren insisted he be allowed to keep his cell phone. As he explained to the rent-a-cop, he was important. A US congressman. The security officer finally relented.

Cleared through security and directed to the third floor, Warren took clean strides toward the elevator. He would have to countermove every gesture by every government agency. To do that, he needed to know the game plan. This man Demott was his best bet. The FBI had no information.

At least not that they would share.

He mentally went over his speech to the marshals as he rode in the elevator. He would implore them to share information—show his outrage that this legal monstrosity had gone on so long—would plead, if necessary, to be kept in the information loop. Although pleading would be his last resort.

Warren sucked in air as he exited the elevator and entered the US Marshals office. He'd just left the district attorney's office and wasn't in the mood to get the runaround. Not anymore. He'd taken as much as he was going to. He'd get answers, and he'd get them now.

He straightened his jacket and squared his shoulders. He made his steps with careful deliberation, paced, smooth, and fluid. A raven-haired young secretary, clad in a skirt entirely too short for office attire, rushed from around her desk. The Colonel had been right—women were men's downfall.

"Sir, you can't go down there without clearance. Sir . . . sir?"

He kept walking down the hall, ignoring the woman's high-pitched voice ordering him to stop.

A closed door drew his attention. He stopped and pushed open the door—it slammed against the wall with an echoing thud. Demott and that Roark Holland fellow stood in a conference room. Warren crossed the threshold and shut the door on the little sex kitten tailing him. "Gentlemen." He gave a nod to both men.

"What're you doing here, Congressman?" Roark struck a defensive pose—legs spread about a foot apart, arms folded across his chest, hands tucked in the armpits. A smart move to automatically go on the defense. He rose a level in Warren's estimation.

"Yes, Congressman, what are you doing here?" Demott moved to stand in front of his employee.

Warren shoved his hand toward the chief marshal. "I think we got off on the wrong foot, Marshal Demott. I'm here to help with the investigation in any way I can."

Demott shook his hand but without a tight grip. One could tell a lot about a man in the way he shook hands. Warren detested a weak handshake.

"We aren't handling the investigation, Congressman. We're only here to support the FBI in their investigation." Demott held on to the back of a government-issued metal chair. His knuckles were ghostly against the dark gray. Warren would bet perspiration marks would linger once Demott lifted his hands.

"I'm on my way to visit them next. I understand your guys have done a bang-up job and have been instrumental in the case." The lie scorched his tongue. By the narrowing of Holland's eyes, he recognized the falsity as well.

Warren directed his next comments to Holland. "I know I said some heated things earlier, but I assure you, I was merely distressed. And disappointed."

Holland cocked his head, but Demott wore the beginnings of a grin. Success, even if only a slight tilt. "We understand, Congressman. We're all disappointed." The chief marshal let out a heavy sigh and lifted a file from the table, tucking it under his arm. "All we know at this point is the accounting papers Mr. Wilks left with the FBI are being scrutinized by the NSA."

"And when do you expect an answer from them? Any rough estimate?" There was no way he'd get anything from the NSA—those guys didn't care who asked. He wouldn't be a bit surprised to learn those geeks didn't even jump when the president called, much less a congressman.

Demott shook his head. "Your guess is as good as mine. They don't report to us. The FBI will let us know."

"Only if they need us," Holland interjected.

That marshal really didn't like him. Warren gave a mental shrug—he didn't much care for Roark Holland, either. As he stared into the man's cold eyes, he knew Holland would have to be taken care of . . . soon.

Permanently.

Monday, 6:50 p.m.
Suburb South of Townsend, Tennessee

THE TIME HAD COME.

Mai let out a slow breath as the headlights from Madam Nancy's car pierced the darkness of the room. Her heart skipped a beat. This was it—their captor had left.

No snow fell from the starry sky. A hush hovered over the landscape. Trees cast shadows on the banks of snowdrifts piled along the driveway.

"Can we go now?" Kanya whispered, reverting to Thai.

"No. We have to wait for Fred to check on everyone before he goes back with Oneia." Mai hoped Fred would stick to his routine the other girls had sworn he had. Their escape depended on it.

Kanya shivered, although Fred had kicked up the thermostat as soon as Madam Nancy shut the door behind her.

Mai squeezed her friend's shoulder. "It will not be long now. Get the bags loaded."

They had stolen two pillowcases from the laundry area. The girls would shove the food and supplies inside so they would be easier to carry. For the first time, Mai allowed her hopes to soar. The bags were not heavy. They had stolen clothes so they could dress in layers, and they had even found Madam Nancy's four pairs of snow boots. They could do this. They would make it. Freedom called.

Heavy footsteps echoed in the hall.

Mai yanked the bag from Kanya's hands and shoved it with hers in the darkened corner. Her heart pounded as doors in the hall creaked open, a long moment ensued, then the click of the door shutting. One by one, Fred checked on everyone.

"Quick, lie down and pretend we are asleep," Mai whispered.

The two girls slid stocking feet across the floor, then dropped to the mattress. It sagged where the now-empty holes had been dug out.

Fred's footsteps paused outside their door. A creak split the silence, then light filtered into the room from the hallway.

Mai held her breath, not daring to move.

"Y'all okay?" Fred's deep voice filled the space.

Kanya rolled over and faced him. "Yes."

Why did she speak to him? The plan was to pretend to be asleep. Mai clenched her hands into balls under the sheet.

"Fine, are ya?"

Just leave. Just go. Mai's heart tightened. Kanya tensed beside her but remained silent.

"I asked ya a question." His boots shuffled against the floor as he moved into the room. "Answer me."

Oh no. Kanya had drawn his interest.

"S-sleep."

He did not respond. Mai struggled against the pounding of her heart. Surely he could hear it?

"Don't look like you're asleep now." He moved farther into the room.

Stupid! Stupid! Mai raced through ideas. What could she do now?

His feet stopped beside the mattress. "Looks like you're awake to me."

He was not going to leave. What to do? Mai rolled over, jerking her arm over her eyes. She filled her voice with a sleepy tone. "W-what?"

Fred laughed, full and throaty. "Nothing. You just sleep. I'm gonna visit with your friend here for a little while."

Before Mai could register his movements, he grabbed Kanya by the arm and jerked her to her feet. She sobbed.

"Come on. Stop it." He dragged her toward the door.

Mai dared not sit up or move to help her friend. She knew the consequences.

Kanya looked back at Mai, tears streaming down her face. Her body struggled against Fred.

Smack!

Fred's hand made contact with the side of Kanya's face. She cried out.

"Now, come on. I'm not playing with you, girl."

Mai had no choice but to watch them leave. The door slammed shut.

Her stomach ached. Fred would be occupied with Kanya for at least a good hour, which would give Mai plenty of time to sneak out. But she couldn't leave Kanya.

Sitting up, she stared out the window. Freedom, so close. All the planning, all the stealing . . . for what?

She could not leave Kanya.

But it had been *her* plan. She had the idea. She plotted how they could do it. She could still do it alone.

She could not leave Kanya.

She could not stay here. Death was more appealing than staying here.

Everything was lost. Or was it? She could make it. She could escape and send help back for Kanya and the others. Yes, she needed to go. Needed to get help for everyone.

A screaming sob pierced the darkness. Mai's heart dropped to her toes.

She would not leave Kanya.

TWENTY-ONE

Tuesday, 8:12 a.m.
Abrams Creek Ranger Station
Great Smoky Mountains National Park, Tennessee

HEALING PROCESSES CREPT TOO slowly for Brannon's liking.

She hobbled from her living space into the ranger station and plopped on the couch in front of the television.

"Want a cup of coffee? Just made a fresh pot." Steve lifted the pot off the coffee station in the corner.

"Sure. Thanks." She flipped through channels until she landed on a news broadcast. "Where's Lincoln?"

"Out in the Jeep, showing Jefferson around."

"Hmm." She swallowed her distaste. "Heard how long my Dolphin will be in the shop?"

"At least a couple of weeks." Steve took a loud slurp from his mug. "The district's waiting to see how much it'll cost to have it repaired."

Her fault. All her fault. "And?"

He shrugged. "If it's too expensive and insurance doesn't cover the expenses, District can't afford to buy another one."

"What'll happen?"

A cloud of emotions covered Steve's face. "Let's wait and see if insurance covers everything before we jump to conclusions."

Her heart pounded. "No, tell me. What will happen?"

"I don't know, Brannon." Steve set his cup on the table and put a hand on her arm. "But District said they'd have to analyze your last mission, see if you made any mistakes that could have prevented the damage."

"Like I could have prevented being shot at? What'd they want me to do? Go out and shield the Dolphin with my body?"

Steve squeezed her forearm. "Don't go getting all upset. They're gonna review the reports, look at everything."

Upset? She wasn't upset—she was mad. "Being shot at wasn't exactly on my list of things to do."

"People lost their lives after you rescued them, Brannon. District would be irresponsible if they didn't call for a full review."

The hesitation in his voice told her what he didn't say. She took a sip of coffee, hoping to squelch the disappointment and pain searing her throat. It didn't.

"Don't take this personally. It's standard policy."

Policy? Since when? They'd lost hikers and campers over the years, and she'd never known them to be under review.

The door opened, blowing in Lincoln and Jefferson who laughed like old friends. Brannon's heart nose-dived. Her partner was buddying up to the enemy?

Lincoln hung up his coat and ruffled her hair. "Morning, sleepyhead. How're you feeling?"

Sleepyhead? Was that a slur that she'd reported for work late? "Fine." She couldn't keep the edge from her tone.

Lincoln cocked his head and studied her. "Really? You don't sound fine." He shifted to sit on the couch beside her. "Is the pain not getting better?" He moved to inspect her ankle.

She jerked her leg away. "It's fine. I'm fine." But she wasn't. Not even when Wade had . . . when she'd lost Wade. At least then she'd had Lincoln to pull her up. But with him cozying up to Jefferson . . . Well, she felt alone.

She wasn't fooling her friend. He nudged closer to her. "Hon, what's up with you?"

"Just watching the local news."

Jefferson grabbed a cup of coffee, then sat on the other side of Lincoln. The hairs on the back of Brannon's neck stood at alert.

"'A man of many companions may come close to ruin, but there is a friend who sticks closer than a brother.'"

How did he always seem to read her mind? It was like the Holy Spirit spoke to her through her partner. She smiled. "Proverbs."

Lincoln winked. "Chapter and verse?"

"Um . . ."

"Come on, hon. You know this one."

She laughed, an honest feeling that banished her fears and uncertainty. "Chapter 19, verse 24."

Lincoln shook his head. "Close, but it's chapter 18."

"I'm being silly," she whispered.

"I love ya, Brannon, and you know it."

Tears threatened to choke her. "I know."

"Hey, isn't that the marshal y'all rescued?" Jefferson interrupted as he turned up the volume on the television.

Brannon's full attention rested on the newscast. An FBI agent spoke to the reporter, but Roark stood in the background, looking as gruff and unhappy as ever. Her heart hiccupped, and she leaned forward to listen.

"At this time we have no evidence of any child-trafficking ring in Tennessee," the FBI agent reported.

Roark's face twisted into a grimace.

Brannon understood. There was such a ring operating right under all their noses. Her heart caught. Without the witness, officials would never catch those involved. And those poor children would continue to be exploited.

The newscast ended with the agent and Roark shuffling back into the federal courthouse. Neither walked with the air of confidence normally reflected in men of their profession.

How common was child trafficking? Was it really something the Justice Department had set up a committee to prevent? Had she been living in a shell about such a serious issue?

Brannon hobbled to the desk and accessed the Internet. She Googled "child trafficking, United States" and was appalled at the number of hits returned. Five hundred thousand? Could that be right? She clicked on the first Web site. Her heart sunk as she read that child trafficking is nothing more than modern-day slavery.

Not only was it exploitation of these poor children, but there were enough instances to justify the passing of the Trafficking Victims Protection Act of 2000. Statistics reported approximately 17,500 children were trafficked into the United States every year—to be victimized. And the number continued to grow.

How could she be unaware of such nightmarish statistics? Was she truly so wrapped up in her life that she'd ignored the abuse of these children?

Oh, Lord, I'm so sorry I haven't paid attention to the dreadful plight of Your children. Please grant me wisdom on how to help. How to reach out and do something.

Her heart lodged in her throat as she lifted the phone. She punched numbers.

"Who are you calling?" Lincoln asked.

"Roark." She caught his censored expression from across the room. "I want to see if there's any information they aren't releasing." She waited for the call to connect. One ring. Two.

"Holland."

She questioned the wisdom of calling. "Hi, Roark. It's Brannon." His voice did strange things to her. His image had haunted her dreams the past couple of nights, leaving her restless and anxious.

And wondering why she couldn't ban him from her mind.

Tuesday, 8:35 a.m.
US Marshals Office, Howard Baker Federal Courthouse
Knoxville, Tennessee

JUST HER VOICE. THAT'S all it took to tie his stomach in knots. "Hi, Brannon."

"I saw the news. Are there no other leads?"

Nothing definite. They hadn't found any connections of Milton's yet, even though they'd located where he'd been living. The FBI scoured the place, as well as tried to track down Wilks's stepson to see what he knew. And Roark wanted to tell her all this, but he couldn't. Not yet. Not without proper clearance. "They're still working on deciphering the paper trail but haven't come up with anything yet."

"It's horrible. What can I do to help?"

Come up and see him? Whoa! He couldn't just blurt that out. "Um, nothing. There's nothing any of us can do right now." But his conversation with Demott replayed through his mind. "Except pray."

Her intake of breath was enough. "O-Of course. Lincoln and I will be praying." He'd shocked her.

Shocked himself, too. Since when did he ask people to pray? "I'll let you know if I hear anything."

"And if I can do anything else to help, just let me know."

He wanted nothing more than to keep talking to her. How long had it been since someone offered *him* help? Too long. But Demott had already motioned at his watch twice. "I will. Thanks." He shut his cell phone and headed toward the courthouse exit.

Since his debriefing, the powers that be determined he needed to visit Dr. Martin again. More torture. Demott had let him know it wasn't a suggestion—it was a condition of his staying on the case. He couldn't let the case go. Not this one. He had to bring those responsible for the irreparable harm to children to justice.

Maybe then he'd be free of the nightmares about Mindy.

The drive to Dr. Martin's office took twenty minutes on a good day. Today it took him almost forty, and he was already late. But talking to Brannon, hearing her voice, made being late worth it. What did that say about him?

The receptionist ushered him into Dr. Martin's office as soon as he arrived. A twinge of guilt that he'd messed up the lady's schedule hit him, but he shoved it away. It wasn't like he chose to come here. No, he'd been forced. Just as he had from the beginning.

"Good morning, Roark."

He settled onto the leather couch as Dr. Martin took her seat in the wingback chair facing him. "Dr. Martin." He gave a curt nod.

"I've read your report. A helicopter crash and being fired upon multiple times. How'd you handle that stress?"

Why did shrinks ask about feelings and handling stress? If he had it under control, why did Demott make him continue to come? "Okay, I suppose. I survived."

"Heard you got stuck in a cave. How was that for you?"

Was she kidding? How did anyone feel about being stuck in a cave? "Wasn't fun, if that's what you're asking." He brushed imaginary lint from his slacks.

"I suppose not. Did you experience bouts of claustrophobia?"

He ignored his pounding heart as he recalled crawling through the small tunnel. "A little. But I had a job to do and knew I couldn't fall apart."

"Good. At least now you're admitting small spaces make you very uncomfortable."

"Look, I had a little girl in an elevator shaft who died. Someone I was supposed to protect. Wouldn't small spaces make you uncomfortable if you were me?"

"I'd feel very uncomfortable. But I'm not you. We're talking about how you're dealing with the incident. How you cope."

"I coped, didn't I? Got out of the cave and completed my assignment." He laced his fingers together and rested his hands in his lap.

"You did. And you did it successfully."

He let out a harrumph.

"What?"

"I don't know if I'd say it was a success."

"Correct me if I'm wrong, Roark, but your assignment was to escort an organ to a hospital in Knoxville, right?"

"That was the assignment, and we did that. But the end result wasn't what we hoped." He speared his fingers through his hair. "Innocent children are still being exploited, and we can't do anything to help them."

"And I can understand. Natural responsive feeling."

He swallowed. "Dr. Martin, do you believe in God?"

Her eyes widened as she looked up from her notepad. "God?"

"Yeah, Creator of the universe and all that."

"Why do you ask?"

Just like a shrink—answering a question with a question. "I only wanted to know your beliefs."

She poured a glass of water from the pitcher on the side table. She took a sip, then set down the glass. "I thought you didn't believe in God anymore. Had come to the conclusion that religion was a crutch weak people clung to instead of facing reality."

"I did, but . . ."

A long moment followed. When he didn't add anything more, she put aside her pen and notebook. "But what? Has something happened to change your mind?"

"Lately I've noticed how some people really believe all the God-stuff. They aren't weak, aren't using it as a crutch. These are strong people, good people."

"And that's made you question your stand on Christianity?"

He lifted a casual shoulder. "Some. I'm wondering if maybe I was wrong."

"You're admitting you could be wrong?" Dr. Martin sounded shocked.

"I don't always have to be right." He crossed his arms across his chest.

A smile teased the doctor's lips. "What's her name?"

Busted! "Her name? How do you know it's a woman I'm talking about? Demott is a Christian and talks about it a lot."

The smile broke into a full grin. "Roark, I'm a psychiatrist. Don't try to fool me. You've worked with Gerald Demott for years, so you're accustomed to hearing about his faith. Only someone new, a woman, could've gotten under your skin to make you question your core beliefs."

He hated that she was right.

"Her name?"

"Brannon. The National Park Service ranger-pilot who rescued us."

Dr. Martin pressed her lips together to form a tight line. "What?"

"And this Brannon . . . she believes in God?"

"Strongly." But he'd get back to that in a minute. "What's got you biting your tongue, Doc?"

"Well, you have to admit, it's a bit ironic, wouldn't you say?" She was having way too much fun at his expense.

"What?"

"That you'd question your beliefs because of a woman who's a rescue pilot."

"I don't see the irony."

"Someone who is strong, in a position of helping others, a pilot, which is still a male-dominated career. . . . See my point?"

Not really. "So, what're you getting at?"

Dr. Martin smiled once again and took another sip of her water. "That you no longer have to be the most aggressive and dominant person." She jotted in her blasted notebook. "You've made great progress and are on course for continuing to enhance your own life. I'm proud of you." She set the book on the little table. "So much so that I'm going to recommend we reduce the number of mandatory sessions we have each month."

Just when he needed to talk more.

TWENTY-TWO

Wednesday, 3:15 p.m.
Abrams Creek Ranger Station
Great Smoky Mountains National Park, Tennessee

"Hello."

"Brannon?"

Her heart raced, and she gripped her cell phone tighter. "Roark?" She lowered herself to the couch, ignoring Steve's inquiring glance.

"Hi there."

"Uh, hi." Great. She sounded like a bumbling idiot. She hadn't had any trouble talking to him in person. Why was she now tongue-tied talking to him on the phone?

Maybe because he'd consumed her every waking thought since she left him at the hospital.

"Listen, we need Lincoln and you to come in. My boss needs to close the report but can't until you two review and sign your statements."

He needed her signature, nothing more. "Oh. Okay." Disappointment stung worse than any insect bite she'd ever incurred.

"Do you think you could come this afternoon?"

If it weren't for her blasted ankle, she'd hop in her Dolphin and head right over. But her ankle and damaged Dolphin kept her from hopping to do his bidding. Although . . . there was Jefferson and the loaner helicopter. "Sure. I think we can swing it. What time?"

"Whatever is best for you."

Did he really want to see her? Or was he just trying to close out his report? She glanced at the clock. "We'll be there sometime in the next couple of hours then."

"Thanks. Looking forward to seeing you." The connection clicked off.

Had he meant that in a personal way?

Lincoln and Jefferson stomped into the station on the waves of male laughter. Brannon's heart did a little side step. No, she wouldn't be like that. Lincoln was only being nice to the newcomer because that's who Lincoln was. She needed to stop reading more into everything. What was it with her emotional roller coaster lately?

"Hey, Brannon. Beautiful afternoon out today." Lincoln plopped down beside her. "Want to go up and give Jefferson more of the pilot's tour?"

"Roark called. They need us to come in and review and sign our statements."

"When?"

"This afternoon." She glanced at Jefferson standing behind Lincoln and swallowed back her distaste of feeling helpless. "Can you fly us? I don't think my ankle's strong enough just yet."

"Sure. Sure." Jefferson crossed the room to stand in front of the fireplace. "Just let me know when."

Brannon glanced over at her supervisor. "Okay with you, Steve? That we're all out?"

"Sure. I can radio if I need y'all."

"Shouldn't take too long." But she kinda hoped it would—it'd be more time she could spend with Roark.

She gave herself a mental shake. She shouldn't be so obsessed with a man she'd only known for days. Had she taken total leave of her senses?

And it hit her—Wade had slipped into her heart just as fast.

Her insides flipped. She wasn't supposed to fall for a man again. It was too painful. Being left behind . . . She couldn't take it again. Roark? Seriously? He wasn't even her type. Most important, he didn't live for Christ.

And that meant she could never, ever become involved with him.

Then again, he'd asked her to pray for the situation. Did that mean he'd come back around to God? Hope surged through her heart.

"It's after three already. What time do you want to leave?" Jefferson interrupted her private argument.

She didn't even have makeup on, much less have her hair looking decent. "Give me a few minutes to change and get ready, okay?" Brannon stood, not nearly as wobbly as the day before.

"You look fine." Lincoln grinned, as if knowing what'd been running through her mind.

"Not to a bunch of suits." She slapped him playfully on the shoulder as she passed him on the way to her living quarters.

Lincoln reached for the phone. "I'll call Roark to see where we can land and give him an ETA."

Brannon entered her bedroom with a nod.

Fifteen minutes and makeup later, Brannon hobbled back into the station's main room.

Steve let out a low whistle. "You clean up nice."

Heat climbed the back of her neck. "Oh, stop it. It's just a little mascara and lip gloss."

"Well, you look really nice." Lincoln stood and reached for the coatrack.

The heat spread to her face. "Are you implying I don't normally look nice?"

"Never said that, hon." He helped her into her jacket.

She spun and studied his expression. "Go ahead, spit it out."

"What?" He feigned innocence.

"Lincoln," she all but growled.

"'The LORD does not look at the things man looks at. Man looks at the outward appearance, but the LORD looks at the heart.'"

She so didn't want to quarrel with her friend over this. "Too easy. First Samuel 16:7." Brannon flashed a weak smile. "And my heart is fine, thank you very much." And she prayed Lincoln would let the matter drop.

He hesitated a moment, then gave her a smile and nod before turning to Jefferson. "You ready?"

"Let's do this."

She climbed into the copilot's seat of the loaner and waited for Jefferson to finish his preflight duties. He climbed into the cockpit and settled his headset. He radioed in to ATC, checked with Brannon and Lincoln to ensure they were ready, then lifted into the air. As they climbed above the tree line and began to turn, Brannon stared over the landscape.

Lincoln nudged her shoulder. "You okay?"

"I'm fine."

Although the flight time was only thirteen minutes, the helicopter seemed to hover over Knoxville much sooner. Brannon's stomach contorted. She ran her slick palms over her slacks as Jefferson piloted the helicopter to the landing pad Roark had instructed them to use. He would be waiting with a car to take them to the federal courthouse.

The landing wasn't as smooth as Brannon's, but all in all, Jefferson had done a good job. She pressed down her competitive streak, letting her nerves at seeing Roark again overcome her.

They shut down the helicopter and ducked out the doors. As promised, Roark stood at the rooftop's door, waiting.

Her heart hammered faster than rotors at maximum speed.

Wednesday, 4:20 p.m.
Market Street
Knoxville, Tennessee

AS IF SHE'D STEPPED straight out of his dreams, Brannon stood before him.

Roark checked his pulse and tightened gut. He shouldn't be having such a physical reaction to seeing her again.

Shouldn't, but did.

"Hi." She appeared as breathless as he felt, her face flushed and her mismatched eyes as animated as ever.

But she was real and right in front of him. He clenched his fists not to touch her. "Hi, yourself. How was the flight?" Why did his tongue feel like a twisted pretzel?

"Good."

Lincoln joined her. Roark extended his hand. "How're you?"

"We're doing well." Lincoln shook his hand firmly.

Roark glanced at Brannon again. "How's your ankle?"

"Healing. Should be back to flying this weekend." She offered a shaky smile.

"No need to rush it. I can handle any flights." The tall blond hovering behind them looked familiar to Roark, but he couldn't place from where.

Brannon's jaw tightened. Most people wouldn't have noticed, but Roark caught it. "Oh, this is the NPS's new pilot, Jefferson Montgomery." She gestured to the man. "Jefferson, this is Marshal Roark Holland."

No way. Jefferson Montgomery? Couldn't be the same one. That'd be too much of a coincidence. But Roark's muscles bunched. "Jefferson Montgomery, huh? You wouldn't happen to know a Jonathan Wilks would you?"

The young man's face scrunched. "He's my stepfather. Why?"

Brannon gave a quick gasp.

Roark smiled. "We've been looking for you. Tried your listed number but got the recording it was no longer in service."

"I just use my cell. Why are you looking for me?"

"It's about your mother and Wilks—a long story. Can you join us at the courthouse?"

Jefferson shrugged and glanced at Brannon and Lincoln. "I guess."

Brannon nodded. "I'll help you secure the helicopter."

"What a lucky coincidence," Roark said as Brannon and Jefferson moved to the aircraft.

Lincoln chuckled.

Roark glanced at the rugged ranger. "What?"

"Coincidence?"

"Yeah." What else could it be?

"I don't believe in coincidences." Lincoln's features were somber.

"Then what would you call it?"

"Divine intervention."

God again. Okay, okay . . . Roark got it. "You really think so?"

"I know so." Lincoln looked confident. Not smug, just assured. "Nothing on this earth is by mere coincidence."

When Brannon and Jefferson had secured the helicopter, the three rangers followed Roark into the elevator and out to the parking garage of the building. Surprisingly Roark didn't even breathe heavy in the confined space of the elevator with four people inside. The ride to the courthouse was short, with a minimum of small talk.

Roark's mind raced. They were on the brink of blowing this case wide open—he could feel it.

And then there was Brannon—the clean smell of her hair as she flipped the length over her shoulder . . . the fire in her different-colored eyes . . . the way her smile did strange things to his gut.

All too soon they arrived at the courthouse and scrambled inside. Roark couldn't wait to see Demott's face when he introduced Jefferson. He didn't have to wait long.

Demott was in the conference room, Brannon and Lincoln's typed statements resting on the table. He greeted Brannon and Lincoln, then stared at Jefferson before shooting a quizzical glance at Roark.

"You'll need to call the FBI and Mr. Markinson. Allow me to introduce Jefferson Montgomery." Roark paused, waiting for the name recognition to flash across his boss's face. When it did, he grinned. "Jonathan Wilks's stepson."

Wednesday, 4:30 p.m.
Suburb South of Townsend, Tennessee

"I DON'T UNDERSTAND WHY we've had to cease operations." Madam Nancy's shrill voice pierced Mai's afternoon nap. She rose and moved closer to the wall, pushing her ear against the paneling.

"All I know is Zimp said the boss sent down the order to stop everything right now." Poppy Fred's deep voice caused Mai to shudder.

"Strange, don't ya think? They've never stopped everything before. Wonder what's going on."

"Heard Tom Hurst's been killed. And nobody's heard from Milt."

Madam Nancy gasped. "Are the cops moving in? Should I send all the girls to Colorado and get out of Dodge?"

"Don't know. All I know is what Zimp tells me the boss says."

"Hmm."

"Zimp even changed his phone number again, but he might just be paranoid."

What was going on? Mai could make out the stress in both her captors' voices. Who were Zimp and Tom Hurst? And Milton—was that Uncle Milt? Was she in Dodge? She thought they were in Tennessee. Mai pressed closer to the wall.

"I think I need to go see Zimp. Find out what's going on." Madam Nancy's tone wavered.

"Can ya do that? Is it smart?"

Madam Nancy huffed. "What isn't smart is staying here if heat's coming down. No way am I gonna be a sitting duck and take the rap if everything goes south. No siree, Bob. I'm not gonna be a fall guy."

Heat? Duck? Go south? Fall guy? Mai shook her head, but the confusion stayed. Were Madam Nancy and Poppy Fred talking in code?

"Ya think that's what's happening?" Now Poppy Fred sounded worried.

"What else could it be? They haven't been in contact with me in days. Has Betty heard anything?"

"Nope. She's been sitting by that cell for days, too. Not a single call."

"Something's going on, Fred. I intend to find out what. They aren't gonna leave us holding the bag."

"Whatcha wanna do?"

Mai held her breath, waiting. Although she did not under-stand what Madam Nancy and Poppy Fred talked about, she knew they were scared. She could pick out fear in anybody's voice. She should—she had lived with it ever since boarding the plane to America.

"I'm going to see Zimp and get some answers."

"When?"

"Now. Can you stay and watch the girls?"

The echo of drawers slamming vibrated against Mai's ear, and she jerked away from the wall. She did not need to be so close to hear Poppy Fred's reply.

"Yep. I'll call Betty and let her know. You be sure to keep us in the loop."

"You got it."

The office door creaked open, followed by the front door. It slammed shut, then the revving of Madam Nancy's car filled the silence.

Mai pressed her lips together, pushing back the thudding of her heart. She needed to find Kanya.

The door to escape had just swung open.

TWENTY-THREE

"YOU MEAN TO TELL me you had no idea your stepfather was here, in a drug-induced coma?" The Special Agent in Charge, Greg Daly, circled Jefferson in the conference room.

Pity for the ranger crawled over Roark. Jefferson had recounted finding his mother's body and calling the authorities, sticking to the account in his report. To the letter. Roark didn't think Jefferson was lying, but the FBI agent seemed relentless in his interrogation. For a brief moment Roark regretted waiting on the agents to say anything to Jefferson.

But the case needed a break. Desperately. The US attorney hovered in the corner, taking notes. Noah Markinson would try the case if they ever got enough evidence to charge anyone.

"I've told you just as I told the police when I found my mother's body—I didn't know where Jonathan had gone. No clue. We weren't close at all."

"But he raised you from a boy," Daly all but spit out.

Jefferson sighed. "Yes, but he wasn't a man to show emotion. At least not to anyone other than my mother."

"Tell us about her cancer cocktail," the other agent interrupted.

"I don't know what it was. All I know is my stepfather had hooked her up with some new medications several years ago, and they seemed to work. She hadn't undergone chemo or radiation in years."

"And you didn't find that strange?"

192

Jefferson glared at the agents. "I didn't care. All I knew was my mother was alive and not in pain."

"So you don't know where he got the drugs?"

Jefferson shrugged. "I assume from a doctor."

"Those drugs aren't available. There's no FDA approval on them. And the combination of the three has never been documented before."

Jefferson's eyes narrowed. "What are you saying? How do you know what drugs she took?"

Daly tossed a file onto the conference table. "We got a copy of the autopsy report. Didn't you find the toxicology report a little interesting?"

Jefferson shook his head. "I wouldn't know what those numbers were. Are you saying my mother took black-market drugs?"

"That's exactly what we're telling you. Think—can you recall anything your mother or Mr. Wilks said about the medications?"

The ranger closed his eyes. Roark could almost see the wheels in his mind turning. Jefferson shook his head again. "Nothing that I haven't already told you."

One of the FBI agents paced the small conference room. "We're looking for a set of books or some documents with a lot of numbers. Can you recall seeing anything like that at your mother's house?"

"No, but I hadn't visited Mom and Jonathan in several months."

"Mr. Montgomery, this is critical to the child-trafficking case. We've searched their house and their holdings and found nothing. Can you think of any special place they would've put important documents?"

Jefferson ran a hand through his sandy hair. "The safety deposit boxes?"

"We've looked. Only passports, birth certificates, and life insurance policies."

Eyes alight, Jefferson sat forward. "Not their joint one. My mom's."

Daly stopped pacing and bore down on the poor ranger. "Your mom's?"

"Yeah. She kept one in her maiden name."

"Do you know which bank?"

Jefferson nodded. "Keystone."

One of the other agents wrote on a legal pad. "What's your mother's maiden name?"

"Daniels."

Daly returned to walking a hole in the floor. "What about money? Mr. Wilks ever mention anything to you about offshore accounts?"

Jefferson let out a caustic snort. "Are you kidding? Jonathan wouldn't ever discuss finances with me. He thought of me as nothing but a kid, even when I earned my wings."

"What about your mother? She ever say anything?"

"My mother and I didn't discuss money. She'd have no idea how much money was in their account. Jonathan handled all their finances. Always has ever since I can remember."

The agent stopped pacing and dropped into the chair across from Jefferson. Even from the corner, Roark could tell the FBI made the ranger nervous. "What can you tell me about Mr. Wilks? His personality?"

"He adored my mother, I'll give him that much."

"What about the two of you?"

Jefferson shrugged. "Like I said, he wasn't exactly a man of many emotions. He tolerated me. Appreciated that I didn't get into trouble as a teen."

"What about his friends? People who visited or he spent time with."

"I don't know. I never knew him to have friends. He and Mom used to go dancing now and again at the American Legion Hall, but that was before she got sick. He pretty much kept to the house, even before he retired. Didn't golf or anything if that's what you're asking."

Roark could feel the frustration from the FBI agents.

Jefferson stood. "Look, is there a restroom I can use?"

"Sure." Demott pushed off the wall and pointed at the door. "Down the hall and to the left."

"Thanks." The ranger rushed to the door. It creaked shut behind him.

"Maybe you should follow him," one of the agents said to Roark.

"Why? Does he need to be guarded?" Roark had about enough of the man's attitude.

Daly glared. "He's being evasive if you ask me."

"I don't think so. I think he's been up-front and honest."

Daly shook his head and shot Roark a condescending glance. "Good thing you aren't the one in charge of this investigation then."

The hairs on the back of Roark's neck stood at attention. "What could he possibly be hiding?"

Daly fisted his hands on the table. "Did it ever occur to you that he might be in the ring with Wilks? That maybe, just maybe, he knows about the records, understands them?"

Roark laughed. "Are you kidding? That guy's as clueless as they come. If he was involved, why'd he volunteer about his mother's safety deposit box?"

"A wild goose chase? Maybe he's already cleaned it out and knows nothing's in there. Knows we have nothing to implicate him."

"Please. You heard him—doesn't sound like he and his step-father even got along."

"A perfect ploy to make us believe he isn't involved."

Roark shook his head and glanced at his boss. "Think I'm gonna go check on Lincoln and Brannon." He cut his eyes over to the agents. "I suddenly feel the need for some fresh air."

Wednesday, 5:20 p.m.
Suburb South of Townsend, Tennessee

Now.

Mai gripped Kanya's hand tighter, listening for signs of Poppy Fred lumbering back down the hall. Silence prevailed. Her heart pounded hard against her ribs. "We can go," she whispered to her friend.

Eyes wide, Kanya nodded and lifted her pillowcase. Together the two girls crept toward the kitchen door. Mai eased it open—the hinges barely gave a squeak. She held her breath, waiting for Fred's bellowing. After a heartbeat with no sound of Fred, she slipped out the door into the frigid air. Kanya followed. They shut the door as quietly as they had opened it.

Freedom raced into Mai's bloodstream, shooting adrenaline through her veins. She grabbed Kanya's hand and ran. And ran.

Over the snow-covered backyard. Into the clump of trees. Dodging saplings and firs, she ran, dragging Kanya in her wake. The clumps of snow weighted down her pace, but she kept moving.

She ran through the woods, icy limbs slapping against them, until she reached the road she had heard the men describe. Mai crossed the pavement and quickened her pace into another set of woods, heading toward the mountains she could just make out from the last rays of the setting sun.

Her legs burned from running so fast and so hard, but she didn't stop. Not even when Kanya cried out she could not go any farther, Mai kept running, kept pulling her friend behind her. Her heart expanded as if it would explode in her chest, but still she ran.

This was their only chance. If they were caught . . . Well, she would not think about that. Mai kept putting one foot in front of the other, putting as much distance between them and Madam Nancy. They had to get away. Find help for the others. Find help for herself and Kanya.

A howl split the darkening woods. Terror snaked up her spine and her steps faltered. No, they could not stop yet. They had only been running for about fifteen minutes. Not enough time, not enough distance. Mai bent at the waist, gulping in air. They would catch their breath and be on their way again.

The howl shattered the rasping of their ragged breathing.

"What is that?" Kanya asked, the whites of her eyes barely visible in the rising moon.

Mai swallowed. "I do not know." She straightened and looked in the direction from where they had come. "We have to keep moving."

"I am tired. And scared." Kanya sat on the forest floor shrouded in white.

Anger crashed into the fear in Mai's heart. "We cannot stay here." She jerked Kanya's shoulder. "We have to keep moving."

Snow and ice crunched under the boots they had stolen from Madam Nancy. The wind whipped around them, cloaking them. Mai paid no mind, just kept running. A chant formed in her mind, keeping rhythm with her stride . . .

Run, run, get away.

Run, run, must escape.

Branches lashed out and slapped Mai in the face. It stung so hard, tears blurred her vision. But it was no more painful than being hit by the American men.

Run, run, get away.

Run, run, must escape.

The evening turned so dark Mai could not see more than inches in front of her face. She stumbled, causing Kanya to trip as well. Ice burned into her palms and wet the knees of her pants.

"I am cut. Can we stop?" Kanya whined.

Mai shoved to her feet, jerking her friend with her. "No, we have to keep going. We cannot rest yet."

Run, run, get away.

Run, run, must escape.

Kanya cried, but Mai tugged her hand harder. They had to continue moving, get as far away as possible before Poppy Fred noticed they were missing. When he came after them, he would be angry. And if he caught them, the punishment would be worse than anything they had ever experienced. Mai shuddered at the thought.

"Come on, Kanya. We have to hurry." Mai's movements felt unsure on the uneven terrain. The too-big boots flopped with every step, rubbing against her sockless heels.

Run, run, get away.

Run, run, must escape.

Faster and faster she led Kanya through the woods and into the mountain range. Surely safety would be just over the crest. Or at least a place she could feel safe.

"Ouch!" Kanya froze, snapping Mai backward.

"What?"

"My hair. Something grabbed it." Panic seeped into Kanya's voice.

"Calm down. Let me see." Mai ran her fingers along her friend's scalp. She followed the long tresses in the darkness until her hand met with wood. "It is caught in a branch. Hang on."

She struggled against the tangle, the moon not providing enough light to see what her fingers felt. Impatience surged inside as Kanya cried with each tug.

"Hold still. I cannot see." She pulled and pried, but the hair would not come free. Kanya's cries turned to wails.

"Shh. Somebody will hear us."

"It hurts, Mai. Help me."

Mai gritted her teeth and tried again. The hair still held firm in the unforgiving branches. She needed to think.

"I need to get something out of my pocket. Be still." She reached for the item she had hidden away. A pocketknife one of the men had dropped. Her nail sought the groove to open the blade. It opened with a quiet click.

She licked her lips with a dry tongue and reached for Kanya's hair. Her beautiful tresses were almost as long as Mai's. But they had no time to try to untangle it. Not in the dark. And not with the possibility of Fred already tracking them.

Run, run, get away.

Run, run, must escape.

Mai took a deep breath, then sawed through her friend's hair until Kanya was free. Closing the blade, she shoved it back into her pocket and lifted her pillowcase. "Come on, time to go."

Kanya ran a hand over her head. "My hair!"

"Shh. It will grow back. It is more important that we get away, right? Now, come on."

Kanya lifted her pillowcase and took Mai's hand but sniffled under her breath. Mai did not care—she, too, was tired, scared, and cold, but they could not stop. Not yet.

Run, run, get away.

Run, run, must escape.

TWENTY-FOUR

Wednesday, 6:10 p.m.
Howard Baker Federal Courthouse
Knoxville, Tennessee

ROARK'S CELL PHONE TWEEDLED. He flipped it open and stuck it against his ear.

"Hey, Holland."

His retired partner's voice soothed his agitation. "Hey, yourself. What's up?" Roark ducked into an unused conference room.

"You asked me to run my own check on someone named Zimp? And to quietly look into Congressman Warren McGovern?"

Roark's chest tightened. "Yeah. Got anything?"

"I do. Funny thing, there's a connection between the two men."

"How's that?"

"My check on Zimp reflects a couple of interesting things."

"Such as?" Roark gritted his teeth but knew he couldn't rush his friend.

"That cell phone, Zimp's?"

"Yeah?"

"Guess who paid for it?"

"McGovern?"

"Yep. Have a transaction receipt. Well, a copy of it anyway."

Here was proof McGovern wasn't as lily-white as he proclaimed. Roark studied the darkened room. "What else?"

"That's it, for now."

Would it be enough? Roark thanked his friend and shut the phone. He needed to tell Demott and Daly what he'd found. He headed back toward the conference room where they continued to question Jefferson Montgomery. He opened the door, prepared to call Demott out, only to have his boss glare at him and hold up a finger. The message was clear—wait.

Wednesday, 6:19 p.m.
Howard Baker Federal Courthouse
Knoxville, Tennessee

"SHEESH, HOW MUCH LONGER do you think they'll be? I'm hungry." Brannon stopped pacing and plopped onto the chair beside Lincoln. Her ankle didn't bother her at all. "We've been here for hours. What do you think they have to talk to Jefferson so long about?"

"Hon, patience is a virtue."

She huffed and slumped back in the chair. "Of which I'm sorely lacking."

Lincoln chuckled. "I don't know what's taking so long. Maybe Jefferson's helping them, giving them a lead."

"I hope so. It rips my heart up to think about those poor children."

"I know." Lincoln patted her knee and glanced around. "Why don't you look for a vending machine? There's gotta be one around here someplace."

She stood and dug in her pocket for quarters. "Want anything?"

"Potato chips would be nice."

"Gotcha." Brannon made her way down the hall toward the elevators. Now where would the vending machines be hiding? Hmm. Probably near the restrooms. Water fountains and vending machines seemed to lurk near the bathrooms.

She rounded the corner and spied the alcove housing the machines. Brannon smiled as she slipped into the darkened space and studied the offerings. What was she in the mood to snack on? Sweet or salty? Better yet, which would take longer to eat?

A cell phone's buzz tightened Brannon's fist around the coins.

"Yes?" A man's abrupt voice split the quiet of the alcove.

Brannon peeked around the corner. That arrogant congressman stood near the wall, cell phone pressed against his ear. She certainly didn't want to run into him. Jerking back into the shadows, she shoved her spine against the edge of the soda machine.

"What do you mean two are missing?" His tone left no mistake that he wasn't happy. "Where is Nancy?"

Brannon held her breath and inched farther into the alcove's recesses.

"Why is she with you? Who's watching the place?" He paced up and down the hallway, his steps heavy. "And Fred has no clue how long they've been gone?"

Although she could only hear half of the conversation, Brannon paid close attention. She didn't know why, but everything in her told her to be on alert.

"Look, send Nancy back. Call Betty and have her go out with Fred. They need to find them. Now." His voice shook with anger. "Call me as soon as they've found them."

Brannon swallowed a gasp. What all did it mean?

The snap of the phone shutting echoed off the wall, followed by the congressman cussing under his breath.

She needed to get out of here, get to Roark, and tell him what she'd heard, but she dared not reveal herself now.

The congressman continued to rant under his breath in the hall. His curses grew louder—he was coming closer. Brannon sucked in air and willed her heart to stop pounding. She shoved herself as far into the corner as she could. If he caught her hiding, he'd know she overheard his conversation. What would he do to her?

God, please don't let him see me.

His cell phone rang again.

"Yes?" Amazing how calm he sounded just seconds after cussing a blue streak. "When?" A short pause felt like an eternity to Brannon. "Fine. I'm on my way." He spun and strode down the hall toward the elevators.

Brannon let out the pent-up breath of air with a whoosh. *Thank You, Father.*

Only problem was, she didn't know where the congressman headed. What if he waited just around the corner? Would he suspect she'd eavesdropped?

She let a good two minutes pass before peeking out of the alcove. No sign of him. She inched into the corridor to the corner and peered around. No congressman in sight.

Letting out another sigh, Brannon hustled back to the hallway where Lincoln sat waiting. He glanced up as she rushed toward him. "Did ya get lost? Hey, where are my chips?"

"Shh. Listen to what I heard." She dropped into the chair beside him and repeated the congressman's conversation.

"You need to tell Roark." Lincoln stood.

Brannon joined him on her feet. "I know, but I can't barge in there."

"Text him. Tell him you need to speak to him."

"Good idea." She reached for her cell, only to remember security hadn't allowed her to bring it into the courthouse. How did the congressman have his? "I don't have my cell, remember?"

"Oh, yeah." Lincoln stared at the closed door. "I guess we don't have any other option but to wait until they come out."

Great. Back to waiting. Brannon gnawed on her cuticle as she paced the hall.

What did the congressman have to do with all this? He sat on the council or whatever that was supposed to help expose child traffickers and help the children. How was it all connected?

Wednesday, 6:20 p.m.
Northwest of Little River Road
Great Smoky Mountains National Park, Tennessee

SUCCESS! THE FIRE CRACKLED and popped to life.

Mai smiled against the heat tickling her chilled face and glanced at Kanya. "I told you I could build a fire."

Her friend huddled closer to the growing flames. "I am so cold."

"You will not be for long." Mai dug in her pillowcase and pulled out a piece of beef jerky. She broke it in two, then handed half to Kanya. "Here, we have to keep up our strength." She bit into the bitter stick, grinding her teeth as she chewed.

Kanya ate in silence, her gaze locked on to the fire.

A growl sounded in the distance.

"What was that?"

Mai struggled to appear unconcerned. "Some animal settling in for the night is all. They will not come near the fire." At least, that was what she had heard the men say when they would tell their stories. She hoped they were right.

"I am thirsty."

Biting back a sigh, Mai pulled a can of diet soda from her case and popped open the top. "Here, but do not drink too much. We need to save as much as we can."

Kanya took a long draw off the can.

Mai snatched back the soda. "We have to keep enough to last us." She took a tentative sip and grimaced as the rank flavor hit her taste buds. How did Madam Nancy drink this too-sweet stuff so much? Nasty, that was what it was. She set the can at her feet, out of Kanya's reach.

A rumble filled the air, closer than the growl had been.

Kanya jumped almost into Mai's lap. "It is coming for us."

"No, it is not." At least, Mai hoped not. But in case it was, she needed to find a weapon of sorts. The knife was a backup—she had no desire to get that close to any wild animal.

A long stick lay just on the edge of the clearing they had found to build their fire. Mai grabbed it and shoved just the end in the flames. If anything, either animal or man, came at them, she would jab it in the eye.

No way would she not be free. Not after everything she had suffered.

"Do you think they know we are gone?"

Mai considered lying to her friend, then realized she could not. If Fred came after them, both would have to be on the lookout. "I am sure by now they know."

"What do you think they are going to do?"

"Look for us, I guess."

Kanya's eyes overflowed with fear. "They will not find us, will they?"

Mai shook her head. "We will rest here for a few more minutes, get warmed up, then head out again."

"But they will keep coming after us."

"They do not know which direction we went."

The growl came again, followed by the snapping of branches and underlying bushes.

Both girls jumped. Mai rested her hand against the stick. Her heart leapt into her throat, burning.

"What is that?" Kanya whispered.

"I do not know."

"Are you sure it will not come by the fire?"

Mai tightened her grip on the stick. "Animals are scared of fire."

She really, really hoped that was true.

Wednesday, 6:30 p.m.
US Marshals Office, Howard Baker Federal Courthouse
Knoxville, Tennessee

THEY'D BEEN AT IT for almost another hour. Roark didn't know how much longer he could stand the FBI drilling poor Jefferson Montgomery. They'd asked him the same questions in a million different ways already, and not once had he deviated from his statement. Not even by a sentence.

And Roark needed to let Demott know about the connection between Zimp and McGovern.

The poor ranger's eyes drooped at the corners—all the dim lighting used for interrogation purposes. His shoulders sagged— worn down by the relentless questions.

Roark pushed off the wall. "Hey, guys, why don't we take a break? I sure could use a cup of coffee, and I'm guessing Mr. Montgomery could as well."

Demott stepped into the center of the room. "I think that's a great idea. Give us time to refocus." But he shot Roark a look that stated they'd discuss Roark's interference later.

Jefferson sighed. "Thanks, I could use a break."

Roark grabbed his boss and informed him of what his friend had uncovered.

Demott pulled Daly to their little circle and had Roark repeat what he'd heard. "Is it enough to get a warrant to search McGovern's place?"

The SAC shook his head. "On hearsay? No judge will grant a warrant on a congressman without some tangible proof." He stared at Roark. "Can you get your friend to fax you a copy of that receipt? That'd be enough, I think."

"I'll get it." Roark lifted his phone, texted what he needed, and gave the fax number. "I'll go wait by my fax." He swung open the door. Brannon was on her feet in a second, her eyes flashing with excitement.

"Listen, I have something important I need to tell you." She grabbed his arm and pulled him down the hall.

Electric current shot up his arm into his chest as he followed her and Lincoln.

Her words tumbled over one another as she repeated a conversation she'd overheard Congressman McGovern having on a cell phone. The implications of what she said jabbed adrenaline into Roark's every muscle.

"I'm not sure what it means, but considering what I just learned about McGovern, I know he's connected."

She nodded. "Right."

"He named a Fred and Betty?"

"And a Nancy."

Anticipation thrummed against his mind. The congressman linked to the child-trafficking ring—the proof was just out of reach.

"Holland, thought you were going to wait by the fax."

Roark turned at his boss's voice. "Am about to."

Demott stood in a cluster with the two agents conducting Jefferson's interview, as well as two other men in navy suits. Demott motioned him to join them. Roark squeezed Brannon's shoulder. "I'll be right back."

He crossed the corridor, ready to take the chewing out for interfering. "Look, I have—"

Daly narrowed his eyes. "We've just received word from one of our agents that we've gotten the warrant to search Mrs. Wilks's personal safety deposit box. Agents are en route to the bank."

Demott shot Roark a questioning look. "Has the fax arrived?"

"I'll check in just a minute." He nodded at his boss. "Brannon overheard Congressman McGovern on a phone conversation, during which he mentioned some names. And specifically talked about the *girls*."

Demott clamped Roark's shoulder.

"Is she positive?" Daly wore a skeptical expression as he stared down the hall at Brannon.

"Yes."

"Can she be trusted?"

Roark ground his teeth. "Yes."

"We need to talk to her ourselves. You go get the fax." The SAC made strides toward Brannon. "Ms. Callahan?"

As they approached, a man turned the corner, almost running smack into Brannon and Lincoln.

Congressman McGovern straightened his tie and frowned at Brannon. "What are you doing here?"

TWENTY-FIVE

Wednesday, 6:40 p.m.
US Marshals Office, Howard Baker Federal Courthouse
Knoxville, Tennessee

IT SEEMED EVERYONE WAS in the loop. Except him. Warren frowned. "I asked what you're doing here, Ms. Callahan."

Her face went pale. That Marshal Holland stepped in front of her. A definite protective move. Why?

Holland crossed his arms over his chest. "She's here to sign her statement and answer a few questions."

"About the rescue?" Hadn't she already been debriefed? What additional information could she have? .

"The FBI has a couple of questions for her."

As if on cue, two agents appeared at his side. "Ms. Callahan, if you'll follow us. We need to go over a few aspects of your statement." They whisked her toward a conference room, leaving Warren staring after her.

"What are you doing here, Congressman?"

He focused his attention on the marshal. "I understand the witness's stepson has been located."

"And you heard this where?"

The nerve of this man to question him. Warren struggled not to show his annoyance. "Justice keeps me well informed on this investigation, Roark. I *do* head up the Coalition Against Child Trafficking, which gives me a vested interest in the case."

Roark's brows shot up. "Really? Then you know the FBI is still questioning the potential witness."

This marshal dared to toy with *him*? Warren cleared his throat. "Yes, but they're questioning him here, in the marshals' office." He narrowed his eyes. "Surely you have some information regarding how the interrogation is coming along."

"I only know what they tell me."

The urge to smack the arrogant marshal's face tensed Warren's hands into tight fists. "But I understand you've been in the interrogation room throughout the questioning."

"I'm not at liberty to discuss anything, Congressman. I'm sure you understand my hands are tied."

"I see." And he did. They'd gotten some sort of lead from the witness and wanted to protect the information. But what did they know? "Well, I'll go see the director of the FBI and see what information he can share."

"You do that, sir." Roark nodded and moved toward Ms. Callahan's partner.

Wait a minute—they needed to ask her questions regarding her statement, but not her partner? Or were they going to question them separately? Something didn't feel right about the situation. And Warren didn't like being uncomfortable.

He spun on his heel and strode down the hall, pulling out his cell phone. He punched in the speed-dial number for his aide and didn't bother with pleasantries. "Kevin, get back in touch with your source in the FBI. Find out what Wilks's stepson has told them and if it's a legitimate lead. Then find out what those rangers, Callahan and Vailes, are doing with the FBI."

Shutting the phone, Warren waited by the elevators. The sense of getting caught in a house of cards during a windstorm wrapped around him. If only the complications would cease . . .

No, he needed to find out everything he could about what the FBI knew. Until Zimp called back to report the situation was under control, Warren wasn't safe.

He jabbed the elevator button again, feeling the earth shift under him.

Wednesday, 6:55 p.m.
US Marshals Office, Howard Baker Federal Courthouse
Knoxville, Tennessee

HAVING ROARK IN THE room brought Brannon unexplained comfort. He'd slipped inside minutes ago, giving a piece of paper to his boss.

"And you're positive to what you've stated?"

She sighed, weariness creeping into her very being. "For the umpteenth time, yes, I'm positive."

The special agent in charge opened his mouth—undoubtedly to ask the same question yet another way—when the door swung open and another agent rushed inside. He leaned toward the interrogating agent and whispered, but excitement lifted his voice enough for Brannon to overhear.

"They've retrieved books from the wife's safety deposit box and are on their way here. We need to get Montgomery back in the interrogation room."

Roark shuffled from his corner. "Are those books encrypted like the ones brought into the office by Wilks?"

The new agent shook his head. "We don't know. All we know is a set of accounting books are on their way."

Brannon's heart jumped. *Please, Father, let them get the break they need to identify all the people involved in the child-trafficking ring.*

The SAC glanced back at Brannon. "I think we've covered about everything." He nodded to Roark. "Is the congressman still lurking out there?"

"Nah, he stomped off when I wouldn't give him any information. But there's a leak somewhere because he knew we were talking to Montgomery."

"Fine. Take Ms. Callahan back to the waiting area. I'll have them bring Montgomery back in." He snapped his fingers at the other agent. "Those books are to come to me as soon as they arrive. Got that?"

The young agent bobbed his head. "Yes, sir."

"Roark, get Demott and Montgomery and meet us in the interrogation room."

Before Brannon could mutter a word, Roark had her by the elbow and led her back into the hall. He stopped in front of Lincoln. "This could be our break."

"What's going on?" Lincoln asked.

"Let Brannon fill you in." Roark leaned over and brushed his lips against her temple. "We'll figure out how the congressman is involved, too." Then he hustled down the hall to where Jefferson sat with two agents.

Brannon's pulse continued to race as Roark reached the group and led Jefferson into the interrogation room.

"What's the deal?"

She gestured for Lincoln to return to his seat, then filled him in on the latest development.

"So everything's starting to come together?"

Swallowing, she nodded. "Little by little. Oh, Lincoln, pray they'll be able to understand what's in the books."

"I will. I hope they have something to do with the ring and aren't some tax return copies or something benign."

"Don't say that." She couldn't even think it. This had to be a break. Brannon's heart bled for those poor, exploited children.

Lincoln shoved to his feet. "Why don't we get some fresh air? Who knows how long Jefferson will be."

"Good idea." She followed her partner to the elevators, then to the lobby. She picked up her cell phone at the security desk before walking into the crisp evening air.

"I have four missed calls from the station. Steve's probably wondering what happened to us." She held down the number programmed with the ranger station's number.

The wind swirled around them, snowflakes dancing on the gusts. Brannon took Lincoln's offered arm so she didn't slip on the icy concrete.

The call connected. Steve answered on the first ring. "Abrams Creek Ranger Station."

"Hey, Steve. Thought we abandoned you?" She leaned against the side of the building.

"Brannon, thank goodness. I've been trying to reach you."

"What's wrong?"

"We've gotten three different reports of smoke spotted just north of Little River Road. I can't get anyone over at the Elkmont station to reply."

Elkmont was pretty close to that location. "Is the radio out?"

"Not that I'm aware of. Their reception might have been knocked out by the blizzard."

Reports of smoke? After the blizzard they'd had? Most likely meant someone stranded by the blizzard. Brannon's hands trembled with adrenaline. "Jefferson's being questioned by the FBI, but Lincoln and I can do a flyby and check it out." She gnawed the edge of her finger.

"Why's he being questioned by the FBI? Thought you and Lincoln just had to sign your statements."

"Long story. We don't know how long he'll be tied up."

"But your ankle—"

"I'll be okay, Steve. I can do this."

"Well . . ."

"I'll radio you for the coordinates once we're in the air." She closed her cell before Steve could offer more argument.

"What's up?" Lincoln asked, studying her face.

"Reports of smoke near Little River Road. Steve can't raise Elkmont Station. We need to check it out."

"Your ankle—"

"Can handle the flight." She picked her way across the ice to the courthouse's doors. "Come on, we need to get someone to take us back to the helicopter."

Wednesday, 7:10 p.m.
US Marshals Office, Howard Baker Federal Courthouse
Knoxville, Tennessee

BRANNON WANTED A RIDE to get back to the helicopter?

Roark reread the note the agent had slipped him. Why would she want to go to the helicopter now? Did she need something from it?

The room was silent, save for the breathing. Jefferson sat at the table, unaware the agents had accessed his mother's safety deposit box. The agents hadn't yet arrived with the books. Roark nodded to Demott, then slipped out.

Brannon paced the hallway. "Good, you're here."

"What's going on?"

"I need you to take us to the helicopter. We've got a call."

"I don't understand."

She sighed. "Steve called. There have been reports of smoke in the park. I need to check it out."

"But you can't fly yet."

"Are you done with Jefferson?"

"No. We have to wait until the books arrive."

"Then I can fly."

"But your ankle—"

She held up her hand. "I can fly. This is my job, Roark. Smoke right after a blizzard usually means someone's stranded out there. While the snow's stopped, it's still below freezing. I have to go."

"Okay. I'll take you. Let's hurry. I want to be back to see the books the agents bring."

Together the three headed into the blistering cold and to his car. Brannon buzzed with excitement. Her face flushed and her eyes glistened. Very attractive.

Roark shifted his attention back to driving the short distance to the building where the helicopter waited. His headlights split the darkness. Could she fly in the dark? He couldn't explain his sudden concern for her, but he felt it nonetheless. What was going on with him?

He turned into the parking lot, then started to get out of the car. Brannon's hand on his forearm stopped him. "You don't have to go to the roof with us. We know the way."

"But—"

She smiled, pushing his heart into twists. "I know you want to get back to look at those books. I understand." Brannon leaned over and her lips whispered against his five o'clock shadow. "We'll be praying this is the break you need. Let me know if you can."

Wanting nothing more than to pull her to him but knowing he couldn't, Roark clenched his teeth and nodded.

With another soft smile, she was out of the car, head down, rushing toward the building.

"Thanks," Lincoln mumbled before he exited the car and followed her.

Roark watched them duck inside but didn't put the car in reverse. Something felt wrong, really wrong, but he couldn't put his finger on what. Maybe it was Brannon leaving. The woman did strange things to his emotions. He needed to pursue these feelings for her.

But he had a case to solve first.

Shoving the car into reverse, Roark backed out of the parking space. He put the car into drive and eased back to the road. Overhead, the steady beat of rotors thrummed.

Fear for Brannon tightened in his gut. Roark paused, letting the mental image of her smile, her concern for others fill his mind. Her strong faith that seemed to call into his very soul. For the first time in years, his breath caught as he prayed.

God, it's me. I know I haven't exactly been talking to You, and I'm sorry about that. But I really need You to watch over Brannon. Something's going on—I can feel it. And help us get a break in this case. We're trying to do the right thing down here. We sure could use Your help.

TWENTY-SIX

Wednesday, 7:35 p.m.
Northwest of Little River Road
Great Smoky Mountains National Park, Tennessee

THE GROWLING SOUNDED AGAIN. Closer.

Evening cloaked the woods of the mountain in darkness. Even the moon sat muted in the sky. Wind rustled through the icy tree branches. Strange noises echoed against the silence.

Mai gripped the end of the stick tighter. Her heart caught in her chest. Kanya scooted closer. "I am scared."

Mai was, too, but she could not tell Kanya. The girl would panic, and then where would they be? "The fire is keeping it away. We are safe." She forced confidence into her voice. A confidence she didn't feel.

"But Poppy Fred can see the smoke and know where we are."

Stupid. She had been plain *khlao*. Of course, Kanya was right. It was probably him out in the woods growling. Toying with them. Scaring them. So close. Ready to jump out and grab them.

No. If Fred knew where they were, he would already have them. It was an animal in the woods, not Fred. Still, she needed to put out the fire so Fred could not find them.

But then what would keep the animal in the woods away?

"Mai?" Kanya's voice trembled with fear.

"Let me think for a minute." Mai swallowed, going over her options again. They did not have many. What could she do? Face Fred or a wild animal?

What should she do?

Another growl echoed from the woods.

Definitely should not put out the fire. Not yet, with the animal so close. Mai glanced up. The tree branches, bare of leaves but heavy with ice, made a thick canopy, so dense she could not see the sky clearly. Only the moon peekabooed through the limbs.

Which meant Fred probably could not see the smoke. Or, if he could, he would not be able to tell their location. Not as fast anyway.

She let out a sigh. "The trees are blocking the smoke, Kanya. Fred will not find us. We are going to make it. We will rest and then find a way out of here. Help will come, I promise." Mai hoped she would be able to keep that promise.

"But the animal out there. The growls . . ."

"It will get tired of waiting and leave. Then we will start moving again."

"In the dark? With wild animals?" Kanya voiced Mai's own fears. "What if it follows us? Attacks us?"

"We do not have a choice," Mai whispered. How she wished she had thought this plan through a little better. They were hungry, cold, and scared. Animals threatened them, and Fred had to be close behind them.

Kanya sobbed into her hands. "We are going to die. All this running, and by morning, we will be *dap*."

"Stop it, Kanya. Do not be silly—we will not be dead. We are not going to die. Stop crying. We need to think and be smart." But Mai did not know what to do either. If only she could reach help.

The growl came again, throaty and close.

Kanya's sobs intensified. Mai wanted to cry, too. What if they did die out here? What if the fire went out and a bear or big cat came and got them? She had not only gotten herself into a dangerous mess, but she led Kanya in right along with her. Mai fought against tears.

A thumping sound beat overhead.

Mai jumped, looking through the trees. A beam of light pierced the canopy.

"What is it?" Kanya leapt to her feet.

"I think it is an aircraft." Mai still gripped the end of the stick. Could help have arrived?

"Like the plane that brought us here?"

"No, something else." Mai shielded her eyes from the beam of light. She could not make out what it was.

"What do we do? Run?" Kanya hugged her arms.

Mai stared at the light. They could not be too careful. Not with all they had already been through. "Grab our stuff. It might be Fred."

Wednesday, 7:40 p.m.
Northwest of Little River Road
Great Smoky Mountains National Park, Tennessee

"CAN YOU SEE ANY movement?" Brannon flexed her fingers around the cyclic, piloting the helicopter two degrees to the left. "The smoke's coming from right down there."

Lincoln pressed the night-vision binoculars to his eyes. "I'm looking, I'm looking."

She adjusted the collective, dropping the helicopter lower. The skids hovered mere inches over the tips of the trees.

"Movement. I see something."

"We're going in." Brannon glanced over the area. Up ahead, about a klick to the north, a space large enough for the aircraft waited. She aimed for the small clearing, hovering the helicopter just long enough for steadiness, then landed.

Lincoln had his headset off and his feet on the ground before the rotors stopped turning. Brannon radioed Steve, then reached for her box. And came up short. Her SIG was back at the station, and this helicopter had no weapons box. She followed Lincoln into the darkness, unarmed.

Ice and snow crunched under their feet. She picked her way, mindful of her ankle even though it only felt a little sore.

"Hello? Where are you?" he hollered.

Brannon went in the opposite direction of her partner, making a wide arc. Sometimes survivors who got lost became disoriented and ran from their rescuers. "We're National Park Service rangers, here to help you." The wind stole her words.

Eyes to her right peered out from the darkness.

Not wanting to alarm anyone, Brannon spoke in an even tone. "Hello, we're here to rescue you." She crouched lower, ducking under ice-heavy branches.

Lincoln closed the arc. The eyes recessed farther into the woods. Brannon held up her hand to halt him. Could this be a lost child? How come no one had reported them missing?

She crouched on the ground and added a soothing tone to her voice. "I'm a ranger, here to take you out of here. Come out. Are you hurt?"

Another set of eyes appeared beside the first. Brannon judged the height—no more than four feet, for either of them. *Two* lost children? She inched toward the edge of the woods, ignoring the twinge in her ankle. "I'm not going to hurt you. I'm here to save you."

She held out her hand, trying to make out their outlines in the dark. A figure stepped forward, slowly, holding a threadbare pillowcase. The other came on her heels, also with a similar pack. Their steps were hesitant, leery. They finally came into view.

Two Asian girls, approximately ten to twelve years old. Dirty, thin, without clothes appropriate for the weather.

Brannon swallowed her horror and pasted on a smile. "Hi. I'm Brannon, a park ranger. We saw your smoke and came to rescue you."

The taller of the girls, probably the oldest, stepped forward. "My name is Mai."

"Hello, Mai." Brannon's smile widened and she glanced at the second girl.

"I am Kanya."

"Hello, Kanya." Brannon glanced over her shoulder at Lincoln. "That's my partner, my friend, Lincoln." She warned him with her eyes to approach with caution. "Come say hello, Lincoln."

He moved beside her. "Hello, Mai and Kanya."

The girls' focus dropped to the ground.

Brannon pressed her lips together. They were scared of men. She motioned Lincoln back while taking Mai's hand. "Let's get out of here. I'll take you back to our station where it's warm. You can get something to eat."

Kanya's head jerked up, her eyes widening.

"Okay?" Brannon slowly rose, not wanting to frighten the children. What had happened to them? Were their parents around? They didn't look like sisters, but they could be. "Are you out here by yourselves?"

Mai pulled her hand out of Brannon's grip. "Yes. We are alone."

A lie, but Brannon would let it stand for now. "Okay. Well, let's go." She turned and led the way to the small clearing. Lincoln doused the fire, then raced to reach the helicopter before them.

As they drew closer, both girls clung to one another, staring at the aircraft. They'd probably never seen one before. Especially not up close. She smiled at them. "This is my helicopter. I fly this every day to save people who need help in the mountains."

Mai nodded and let Brannon and Lincoln help her into the backseat. Brannon reached for Kanya next.

Crack! Crack!

Gunshots . . . again? Brannon lifted a trembling Kanya and put her in Lincoln's hands, then hopped into the pilot's seat. Why hadn't she brought her gun? She secured the headphones over her ears and started up the helicopter.

God, not again. Don't let them hit us. Don't let them damage the helicopter. Not with these girls. Please, Father. Help us.

"We're good." Lincoln crawled into the front seat. "They're secure."

Brannon didn't have time to glance at the girls. More shots echoed in the woods. She engaged the helicopter and lifted them into the air. She didn't hover, just pulled on the cyclic and collective and steered them toward the station. Once she was far enough away that shots wouldn't make contact, she activated the headset comm. "Are they okay?"

Lincoln glanced over his shoulder, then back to Brannon. "Scared and shaken, but I think they're good."

"Those people shooting at us . . . they were after these girls."

"Parents, maybe?"

Brannon shot him a scathing look. "Right. Armed and shooting at their kids? I don't think so."

"How'd they get out there? What were they doing by themselves? Runaways?"

"I don't know. I need to radio Steve." She changed frequencies and hailed the ranger station.

Steve came back in a heartbeat. "You guys okay?"

"Fine. We found the source of the smoke. En route to the station with two children. Shots fired at us."

"And those firing at you?"

"Unidentified. Stand by with first-aid supplies. ETA five minutes."

Wednesday, 8:05 p.m.
Congressman McGovern's Home
Knoxville, Tennessee

"What do you mean they got away? They're only children." Warren took another sip of his Scotch. The liquid seared his throat. His head pounded—a promise of the migraine to come.

Zimp's voice squeaked over the phone. "Rangers in a helicopter picked them up."

Brannon Callahan! Everywhere Warren turned, the woman showed up to complicate his life. "Tell Fred, Betty, and Nancy to get to that ranger station. Those girls can't live to talk."

"Yes, sir. Abrams Creek Station, right?"

He was surrounded by idiots. *"Yes."* He ground out the word through clenched teeth. "Call me as soon as it's done." Warren studied the amber liquid in his decanter. "And take out the rangers as well. We can't have any witnesses."

That would handle the woman pilot's meddling once and for all.

TWENTY-SEVEN

Wednesday, 8:06 p.m.
US Marshals Office, Howard Baker Federal Courthouse
Knoxville, Tennessee

ANTICIPATION BUILT INSIDE THE interrogation room to the brink of exploding.

Roark along with the FBI agents and Gerald Demott held their breath as a consulting CPA studied the books retrieved from Wilks's wife's safety deposit box. Jefferson Montgomery had already stated he didn't recognize them, nor did he have any information about them. Now the CPA had flipped pages and pulled out Excel spreadsheets for the better part of ten minutes, leaving the others in the room waiting. And waiting.

Seconds fell off the clock over the window. The hands made steady clicking noises. The hum of the fluorescent light increased.

Click. Click. Click.

So much rode on these books. If they could be deciphered, the money trail could lead to all those involved with the child-trafficking ring. Roark clenched and unclenched his fists, just for something to do.

Click. Click. Click.

No one moved. Nervous energy bounced off the walls, nearly suffocating the room's occupants. Roark fought the urge to pace or slam the table and demand the CPA tell them if he could make heads or tails of the books. Neither would be productive, so Roark continued to make and release fists.

Click. Click. Click.

Finally the CPA closed the books and met Greg Daly's gaze. "It appears the transactions can be traced."

A collective sigh exploded.

The CPA held up his hands as he stood. "It won't be easy, but the account numbers are consistent, which should allow you to detect the account holders' names."

"Can you tell anything else?" one of the agents asked.

"I can't be sure, but there are a lot of references to Black Forest, Colorado, and Townsend, Tennessee. If I were to guess, I'd think the base of operations was in one of those locations."

"Thank you, Mr. Holt." The SAC shook the CPA's hand. "We appreciate your coming in at this late hour and taking a look at this for us."

The man bobbed his head. "No problem."

One of the other agents hovered at the CPA's elbow. "I'll show you out."

As soon as the door closed behind them, pandemonium erupted with everyone talking at once. US Attorney Noah Markinson whistled, and silence settled over the group. He pointed at the two senior agents. "Get these books over to NSA. Now."

The agents grabbed the books and hustled out the door.

Greg Daly continued to issue orders. "Get a team ready. I want agents in Townsend as soon as possible. I'll call our Colorado office and alert agents there."

An agent almost knocked over a chair to do his boss's bidding.

Mr. Markinson turned to Roark. "Now what's this about Congressman McGovern possibly being involved?"

Roark relayed what Brannon had overheard, then handed him a copy of the fax. A pregnant pause followed. Finally the US attorney pinched the bridge of his nose. "That's not enough to get a search warrant. Might be enough to get his phone records, but no judge will get a warrant based on someone's statement regarding an overheard conversation."

"What about the fax?" Roark's chest tightened.

"This merely implies a connection. It's not signed by the congressman, so he could state his credit card was stolen and used to purchase this."

The SAC pointed at the last agent in the room. "Quietly assemble a covert team. They are to unofficially monitor the congressman's moves. This is off the grid, got it?"

"Yes, sir." The agent rushed from the room.

"If he finds out—" Markinson began.

"He won't." Daly stood tall. "My agents are good. He won't detect them."

Roark shifted his weight from foot to foot. "What about Jefferson Montgomery? He's still in the conference room."

Markinson sighed. "You can release Mr. Montgomery for now. But remind him that he isn't to leave the state without notifying us."

Roark nodded and headed out the door. Excitement soared. This was it—he could feel it. All the loose pieces of the case were finally coming together.

He entered the conference room, startling Jefferson. "Sorry."

"It's okay." Jefferson yawned and ran a hand over his face. "Time for more endless questions?"

Roark laughed. "Nope. You're good to go. But the FBI asked me to tell you not to leave town."

Jefferson grinned. "Kinda like in the movies, right?"

"Guess so."

The ranger ambled to his feet. "Bet Brannon and Lincoln are ready to get out of here. Almost as much as I am."

"Actually, they've already gone." Roark led the way down the hall to the elevators.

"How? Why?" Jefferson stepped into the car as soon as the doors slid open.

"They got a call of smoke reported. I took them to the helicopter about an hour ago."

"But Brannon isn't cleared to fly yet."

"Try telling her that." Roark exited the courthouse.

The burst of icy wind blasted their faces as they ducked toward the car.

"So how am I supposed to get back to the station?"

"I'll drive you. It's less than an hour away." Roark unlocked the door, then slipped behind the steering wheel.

Jefferson clicked his seat belt. "Whatever works. I'm just ready to get out of here."

Wednesday, 8:10 p.m.
Abrams Creek Ranger Station
Great Smoky Mountains National Park, Tennessee

"STEVE, THIS IS MAI and Kanya." Brannon led the shivering girls into the ranger station and out of the cold night.

"Hello, there." Steve's voice held a soothing tone, for which Brannon was grateful. Still the girls shied away from him.

Brannon led them to the couch and pulled an afghan over them. "Let me get some medical supplies and check you both."

Mai shook her head. "Fine."

Brannon smiled as she squatted before the girls. "I'm sure you are, but would you let me check, please? Just to make sure you don't have frostbite on your toes or scratches?"

Mai hesitated a moment, then nodded.

"Good." Brannon stood and slipped out of her coat, passing it to Steve. "Hand me the first-aid bag."

Lincoln spoke behind her. "I can probably check them over quicker."

She nodded at him. "But they're scared of you." She glanced at Steve. "Of all men, it seems."

Steve rubbed his stubbled chin. "Abusive father, maybe?"

"Could be." Brannon wouldn't think of what could make the girls so frightened of men. It made her stomach turn. "One of you needs to call the authorities. While I'm checking them over, I'll try to get more of their story."

"I'll call." Steve strode to the desk.

Brannon lifted the black bag and returned to the girls. She explained what each item was as she withdrew it. As she checked the girls' hands, she cleaned cuts and scratches. "What were you girls doing out there all by yourselves? At night, in this cold weather?" She tried to keep her voice casual. Anything could spook these two.

Neither girl responded, but Brannon knew they understood her. Their comprehension of English seemed more than adequate. She finished bandaging Mai's hands, then moved to Kanya's. "Were you with a group and got separated?"

Again, no response, but Brannon noticed the eye contact between the two. They had a story but were too frightened to tell it just yet. She finished dressing Kanya's hands, then removed the girls' boots. Neither had socks. The tips of their toes were already changing colors. "Hang on, I'll be right back."

"Lincoln, get me a bucket with cool water, please." She headed toward her living quarters. "I'm going to get the girls some dry, warm clothes."

She rushed through her room, grabbing socks and sweatpants and sweaters. When she entered the station's common area, Lincoln had the bucket of water in front of the girls. They clung to each other, guarded eyes watching his every move. Brannon smiled her thanks and set the pile of clothes on the couch.

"You have beginning stages of frostbite. I need to put your feet in the water. It's going to be cold at first, but we can add warm water once we bring up your temperatures a little."

Mai allowed Brannon to submerge her feet. Kanya followed suit. The girls grimaced against the sting and bite, but they didn't withdraw their feet from the bucket. So young but already accustomed to pain. Brannon blinked back tears.

God, please watch over these girls. I don't know what they've been through, but I have a feeling it's pretty bad. Guide me to help them.

Sticking her hands in the bucket, Brannon massaged the girls' feet. Slowly she felt the cold lessen. She nodded at Lincoln, who stood with another bucket of water. He poured it into the bucket with their feet.

Warm water caressed Brannon's fingers as she continued to massage Mai's and Kanya's feet. "Did someone leave you out in the woods? I'm trying to help you, but I need to know what happened. Can you tell me?"

"We ran away." Mai's voice could barely be heard.

Brannon's heart caught. Runaways? So young? What had caused them to run away in this winter weather? Child Protective Services would need to be contacted.

She took their feet and dried them with the terry-cloth towel Lincoln gave her. She pulled the socks over their feet, then handed them the sweatpants and sweaters. "Go put these on. They'll be too big, but they're dry and warm." She pointed them to the bathroom.

Without a word the girls shuffled to the bathroom, then shut the door behind them.

Brannon spun to face Steve and Lincoln. "Those girls are runaways."

"I've already called the locals. They said they'd send out CPS and have a unit out here within a couple of hours," Steve said.

"Doesn't explain someone shooting at us." Lincoln reached for coffee mugs. "Why would anyone shoot at us for rescuing two runaway girls?"

"Maybe they weren't interested in the girls at all. Maybe we were the targets. Because of our rescue of Roark." Just saying his name made her heart quicken.

"Could be." Lincoln passed a mug to her. "But I don't see what purpose it'd serve now."

"Me either." Brannon took a sip of the scalding coffee. Lincoln had doctored it just the way she liked it.

"How's your ankle?"

She glanced down her leg. She hadn't even noticed her injury. "Fine. I'm in no pain."

"Good." Steve lifted his own cup.

Brannon took another sip. "Maybe the girls will talk more once they're more comfortable."

"I have hot chocolate ready and waiting," Lincoln said with a smile.

Wednesday, 8:35 p.m.
Abrams Creek Ranger Station
Great Smoky Mountains National Park, Tennessee

"WE HAVE TO TRUST them." Mai pulled the sweater over her head and stared at Kanya. "These people are here to help us. Like I told you."

"Poppy Fred might still be coming after us."

Mai nodded. "I think that is who shot at us."

"Then you have to tell them."

"I will try." Mai opened the bathroom door and shuffled back to the couch. So warm . . . Mai could not remember the last time she had been warm through and through.

"There you are." The woman—Brannon—smiled and brought over two cups. "We've made you some hot chocolate."

Mai took a tentative sip. She never tasted anything so wonderful. And warm.

Brannon sat on the table in front of them. "Can you tell me who you ran away from?"

She had to trust someone, and this woman had been nothing but nice to them. Mai nodded. "Madam Nancy. Poppy Fred."

"Nancy and Fred? Are those relatives of yours?"

"No."

Brannon frowned. "Where are your parents?"

The thought of *Maae* and *Phaaw* made Mai's chest hurt. "Thailand."

"Why are you in America?"

This was the part that hurt the most. "*Phaaw* wanted me to get proper English lessons."

"Who's *Phaaw*?"

Mai shook her head. "*Phaaw* not his name."

Brannon tilted her head to the side. "Is *Phaaw* your father?"

"Yes."

"And he wanted you to get an education in America?"

It was too painful for Mai to admit her father had sold her to Fred and Betty. He and *Maae* needed the money for food. And Fred promised she would get an education.

"So how did you get to America?"

"Poppy Fred. Aunt Betty."

"Where are they now?"

"Fred is following us. We run away."

Brannon's eyes widened. Mai noticed they were light in color but not the same color. "Was Fred the one who shot at us?"

Mai shrugged. She did not know for sure, but most likely it had been him.

"Why did you run away from Fred? Did he hit you?"

Mai's hand went to her cheek. She could feel the sting by remembering alone. "Yes."

"What about Betty and Nancy? Did they try to help you?"

"No." Nancy's slaps were the worst.

"Did they hit you, too?"

"Yes."

"Where were you? Camping?"

Mai shook her head. "Br-brothel."

The lady sucked in air. "A brothel? Are you sure? Maybe you mean a motel or a hotel?"

Maybe she had pronounced it wrong. It was not one of the English words Mai had learned back in Thailand. She tried again, just like she had heard Nancy say it. "Broth-el."

Brannon rocked back on the table. "You mean, with men? Doing things to you?"

Mai could not stop the tears. She dropped her head. Humiliation burned in her chest. She made eye contact with the nice lady. "Yes."

Brannon reached out and laid her hand over Mai's. Warmth seeped deep into Mai's bones.

Ka-boom!

Glass from the window shattered. Brannon shoved her and Kanya to the floor, lying on top of them. Mai's face pressed against a worn rug.

"Lincoln, Steve—are y'all okay?" Brannon yelled over the loud eruptions.

Mai cried. Her nightmare had come true.

Fred had found them.

TWENTY-EIGHT

Wednesday, 9:01 p.m.
Congressman McGovern's Home
Knoxville, Tennessee

"FRED CALLED IN FIVE minutes ago. He's at the ranger station." Zimp's voice pitched higher than normal, grating on Warren's last nerve.

Warren gripped the phone tighter. "Call me when everything's taken care of."

"Sir, um, there's a complication."

He ground his teeth. More? There had been too many mess ups and complications. He let his silence speak.

"It's Nancy."

Why wouldn't the moron just spit out the information?

"She's gone."

"What?" Had she lost her ever-loving mind? "Where did she go?"

"I don't know, sir. She called and said she wouldn't be a scape-goat. When I called her back, one of the girls said Nancy left." Silence filled the connection. "I think she ran."

"And left the girls alone?"

"Yes, sir. Both Fred and Betty are at the ranger station. Milt and Tom are dead. There isn't anyone left to watch the girls."

The idiots—they were going to blow everything if he didn't rein them in. He needed to stay calm. Make sure the morons didn't panic. *Think, McGovern, think. If authorities find that house, if those girls talk . . .*

He'd been careful. Nothing connected him to this except the money trail. And with Wilks out of the way and the agencies unable to decipher his notes—Zimp remained the only loose end left.

"Listen carefully, Zimp. Pack up base and come straight to my house. We'll contain the situation."

"Come there, sir? To your house?" Fear edged Zimp's voice.

Something Warren couldn't allow. He needed the middleman to come.

To be silenced.

"Yes. Come to the house. We'll figure out the safest place to send you. Bring all the phones. And pack. You'll leave on a flight tonight."

"Yes, sir." The wimpy man didn't sound so scared now. "I'll be there in fifteen minutes."

Warren hung up the phone and opened his top desk drawer. His mother's pearl-handled .380 handgun glistened in the overhead lights.

Come, Zimp, come.

Wednesday, 9:02 p.m.
Abrams Creek Ranger Station
Great Smoky Mountains National Park, Tennessee

WHERE WAS HER GUN?

On the stand by the door.

The firing had ceased. Reloading? Brannon touched the girls' shoulders. "Stay here and stay down."

The girls nodded, fear on their faces. These poor things were part of the child-trafficking ring. She had to do something. This was her chance to act.

Help me, God.

Brannon pressed her lips together and belly crawled to the stand holding her belt with her gun. Using her toes shot pain into her ankle. She put weight on her knees instead. "Lincoln, are you armed?"

"No, but I'm hit."

Her gut spasmed. "How bad?" She knocked the stand to the floor. Wood clattered against wood.

"In the knee. Hurts like all get-out."

Oh no. She grabbed her Sig and looped Lincoln's belt holster over her shoulder. "What about you, Steve?"

"I'm okay."

"Are you armed?"

"No. Heading to the gun case."

She bit her bottom lip as she crawled to where Lincoln hunched behind the chair. "Can you get me some extra ammo, Steve?"

"I think so." Scuffing sounded across the wooden floor. "Got it. Ready? I'll toss it."

She turned to find Steve but caught sight of Lincoln. He leaned against the back of an overturned chair, tightening his belt around his thigh. Crimson covered his pant leg. Brannon slid his gun across the floor to him. He caught it with ease, but sweat lined his upper lip.

"Are you okay?"

"I think so." He wiped his brow. "Think it's the same guy who shot at us in the mountains?"

"Pretty sure. He's gotta be with the child-trafficking ring."

Lincoln nodded. "Mai and Kanya—"

"Are some of the children in the case Roark's working on."

Pop! Pop!

More glass shattered. The girls cried out.

"Stay down!" Brannon turned and took a crouched firing position. She held her Sig at the ready, took aim at the window the last shots had entered through, and pulled the trigger.

Once. Twice. A third time.

Return fire overflowed in the station, drowning out the girls' heart-wrenching sobs. Sounded like a nine millimeter to Brannon.

She slumped lower behind the edge of the couch, resting her weapon-yielding hand on the top and squeezing the trigger two more times.

Smoke filled the room. The acrid stench of gunpowder assaulted her senses.

A loud explosion sounded behind her—a shotgun firing at the window. "Catch, Brannon," Steve hollered above the noise.

She turned and caught the magazine he threw her, discharged her empty clip, and shoved the new one in the Sig. "Kill the lights." Harder for them to see inside, easier for her to detect the muzzle flashes.

Silence echoed in the haze. A click sounded, then darkness covered the station. The girls sobbed.

Brannon crawled back to Lincoln. He lay still, his Sig tight in his hand.

Oh, God, no. Please, no.

She pressed her fingers against his neck. "Lincoln." His pulse popped against her fingers, steady. He must've passed out from the pain.

Bam! Ba-bam! Bam!

Shots came through the other window. Brannon grabbed Lincoln and pushed him into the hallway, safe from all angles of the windows.

The shotgun exploded.

She raised her gun and fired ten times. She pulled the trigger an eleventh time, but only a click sounded.

Time to reload.

"I'm out." Brannon released the empty magazine, flipped onto her stomach, and crawled toward the gun cabinet.

"I'll cover you." Steve fired again. The boom resonated, vibrating the wooden planks.

She scrambled across the floor and reached the cabinet. Jerking open the drawer, she felt around for magazines. She pulled out two clips, shoved them into her pocket, then inserted a third into the Sig with a resounding click. "Armed and ready."

Steve fired once more. "I'm heading to the radio to call for backup."

"I've got your back." Taking a deep breath, she leapt to her feet and rapid-fired toward the window. She emptied the magazine, crouched, dropped the clip, and popped a new one in, taking only seconds.

"Made it."

Brannon crawled to the girls. Both cried uncontrollably. "Listen, I need you to get to the hallway where Lincoln is. It's the safest place. Follow me, but keep down, okay?"

Neither girl responded.

More bullets entered the cabin, littering the floor and lodging into the wood.

She didn't have time to placate the children. Brannon shook Mai's shoulder. "I need you to stay down and follow me. Now."

Mai nodded.

Brannon shoved her gun above the back of the couch and fired off several more shots. When no return fire sounded, she nudged Mai. "Now."

Keeping to a belly crawl, Brannon led them to the hallway. Once there, she leaned against the wall, catching her breath. She glanced over at Lincoln. He was backlit by the lights in her living quarters. His eyes fluttered open. "You're going to be okay, Linc. Hold on. Watch the girls while I check on Steve."

He gave a weak nod. She hated leaving him, but she had to stop whoever shot at them. Maintaining a crouch, she crawled to the desk.

Steve held the shotgun at the ready. "Phones are down, but I got the call out over the radio. Backup should arrive soon."

"We have to hold them off."

In the silence of cease-fire, the unmistakable sound of tires on gravel ground out.

Brannon turned around, staring out the broken window. Headlights pierced the darkness. Her heart caught. Help couldn't have gotten here so fast. She gripped her Sig tighter.

The bad guys' backup had arrived.

Wednesday, 9:15 p.m.
Abrams Creek Ranger Station
Great Smoky Mountains National Park, Tennessee

LIGHTS BLAZED FROM THE back of the building but not from the station area. Roark's nerves bunched—he'd get to see Brannon again. Funny how that made his heart race.

"Guess they're not waiting up for me," Jefferson joked as he reached for the car's door handle.

Crack!

The windshield shattered. Roark grabbed Jefferson's arm and ducked, pulling the ranger facedown into the seat.

"What in the—?"

"Shh." Roark eased his Beretta from its holster. No further gunshots echoed in the area. He eased open the driver's door. "Stay put," he ordered Jefferson.

He lowered his feet to the ground. No shots fired. He slipped from the car, crouching behind the door.

Pop! Pop!

Holding his gun, Roark peeked around the door's frame, then opened fire into the darkness. He stopped after shooting six rounds.

No return shots came.

What in the world? Shivers snaked up his spine. Brannon! Was she okay? Or hit—lying in the station hurt?

God, please take care of her. I know, I know . . . only calling on You when I need Your help. But please don't let anything happen to Brannon. Please, God. I promise I'll give my life back to You if You'll just protect her.

Roark knew he couldn't bargain with God, but he hadn't been able to stop the words from crossing his mind and entering his prayer. If something happened to Brannon . . .

"What's going on?" Jefferson whispered.

"I don't know."

Shots fired into the station. Roark studied the muzzle flashes before lifting his gun and discharging. Two shooters. A succession of answering shots came from inside the station. If he wasn't mistaken, and Roark normally wasn't about ammo and weapons, a Sig and a shotgun were used. That meant at least two people were inside and capable of shooting.

Please, God, let one of them be Brannon.

"Stay here, Jefferson. You're unarmed." Roark rushed to the nearest clump of trees, keeping low.

More shots rang out directed at the station. Again, return fire sounded.

Roark raced toward where he'd caught the muzzle flash. He pulled off six rounds, then ran closer to the station, using trees as cover.

The exchange of gunfire continued. He'd shoot, move forward. Wait and watch. Pull the trigger, move forward. Wait and listen.

The shots into the station seemed to lessen. Out of ammo? Reloading? Roark waited. Still, the second shooter wasn't engaging. Had they hit him?

He crept closer, keeping his cover in the trees and firing, waiting and watching. And listening.

Off in the distance, from behind the station, the rumble of an ATV sounded. Louder . . . louder.

Roark faced that direction, his weapon ready to fire when the vehicle came close enough.

But the sound of the ATV grew fainter. It'd changed directions and headed away from the station.

In his peripheral vision, Roark caught the movement of a figure silhouetted by the moonlight. The figure moved to the front door, paused for a split second.

Roark raised his gun and ran closer.

The figure kicked in the door and opened fire.

Roark ran forward at top speed.

Brannon!

TWENTY-NINE

Wednesday, 9:30 p.m.
Congressman McGovern's Home
Knoxville, Tennessee

WARREN HEADED TO THE foyer to answer the front door. Zimp arrived, a few minutes late, but here nonetheless. Now to follow through with the plan. Too bad Tom had gotten himself killed. Shot by that roguish marshal. Holland would be a problem dealt with later. For now . . .

Warren opened the door, a plastic smile in place. "Hello, Zimp. Come in." He waved the acne-scarred young man into his home.

Zimp's muddy work boots scuffed across the marble floor. Great, Warren would have to have it buffed and polished. He gritted his teeth and motioned toward the study. "Would you like a drink?" Warren stood at the wet bar, studying the middleman. He'd never met him in person before.

"Uh, yeah. That'd be nice, Mr. McGovern."

That would be *Congressman* McGovern. One day, Mr. President. But Warren had to contain the situation. Now. "Whiskey? Scotch? Brandy?"

"Uh, brandy, I guess."

Of course—a lady's drink. Warren opened the snifter and poured Zimp half a glass before pouring himself two fingers of Scotch. Not the cheap stuff, either. Johnnie Walker Blue Label, King George V edition. The best five hundred dollars he'd ever spent.

"Thanks." Zimp took the glass and guzzled it. He made a slight grimace. Probably used to bottled beer, and not the imported kind.

Warren would do the world a favor by getting rid of this lowlife. He'd served his purpose but now was only a liability.

Warren sipped his Scotch, enjoying the smooth warmth traveling down his throat. "Have you thought about a place you'd like to go to ride out this situation?"

Zimp set the glass on the coffee table. Warren struggled not to smack the boy. Didn't he know about water rings? No, he probably used milk crates for end tables. Warren carried the glass back to the wet bar and set it in the sink.

"I was thinking about Jamaica. I hear it's nice."

More than likely, with visions of girls clad in string bikinis.

"It is."

"Um, how am I supposed to get my money?"

Uncouth, bringing up money. Yes, Warren would do society a favor in eliminating Mr. Buddy Zimp. "Once you get to your destination, we'll set up a wire transfer to your offshore account."

"How long will that take?" Zimp shifted his weight from one foot to the other. "I mean, I don't have any traveling money or funds for a hotel."

"I'll take care of it." Warren set his glass in the sink beside the other. "I'll arrange the flight and your reservations and give you several thousand to hold you over until you can open an account."

Zimp smiled, revealing straight teeth. "That'd be great, Mr. McGovern."

"Did you bring the phones and your laptop?"

"Yes, sir." Zimp lifted an attaché case. "Everything's in here."

"Perfect." No trail. Warren took the case and placed it in his desk's bottom drawer. "Well, let me call my pilot and get your flight arranged."

Zimp nodded, looking more relaxed.

Warren lifted the phone and dialed his cell phone number, which he'd already turned off and put upstairs. "Yes, Paul, I need to arrange a flight to Jamaica tonight." He waited a moment, aware that Zimp hung on his every word. "Certainly. As soon as possible."

Zimp rocked back on his heels, smiling when he thought Warren wasn't watching. Clueless . . . utterly naive.

"Yes, that's fine. We'll be there directly." Warren replaced the receiver to its cradle and met Zimp's stare. "You'll fly out in less than an hour. We'd better hurry and get you to the airstrip."

"Great."

"Where's your car?"

"Out front."

Another item to take care of. No matter, Warren thought well on his feet. And suddenly he knew what to do. "Why don't I drive you in your car, then bring it back here and hide it in my guest cottage's garage?"

Zimp shrugged. "Works for me."

"Then let's go." Warren pulled the driving gloves from his pockets and slipped them on. "It's getting colder out since the sun went down."

"Ain't that the truth. Really nasty weather. Worst we've seen here in years." Zimp's nervous chatter wore on Warren's nerves. Soon it'd all be over.

He slipped behind the wheel of the jalopy Zimp had left in his driveway. Warren would have to make sure there were no oil stains on the red bricks. The car started easily enough. Warren couldn't help but wrinkle his nose at the odor in the car. Fast food. His stomach turned. He'd have to send this suit to the cleaners.

Steering the car out of the driveway, Warren headed toward the back roads out of town. He kept his speed at the limit and his gaze peeled for any other vehicles. Wouldn't do him any good to have someone see him driving this piece of garbage.

"Why are we going this way?" Zimp's knee bounced.

"We don't want anyone to follow us."

Zimp whipped around to look out the rear window. "Do you think someone is?"

"Not right now, but we have to be careful." Warren swallowed the laugh. Poor Zimp looked positively ashen with paranoia. "We'll keep to the back roads until we get closer to the airstrip."

"Oh. Good." But Zimp kept stealing glances behind them in the car's side mirror.

Once they'd gone about half a mile, they came to a gravel road. Warren turned. He drove for a few minutes, then slowed and eased the car to the side of the road.

"What's wrong?"

"I think we have a flat or a low tire. A rock might have punctured it." Warren killed the engine and opened the driver's door. "Check your side."

Zimp opened his door and stepped outside.

Warren moved to the back of the car. "It's mine. Do you have a spare tire?"

"I think in the trunk." Zimp joined him at the trunk and opened it with the press of a button. He leaned over. "I think I have a jack in here somewhere, too."

Hand over the pearl handle, Warren withdrew his mother's gun from his coat pocket. With steady hands, he raised the .380, leveling it with the base of Zimp's head. Without hesitation he squeezed the trigger.

Zimp fell over into the trunk.

Warren checked the backseat. Sure enough, two large plastic cups littered the floorboard. He grabbed them, then popped the hood. He cut the fuel line, draining gasoline into the cups. When they were filled, Warren set them aside, then laid the fuel line over the engine, letting gasoline flow over.

He took the cups and saturated Zimp's body and the trunk with gasoline. He took a match from his pocket, struck it, and threw the match into the trunk before closing it. Next, he tossed a lit match under the hood and shut it. Finally, he lit two of the fast-food bags in the backseat.

As the car lit up in flames, Warren smiled. Then sighed. He'd have to walk back home.

Oh, well . . . some things were worth the effort.

Wednesday, 9:35 p.m.
Abrams Creek Ranger Station
Great Smoky Mountains National Park, Tennessee

THE FRONT DOOR CRASHED open.

Brannon stood and took aim at the bulk filling the doorway. He swung, pointing his gun at her. She squeezed the trigger. Again. And again.

The man fell facedown on the wood floor.

Her palm cramped around the butt of her Sig.

"Brannon!"

Suddenly her handgun weighed heavy in her hand. "Roark?" She lowered her weapon to her side.

Roark rushed to the doorway, halting as he spied the man on the floor. He kept his gun ready as he felt the man's neck. "Somebody hit the lights." The station washed in light. Roark jerked up his head. "Brannon." He stepped over the body and hurried to her side. He drew her into his arms, teasing her temple with feather kisses. "Are you okay?"

"I'm fine. Lincoln's shot." While his arms made her feel safe and secure, she had to get Lincoln to the hospital. Now. She moved out of his embrace. "I'll fly Lincoln to the hospital. It's quickest."

Roark nodded at the man lying in the doorway. "He's dead. There's another shooter getting away on an ATV. I'm going after him."

Was it smart to run after someone with a gun? He was a marshal, not an FBI agent.

Steve handed Roark a key. "Take the four-wheeler out back. You'll never catch him on foot. The authorities have already been called."

"Thanks." Roark met her gaze. "I'll get 'em." Roark placed a hard kiss on her mouth. "I promise."

Her heart fluttered, despite the circumstances. "Be careful."

He ran from the station, Beretta in hand. Fear for his safety nearly had her chasing after him. But she had to take care of Lincoln.

She'd never felt so torn before. She'd gone into the professions she had so she could save people. What if something happened to Roark? Brannon didn't know if she could handle losing him.

Father, please watch over Roark. Keep him safe. Bring him back to me. Please.

Jefferson ran inside. "Everybody okay?"

Brannon rushed to the hallway. "Lincoln's hit. In the knee. He's lost a lot of blood. I'm taking him to the hospital."

"I'll pilot," Jefferson said.

"No, I'll do it." No way would she *not* fly her best friend to the hospital.

The two girls were backed against the door to her living quarters, both trembling and crying. "Shh. It'll be okay."

"Who are they?" Jefferson asked.

"Fill you in later. Right now, we need to leave."

Lincoln lay unconscious again but with a pulse. Weaker than before but still detectable.

"Let me get him." Jefferson moved beside Lincoln and nodded at her ankle. "Despite what you think, you're still injured."

"Let's get him into the helicopter." Steve helped Jefferson lift Lincoln.

Brannon rushed to the aircraft and did a quick preflight. In minutes Lincoln was secure in the backseat, she in the pilot's seat, and Jefferson ready in the copilot's chair. She smiled at Steve. "Take care of the girls until I get back."

"Will do."

She maneuvered the controls, and in seconds the helicopter was airborne. She radioed ATC, then patched to the hospital. Once she'd given as many details as she could, she clicked off the comm.

"Want to tell me about those girls back at the station?"

"As soon as Lincoln's at the hospital, okay?"

Jefferson nodded, then glanced over his shoulder. "Hey, buddy. You're gonna be fine. We're taking you to the hospital in Sevierville. Will take us less than ten minutes to get there." He caught Brannon's eye. "He's coming to."

"Hey, Linc. About five more minutes, and we'll land."

"What?" Jefferson undid his harness and slipped into the backseat. "I can't hear you." He leaned over Lincoln's head.

"Uh, okay." Jefferson slipped back into the copilot's seat.

"What'd he say?"

"I hope I remember this right. He said to tell you, 'But for you who revere my name, the sun of righteousness will rise with healing in its wings. And you will go out and leap like calves released from the stall.'"

Brannon smiled and glanced over her shoulder at her partner. "You'll be fine, Lincoln. You'll be leaping soon enough."

Wednesday, 9:37 p.m.
Woods North of Abrams Creek Ranger Station
Great Smoky Mountains National Park, Tennessee

ROARK KILLED THE FOUR-WHEELER'S engine. He trained his ears to pick up the other ATV's location. Over the cold silence of night, the distant hum came. Up and to the left.

He turned the key, the Polaris hummed to life, then he sped in that direction. He'd catch this other shooter. Get answers as to why they fired on Brannon's station.

She'd shot and killed that man. Not that he wasn't glad—he was ecstatic she was safe—but he'd never pictured her killing someone.

Yet she was trained to do so.

He raced over rocks and bumps, pushing the four-wheeler as fast as it would go. His mind kept going back to Brannon.

Never in his life had his heart ached as much as when he'd seen the man bust open the door and fire, knowing Brannon was inside. What did that mean?

She'd stolen his heart.

And she was safe.

Okay, God. I'm a man of my word. You kept her safe. Forgive me for being so angry with You. I want to follow Christ. Change me, God, to be the man You want me to be. Amen.

Ahead, he could make out the outline of the ATV. The rider didn't seem to realize he was being followed. Roark pulled his Beretta out, targeting the vehicle's back tires. He accelerated to get closer, steadied his aim, and pulled the trigger.

The vehicle fishtailed, then flipped.

Roark jerked to a stop and hopped off the four-wheeler. Keeping his gun ready, he approached the person lodged under the overturned ATV. The shooter was a woman. A nine millimeter lay on the ground beside her and the ATV. "Don't move."

Her sobs brought him up short.

"Help me. I can't breathe."

He dared not holster his Beretta, in case she had another handgun. But he couldn't leave her trapped. He needed to take her in. Find out what her story was.

Passing his gun to his left hand, Roark rocked the ATV back right side up. He pointed the gun at the woman. "Get up."

She coughed, rolling over onto her hands and knees.

"Get up slowly. Keep your hands where I can see them."

She stood, still coughing. "Who are you?"

"US Marshals and you're under arrest for attempted murder."

THIRTY

Wednesday, 10:45 p.m.
Fort Sanders Sevier Medical Center
Sevierville, Tennessee

"SURGERY?" BRANNON COULDN'T BELIEVE Lincoln needed surgery. Her heart clenched, and she glanced at Jefferson.

Dr. Miller nodded. "Both the femoral component and the patella are shattered, as well as the damage sustained to the femur. We'll have to perform a total knee reconstruction and replacement. It'll take about three to four hours."

"Three hours?" Her nerves bunched.

"Three to four, yes, ma'am."

"He's a park ranger. Will he be able to walk?"

"Walk, most probably. Climbing like rangers do?—depends. I make no promises or guarantees." Dr. Miller adjusted her watch. "He'll have months of physical therapy after the surgery, but he should graduate to walking without a cane."

Lincoln, with a cane? Tears burned Brannon's eyes.

The surgeon gazed about the waiting room. "Why don't you get something to eat, call somebody or something? There's nothing you can do. You can go up to the surgical waiting room around the time he gets out of surgery. I'll talk to you after the surgery."

"Th-thank you." Brannon released Jefferson's hand and pawed at the tears as the doctor strode down the hall. "I'm going to check in with Steve." Her voice was thick with the words she wouldn't voice. She withdrew her cell and dialed the station's number. It rang six times before she closed her phone.

Jefferson gave her a questioning look.

"Phone's still down." And she hadn't heard from Roark, either. Had he returned the four-wheeler? Did he get the other shooter? Was he okay?

"Why don't I head back to the station? Check on Steve and those girls. Find out what's happened."

But the girls . . . "Mai and Kanya don't know you. They're scared of men. I'm worried how they're faring with Steve as it is. You'd terrify them." She smiled. "No offense."

He grinned back. "None taken. How's your ankle?"

"Fine." She rotated it as an example. Only a little twinge burned. "So you go and I'll stay here."

"I can't leave Lincoln. He's my partner. He's like family." What about his career?

Jefferson rested his hand on her shoulder. "You heard the doctor—this'll take about four hours. It's a short flight to the station."

She couldn't leave Lincoln here, could she? But what about the girls? Steve? Roark?

"Look, I'll call your cell if anything happens." Jefferson held up the Boy Scout fingers. "I promise."

Lincoln would demand answers when he came out of surgery. The surgery that might cost him his career. Brannon chewed at the thick skin beside her nail. Just being on crutches for a couple of days had driven her up the wall. A long regimen of physical therapy . . . She couldn't imagine.

"Brannon, go. You can't do anything here. You'll be back before he comes out of surgery."

"Okay. You call me if there's *any* news. Anything at all."

"I will."

She ran her hands over her jeans. "I'll be back as soon as I check on everything."

Her steps were like sludge as she made her way to the helipad. How could she leave her partner? Lincoln had never left her side when Wade died. Even when she tried to force him to leave, he dug in his heels and stayed. Pulled her out of the pit of depression. Gave her hope and restored her faith.

She hesitated before climbing into the helicopter. Could she leave Lincoln in surgery, not knowing if he'd be okay?

"And the prayer offered in faith will make the sick person well; the Lord will raise him up. . . . The prayer of a righteous man is powerful and effective."

Brannon smiled. James 5:15–16—very powerful Scriptures Lincoln had encouraged her to memorize when she'd lost Wade. The power of God's Word washed over her, and she bowed her head and prayed for the man she loved like a brother.

Heart not as heavy, she lifted the bird in the air and turned toward the ranger station. Home. Her mind drifted to Roark. Was he okay? What if he'd been shot and left for dead?

Twelve minutes later Brannon touched the skids to the helipad at Abrams Creek. Flashing lights atop cars lit up the night. She completed her postflight duties, then rushed to the door. She paused at the threshold.

A tape outline of the man she'd shot stopped her cold.

She'd killed a man. A human. A child of God.

Tears swam in her eyes, blurring her vision. She'd never killed someone before. *Oh, Father, forgive me.* She knew He did—she'd had no choice as the man would've killed them all—but remorse shook her hands.

"Brannon."

She glanced at the officers and agents swarming the station. Men and women filled the room to capacity. Steve sat on the couch with Mai and Kanya, their eyes wide as they took in all the commotion. Brannon crossed the room and knelt before them. "Hi, girls. How are you?"

"Okay," Mai said.

Brannon smiled. They were okay because she'd protected them. The fact did little to ease her conscience.

"How's Lincoln?" Steve asked.

She sobered. "In surgery. His knee needs reconstruction and replacement."

Steve grimaced, rubbing his knee. "Doesn't sound good."

"No." Brannon swallowed the lump lodged in her throat. "Have you heard from Roark?"

Steve nodded. "He brought the four-wheeler back. Arrested the other shooter and took her in for questioning. Left with two FBI agents."

"Her?"

"Yeah. Shocker, huh?"

What in tarnation? She ignored the voices and sounds of the people around them, focusing on her supervisor. "Did Roark see Mai and Kanya?"

"No. He didn't even come inside. Told me to wait here and one of the agents would take my statement."

So he didn't know. She stood and squared her shoulders, running her gaze over the room. "Who's in charge?"

No one answered. No one even stopped and looked at her.

She tried again, this time raising her voice. "Who's in charge?"

One of the men in an FBI coat moved to her. "I am. Special Agent Greg Daly. And you are?"

"Remember me, Ranger Brannon Callahan?"

"Right." He shouted out for two of his men to take some more photographs, disinterested in the conversation with her. "We'll need your statement as well. Give us a few minutes, and we'll take you in."

"No."

He stopped and glared at her. "Excuse me?"

"No, I won't wait a few minutes. I have crucial witnesses in an ongoing investigation. I need to speak to US Marshal Roark Holland."

"Lady, he's at the courthouse with a suspect. You'll have to wait." Mr. Special Agent in Charge spun and barked orders to those milling about.

Wait? Not hardly. She gestured to Steve. "Get them some coats."

"But he said to wa—" Steve must have seen something in her expression because he shoved to his feet.

"He's wrong. Roark needs to talk with Mai and Kanya now."

"You'll never get the Jeep out of here. Did you see all the cars and lights?" He reached for coats anyway.

"I have no intention of driving out of here. I'm going to fly them out."

"Brannon, I don—"

She grabbed the coats from him and eased them onto the girls. "Trust me, Roark needs to talk to them. It's critical to their investigation."

"But—"

"It's okay, Steve. I'll call Roark on his cell now. Will that make you happy?"

"Yes."

She pulled out her cell and dialed Roark's number. It rang once. Twice.

"Brannon, are you okay? How's Lincoln?"

"I'm fine. Lincoln's in surgery. Listen, I need you to meet me at the landing site by the courthouse in fifteen minutes."

"I'm kind of in the middle of an interrogation right now."

"Trust me, you'll understand. I'm bringing you two witnesses." She glanced at Mai and Kanya, not wanting to alarm them more than necessary.

"Witnesses?"

"Two *young* witnesses."

"Are you saying—?"

"Yes. Will you meet us at the roof in fifteen minutes?"

"I'll be there."

Wednesday, 11:10 p.m.
Downtown Area
Knoxville, Tennessee

BRANNON HAD FOUND SOME of the trafficked kids. Roark dared to hope for more. Had she isolated the location?

He lifted his collar as the helicopter approached. Brannon Callahan was one unique lady. And almost losing her had made him realize how much he cared about her. He forced his thoughts to the case. The kids. The job.

As graceful as a machine could be, the helicopter touched down on concrete. The deafening roar of the rotors dulled, then faded away. The pilot's door opened, and Brannon filled his vision. His heart caught and wouldn't let go.

She ran to the other side of the aircraft and opened the door. In the lights on the roof, he couldn't quite make out who she helped from the passenger side. He waited as she approached. Her silhouette moved beside two smaller ones. Young girls.

His gut knotted as they drew close enough for him to estimate their age. Barely in their teens.

Children. Asian.

The two girls clung to Brannon as if she were their lifeline. She flashed him a shaky smile. "Roark, these are my new friends, Mai and Kanya." She wrapped her arms around each of the girls' shoulders. "Girls, this is my good friend, Roark. He's been looking for you."

The girl she'd gestured as Mai looked up at her. "For us?"

Brannon nodded. "To help you and the other girls."

The wind gusted, whipping around the roof. Roark motioned toward the roof access door. "Let's get out of the wind."

Brannon and the girls followed him. Silence hung heavy as they made their way into the car and steered toward the courthouse.

"Heard anything more on Lincoln?"

He didn't miss the slight tremble of her chin. "He's still in surgery. Total knee replacement."

And he understood all too well what that implied. He reached over the console and grabbed her hand. "I'll be praying for him to make a full recovery."

Her hand inside his shook. He'd shocked her. Smiling to himself, he patted her hand, then returned his to the steering wheel.

In minutes he'd parked in the courthouse lot and ushered Brannon and the girls inside, past security, and into the marshals' office. Demott met him in the main room. "Where have you been?"

"Had to pick up some important witnesses, sir." He gestured to the two girls cowering behind Brannon.

Demott froze, his stare locked on the two young faces. "Are those—?"

"I haven't had time to get any details. I brought them here."

"Good." Demott straightened and met Brannon's concerned look. "Why don't you take them into this room, Ms. Callahan?" He gestured to the larger interrogation room.

"Come on, girls. Let's get out of these heavy coats." She led them into the room, then eased the door shut behind them. Her soothing voice calmed even Roark's excitement.

"What . . . where . . . how?"

Roark held up his hands, knowing how his boss felt. It was all coming together at once. The feelings rushed over him, overwhelming him. "All I know is Brannon brought them in. I don't know anything else."

"The FBI should be part of the interview. These girls could lead us to an operations site for this ring."

"Sir, those kids are terrified. Of men. Did you notice the way they clung to Brannon?"

"What do you suggest, Holland?"

"I'd recommend the FBI bring in a female agent for the questioning. And let Brannon stay. They seem to trust her."

Demott nodded. "Makes sense. If she rescued them, they view her as a savior."

And in many ways Brannon had helped Roark back to his Savior. His throat tightened. "Right."

"I'll talk to the FBI. See how fast they can get a woman agent here." Demott shifted toward the opposite end of the hall. "We'll need to get Ms. Callahan's statement while she's here as well. Agents on-site will take the chief ranger's statement." He paused. "And her partner—how's he?"

"Still in surgery on his knee." Roark grabbed his boss's arm. "Did you get anything more out of Betty?"

"She's still not giving up details. The man Callahan killed has been identified as Frederick Noslen."

"Her husband?"

"Yes. When we told her, hoping it'd get her to open up, she almost passed out." Demott shook his head and stabbed his fingers through his hair. "We're pulling records now. The FBI believes the Noslens brought the girls over from Thailand. Agents are searching their residence."

Roark raked a hand over his face. "What's the status with the books?"

"NSA finally broke the code. All the funds flip around multiple times before landing in seven different offshore accounts. The FBI's securing warrants to obtain the names belonging to the numbered accounts. There's a lot of money. This ring's been operating for some time." Demott flexed his hands, then shook his head. "To think it happened right here, under all of our noses."

"How could one couple have brought over so many girls? The numbers seem staggering."

Demott grimaced. "Fake adoption service."

Sickening. Roark couldn't comprehend people who possessed such malicious intent. And toward children. "Government involvement?"

"Almost has to be. Adoption services overseas require a government permit."

"Could it have been forged?"

"Not likely. Not with TSA and Customs cracking down on regulations."

One man's image flashed before Roark's eyes. Congressman McGovern. "Have we heard from the agents following McGovern?"

"Last I heard they reported he had a visitor who left shortly after arriving at the congressman's house. Since then, no activity."

McGovern was wrapped up in this mess—Roark just knew it. Now to find the evidence to prove it.

THIRTY-ONE

Wednesday, 11:30 p.m.
Congressman McGovern's Home
Knoxville, Tennessee

HAD ZIMP GIVEN HIM the wrong number for Fred? Warren had called the number from his trash cell at least ten times since returning to the house. It went straight to voice mail. Wouldn't that be just like Zimp to give him the wrong number? The kid always felt he was indispensable. Bet he didn't think so now.

Warren swallowed the grin and moved to Zimp's attaché case. More than likely, the laptop contained everyone's phone numbers. Might as well see what the boy wonder saved.

He withdrew the laptop, set it on his desk, and opened the top. As he waited for the system to boot up, Warren stared into the darkness. Had he covered himself well enough? Those fools at NSA, CIA, and FBI hadn't been able to break the code Wilks set up for the books. Would they? Even if they did, could they link the names to the accounts? Wilks had sworn there would be no paper trail. Had he been wrong?

The laptop hummed to life. Warren accessed the Documents folder, then scrolled through the file names. Zimp wasn't overly intelligent so finding the phone numbers shouldn't be too hard. Seriously, some of the file names were laughably naive My Checking, My Savings, Passwords.

Letter to FBI.

Warren's heart hiccupped. He double-clicked on the file and waited for the word processing program to open. It had to be a joke of some sort, although Zimp hadn't seemed particularly witty.

The document opened. The more Warren read, the tighter his gut knotted. Zimp had outlined their operation in great detail. Listing names. Dates. Details. If he hadn't already killed Zimp, he would now.

Warren studied the letter again. No date. When had Zimp written this? Had he already sent a copy to the FBI? He closed the file and hovered the mouse over the file name. Date of last save, this morning.

What had the moron done?

Warren scrolled through the rest of the documents and found nothing interesting. What had Zimp planned to do with the letter? Safety net? Maybe. But he'd been nervous when he'd arrived. If he intended to use the letter as insurance . . .

Warren accessed the e-mail program and scrolled through the Sent folder. Mostly benign e-mails, but one stuck out at Warren—Urgent. He checked the creation date. This morning. He clicked on the e-mail and waited for it to open.

All his careful planning . . . covering his tracks . . . was it all about to come undone because of one ignorant man?

The e-mail appeared on screen. Warren's stomach flipped as he read.

> Bucky,
> In case you don't hear from me by midnight
> tomorrow, print the attached letter and take it to the
> cops. Doesn't matter if they're local or not. They'll
> know who to get it to.
> Thanks,
> Zimp

A headache pounded at Warren's temples. He dropped his head into his hands, massaging his skull. The kid was smarter than Warren gave him credit for being. He'd realized their house of cards was crashing down around them and had taken safeguards.

Didn't matter now if the girls were recovered or not. Warren glanced at the clock—less than thirty minutes until midnight. This

Bucky character would take the letter to the authorities soon, and the gig would be up.

Time for plan B. Time to leave.

Warren slammed the laptop shut and shoved it back into the attaché case. He only needed to grab the suitcase he kept packed in the closet. Like the Boy Scouts, always be prepared. He turned and headed toward the stairs.

Buzz. Buzz.

What in the—

A cell phone set to vibrate. Coming from his office. From Zimp's attaché case.

Warren rushed back to the desk and opened the case. Three cell phones nestled in the outer pocket. He grabbed the one dancing on the crushed velvet. "Hello."

"Zimp?"

"He's not available right now. Who is this?"

"This is Bucky. Who's this?"

Bucky. Warren's pulse kicked up a notch. "This is Zimp's friend. He's been trying to get in touch with you." He fought to keep his tone even. He could save everything.

"Really? I'm not showing any missed calls."

Warren tightened his grip on the cell phone. He had to relate to this Bucky character on his level. "I don't know about that."

"Well, let me talk to him."

"Like I said, he's unavailable."

"How's that?"

Warren pressed his lips together. Think. He could contain the situation. Save himself. "He's packing."

"Packing for what?"

"Jamaica. Didn't he tell you the plan?"

"Jamaica?!" Heavy breathing pulsed against Warren's ear. "What plan?"

"He's going to Jamaica. Said he needed to get away until things died down." Warren needed to think carefully. He had to play this just right. "That's why he's been trying to get in touch with you. He wants you to go with him."

"Why?"

"I don't know. Zimp told me if you called to give you the message to meet him at the McGhee Tyson Airport no later than two a.m. Oh, and he said to bring the letter." Warren paused for effect. "Whatever that means."

"Hmm."

The guy wasn't buying it. Warren almost sighed. He'd been so close. This one character, Bucky, would blow everything apart. "Well, that's what Zimp said. I did what he asked. I'm taking him to the airport as soon as he packs things up." He had to get this guy on board. "Should I tell him you'll meet him at the airport?"

"I'll see." The connection broke.

What was it with the rudeness of people these days? Not even ending a conversation before hanging up. Warren tossed the cell into the attaché, then hurried up the stairs. Maybe he'd gotten through to Bucky, and he'd show up at the airport. At that hour it should be easy enough to take care of one more person. Get this Bucky out of the way, then it'd be smooth sailing.

But if he wasn't lucky, he'd institute his backup plan and catch the next flight to Jamaica. After all, it *was* nice there.

Wednesday, 11:45 p.m.
US Marshals Office, Howard Baker Federal Courthouse
Knoxville, Tennessee

"HELLO, MS. CALLAHAN AND girls. I'm Krista Thomley with the FBI." The lady slipped into the interrogation room with Roark, his boss, and two other FBI agents on her heels. "In order to continue our investigation, I need to ask you girls a few questions if that's okay?" She made eye contact with Mai and Kanya as she eased into a chair across the table from them.

The girls pressed against Brannon to the point they almost fell into the chair with her. She gripped their small hands in hers and shot Roark a warning look.

He grasped her silent message as he guided the other men in the room to the shadows of the corner.

"Hi, Ms. Thomley." Brannon infused her voice with a chipperness she didn't feel. But if the girls picked up on her mood . . . "This is Mai and Kanya." She nodded to each girl as she introduced them.

"Hello, Mai and Kanya." The agent opened her notebook. "I'm here to ask a few questions. To get help for the other girls. Okay?"

Mai hesitated a moment before bobbing her head. Brannon squeezed her hand. *Please, Lord, let this be easier on them.*

"Where are you from?"

"Thailand."

Ms. Thomley's pen flowed across the paper. "Both of you?"

Kanya nodded.

"How did you get to the States?"

Neither girl moved. Brannon released Mai's hand to stroke her hair. "It's okay. Ms. Thomley just wants to help you."

Mai ducked her head. "Poppy Fred and Aunt Betty." Her words were muffled but understandable.

Brannon swallowed back anger. All these girls had been through . . .

Ms. Thomley made notes, then pressed her lips together. "But they aren't relatives to you, are they?"

Mai shook her head.

Bit by bit, the FBI agent drew out the girls' stories, just as Brannon had. Their parents selling them for adoption in order to survive, the girls having such high hopes and dreams for a new, better life, then having their dreams murdered. Brannon wanted to throw up hearing it all again.

Tears burned Brannon's eyes as well. Suddenly she didn't feel so guilty about killing Fred anymore. *Forgive me, Father, but I'm not sorry. Not after hearing what this man did.*

Silence fell over the room when Mai finished the details of how she'd been brought to the States and what had happened then. Finally Ms. Thomley set her pen down, tears visible in her eyes, and addressed the girls. "I'm so sorry for what happened to you. We're going to make sure this doesn't happen again."

The door to the interrogation room creaked open and an agent stuck his head inside. "Child Protective Services is here."

One of the agents from the corner slipped out of the room.

"Now I need to ask you details about your escape," Ms. Thomley continued. "You've told us how you got supplies and extra clothes. Can you tell us about the place you stayed?"

Mai shrugged.

Hopelessness washed over Brannon. If they were to find the other girls . . . No, she would not allow herself to think so dejectedly. She shifted in her seat to face Mai. "When you left, you said you went out the kitchen door. Was that in the back of the house?"

"Yes."

Ms. Thomley caught on. "Did you run behind the house, or circle around and run away from the front of the house?"

"Back."

"How long did you run before you made the camp where I found you?" Brannon grabbed a piece of paper from Ms. Thomley and jotted something down.

"I do not know." Mai's bottom lip trembled.

Brannon patted her hand. "It's okay." She slid the paper across the table to the FBI agent. "Here are the coordinates where I found them."

The male agent returned. "Excuse me, but CPS said to let them know whenever you're ready. They'll take the girls to the hospital before being escorted to the safe house."

Brannon glanced at the girls. Their lids were weighted down. She made eye contact with the lady agent. "They've had a long day and are exhausted. I don't think you'll get anything more from them right now."

Ms. Thomley understood. "I think we're done here anyway. Let CPS in."

The agent slipped back outside. Ms. Thomley addressed the girls a final time. "Thank you both. One last question, if you can answer. About how many other girls are at the house?"

The agent returned, this time with two ladies wearing CPS badges.

Brannon stood and helped Mai and Kanya to their feet as the CPS ladies hovered over them, ushering them out.

Mai stopped at the door and faced Ms. Thomley. She held up her hands, separating her fingers.

Ms. Thomley gasped. "Ten?"

Mai shook her head. She closed her hands, then opened them. Once, twice.

Thirty other girls.

Wednesday, Midnight
US Marshals Office, Howard Baker Federal Courthouse
Knoxville, Tennessee

"GET ME AN AREA map." Roark cleared the table of the interrogation room as chaos erupted.

CPS escorted the girls from the courthouse. He didn't worry about them—they'd be kept secure at a safe house. But their tearful separation from Brannon almost ripped Roark's heart from his chest. He probably could have gotten her clearance to go with the girls, but he needed her here. She knew the area better than anyone in the building.

To save the other girls, time was of the essence. Thirty girls . . . right under their noses. He focused on one of the agents. "Take this info to Betty Noslen. See if she'll break and give us the location of the brothel."

The agent rushed from the room.

Roark spread out the map another FBI agent brought him, then glanced at Brannon. "Where'd you pick them up?"

She leaned over the table, her silky hair spilling over the side of her face. She pointed to a place on the edge of the Great Smoky Mountains National Park.

Everyone hunched over the map.

Roark set his finger on the only town close enough for the girls to have run to the area Brannon indicated. "Townsend."

One of the FBI agents lifted his cell phone. "We already have agents in the area. I'll get them to check the outlying areas south of the city."

"Get more teams in the area," Ms. Thomley added.

Everyone milled about, talking into cell phones or radios. The FBI agents geared up for a full launch, flooding from the courthouse to their office blocks away to arm themselves.

Roark glanced at Brannon. "Guess we'll have to wait to hear how it goes."

She shot him one of those quirky smiles of hers. "Not really. I happen to have a helicopter close by, and I know the area." She cocked her head. "Wanna come fly with me?"

THIRTY-TWO

Thursday, 12:25 a.m.
US Marshals Office, Howard Baker Federal Courthouse
Knoxville, Tennessee

BEFORE ROARK COULD ANSWER her, the door to the interrogation room flew open, and an agent rushed inside. "Betty's turned and is talking up a storm. She gave us the location just outside of Townsend." The younger man couldn't hide the excitement in his voice.

Exhilaration chased anticipation inside Brannon. Soon they'd have the rest of the girls safe. *Please, God, keep them safe until we find them.*

The other two FBI agents hurried from the room, filling the hallways with orders to dispatch teams to be on their way to the location. Brannon stood to the side, helpless amid all the activity. What should she do now?

Gerald Demott appeared at her elbow. "The FBI is setting up a base downstairs in the conference room on the first floor. Roark, you need to be there."

Roark's boss smiled at her. "You need to come as well. So they can take your statement."

She slowly exhaled. She'd at least get to participate in the outcome. Be in the loop when they rescued the other girls. *Please, God, let no one else be hurt by this ring. Especially no more children.*

She nodded and followed Mr. Demott to the elevators, stretching her stride to match Roark's. Walking beside him, a sense of safety flowed from him. She felt secure. It felt . . . right.

"Any news on Lincoln?" Roark motioned her into the elevator car in front of him and his boss.

She checked her cell phone. No missed calls. "Nothing yet. Thanks for pulling strings to let me keep my phone." Security had tried to nab it, as was courthouse policy, but Roark took her phone and slipped it in his pocket until they'd reached the marshals' office.

"Not a problem. I'm praying Lincoln will be okay." Again Roark allowed her to precede him and Mr. Demott from the elevator. Then his boss took the lead down the hall.

Again a praying comment. Brannon slowed, letting distance grow between them and Mr. Demott. "Um, Roark?"

"Yeah?"

"I've noticed you've made a couple of references to praying." It was a statement, but she hoped he'd answer her unasked question.

"Yeah."

No such luck. He wasn't going to make it easy on her. "I thought you and God weren't on good terms." She held her breath, willing him to explain without her having to probe further.

"We weren't." A long pause hung between them. He chuckled. "But I've since seen the error of my wicked ways."

Something inside her spirit leapt forth. She forced herself to remain calm, even. "Really?"

"Yeah."

"When did this happen?"

He smiled as he opened the door to the conference room for her. "Oh, about the time I prayed for Him to keep a certain lady ranger safe when she was in a shoot-out."

Her throat tightened. She wanted to discuss the topic further, but they'd walked into a hub of activity. Mr. Demott spoke to an agent who gave Brannon a funny look, then hurried off.

"Someone will be here in a second to get your statement," Mr. Demott explained. "Roark, head to the back of the room."

Roark paused, staring at her. Her heartbeat raced under his scrutiny. Her pulse pounded. Time stood still.

"Ms. Callahan?" A young agent stopped in front of them. "If you'll come with me, I'll take your statement across the hall in another conference room."

Roark gave her a quick wink before rushing toward the back of the area.

Brannon sighed and faced the young agent. If only she didn't have to give this statement, if only she could stay with Roark . . .

God, have You sent another man into my life? Roark? I'm feeling all these emotions toward him and am so confused. If being with him isn't what You want, I pray You'll remove these feelings I have for him. I don't think my heart can take being broken again. I'm so scared, God. Scared of being hurt. Scared of being alone. Oh, Lord, I'm a mess. Please, help me—give me wisdom of what to do.

Thursday, 1:05 a.m.
Howard Baker Federal Courthouse
Knoxville, Tennessee

THE FBI UNITS ALREADY in the area left for the location, sirens wailing and lights strobing. The FBI had men in a helicopter heading there as well. Roark wandered around the conference room, waiting to hear that someone had arrived on-site. He should be there. He'd worked the case, followed the leads.

He couldn't even be with Brannon, who sat across the hall, giving her statement. He'd shocked her with his words—he'd seen the expression on her face. But how did she feel about it?

How did she feel about *him*?

"Stop pacing. You're making me dizzy." Demott stood and stretched his arms over his head.

"I hate the waiting."

His boss chuckled. "Then you're in the wrong profession, Holland. You should know better."

"I do. I got filled in on the hurry-up-and-wait method of government years ago."

"Then why so antsy now?"

Good question. "Guess this case is important. The kids. And seeing Mai and Kanya . . . well, it made the horrors real. Personal." He let out a heavy sigh. "After losing Mindy . . . I don't think I could take it if more innocents were hurt."

"I understand."

"And so many have paid a high price because of this case." Roark shook his head. "So useless."

"Marshal Demott and Holland, come see." An agent motioned from across the room.

Maybe there was word already.

They hustled to the agent's desk in the corner. He gestured to the fax machine the US Attorney's office had brought in for them. "Our office got a call from a Blount County sheriff's deputy. Said a guy brought in a letter addressed to the FBI. He's gonna fax it right over."

Letter? Roark leaned against the wall beside the fax machine, willing it to come to life. "From who?"

"Buddy Zimp."

Every nerve in Roark's body jumped on alert. What a break this could be. "What else did the deputy say?"

"The guy dropped it off and mentioned the person who wrote it would be boarding a plane to Jamaica soon, then left."

The fax machine rang, then a sequence of modem tones pierced the room. Roark held his breath as the machine spit out a sheet of paper. A second piece fell before the disconnect click sounded.

The agent grabbed the sheets and scanned them. He passed them to Roark, his eyes wide. Roark grabbed the papers and read. The reason for writing the letter? Fear of being killed. Within the letter Buddy Zimp named everyone involved in the child-trafficking ring:

Jonathan Wilks, moneyman
Tom Hurst, heat
Milton Anderson, heat and transporter
Betty and Frederick Noslen, couriers
Nancy Blackship, overseer of prostitutes
Buddy Zimp, go-between man from boss to others
Congressman Warren McGovern, boss

Roark's heart paused. He lifted his gaze to Demott's. "Bet we can get that warrant for McGovern now."

Demott nodded. "I'll call Noah Markinson. He'll find a judge to sign." He glanced at the FBI agent. "We need to call NSA. They should be able to link the accounts now that we have the names. And get Daly in here."

Proof the congressman *was* involved sat in his hands. Roark had known it. Now he'd get to arrest the scum of the earth. He looked at the FBI agent. "Get your agents watching the congressman on the phone, please."

Thursday, 1:26 a.m.
McGhee Tyson Airport
Alcoa, Tennessee—Fifteen Miles South of Knoxville

THE AIRPORT WAS AS dead as Zimp.

Warren sat in a borrowed car in the parking lot, monitoring activity. Even the airline representatives were missing from the front counters. Only a couple of TSA employees wandered about inside. Good. If Bucky showed up, Warren would handle the loose end.

If Bucky showed up.

Warren had been careful. He'd snuck to his next-door neighbors' who were out of town, used the key they'd left with him, and borrowed their car. No sense having his car seen out in the area if he could take care of Bucky. And if he didn't . . . He glanced at his E-ticket. A 5:10 flight to Atlanta. From Atlanta he'd head to Montego Bay.

If Bucky didn't show. That would be the only reason Warren would leave. Because if the character came to the airport, Warren would eliminate the threat he posed. Get the letter, contain the risk. Then back to business as usual.

Surely Bucky would come. What half-wit wouldn't want a free trip to the Caribbean? Sure, he'd sounded suspicious on the phone, but Warren had little doubt the man wasn't rocket scientist material. After all, he'd been close to Zimp, so how smart could he be? He'd come.

Warren pulled the houndstooth bowler hat lower over his forehead. No one would recognize him unless they saw him up close and under lights. In the shadows of the parking lot, that wouldn't happen.

He glanced at his watch—1:45. If this Bucky showed, it would be in the next fifteen minutes. Warren reached into his coat pocket, his gloved fingers grazing the handle of his mother's handgun. How different his life would've been had his mother lived. He still missed her so much.

Growing up with the Colonel had made him strong, independent. The traits men were made of. Superior to women in all ways.

Yet Warren couldn't help but remember his mother. The softness of her skin. Her feathery kisses on his brow before bed. The warmth of her hugs.

He shook his head. No, he wouldn't allow himself to remember. His father had taught him not to live in the past. Not to show weakness—not then, not now, not ever.

To distract himself, Warren flipped on the car's radio. He scanned through stations, most with annoyingly loud guitars and screaming or twangy whining. Finally a newscast flowed from the speakers. A weather report. Cold, but no prediction of precipitation. That was good news. At least if he had to leave, the weather wouldn't delay his flight.

A commercial replaced the droning of the weatherman's voice. Warren flexed his fingers, keeping them limber. He stared out the windshield. Watching for any sign of a vehicle.

Another commercial followed the two previous. This one more stupid advertising for a useless product. Was the general public really that ignorant to fall prey to such ploys? Warren smiled. They were.

"Here's late-breaking news. Following the death of the witness in an alleged child-trafficking ring here in Tennessee, joint efforts between the FBI and US Marshals have led investigators to a location outside of Townsend. Ten minutes ago, units arrived and discovered underage Asian girls. Stay tuned for further information as it develops."

Warren froze. The blood rushed to his head, his pulse drowning out the radio. His hands trembled as an automobile's headlights pierced the darkness of the airport parking lot. No, he was still safe. Nancy had run, and besides, she didn't know him, had never seen him. He'd certainly never gone to the house. Why would he? Those girls were dirty—reminded him too much of his father's mistress. And her daughters. But Warren couldn't be connected to the ring. No one knew about his involvement. No one but Wilks and Zimp, and they'd been eliminated.

That left just Bucky and the stupid letter Zimp had written. Sever the last two threads and he'd be home free. The authorities finding the girls meant nothing. Not to him.

He concentrated on the car parking down the row from him, under the harsh security lights. His mind already turned to the press conference he'd hold later this morning, regaling the success of the FBI's raid.

Once again he'd come out on top. Just like he always did.

THIRTY-THREE

Thursday, 1:55 a.m.
Howard Baker Federal Courthouse
Knoxville, Tennessee

"WE'VE GOT THE WARRANT for Congressman McGovern. Judge Lewis signed it even though he wasn't thrilled about us waking him at this hour." Samuel Harper, a new member of the Marshal team, rushed into the room waving his fist. He grinned at Roark. "Mr. Demott said you get to do the honors."

Roark's muscles tensed. This was it. He nodded to the FBI agent. "Get in touch with the agents watching McGovern. Find out if he's still at the house. Tell them to knock on the door and tell McGovern we have new information." He winked at Brannon, who'd only just rejoined him.

The agent nodded and lifted his phone as Gerald Demott entered.

"You don't want to just show up and arrest him?" Demott stared at him as if he'd lost his mind.

As much as he wanted that gratification . . . "If he gets wind we're on our way, he'll flee. I'd rather be positive he's there."

"Marshal Holland?"

Roark faced the FBI agent.

"The agents on the McGovern detail report there are no lights on in the house and no one answered the door."

Stomach knotting, Roark clenched his fists. "He's gone. How'd he get out without your agents seeing him?"

"They report his car is still in the garage."

"Let me talk to him." Roark held out his hand. The agent spoke into the phone before passing it to Roark. "Hello."

"Agent Watson, sir."

"Agent Watson, how close to his residence are you?"

"Three driveways down. But they're pretty long driveways."

Roark ignored the heavy sigh rising in his chest. "How long ago did he have a visitor?"

"Car arrived around nine thirty. Left about thirty minutes later."

"How many people were in the car when it arrived? When it left?"

"Sir, it's dark out and we're supposed to keep a low profile."

"Are you telling me you don't know?"

"No, sir. We don't."

"Please tell me you at least got a license plate."

"Yes, sir. It's, uh . . ." The rustling of paper grated against Roark's ear. "Tennessee 986 PDQ. Knox County."

Roark wrote it on a scrap piece of paper and passed it to the agent. "Trace it."

"Sir?" Agent Watson asked.

"And no other vehicle has come or gone since then?"

"His next-door neighbor left around twelve thirty. Hasn't returned."

"Did you get that plate?"

"Um, no, sir."

This time Roark released the sigh. "And you're positive McGovern's not in the house? Maybe upstairs or where he can't hear you knocking?"

"No lights are on, sir, and he didn't answer the door. We banged pretty hard. There's nothing—no television, radio, or anything."

Yep, he'd run. And the FBI let him.

"Keep watching. We're sending marshals there with a warrant." Although they wouldn't have anyone to take into custody.

"Yes, sir."

Roark passed the phone back to the agent in the room and turned to his boss. "He's gone."

Brannon's face went blank. "Gone? People don't just disappear."

"I know. He had a friend visit around nine thirty, stayed for about half an hour, then left." Roark nodded at the agent on another phone. "He's running a trace on the plate."

"You think he left with his friend?" Demott asked.

"Probably. But the agents also said his next-door neighbor left around twelve thirty and hasn't returned."

"So, he could have left with his neighbor?" Brannon chewed on the skin beside her fingernail again. Why did he find that nervous trait so endearing? She dropped her hand and flipped her hair over her shoulder.

He caught a whiff of her spicy shampoo. His stomach twisted. He stiffened, willing himself to concentrate. "He could have. He might have." Roark sat on the edge of the conference table and stabbed a hand through his hair. "The question is—where did he go?"

Thursday, 2:00 a.m.
McGhee Tyson Airport
Alcoa, Tennessee

THE YOUNG MAN EASED out of his older car, glancing about the parking lot.

Warren turned off the radio and gauged the man's every step. Bucky? Had to be. Warren flashed the headlights on, then off again.

The man stared at the car, hesitating.

"Come on, Bucky. Come on over," Warren whispered in the darkness. He flashed the lights again.

Moving as slow as Christmas, the man ambled to the passenger side of the car and ducked down.

Warren adjusted his hat even further over his eyebrows and lowered the window. "Bucky?"

"Yeah. Who are you? Where's Zimp?"

"Zimp's inside." Warren delivered the lie he'd carefully constructed. "Had to check his luggage. He'll be right back."

Bucky glanced toward the front counters inside. "I don't see him."

Warren lifted what he hoped looked like a casual shoulder. "Guess he went to the men's room. Left me out in the cold to wait for you."

The suggestion worked as Warren had hoped. Bucky ran his hands up and down his arms. "Is mighty chilly."

Oh, the guy definitely had Zimp's intellect level. "Hop in and get out of the wind. Zimp said he'd return with our tickets." He pressed the button, unlocking the door with an echoing click.

"You going, too?" Bucky's eyes narrowed.

Warren nodded and gruffed his voice. "Yeah. Zimp better not stiff me."

Bucky chuckled and reached for the door handle. "Me either." He eased into the front seat, blowing into his cupped, bare hands. "You know who I am. Who are you?"

"The moneyman of the operation."

Bucky peered into Warren's face. "What operation?"

Time to pick the guy's brains. Well, what he had of them. "Come on, man, don't play with me. Zimp told me he sent you a letter outlining everything."

Bucky nodded.

"Good thing you didn't take it to the cops, huh?" Warren forced a laugh. "Otherwise, we wouldn't get out of here."

Bucky ducked his head.

Warren reached into his pocket. The idiot had sent the letter. Rage burned through Warren's gut as he tightened his grip on the gun. "You sent the letter?"

Bucky's Adam's apple bobbed. "Dude, Zimp told me to deliver it if he didn't call me before midnight."

Clenching his jaw, Warren scrambled to think. "Did you mail it?"

"No, Zimp said to deliver it to the cops."

"Where did you take it?"

Bucky shrugged. "Local sheriff's office."

"When?" As dimwitted as the locals were, they might not have had the intelligence to forward the letter.

"'Bout an hour ago."

And nothing had been on the newscast. Warren mentally thanked the laziness of sheriffs' offices everywhere. "Did you say anything?"

Bucky cocked his head to the side. "Hey, why're you asking so many questions?" His stare darted to the airport's front windows. "And if Zimp's getting our tickets, how come nobody's at the counter?"

Warren slipped the gun from his pocket and lifted the butt.

Whack!

The side of the gun made clean contact with the back of Bucky's head. He slumped forward in the seat.

Warren let out the breath he'd been holding. He finally got to use some of the physical training the Colonel had made him endure.

He glanced at his watch—2:20. He'd have to hurry and find a place to get rid of Bucky, then get back to the airport before four thirty.

Looked like he'd go to Brazil. No extradition treaty to worry about.

Thursday, 2:35 a.m.
US Marshals Office, Howard Baker Federal Courthouse
Knoxville, Tennessee

"AT THE LEAST HE has a two-hour head start. At the most, a little over four hours." Roark paced the conference room.

"He could be almost anywhere." Brannon's entire body ached for Roark. The urge to embrace him almost had her taking a step forward. But she forced herself to focus instead. To think.

"Marshal Holland?"

Roark turned back to the agent. "Yes?"

"We have a hit on the plate."

Brannon's pulse spiked.

Roark stood and moved to the desk in the corner. "And?"

"It's registered to Buddy Zimp."

Facing Demott, Roark shook his head. "No way he left with him. Not after the letter."

"Then he had to have left with the neighbor." Demott rubbed his hands together. "Which means he only has a two-hour lead."

"But that still doesn't tell us where he's gone." Brannon picked at her nail again.

Think. Something was there. A clue. But where? She reached for the information teasing her from the edge of her subconscious. It was right there . . . like a smoky wisp.

She snapped her fingers and stared at Roark. "Before the fax, the guy who delivered the letter to the deputy—what did he say about Zimp?"

"What?"

"He told the deputy something about who'd written the letter. What was it?"

The FBI agent stood from his desk. "Oh, that he'd board a plane to Jamaica soon."

"That's it. We should check to see if Buddy Zimp and Warren McGovern have reservations to Jamaica. Or if Zimp already left."

The agent lifted the phone.

"You think McGovern's going with Zimp?" Roark shook his head. "Doesn't make sense."

"No, I think the deliverer was right and Zimp's already gone. I think the congressman's going to make sure Zimp's out of the picture." Her muscles bunched with pure adrenaline.

"I don't follow," Demott said.

"Zimp comes to visit McGovern. Maybe they argue, maybe not. Who knows? But Zimp leaves. Most likely straight from McGovern's to the airport." Roark's steps bounced as he paced. "McGovern knows Zimp's headed to Jamaica. If he wants to keep his hands clean, he needs to make sure Zimp doesn't talk to us."

"So he doesn't get caught," Brannon added.

"Right. He doesn't know about the letter."

"Marshal Holland?"

"Yes?" Roark turned toward the FBI agent.

"Buddy Zimp didn't fly to Jamaica today, nor does he have any reservations to do so."

No, they couldn't be wrong. Brannon *knew* they were on the right track. "And Congressman McGovern?"

The agent smiled. "Booked on the 5:10 flight to Atlanta out of McGhee Tyson Airport, with continuing service to Brazil."

Roark grinned at his boss. "Let's lock and load, rock and roll."

"Wait a minute." Demott glanced at his watch. "It's nearing three now. His flight is at 5:10, which means they'll board around four thirty. The airport's a good twenty minutes from here." He rubbed his chin. "I'll call the airline and hold the boarding."

Roark nodded. "Good idea."

"Would it help if you could get to the airport in about five minutes?" Brannon asked.

"You bet it would," Demott said. "But even Roark can't drive that fast."

Brannon's chest filled with elation. "Then it's a good thing I can fly."

THIRTY-FOUR

Thursday, 3:00 a.m.
Downtown
Knoxville, Tennessee

FUNNY THING, FLYING IN the small helicopter didn't bother Roark now. His breathing came out in regular rhythm. His heart rate escalated only in anticipation of arresting McGovern. Or maybe because he sat so close to Brannon.

Demott sat in the backseat, checking and rechecking his handgun. Roark understood—he'd checked his Beretta about four times during the short flight.

Roark listened as she spoke with air traffic control over her headset while piloting the helicopter. That didn't make him nervous—her having ultimate control over the aircraft. Odd how he trusted her implicitly.

Maybe it was more that he trusted God again. And it felt really good.

Brannon completed her conversation with ATC and smiled at him. "We're really going to get him."

He grinned. She was as excited as he. A match made in heaven.

Roark stilled and mentally repeated his phrase. A match made in heaven—could it be? Had God orchestrated everything this way? God had used Brannon to bring him back to his faith. Could He intend for Roark and Brannon to end up together?

God, please let it be so.

He couldn't imagine being in a relationship with Brannon, but he sure looked forward to trying it out.

"Okay, we're coming in. The tower has cleared me to land in the back so we're not visible from the lobby." She dipped the helicopter lower over the airport. "This way the congressman won't see us."

"Good. We want to take him by surprise."

"Amen to that," Demott mumbled.

Brannon landed the helicopter with little more than a bump. "Here we are." She flipped controls. Lights on the instrument panel went dim. "I need to do my postflight. Go ahead and get inside. I'll find you."

Demott jumped from the seat and glanced at Roark. "Let's head to the security office. The FBI will meet us there."

"Go ahead. I'll be right behind you." Roark grabbed her hand as Demott ran inside. If something happened to him, he wanted her to know that he cared about her. Deeply. Seriously.

She went motionless, meeting his gaze with wide eyes. "What's wrong?"

"Nothing." Roark leaned over, and as gently as she'd landed the helicopter, he pressed his lips to hers.

At first she went rigid, then relaxed. His heart raced. Roark wrapped an arm around her, pulling her closer. She melted against him. He reached up, grabbing the silky strands of her hair, and deepened the kiss, letting his emotions come through.

She moaned against his mouth, sending his blood pressure through the roof. Reluctantly he ended the kiss and drew back. He rested his forehead against hers, staring into her eyes.

Those mismatched eyes of hers blinked a range of emotional reaction—shock, surprise . . . and yearning.

His pulse reacted by drowning out all sounds around them. His body nearly followed suit and eased in for another kiss, but his mind halted his actions. Right now he needed to arrest McGovern, put the lowlife behind bars. But afterward . . .

"We'll talk later," he breathed.

Brannon's face flushed, the skin around her mouth rosy from where his stubble had grazed her soft skin. She nodded, then swallowed.

He smiled, pecked the end of her nose, then opened the door and jumped from the helicopter. "Either stay with the helicopter or go straight to the airport security office. I'm not kidding around, Brannon."

"I'll, uh, be there. As soon as, uh, I finish. My postflight."

He grinned and ran into the building. Getting to arrest McGovern . . . hope for a future with an amazing woman he could fluster . . .

Today looked to be a wonderful day indeed.

Thursday, 3:12 a.m.
McGhee Tyson Airport
Alcoa, Tennessee

WHAT A KISS! IT'D made her toes curl. And that was a good thing.

Brannon finished her postflight walkaround, running a finger over her lips every so often. She could almost feel Roark's lips on hers and had relived it at least a dozen times already.

She shook her head and rushed toward the airport doors. No matter how breathless the kiss made her—how breathless Roark made her—he was here to do a job. Bring Congressman McGovern to justice for all the horrors he'd inflicted on numerous children.

But once that was done . . . oh, she and Roark would definitely talk.

Brannon welcomed the blast of warm air that brushed against her face as she headed into the airport. She could detect few people in the building. A woman strode to the ladies' room. A man with a white shirt boasting the TSA logo bustled down a corridor. Otherwise the airport sat as still as a tomb. Kind of creepy, in a way. But good. Arresting the congressman without a lot of people about was probably a good thing.

Now where was the security office?

Tweedle. Tweedle.

She jerked her cell phone from her hip and flipped it open. "Hello?"

"Brannon, it's Jefferson. Everything's okay."

Stopping to slump against the wall, she glanced at her watch. "Lincoln's out of surgery?"

"Not exactly."

"I thought you said everything was okay." Her knees felt like oatmeal.

"He's okay. The nurse just came out and told me he'd be in surgery another thirty minutes."

"Why?" *Oh, God, please take care of Lincoln. Please.*

"She said they found more ligament and tendon damage than they'd expected, so they have to repair all that."

Fatigue pressed down on her, pushing her past exhaustion. She turned to face the back entrance to the airport. "But he'll be all right?"

"The nurse said he'd be out of surgery and in recovery soon. I thought you'd want to know."

"Of course."

"Steve's here."

She should be there as well. Waiting and praying for Lincoln. Conflicting responsibilities ripped her heart in two.

"What's happening there? We caught the newscast about the FBI finding the girls."

Brannon didn't have the energy to rehash everything. The long hours and little sleep caught up with her in a draining sensation that left her limp. "I'll fill you in when I get there."

"Don't rush back, Brannon. Lincoln's fine, and he won't be awake for an hour or so at the earliest. Take care of things on your end."

An update that sent her packing for a guilt trip. How could she not be at Lincoln's side?

"We'll stay with Lincoln and catch up when you get here." He disconnected the call before she could argue.

Brannon closed her eyes and rested the back of her head against the wall. *God, please keep Lincoln safe. Let him be o—*

A clammy hand over her mouth and cold steel pressing into her side yanked her from her prayer.

Thursday, 3:39 a.m.
McGhee Tyson Airport
Alcoa, Tennessee

WARREN JABBED THE GUN deeper into Brannon Callahan's side.

Her eyes shot open, panic filling them when she recognized him. Good. She deserved to be scared.

"Don't say a word. Understand?"

She nodded.

"I'm removing my hand, but if you so much as breathe too loudly, I'll shoot you. Got it?"

Again she nodded.

He pulled his hand away, leaning closer to her. "Well, well, well, Ms. Callahan. We must stop running into each other like this." He clucked his tongue and shook his head. "What will people say about us?"

She swallowed hard. Fear shot into her face faster than the bullet had lodged into Bucky's skull.

"Let's take a walk, shall we?"

The terror seemed to have paralyzed her. He dug the gun barrel harder into her side. "I said, let's take a walk outside."

She stumbled for a moment, then allowed him to lead her across the building and out the front doors.

Wind gusted around them, swirling and stealing their breath. Fitting, Warren supposed with a smile. He'd steal Ms. Callahan's life as soon as he learned what had happened. Who had come for him.

How fortuitous to have spied her as soon as he'd entered the airport. Her presence could mean only one thing—they'd received the letter and figured out he would leave town. An ambush awaited him, of that Warren could be certain. But by finding Brannon, he'd thwarted their plans.

The thought of shooting down the arrogance of the FBI put a smile on Warren's face and determination in his grip on the gun.

He shoved her toward the long-term parking lot where he'd left his neighbor's car.

She tripped over loose rocks, then steadied herself. "You won't get away with this, Congressman."

Ah, her spunk and fire had returned. Good. He'd grown weary of besting wimpy victims. He'd enjoy robbing this one of her life. "You think not?"

"No."

He laughed as they reached the car. He pushed her against the hood, meeting her steely gaze. "So tell me, where's good ol' Marshal Holland, huh? Where's he hiding out, waiting for me to show?" He pointed the gun straight at Brannon's head. "And don't insult my intelligence by pretending he's not here."

She swallowed so hard he could hear the gulp. "He's in the security office."

Oh, he enjoyed this more than he had anything in a long time. "So far from the action?"

Her eyes went cold, and she shot him a glare that could freeze an ice cube. Anger . . . hatred . . . he liked it.

"What about those pesky FBI agents? Waiting at the terminal? Hiding on the plane already?"

"No, they aren't here." She lifted her chin, staring at him with those different-colored eyes.

Little spiders of unease skittered up his spine and spread across his shoulders. Goose bumps pimpled his arms.

No, he wouldn't let this woman bluff him, toy with him, and make him second-guess himself. The Colonel would come after him from the grave if Warren allowed a *woman* to get the best of him.

"I suppose I'll just have to alter my plans somewhat." He gestured her toward the driver's door. "Feel up to a little trip, Ms. Callahan?"

"Look, why don't you run? Get away before they arrest you. Leave me here."

"Right." He snorted. What kind of idiot did she take him for? How insulting for this woman to believe she could play him? "Get in the car."

She hesitated.

He leveled the gun barrel at her temple. "I said, get in. Don't make me tell you again. You've tried my patience long enough."

She reached for the handle.

"McGovern!" Marshal Holland's voice exploded behind him.

Warren glanced over his shoulder.

The car door rammed into his side. *Oof!*

He spun and his face met with Brannon's fist. Searing pain shot through his right cheekbone. His head jerked left.

He raised the gun, leveling the barrel at her. She moved fast— her blow smacked against the top of his shoulder.

Stinging advanced down his arm. His hand became incapable of a grip. The gun clattered to the concrete.

Brannon whipped around the door and shoved him to the ground. His hip landed on loose rocks, digging into his sensitive flesh. He moaned as he rolled to his hands and knees. He had to get to his feet. Grab the gun.

"Don't *you* move, Congressman." She stood above him, his mother's gun in her hand . . . pointing at his chest.

THIRTY-FIVE

Thursday, 4:45 a.m.
Fort Sanders Sevier Medical Center
Sevierville, Tennessee

"SOUNDS LIKE I MISSED a great time." Lincoln shifted against the hospital bed in his private room.

Brannon laughed, relieved her friend had come through the surgery well. "I don't know about that. I'm just glad it's over."

Lincoln sobered. "Me too. I'm even more glad the congressman didn't hurt you."

Tears she couldn't blink back welled in her eyes.

"Hey." He reached for her hand, gripping it in his cold one. "It's okay. We're fine."

"But your knee. If I'd acted faster, maybe you wouldn't have gotten shot."

Lincoln squeezed her hand. "Don't think like that."

She sniffed, but the tears demanded release.

"Aw, Brannon. You have no control over stuff like that. 'Why, you do not even know what will happen tomorrow. What is your life? You are a mist that appears for a little while and then vanishes.'"

Smiling through her tears and fighting her tumultuous emotions, Brannon wiped her face. "Book of James."

"Chapter and verse?"

She grinned, never able to stand firm against Lincoln's infectious positive outlook. "Four, fourteen."

"Very good." He adjusted his IV before leveling her with a parental stare. "Now, talk to me about Roark."

Her heart skipped a beat. "He took the congressman back to the courthouse for processing."

"That's not what I mean, hon, and you know it."

She let out a long breath, then forced a yawn. "Don't you need your rest?"

"Oh no. You don't get off that easy. I don't care that you look like you need to be poured into bed. I want to know what's happening with you. And Roark." He winked at her. "Come on, spill."

"How do you know something's going on?" She jabbed him gently in the side. "You think the surgery gave you ESP or something?"

"No, Ms. Smarty, I just know you. I can read you like a book."

"Can you now?"

"Yep, and whenever you mention his name, you blush, and your eyes get all misty." He pointed at her. "So you can deny it all you want, but there's something between you two, and I want to know what."

Busted. She dipped her head, the heat spreading across her face just thinking of Roark. Remembering their kiss. The feelings it sent flooding through her.

"Brannon?" Lincoln's tone turned serious. Dead serious.

She raised her head and met his stare.

"This is it, isn't it? He's the one."

"No. Maybe. I don't know." How to answer such a loaded question? She really couldn't explain. She hadn't had a chance to talk to Roark after he'd stormed onto the scene with the congressman. She'd been whisked off to give another statement to the FBI, then rushed straight to the hospital. Brannon didn't know what to make of their kiss. Of her feelings for him.

"Honey, I know. I can tell."

Misery weighed on her shoulders like an iron shawl. "Is it that obvious?" What if Roark's feelings didn't run as deep?

"Only to someone who knows you like I do." Lincoln took her hand again. "Talk to me, Brannon."

"I don't understand why I'm so hesitant. He's given his life back to Christ, he's not involved with anyone else, and he's a good man.

Why am I so reluctant?" She shook her head. "And no, I don't feel like I'm still committed to Wade, so don't give me that lecture."

"I know you're not. But, hon, it's not doubt holding you back."

"Really? Then what is it, O Wise One?"

Lincoln didn't give in to her joking. His expression remained somber and tense. "It's fear."

"Fear?" Just saying the word made something resonate inside her. Lincoln was dead-on.

"Fear of loving again. Fear of losing."

"But I didn't feel so reserved with Wade." Saying his name aloud didn't hurt this time. The first time ever. But what would Lincoln think of her falling for someone else? Wade was his brother. Did he feel like she'd betrayed him?

"Because Wade was your first love. Everything was roses and candy. You thought y'all had forever. But then you lost him. Now you're scared to love again because you don't want to chance getting hurt again. Of losing someone else you love."

Lincoln nailed her feelings exactly.

He squeezed her hand. "Brannon, Roark isn't Wade. He isn't supposed to be. He won't replace what you felt for my brother." He rubbed his thumb over her knuckles. "Roark's a new love for a new stage in your life. He's the promise of your future."

Silent tears tracked down her cheeks. "But I haven't known him that long."

"And you didn't know Wade more than a few weeks before you were sure." Lincoln sighed. "Sometimes God puts that special someone in your path and you just know. Your heart recognizes the person as *the one*."

"But only after a week?"

"Tell me where there's a time line written for a heart to open up to love?" He shook his head. "I'm not telling you to run off and elope anytime soon, but closing off your heart to the possibility of a lasting love relationship . . . Well, I don't think that's healthy."

"What should I do?"

Lincoln grinned. "I'm not an expert in relationships, obviously. Only you can decide where to go from here." He pressed her hand to his lips and gave it a gentle kiss. "I just don't want you to let fear stop you from being happy. God wouldn't want that, either. Scripture tells us over and over that fear is not of God."

As always, Lincoln spoke the truth in love. She squeezed his hand back. "Will you pray with me to discern God's will for me with Roark?"

Thursday, 5:30 a.m.
Fort Sanders Sevier Medical Center
Sevierville, Tennessee

BRANNON SLEPT IN THE chair in the waiting room, hair splayed across the cheap vinyl. Her lips were slightly parted as her chest rose and fell rhythmically.

Roark stood over her for a moment, watching her sleep. She looked peaceful . . . angelic. Yet she still radiated that quiet inner strength of hers.

He slipped into the chair beside her, then eased her head onto his chest. She settled without opening her eyes. He let his fingertips stroke the sleek strands of her hair. The silkiness caressed his touch. Strange sensations, ones he'd never felt before, did odd things to him. Logic and reasoning fled. His mind warred with his emotions, and he hadn't a clue how to call a cease-fire.

God, thank You for keeping her safe. I don't know what I'd have done if McGovern had hurt her. I think I'm falling in love with her. We've only known each other for a week or so, but I've never been so sure of what I felt.

He dipped his head, planting a feathery kiss on her crown.

Her eyes fluttered, then went wide. She bolted upright. "Roark."

"Brannon." He grinned at her.

She wiped at her eyes and smoothed her hair. "When did you get here?"

"A few minutes ago." She looked downright cute with the remains of sleep hovering in her expression. "Where are Jefferson and Steve? I thought they'd still be here."

"I sent them home to get some sleep."

He tweaked her chin. "Like you don't need any, Wonder Woman?"

A tinge of pink dotted her cheeks. "I wanted to wait and see Lincoln one more time before I catch a few winks."

Roark tucked an errant strand of her hair behind her ear. "How's he doing?"

"Good. They gave him something for pain at 4:30, and it wiped him out."

"What's his prognosis?"

She lifted her nail to her mouth. He grabbed her hand and held it tight. She smiled. "No promises. They can't tell much until the swelling from the surgery goes down and he works through physical therapy."

"That's good. At least the surgery went well."

"There is that." She kept her gaze to the floor, her voice low even though they were the only ones in the waiting room.

"Brannon, what's wrong?"

She met his stare. "I want to talk about that kiss."

Heat burned within him at the memory. "What about it?"

"What do you mean *what about it*?" Her voice raised an octave. She looked even cuter when she was perturbed.

"Brannon, are you asking for another one?"

Her eyes widened and her face flushed. She opened her mouth, paused, then snapped it shut.

He couldn't help it—his emotions took control of his actions. He wrapped his arms around her, turning her to face him. Roark pulled her close. When they were a breath apart, he put his hands on either side of her face. "I'm going to kiss you again. And this time you'll understand what I mean by kissing you."

Roark centered his mouth over hers, putting every bit of what he felt into the kiss. She clung to him, shocking him with her response. He kept his thumbs on her cheekbones but expanded his fingers into her hair, rubbing against her scalp.

She made little throaty sounds against him. Deepening the kiss, Roark let his emotions loose with tenderness.

When he felt as if she would consume him in heat, Roark pulled back but kept his hands firmly cradling her face. His erratic breathing matched her jagged gasps. He waited until his heart stopped racing to even try to speak.

"Do you understand now? Do you realize I'm falling in love with you?"

Tears shimmered in her eyes even while her brows knitted. "Oh, Roark."

So serious, so determined to analyze his intentions and her reactions. He chuckled. "Don't worry about it. We have plenty of time to figure out everything."

He planted a kiss on her forehead and rubbed his thumbs over the delicate skin of her cheeks. "And I'll give you lots of opportunities to understand exactly what my kisses mean."

EPILOGUE

Thirteen Months Later
Howard Baker Federal Courthouse
Knoxville, Tennessee

"WELL, IT'S FINALLY DONE." Lincoln smiled at Brannon and Roark. They stood beside him in front of the courthouse, holding hands.

"I'm glad it's over." Brannon leaned against Roark, her face glowing with happiness.

They were so in love and had overcome great obstacles to find true bliss. Lincoln was happy for them, he honestly was, but witnessing their special relationship was a painful reminder of the loneliness in his own heart.

"I'm relieved the judge gave McGovern the maximum sentence. We won't have to worry about him being eligible for parole anytime soon." Roark untangled his hand from Brannon's and rested his arm across her shoulders.

The sun tiptoed behind a large cloud. The wind picked up, reminding them winter hadn't made its great departure yet. Lincoln knew it better than most. The cold weather played havoc with his knee. After a year of recovery and daily hard work, the physical therapist had finally released him. But he still walked with a limp, the cold weather making it more pronounced.

Instead, he'd ridden desk duty for the past year, praying for a full recovery. Now he had to face facts—that day would never come. He'd never return to 100 percent.

God, what do You have in store for me now? I know You have a plan for me and it will be good.

"We're going to see Mai and Kanya at their new home. Want to join us?" Roark asked.

"I'm so glad the adoptive parents wanted both of them." Brannon's grin widened, if that was even possible.

After Child Protective Services contacted Fight Against Child Exploitation, FACE, based out of Thailand, some of the girls were returned to their families. But not Kanya or Mai. Kanya's parents had been killed, and Mai couldn't go back to her father's home—not after he'd sold her.

"No, you two go ahead. I have some things to take care of." Like spending time with the Father, seeking His guidance.

Brannon touched his arm. "Lincoln?"

She knew him too well. She was like a piece of him. "I'm good. I promise." He started to chuckle, but the sun broke free of the clouds and shone down brightly. A prism shot from Brannon's left hand on his forearm.

His heart tripped as he peered into her face, then at her hand, then back into her eyes. He grabbed her hand. "Brannon?"

She giggled—Brannon Callahan actually giggled. "Isn't it beautiful?"

An engagement ring. A promise of Roark and Brannon's love and commitment. Excitement for them thickened Lincoln's tongue.

"We've set the date. April 10th. Isn't it wonderful?" She snuggled against Roark, beaming.

This was wonderful news. She'd come so far in pushing beyond old pains to embrace the goodness God provided her. Roark, too, had to deal with issues of his past to move toward a promising future.

But Brannon hadn't told Lincoln that Roark proposed. He'd had to notice the ring. Lincoln tried to hide his disappointment and awareness that he was no longer her confidant. "It's great." He extended his hand to Roark. "Congratulations."

Roark shook his hand. "Thanks."

Brannon looped her arm through his. "And I want to ask if you'll give me away." Tears floated in her eyes.

His chest tightened into a knot. "Of course. I'd be honored, hon." And he would.

She hugged him so hard he lost his breath. Laughing, she let him go and returned to her fiancé. "We'll discuss details soon, okay?"

"You betcha."

"Are you sure you don't want to go with us?" she asked.

"Positive. I'll catch up with you at the station later."

"Okay." Brannon gave him a quick hug, then she and Roark headed off toward the parking lot, arm in arm.

Lincoln's feet refused to move. He was so glad for Brannon. She deserved every happiness in the world. And he was honored she had asked him to give her away. But that hurt, too.

He'd be giving away his best friend. Giving away the final link to his brother.

Lincoln took a stiff step toward his own car as realization hit. Brannon had Roark to love and Jefferson as her partner at work. Maybe Lincoln's whole purpose in being a ranger had been to help her. Now she no longer needed him.

Lincoln stared heavenward, anxiety thrumming through his veins.

What now, God? Where do we go from here?

READER'S GUIDE

1. Brannon and Lincoln were loyal friends. Lincoln helped Brannon get through a personal tragedy, using Scripture and faith to strengthen her resolve. Many times in life, we need a friend to speak to us in truth and to encourage us. Looking at your own friendships, how can you be more of a biblical blessing to your friends? (See Proverbs 17:17; Proverbs 18:24; and John 15:13.)

2. The loss of loved ones can have a profound effect on people. Brannon chose her professions based on an emotional need to save people. This need was brought on due to losing loved ones. Roark's loss of the little girl triggered a physical response of claustrophobia. Have you ever lost someone you loved? What effect did it have on you—physically, emotionally, and spiritually?

3. It's no secret that parents' attitudes rub off on their children. Congressman McGovern lost his mother at a vulnerable age and had to live with his militant father, who had strict ideas about living life to a particular code. Reflect on how your own parents' ideals (good and bad) affected your childhood. What about this would you have changed if you could? How has this followed you into adulthood?

4. Child trafficking is a serious and real tragedy. In the story Roark has an opportunity to bring those involved to justice. Do you think our current laws are too easy or too harsh on those involved with exploiting children? Discuss how you can help with this issue. (See Psalm 127:2–4 and Matthew 19:14.)

5. Brannon was afraid to open her heart again after losing the man she'd loved. Fear can paralyze people, yet what does Scripture tell us about fear? (See Psalm 23:4; Psalm 27:1; and Isaiah 41:13.)

6. Mai and Kanya were children, innocents, but in a horrible situation over which they felt they had no control. Yet they were determined to improve their quality of life. Have you faced a situation you felt you had no control over yet struggled to improve your life despite the situation? What did you do?

7. Lincoln and Brannon not only had deep faith but lived it. Why should we live according to our faith? How can we exhibit our faith in everyday life? (See Proverbs 14:25; Isaiah 44:8; and Acts 1:8.)

8. When Brannon meets Jefferson, she is annoyed and frustrated that she must train him. Yet she didn't really know him. How can we avoid judging others without getting to know them? What does the Bible say about judging others? (See Matthew 7:1–3 and Luke 6:37.)

9. Roark had chosen to move away from God because of something bad that happened in his life. Have you ever felt disappointed or angry with God because of your circumstances? How did you deal with your emotions? What did you do to move back into a relationship with God?

10. While the congressman's motives were greed and power, Jonathan Wilks's participation in the child-trafficking ring was a means to provide special medication for his wife. Do you believe doing something wrong for the right reason is okay? What does Scripture have to say on the subject? (See 1 Kings 15:11 and Isaiah 1:17.)

11. Brannon witnessed to Roark, and Lincoln questioned her motives. (See Philippians 1:18.) Why do you think God can use selfish motives to further His purposes?

12. Roark and Brannon felt a quick emotional connection to one another. Do you believe people can truly bond that quickly? Why or why not?

13. Brannon had instances where she lacked self-confidence in her job as well as in her status with her best friend. Why do you think she felt that way? What in our own lives can cause us to lack confidence?

14. When Brannon hurt her ankle and had to use crutches for a short time, she felt helpless. What do you do when you feel helpless? How can we overcome such feelings?

Dear Reader:

Some time ago I watched a television special on child trafficking with my husband. As a mother of three daughters, I couldn't stop the ache in my heart long after the show was over. I couldn't get the image of these poor girls' faces out of my mind. The horrors these children endure in their own poverty-stricken country is horrible enough, but to be brought to America and be further exploited and abused is appalling. When my outrage settled inside me, I knew I had to write a story about this most serious issue.

Researching this story line drained my emotions as well as educated me. I couldn't believe how often this atrocity occurs—and I had no clue! While I took certain fictional liberties and invented the congressional coalition, FACE is a very real and very proactive organization in addressing these children's plight. You can visit their Web site at: http://www.un.or.th/ TraffickingProject/FACE/face_home.html. I commend their efforts and presence in Thailand.

I must commend the often unsung heroes of the National Park Service rangers. Until I began writing this book, I didn't realize the enormous job they hold and the intense training they've undergone to be rangers. My hat goes off to these amazing men and women who save lives, educate, and serve the public.

I hope you enjoy the journey into the Great Smoky Mountains National Park as much as I did when writing this story. These characters came alive for me, and I hope this story touches and blesses you.

I love hearing from readers. You can find me on the Web at: www.robincaroll.com.

Many blessings,

Robin Caroll

ONLINE & PRINT SOURCES

Thai Translation

http://www.thai-language.com

Child-Trafficking Facts

http://www.lirs.org/what/children/tcibackground.htm
http://www.childtrafficking.org
http://www.msnbc.msn.com/id/4038249
http://gooddeedsinternational.org/index.php?option=com_
content&task=view&id=41

Medical/Drugs

http://www.appraisercentral.com/research/Bio%20Chemestry.htm
http://www.ncbi.nlm.nih.gov/pubmed/7947884
http://articles.latimes.com/2007/apr/07/science/sci-briefs7.3
http://scienceroll.com/2007/01/31/curing-cancer-the-dichloro
acetate-story
http://www.thedcasite.com
http://puredca.com
http://www.berner.org/pages/medical_treatments/
cancer_thcrapy.php
http://www.news.com.au/heraldsun/story/0,21985,24578841
-662,00.html
http://www.businessweek.com/magazine/content/05_50/
b3963151.htm
http://www.essaysample.com/essay/001839.html
http://www.zimmer.com/z/ctl/op/global/action/1/id/8138/
template/PC/navid/88

Helicopters & Flight

http://sunnyfortuna.com/festivals/disaster/dolphin.htm
http://www.globalsecurity.org/military/systems/aircraft/hh-65.htm
http://itouchmap.com/latlong.html
http://www.csgnetwork.com/slflightdistcalc.html
http://www.pilotfriend.com
http://www.bellhelicopter.com/en/aircraft/commercial/pdf/
    B3_2006_jan_web.pdf
http://science.howstuffworks.com/helicopter1.htm
http://www.copters.com/pilot

Coming August 1, 2010
from suspense author
Robin Caroll

Lincoln Vailes, from **Deliver Us From Evil**, leaves Tennessee to become a police officer in a small bayou town. It doesn't take long for Lincoln to be thrown into his first real investigation— involving big-city gangs and a beautiful young social worker.

Fear No Evil

a novel

Robin Caroll

author of Deliver Us From Evil